The new Zebra Regency [...] on the cover is a photograph of an actual regency "tuzzy-muzzy." The fashionable regency lady often wore a tuzzy-muzzy tied with a satin or velvet riband around her wrist to carry a fragrant nosegay. Usually made of gold or silver, tuzzy-muzzies varied in design from the elegantly simple to the exquisitely ornate. The Zebra Regency Romance tuzzy-muzzy is made of alabaster with a silver filigree edging.

INFAMOUS CONDUCT

"I have nothing whatever to say to you," stated Amanda, instantly contradicting herself by adding in scathing accents, "If I were a man I would hit you, but alas I am not, so I must suppose you will go unpunished for your *infamous* conduct!"

"By all means, go ahead and hit me," he challenged, flashing her another of his oddly disturbing smiles. "I won't strike back, I promise."

"Now you are being ridiculous," she said in a dampening tone.

He looked amused. "And you, my sweet, are being delightful."

Despite Amanda's very real attempt to prevent him, the Marquis easily pulled her close, trapping her arms against his broad chest. Even before his lips touched hers, Amanda's heart was hammering wildly. Never, never in a thousand years would she have believed something like this could be so exciting. And when his mouth finally came down to claim hers, she was even more shocked to discover that a part of her longed to return his kisses . . .

"No, no . . . you must stop," she heard herself cry weakly, as if from a great distance.

In answer, the Marquis drew her closer still . . .

The Scandalous Marquis

Julie Caille

ZEBRA BOOKS
KENSINGTON PUBLISHING CORP.

ZEBRA BOOKS are published by

Kensington Publishing Corp.
475 Park Avenue South
New York, NY 10016

Second Printing: June, 1993

Printed in the United States of America

To my husband, Evan,
who gives me so much love and
encouragement and is always
there when I need him.

Chapter One

The Countess of Besford sipped cautiously at her coffee and eyed with disfavor the stack of mail awaiting her inspection. With a short sigh, she thumbed listlessly through the usual assortment of social invitations. Each day at breakfast, the small silver tray at her elbow contained the morning's postal offerings, and as the London Season drew nearer, so did their number increase.

Such invitations would normally have gained her ladyship's full attention, but on this particular morning she was in no mood for such diversions. Lady Harron's card party the previous evening had seemed sadly flat, and after passing an indifferent night, Lady Besford had awakened feeling more than a little depressed. The endless round of balls, routs, and assemblies, perpetuated by the *beau monde* and enthusiastically attended by her ladyship, now loomed bleakly, and it crossed her mind that perhaps she had grown too old for such nonsense. As a girl she had loved to dance, but now she sat with the dowagers, too plump and elderly to have her hand solicited for anything more exerting than a rubber of whist!

Her lips puckered at the melancholy thought. Oh, if only she had something of interest to occupy her! How thoroughly vexing it was that there was still no word from — but wait! She had almost missed the small, lavender-scented envelope hidden at the bottom of the pile.

"At last!" the Countess murmured under her breath. Hastily, she broke the wafer, spread flat the two sheets of paper, and quickly scanned the contents of the letter. As she read, a sparkle of excitement stole into her eye, replacing the discontent of a moment before. Nodding to herself, she transferred her attention to the other occupant of the breakfast parlor, hidden behind his copy of *The Morning Post*. Her lips curved into an affectionate smile as she regarded the top of her husband's head — the only portion of him that was visible — while she debated the wisdom of interrupting him. When the Earl was absorbed in something, it could be a trifle difficult to get his attention. But on this occasion, the Countess decided, her news was far too important to wait.

"Robert, my love — ?" she ventured, and waited for a reaction.

A full twenty seconds elapsed before the Earl lowered his newspaper to peer rather vaguely over the rim of his reading glasses at his wife. "Yes, Emily?"

That hurdle dealt with, the Countess smiled happily. "I have here a letter from Jane with the best possible news! All is well! Jane has recovered and dearest Eve will be able to have her introduction into society this Season, just as we planned! What with Jane's illness last month, I have been living in trepi-

8

dation that something dreadful would happen." She tapped the envelope with her finger. "I am extremely pleased, not only for Jane and poor, dear Eve, but on my own behalf as well. You must know, Robert, how very melancholy I have been feeling these past few weeks. Depend upon it, this will be just what I need!"

The Earl's response was, to say the least, disappointing, for an interesting editorial had distracted him somewhere in the middle of his wife's speech. "Eve?" he mumbled with an abstracted frown. "I'm sorry, m'dear. I can't quite recall . . ."

"My niece, Robert!" reprimanded his wife severely. "I trust you have not forgotten my sister's only child!"

The Earl's brow cleared. "Oh, aye. Tall chit with yellow hair. Lucky she don't favor her mother!" he remarked, giving the final page of his paper a quick skim.

Lady Besford ignored this last statement. "Yes, indeed. She is a lovely girl, quite out of the common way. I am persuaded she will *take*." She paused to sample her coffee, and added thoughtfully, "I suppose it is possible she may even attain the distinction of becoming a Toast."

"Mmm . . . I think not," murmured his lordship absently.

The Countess blinked. "You don't agree? Well, you may be right. Perhaps she is a trifle tall to become the fashion—"

"Well, perhaps I shall after all." The Earl folded his newspaper, scratched his grizzled head, and looked around. "Where is it?"

"Where is what?" repeated her ladyship, at a loss.

"Blister it, Emily! Can't you pay attention? You offer me toast and then look at me as though I've got a loose tile when I say I want some!"

Lady Besford smothered a laugh. "Oh, Robert! I didn't offer you toast. I was speaking of *Eve*. I was saying I think her beautiful enough to become an accredited Toast. You know, like Cordelia Rowland's daughter, last Season. What do you think?"

The Earl stared at his wife. "I don't know," he replied flatly. "You're the expert on things of that nature. As long as she don't come out all mealy-mouthed like your sister."

"Jane is not mealy-mouthed," protested her ladyship mildly.

"All right, she's not mealy-mouthed," retorted the Earl. "Ten to one I've missed something, so you'd better start over and tell me the whole. I can give you twenty minutes or so before I'm off to my club."

The Countess heaved an exaggerated sigh. "It's not a particularly long story, Robert. Eve is coming to us for the Season and I am to see that she has a proper introduction into society. Jane's health does not, of course, permit her to bring the girl herself. I must say I'll be glad to have her here! It should do me a world of good to have someone young in the house again, for it's never been the same since Priscilla left, as you know. Of course, I have the comfort of knowing she is happiest in the country with Sir Julian and the dear children, so I know I must not repine. It's only that I need something to do!" she added fervently.

The Earl shot a keen look at his wife. "If that's what'll do the trick for you, m'dear, then I'm glad the girl is coming. Come to think of it, I did notice you were looking a trifle hagged this morning." He made as if to rise but was halted by her ladyship, who could not resist elaborating while she was still certain she had her husband's ear.

"And when I think of all that poor girl has been made to suffer, my heart just goes out to her! Do you realize, Robert, that Eve is all but twenty and has not yet been formally introduced? First her grandmother died and she was forced to give up *that* Season. Then last year, right after Christmas, her father's death! One would be tempted to say, if such a thing were possible, that the Marlowes have actually been *conspiring* to keep her at home!"

"I'm sure old Hugo went out and broke his neck solely to disoblige his daughter!" remarked the Earl ironically.

"Well, of course he did not, but don't you see it amounts to the same thing? The poor girl has been in blacks for two whole years!"

"Foolish custom!" growled the Earl with sudden contempt. "Forcing the living to wallow in their grief. A classic example of civilized barbarity!"

"Er, exactly so, my love," agreed Lady Besford meekly. "Anyway, I know how very much you dislike fuss and botheration, *dearest* Robert, so I did want to be sure you understood precisely why it is so important that I do this. You don't mind, do you?" the Countess inquired anxiously.

The Earl yawned and rose to his feet. "No, why should I? As long as you don't dig up some reason to drag me to all those plaguey balls!"

"Oh, I am so glad! I should hate for you to object

11

when I am already committed to the project!" Her ladyship beamed happily for a moment, then a small cloud descended upon her brow.

"Well?" inquired the Earl.

"There is just one other thing," said his wife slowly. The Earl sat down.

Lady Besford unfolded her sister's letter and scanned it with a pensive air. "Roger's daughter is living at Birchfeld Manor also, on account of her own bereavement. She is just nineteen, Robert, and ought also to be presented."

The Earl closed his eyes for an instant. "As ever, Emily, the intricacies of your mind elude me. Who, may I ask, is Roger?"

"Why, Sir Hugo's brother, of course!" answered the Countess in some surprise. "Surely you remember my telling you about the tragedy? He married Katherine Haines-Scott, a very good match indeed for a penniless younger son. It was thought to be a shocking mesalliance at the time! I still shudder when I remember who she turned down to marry Roger Marlowe. Think of it, Robert! Two earls, a viscount, and the heir to a dukedom!"

The Earl digested this information. "Aye, I remember. She turned down Farnborough, the old rapscallion! She wasn't beautiful, but she had something, by jove. Dead now, ain't she?"

Lady Besford nodded sadly. "And her husband with her. Such a dreadful accident! The coachman was foxed, they said. And *he* survived without a scratch! I tell you, Robert, there is no justice in this world!"

As she spoke, the Countess's cheeks turned quite

pink with indignation, and her large blue eyes glimmered with the suspicion of a tear. Her husband noted these signs, and became resigned.

"I see," he remarked, "that you have found a Cause, Emily. You are longing to take this motherless girl, whatever-her-name-is, under your maternal wing, whether she wants it or not."

"Her name is Amanda," said the Countess simply. "And yes, I want to help her."

"I suppose this Amanda has no family of her own?" inquired his lordship, gloomily grasping at straws.

"None at all, but at least the poor child has not been left destitute. Her grandmother Haines-Scott left her a sum of money, I understand. Not a fortune, sadly, but enough to provide her with an income, of sorts. Her grandfather was reputed to be an excessively difficult man. He utterly disowned Amanda's mother after she eloped—remarkably shabby behavior in my opinion, but just what one would expect from such a stuffy old nip-farthing! Poor Amanda! I intend to write to Jane and insist that she accompany Eve to London! Then I shall do my best to see them both creditably established."

At this point, the Countess became reflective, her mind running down a mental list of matrimonial candidates. "There is Lord Castlebury or Sir Edward Tymalt. Neither of them needs to marry a fortune and both must wed soon, and set up a nursery. Then there is Mr. Wilcox, who is a younger, more scholarly man, a bit like Roger Marlowe, in fact."

"Emily, you never cease to amaze me!" mocked the Earl, shaking his head.

"I don't know why that should be so," replied his lady tranquilly. "These matters are not so difficult to arrange if one only knows how to set about getting started. You must own that I had plenty of practice with our darling Priscilla. And by the by, Robert, you must be very kind to Amanda, and not bark at her the way you do upon occasion. After all, we will be complete strangers to her. She will no doubt be feeling very shy and out of place."

His lordship chuckled. "If she resembles her mother, I don't fancy she'll be in much difficulty. I can't imagine Kate's girl being anything but up to snuff. You need only hope she don't outshine Jane's girl too greatly!"

"I can imagine very few girls who could hold a candle to our niece," remarked the Countess dryly. "In any case, nothing would please me more than if Amanda turned out to be a Beauty. It would make the task of seeing her settled all the easier."

"You'll have all the Matchmaking Mamas at your throat, if she is. A Beauty and a Toast residing under the same roof! The mind totters to contemplate such an arrangement!"

Lady Besford's eyes gleamed. "Wouldn't it be a marvelous circumstance, indeed. I vow it's been an age since I've looked forward to anything as much as this!"

The Earl tipped back in his chair and regarded his wife with amusement. "You're rushing your fences, Emily. She may be a bran-faced Antidote with a club foot and a squint. Then you'll have your work cut out for you!"

Her ladyship raised one well-defined eyebrow.

"Kate's girl? Oh, surely not."

The Earl grinned. "That rankled, did it? Rest assured I was never among those who formed her court. I was head over heels for you before I ever clapped eyes on Kate Haines-Scott!"

"And you were far more handsome than any of her suitors," remarked his loving wife complaisantly. "I know I've no cause for complaint so don't think it. You're a good husband to me, Robert."

"Well, well!" mumbled the Earl, gruffly clearing his throat. The tips of his ears had grown a trifle pink, and the Countess concealed a smile as he made a great business of digging through his pockets for his gold watch, which he found, after a thorough search, in his watch-pocket.

"Do you have to leave now?" Lady Besford inquired.

"Soon." The Earl pushed back his chair, and gazed for a moment at his wife. "Well, I'm glad to see you in such spirits, m'dear. If this is all it takes to keep you from being cast into the dumps, then you may have both Jane's girl and Kate's girl here with my blessing! In fact, you can invite every confounded girl in Hampshire if it makes you happy! We'll find 'em all husbands!"

Once again, he rose, and was about to leave the room, when he was struck by a thought. "You know, I don't recall you being in quite such a dither of joy when you brought Priscilla out."

Lady Besford looked embarrassed. "Well, I suppose that is true, to a degree. When it is one's own daughter, one is so very anxious for her to do well, and hence it is much more difficult to relax and enjoy

15

oneself. Besides, Eve is so very lovely, I am persuaded she may aim as high as she chooses for a husband. I'm afraid Priscilla—though a dear lamb, of course!—was of such a retiring nature that—oh dear! You will think me a most unnatural parent!"

The Earl reached across the table and gently pinched his wife's chin. "I think nothing of the sort, my love. Here is a chance for you to give your matchmaking instincts free rein. I understand perfectly! Which paragon have you selected for the Toast? One of the Royal Dukes?"

"Now you are talking fustian, Robert! As a matter of fact, I have reason to hope that she will contract an alliance with the Marquis of Vale."

"What?" ejaculated the Earl, his eyebrows flying up. For the third time, he dropped back into his chair. "Have you taken leave of your senses, Emily? Vale leg-shackled!" He laughed. "Lord, I'd give a monkey to see it!"

"No, Robert, I have not taken leave of my senses!" said her ladyship tartly. "Men of his rank must eventually marry, and why not to our niece?"

Ignoring her question, the Earl demanded, "Where in the world did you get such a crack-brained notion?"

His wife bristled. "Of all the unjust—! You know perfectly well—or if you do not, you should!—that Sir Hugo and the present Marquis's father were fast friends. Jane told us years ago that there was some sort of an informal agreement between the two men that their children should marry. I don't claim it's common knowledge but—"

"Well, you'd best keep it from becoming common

16

knowledge!" interrupted the Earl with some severity. "Vale won't thank you for interfering, and it won't do the girl a whit of good to start the tongues wagging again! I'd lay handsome odds that boy has no intention of dropping the handkerchief for any girl at his time of life! Why should he? He ain't more than eight-and-twenty, and obviously prefers rubbing shoulders with a different sort of female — judging from the number of highfliers he's kept under his protection!"

"Robert!" gasped Lady Besford. Normally, the introduction of such an indelicate subject would have drawn from her a reproof, but the wound to her self-esteem outweighed the shock to her sensibilities. Displeased with the implication that she was not the soul of discretion, she glared across the table at her spouse.

"How can you suggest — ? As if I were going to run out and announce it to the world! Or perhaps you thought I would simply dash off the announcement and send it to *The Gazette?*" she inquired sweetly.

"Oh, for land's sake, Emily!" returned the Earl, somewhat testily. "You know that ain't what I meant. No need to bite my nose off! The thing is, you've only to mention it to one person — in complete confidence, of course! — and it'll be all over town by nightfall. The tabbies prey like vultures on Vale! Always have!"

"Well, I'm sure that is no reason for him not to marry! As ramshackle as Lord Vale's past behavior has been, I am sure he knows his duty. Eve possesses not only unexceptionable birth and a handsome fortune but more than her fair share of beauty. Why

17

should he not wish to marry her?"

"Because he ain't the marrying kind!" her husband told her bluntly. " 'Pon rep, Emily, if you haven't heard the stories, I have. He gambles, drinks—he fought that duel with Henry Scorpe last fall, and nearly had to flee the country because of it! It was God's own miracle the man survived! What kind of a man is that to husband your niece?"

Lady Besford sighed, temporarily daunted. "Oh, Robert! Is he truly so very bad? He has such a charming smile."

"Bad? No, he's not bad." Lord Besford leaned forward, his palms pressed flat on the table in front of him. "He's a boy, Emily. Just a wild and spoiled boy. But mark my words, he ain't the man for your niece."

"But you cannot deny that from a worldly standpoint he is an extremely eligible *parti*," persisted his wife. "And many young men are vastly improved by marriage."

"Twaddle!" snorted the Earl. "And what of that business with Frome's sister? Has that ugly little scandal slipped your mind?"

The Countess's eyes dropped. "No, Robert, but I have always believed the story to be greatly exaggerated. These rumors often start out of nothing, you know."

The Earl shrugged. "The young pup toyed with her affections, that much is clear. Think about it, Emily! The girl kills herself and the same evening he strolls into White's and enters into a card game with the Duke of Portland. Wins, too! When the girl's name is mentioned, does he glance up? No! Does he show

18

signs of despair? Not a one! He makes his next bid, that's what he does. Pretty cool, I'd say! And that story's no hum, for I witnessed the whole of it myself."

The Countess bit her lip. "But surely such behavior suggests a clear conscience, Robert. After all, I never saw him do more than stand up with her for a few country dances! It's my belief that she threw herself at him in a most improper fashion!"

The Earl's patience began to desert him. "So now it was *her* fault, was it? You're a naive idiot, Emily!"

Lady Besford pouted. "I won't listen to you, Robert! I don't for a moment believe he seduced that girl and neither do you. Why, you just said yourself he was only a spoiled boy. And besides, I have always found him perfectly charming and well mannered."

"Fiend seize it, of course he's charming! How do you think he's earned his reputation? He wouldn't have half the trouble he has if the entire female sex didn't behave like a parcel of damned fools over him!"

"Robert! Your language!"

"Beg your pardon, my dear," apologized the Earl, struggling with his rising temper. "But I think you're making a mistake. You'd be wise to point your niece in some other direction. A man of his kidney ain't likely to change."

"We shall see!" countered her ladyship.

It was true, she thought later, that there had been some shocking rumors concerning the Marquis of Vale, but he was the type of man to attract notoriety. After giving the matter careful consideration, Lady Besford dismissed it from her mind. It was old gossip, after all. More than six years had passed since Charlotte Wythe had taken that overdose of laudanum, and scandals, like flames, tended to flare high for only a short while and then burn themselves out. Miss Wythe would not have been the first girl to mistake flirtation for serious intentions, nor the first to lose her heart to a man who made it his practice to be agreeable to women.

No, she decided, the man's only crime was being single. Nothing could alter the fact that the Marquis was one of the most eligible bachelors in England. That he was arrogant and spoiled, a gambler and a womanizer, must be the natural outcome of his upbringing. To reform a rake, to find and tame the spoiled boy beneath the cynical facade—this was too enticing a fantasy for many women to resist, and the Countess was no exception. Had she been thirty years younger she might have set her cap for him herself. Lady Besford shivered at the thought. No, that was ridiculous—no one could replace dear, predictable Robert! But someone, she reflected, really ought to undertake the taming of that dashing young man.

Well, whatever transpired, she supposed this Season was not likely to be dull. She felt sure that Eve and Amanda would take care of that.

John Jasper Nicholas Brinvilliers, Fifth Marquis of Vale, strolled into White's, blissfully unaware that his taming was being contemplated with some relish by a woman he scarcely knew. If he had known, he would have laughed, for his downfall had been plotted any number of times, unsuccessfully as it were, by women far more adept at scheming than the Countess of Besford. However, his laughter would have held a rueful note, for he was aware that ultimately one of them would have to be successful. As the head of an old and aristocratic family, it was both his duty and his fate to don connubial shackles. The ghosts of centuries of ancestors and the law of primogeniture demanded it. His conscience also demanded it.

The Marquis paused as he entered, and raised his quizzing glass in silent surveillance of those members of the club within his view. Nodding coolly to a trio of acquaintances, he sauntered through several of the rooms, until he found the person he was seeking. The corners of his mouth twitched and an amused look crossed his handsome countenance as he regarded the slim, auburn-haired gentleman dozing in a large wing chair in a corner.

The Honourable Charles Perth, heir to a viscountcy, had been his closest friend for many years. They had been at Eton together, and again at Oxford, and had emerged from behind those hallowed walls of learning with as firm and unswerving a friendship as two men may have. Charles was just the person he needed to give his spirits a boost, the Marquis decided.

A mischievous light that Charles would have regarded with some misgiving entered Vale's eyes as he bent over his friend. Shaking the sleeping man in an urgent manner, he whispered, "Wake up, Charles! Quick, man! Your grandmother's here!"

Roused from his slumbers, Charles's reaction to this cryptic utterance was extraordinary. His eyes shot open, his mouth snapped shut, and he sprang out of his chair like a startled cat.

"Where is she?" he croaked, tugging nervously at his cravat. Finding himself in the middle of his club in St. James's Street rather than at some family gathering or dinner party as he had for one awful moment supposed, he shifted his indignant gaze to the Marquis, who was making no effort to contain his mirth.

"Dash it, Jack!" he expostulated. "What the devil do you mean scaring me like that? A shock like that's enough to make a fellow lose his appetite for a week!"

"You, Charles?" mocked the Marquis with an unrepentant grin. "Come, come. Surely nothing's as bad as that."

Unmollified, Charles glanced at his watch. "My grandmother is! And you're almost an hour late," he accused.

Vale flipped open his snuffbox. "I apologize for that. I'm afraid I was unavoidably detained."

Charles's green eyes narrowed knowingly. "Alexandra, again?"

The snuffbox closed with a snap. "Yes." There was a tightness about the Marquis's mouth that his friend recognized, but it disappeared almost at once. "You'll be pleased to hear that the lady is going to receive her *congé* very soon."

Charles cast Vale a measured glance. "S'that so? Can't say I blame you. Always thought her a trifle too high-spirited, myself. Never been broken to bridle!"

"On the contrary, I never object to high spirits. It's

her propensity for . . . how shall I say it? . . . dispensing her affections a shade liberally that for some unfathomable reason annoys me. Ogmore's idiocy is giving her some queer ideas, too," Vale added with a grimace.

Correctly interpreting this reference to the Earl of Ogmore's recent marriage to his mistress, Charles remarked, "Trying to lure you into the Parson's Noose, is she? Must be a remarkably stupid woman!"

Receiving no reply to this remark, Charles inspected his companion shrewdly. There were dark circles under the Marquis's eyes, and he looked fatigued. "Well, enough talk," Charles said tactfully. "Let's eat, shall we? I'm starved."

"That's the ticket," agreed Vale, with a tired but amicable smile. "When all else fails—!"

As they dined, the conversation centered upon pugilism, a sport in which both men took interest. A new bruiser bearing the doubtful name of Horrible Hans had recently come to light, and was to take part in a match at Fives Court the following month. The two men had already witnessed Horrible Hans's fighting techniques, and agreed that they had seldom seen a newcomer handier with his fives. This subject dominated the conversation until just after they were left to their port. There was a brief lull while they both drank from their glasses, and then the Marquis brought up what Charles Perth would have considered the last subject on earth his friend might wish to discuss.

Lounging at his ease, one exquisitely booted foot propped against a neighboring chair, the Marquis said in his cool way, "By the way, Charles, you may soon have reason to felicitate me. I am thinking of getting married."

Charles had been staring rather critically into his wine, wondering if a small speck in the bottom of the glass was worth the trouble of removing. At the Marquis's words, he looked up, fully expecting to see the wicked grin that would have assured him that Vale was joking. He did not see it.

"You must be bamming me!" he said involuntarily.

Vale's brows rose haughtily. "Why?"

"Well, burn it, Jack!" floundered Charles. "It's obvious! I mean, you just ain't the domestic sort. Me now, maybe. I ain't saying I ever will tie the knot, mind you," he added cautiously, "but I might. You? Never! Why, you've only to take a look at yourself!"

Despite his somber mood, the Marquis was amused. "How unkind of you, Charles," he said, the faintest quiver in his voice. "I'd no idea I was such a quiz."

"No, no!" protested the other man, fortifying himself with a gulp of port. "No bone to pick there. Hang it, that's half the problem! There's more women than you know what to do with throwing themselves at your head, and you ain't exactly pushing them away! Ask yourself this—what sort of a husband would you make?"

"Now that," responded the Marquis, sounding quite bored, "is a matter I really haven't considered."

"Well, you should!" said Charles frankly. Curiosity finally won out over disapproval. "Who is she, anyway?"

"Can't you guess?" The Marquis fingered his wine-glass, holding it up to survey its ruby contents with

24

an appraising air.

"Well, I could try, but I don't choose to! I just hope you ain't corkbrained enough to offer for Miss Warfield. She may have a beautiful face, but she's nothing but a curst shrew when it comes down to it. Tries to gull you into thinking otherwise, of course."

Vale sipped his wine. "Rest assured, my dear Charles, that Miss Warfield has not succeeded in deceiving me. How do you think I've avoided the noose as long as this?"

Charles eyed him dubiously. "Well then, who?"

"She is Emily Besford's niece. Her name is Eve Marlowe."

"Eve Marlowe . . ." repeated the other man with a thoughtful frown. "Has a familiar ring." His eyes widened as the memory hit him. "I say, she ain't that filly your father wanted you to marry, is she? Daughter of some baronet? I remember you swearing you'd be damned if you'd let your father choose you a wife. Dash it, I remember! Said you wouldn't have anything to do with her!"

Vale sighed. "Yes. It's the same girl."

An idea began to form in his friend's mind. "By jove, Jack! Don't tell me you've gone and fallen in love! Out with it, now! Is this a love-match?"

The Marquis's lip curled cynically. "Don't be absurd, Charles. I haven't seen the girl since she was twelve. And what the deuce has love to do with marriage? All I desire in a wife is beauty, docility, and fertility."

As used as he was to his friend's sarcasm, Charles was a trifle shocked. "Gad, Jack, what a bloody cold-hearted devil you sound!" He cast a knowing look at the Marquis. "Though I ain't so sure you really mean it."

Vale regarded him mockingly. "Trying to make me better than I am, Charles? It won't fadge. I haven't a grain of proper feeling in me."

"What a rapper!" Charles Perth rejected this statement with visible scorn. "Wouldn't be sitting here eating with you if you was as bad as that. Don't much care for that sort of fellow, myself. Bad *ton!*"

A hint of a smile entered the Marquis's blue eyes. He said mildly, "Spare my blushes, Charles, I beg you. Such devotion!"

Charles responded with an absent grin. "Gammon! Anyway, no use in denying that hearing you talk of marriage is devilish strange. And to a girl you haven't clapped eyes on in years! Good lord, Jack, why?"

Vale hesitated. "God, Charles, I don't know," he answered, his expression clouding. "My father always had to have his way, you know. If he were alive, it would be one thing, but dead—! How am I to fight the guilt? All I can do is give in, and hope it's enough . . ."

The Marquis was staring at the floor, and so did not see the quick pity leap into his friend's eyes. For once, Charles was at a loss. What could he say that he hadn't already said many times in the past? The irony was that while the world thought the Marquis a hard and cynical man, he was very much the opposite. His give-a-damn-about-nothing act was so good, even Charles occasionally forgot the truth.

"My actions caused my father so much grief. Why he never told me his heart was weak, I'll never understand." The Marquis closed his eyes at the memory.

"I was not a good son to him, Charles."

"Nonsense!" Charles cut in gruffly. "What happened was not your fault. You must stop blaming yourself."

Vale dismissed his words with an impatient wave of his hand. "It could all have been avoided. Had I been wiser, I would not have become involved with the girl in the first place."

"But how could you have guessed she was unstable?" said Charles indignantly. "Should have been her family's responsibility to be on the lookout! Ten to one if it hadn't been you it would have been some other poor devil!"

The Marquis shrugged wearily. "Well, it's all water under the bridge now, Charles. Let's not argue about it, shall we? Suffice it to say that duty compels me to marry, and it may as well be Miss Marlowe as any other girl. I must have an heir. My father could never stomach the thought of Godfrey inheriting. I never thought there was much harm in the man, myself, but he's not, after all, a Brinvilliers. I owe it to my father and to my name."

Charles shook his head in dismay. It was clear that something drastic would have to happen to prevent the Marquis from taking this potentially disastrous step. But what would change his friend's mind? Unfortunately, Charles couldn't think of a thing.

Chapter Two

It had been a full sennight since the post had conveyed Lady Besford's gracious invitation to Birchfeld Manor, the Marlowe home in Hampshire. The two young ladies who had, six days past, penned their acceptances to that invitation had just completed their breakfast and retired to the Rose Saloon, a room they often occupied for its warmth and its pleasant view of the east woods. As was frequently the case, the cousins did not immediately converse, for if they had anything in common it was the mutual understanding that they had nothing in common, and conversation between them was seldom more than a frustrating experience for each. Both in character and physical appearance, attitude and disposition, they bore no more resemblance to one another than a peacock and a sparrow.

Miss Eve Marlowe, the elder by almost a year, was a tallish blonde, whom fortune had endowed with guinea-gold curls and eyes of an arrestingly vivid shade of blue. She knew her figure to be elegant, and her profile, classic, for she had studied them often enough in her mirror, and if she were not precisely vain, at least she knew the value she might safely bestow upon her own assets.

Miss Amanda Marlowe was a small-boned brunette. Though there was no question that her cousin was the more striking of the two, there was a quality about Amanda that almost demanded closer inspection. She was rather like a fine painting which, having been wrongly tucked away in a dark and lonely corner, was simply awaiting discovery by someone of discriminating taste. That person would have no need of the sun's rays to appreciate the rich chestnut highlights that gleamed in her thick brown hair, and would doubtless have no difficulty discerning the stubborn set to the firm little chin, or the honest charm in the sweet curve of her lips. He would probably decide that her eyes were her greatest beauty, for there was a hint of silver in their grayness, and a glimmer of humor could often be found lurking in their depths. At the moment, however, the only emotion those lovely eyes held was indecision, for a matter of great personal importance was preying on her mind.

She had tried to sit, but it was no good. Instead, she had taken to fidgeting about the room, here and there picking up some object, then setting it down again, her hands clenching and unclenching with restlessness. For perhaps the hundredth time that morning Amanda tried to view her situation dispassionately. Why, she wondered, was it so amazingly difficult to reach a decision?

However, she knew the answer to that. There was, after all, a great deal of difference between what she *wanted* to do, what she longed to do with all her heart—and what she suspected she probably *ought* to do. Two voices warred within her, and it was they who were responsible for her quandary. The louder of the two owed its existence to that portion of herself which had always been a shade headstrong and rash, but the other, more cautious, voice was making itself heard, too. It was the second voice that warned her not to be a fool, admonished her for hoping and praying for the miracle that might suddenly make the whole mad scheme seem feasible. It was highly unsettling, to say the least.

Pausing before the mullioned window, Amanda touched her fingers to the cool glass and wished suddenly that she were outdoors, though the rain had been drizzling relentlessly for more than two days. Out there, at least, there was room to move and breathe, and to forget, for a little while, that she was now an orphan. Perhaps out there she might be able to blank out her apprehensions of the future, and forgive her aunt for her many little cruelties. But she must not fall into the trap of self-pity, she chided herself, for that would be as foolish as it was unproductive. Instead, she must direct her energies to—

"Oh, for heaven's sake, *do* come and sit down, Amanda!" complained Eve, her voice slicing so sharply into Amanda's reverie that she flinched. "Why must you pace about so? I find all this . . . this *motion* excessively distracting. It jars upon my nerves," she added pettishly.

With a short sigh, Amanda turned away from the window to take silent stock of her cousin. It occurred to her then, that even with all of Eve's blessings—her wealth and security, her beauty and elegance, her brilliant prospects—even with all of this, she would not wish to trade places with Eve, not for a dozen London Seasons. As dismal as Amanda's life presently seemed, she still found it preferable to the pampered existence her cousin enjoyed. It was a consoling revelation.

And Lord only knew that living with Eve and Aunt Marlowe this past year had not been easy. If only Eve were someone with whom she could have become close, how much more pleasant things would have been. Their backgrounds were as much to blame as their temperaments, she mused. Eve had lived all her life surrounded by luxury, knowing it was her destiny to have that London Season, to whirl gracefully around the floors of glittering ballrooms, partnered by a succession of tall, gallant gentlemen . . .

Involuntarily, Amanda shut her eyes in a futile attempt to blot out the enticing fantasy of herself in those same ballrooms. When she had received the Countess of Besford's invitation to share in Eve's Season, her first reaction had been one of astonishment and delight. Certainly, she had never expected or hoped for the offer, and could recall only too clearly that first, wild elation when she actually thought she was going to go . . . until Eve, with her typical, almost brutal indifference to Amanda's feelings, had pricked this bubble by pointing out the many obstacles to the plan.

How stupid she had been not to have realized it at once. Not to have realized that, of course, she had nothing stylish to wear, and almost no money with which to purchase new gowns. Not to have remembered that she had never been to a dance, and indeed, scarcely knew any of the steps. Not to have recalled how few proper accomplishments she actually possessed—far too few for a young lady preparing to embark upon her first London Season. Not to have seen that, next to her polished and sophisticated cousin, she was bound to appear mortifyingly gauche. And the final objection, perhaps the most important of all, was that it seemed wrong, somehow, to accept such an extraordinary offer from a complete stranger. After all, Lady Marlowe was her aunt by marriage only—her sister, Lady Besford, no relation at all! The last thing in the world Amanda wanted was to appear *encroaching*.

Yet curiously, both Eve and her mother had urged Amanda to accept the invitation, and being herself an essentially optimistic person, Amanda had finally allowed herself to be persuaded. After all, as Aunt Marlowe had pompously pointed out, the opportunity to be introduced to Polite Society under the aegis of no less a personage than the Countess of Besford was not an honor to be lightly cast aside! Aunt Marlowe's sister had been a renowned London hostess for years, and was acquainted with almost everyone of any consequence. And although Amanda shrank from the idea of putting herself on the Marriage Mart—a ludicrous notion when one considered her lack of fortune—she was able to discover (with only a little thought) any number of other excellent reasons for undertaking a sojourn in London. The chance to escape the dreary confinement of her aunt's house reckoned as one of the most powerful, and in the end had proved too tempting for Amanda to resist.

Her optimism over the entire matter had remained high until this morning, when the post had arrived, bearing the draft for her quarterly stipend. Her late uncle's man of business, Mr. Goodall, had, at her request, invested the small amount of money she had inherited so that she might have the benefit of an income for life. Yet the draft was for so paltry a sum that Amanda was immediately disheartened. When all was said and done, financial considerations were simply not as easy to dismiss as an inability to dance or play upon the pianoforte. And under these circumstances, how could she possibly have considered spending a Season in London?

Moreover, in spite of her aunt's assertion that Amanda would be foolish to turn down the chance of a lifetime, Lady Marlowe had offered no practical suggestions for ways in which to remedy the deplorable state of her niece's wardrobe. One could hardly expect to mingle with the *haut ton* when one's clothes so obviously proclaimed one's straitened circumstances. The crisp good sense of this logic was what had so shaken Amanda, and caused her to reconsider her decision.

Perhaps, in the final assessment, it would be wiser to become a governess, she reflected soberly. What did it matter if she didn't go to London? After all, there was a good deal more to life than making friends and dancing and going to the theater and feeling carefree and having fun . . . well, wasn't there?

Oh, how she yearned for a sympathetic ear at this moment, a confidante who had her best interests at heart and the wisdom to advise her! Along this path lay more distressing thoughts, for who but her own dear mother and father had ever performed that service? She had been very close to both her parents, which had made their sudden, senseless deaths that much more difficult to bear. Even after a year, the memory was still painful for Amanda, and the deep breath she drew was shaky with emotion.

"Well, I see you are in the mopes today," observed Eve with sarcasm, laying aside the current month's issue of *Ackermann's Repository,* which she had been perusing. "Is it this beastly rain, or just another one of your nonsensical fancies?"

Amanda forced her lips into a small, mechanical smile. "Oh, a bit of both, I suppose," she said briefly. Abandoning her stance at the window, she joined her cousin on the settee. "But unfortunately it is not at all nonsensical." She hesitated, wondering if she was mad to confide in her cousin. But who else was there?

"Eve," she said finally, in a low voice, "I just cannot convince myself it is right for me to go to London. Under the circumstances, it seems more like . . . like sheer lunacy!"

Eve made an exasperated sound. "Lud, Amanda, it would be lunacy *not* to!" she countered, her expression faintly contemptuous. "I thought we had been all over that. Are you really such a clutchfist that you would throw away a London Season only to avoid spending a few guineas?"

"But I am not!" Amanda protested, stung by such unfair criticism. "There is no question of its being *only a few guineas,* you must know that! I simply do not have the resources that are available to you, Eve. What income I have is barely sufficient for my needs, and certainly far too small to purchase the vast numbers of new gowns that you tell me are of absolute necessity for a Season in London!"

"But you have four hundred pounds!" objected Eve, retrieving her magazine and flipping it open with a snap.

Amanda gazed at her cousin, willing her to understand. "Tied up in stock, Eve. I cannot spend it, don't you see? Anyway, that money may have to last me the rest of my life. Mr. Goodall has advised me most earnestly not to touch the principal so it will—"

"That stuffy old windbag!" scoffed Eve, her eyes on the pages she was turning. "I daresay he has never in his life advised anyone to spend so much as a groat! Save, save, save, then sit around and count it by yourself! You will end up a spinster, Amanda."

Feeling defeated, Amanda sat back, knowing her impulsive confidence had been a mistake. She should have learned her lesson by this time, she thought grimly. Aloud, she said, "Mr. Goodall is a very kind and knowledgeable gentleman and I intend to take his advice."

"Then I shall lend you the required funds until you can repay me," stated Eve in a bored tone, as if that were the end of the matter.

Surprised by the offer, Amanda hesitated, then slowly shook her head. "It is good of you, Eve, but I . . . I cannot accept. It would take much too long to repay you, since it would have to come out of the interest. And such a debt would place me in an excessively awkward financial position."

Flipping another page, Miss Eve Marlowe gave a cynical snort. "Good gracious, Amanda, what fustian you talk! Your husband will do the paying, you ninny. Consider it an investment in the future—all women do, I assure you."

By now used to her cousin's rather worldly remarks, Amanda was unimpressed. "Oh? And suppose no one makes me an offer?" she inquired, calmly determined to make her point.

It was unfortunate that her aunt chose that instant to enter the room, and Amanda flushed slightly, conscious of the penetrating look bestowed upon her by that austere and ponderous female. Even in her youth, Jane Marlowe had been no beauty, and time had not been particularly kind to her. Her face was heavily jowled and her teeth, never her best feature, had yellowed with age. She wore a turban over her graying hair, and was clever enough to abstain from those excesses of fashion which would have done her bulky anatomy no service.

"I am glad to hear you express some concern on that head, Amanda," wheezed Lady Marlowe, launching into yet another of the prosy speeches that set her niece's teeth on edge. With some effort, she lowered her person into a large wing chair opposite the girls. "And none too soon! I sincerely hope that you will exercise a little more control over your tongue when you are at my sister's than you are wont to do in this house!"

Sniffing audibly, her ladyship rearranged her skirts. "In general," she continued, "your remarks are far too unreserved to please, and could very well ruin your chances of contracting a respectable alliance. Gentlemen do not like to have their opinions questioned by ignorant young girls from the country."

As usual, Amanda could feel her temper flaring at her aunt's condescending manner. "But Aunt Marlowe," she retorted, trying to control the asperity in her voice, "I am not going to London to search for a husband. And if I were—which I'm not—the last sort of man I would wish for my husband would be one who . . . who didn't want a wife who could think for herself! Or was willing to pretend that she couldn't. Why, it's the most absurd thing I ever heard! I'd rather stay unmarried than live such a . . . a farce."

As she spoke, her aunt's lips had tightened in disapproval, but it was clearly Eve who was more shocked.

"Unmarried!" she echoed, allowing the magazine to slip from her fingers as she stared incredulously at her cousin. "You don't wish to marry, then? Amanda, you cannot be serious!"

"I didn't say that," Amanda corrected, rather tartly. "Indeed, I hope very much to meet—someday—a person whom I can love . . . and who will return my love." Groping for words that her cousin and aunt could accept, she went on, "What I am saying is that it is not for that express purpose that I accepted Lady Besford's very obliging invitation. And as for ruining my chances of marriage"—she shrugged—"I might not be the quiet, shrinking miss you want me to be, but at least I don't pretend to be what I'm not."

"Shockingly outspoken is what you are!" apostrophized her aunt grimly. "Just like your mother, more's the pity!"

Another surge of anger tapped the reserves of Amanda's patience. "If I am a bit outspoken, Aunt Marlowe," she said defensively, "the man I marry will simply have to love me in spite of it, or . . . or perhaps *because* of it." She paused for a moment, then added, with greater vehemence, "But *certainly* not because he thinks I will sit about with my mouth shut, agreeing with everything he says and never having any opinions of my own!"

Lady Marlowe smiled thinly. "I can see you are of a romantic disposition, Amanda, and I would not be doing my duty if I did not advise you to put aside such sentimental daydreams. Eligible offers do not grow on trees, and you would do well to remember it. With your lack of a proper dowry you will be extremely fortunate to marry within your own class."

She frowned, noting her niece's obstinate expression. "Perhaps Emily can talk some sense into you. I beg you will not forget, Amanda, that this may be the only chance you ever have to go to London as a member of the class into which you were born. And it has come about solely through my sister's generosity! Should you be fortunate enough to receive a respectable offer while under her protection, I sincerely trust you will come to your senses and accept it. Though I cannot consider it likely," she added in repressive accents.

"But, Mama, Amanda still does not think she ought to go to my Aunt Besford's and in truth I own she may be right." Eve's eyes traveled from Amanda's plain gray gown to her own modish attire with unconscious satisfaction. "Really, Mama, how can she go when her clothes are in such a state? She will be the laughing-stock of London!"

Lady Marlowe studied Amanda's simple country frock, and wondered for the first time whether people might condemn her for refusing to furnish her niece with more suitable attire. She saw no reason why she should do so, but said, in a sudden burst of magnanimity, "That is true, Amanda. Something must be done. It's a crying shame your parents were not able to provide more adequately for your future! You've good blood in you, too! It's not as if either one of them came from common stock. Who on earth would they have procured for you to wed, I wonder? Some brandy-faced farmer, no doubt!"

Her ladyship shook her head, dolefully recalling the events surrounding Katherine Haines-Scott's elopement with the old baronet's third son, a lengthy impartation which took several minutes, and caused Amanda to grind her teeth with fury.

"Well, I have thought it over," Lady Marlowe concluded, "and upon reflection I wonder if things might not have worked out for the best. How else could you have secured an invitation to London? The scandal of your mother's elopement is long forgotten. Fate has given you a chance at a respectable future." She bit her thumbnail thoughtfully, unaware of the growing rigidity in her niece's jaw.

"I think the best solution is for me to go through my daughter's things and weed out a selection of items she will not be needing. We can get Mrs. Larson from the village to alter them to fit you." Her ladyship's top-lofty tone proved the last straw.

"No, thank you, ma'am!" Her cheeks flushed with wrath, Amanda jumped to her feet. So her aunt considered it "best" that her parents had died, did she? So that, because they were gone, she might have a respectable future? Oh, how convenient, to be sure!

"I would not for the world put you to so much trouble on my behalf!" she flung at her aunt in a voice trembling with rage. "As I intend to make my own purchases when we reach London, it will be *quite*

39

unnecessary to give me any of my . . . my cousin's castoffs!"

"Sit down, Amanda!" Her bombazine-covered bosom swelling with displeasure, Lady Marlowe's eyes hardened at her niece's insolence. "If that is your decision, then so be it! At least I know I made the offer. Your actions make it clear that you intend to make as much a mull of your life as did your poor mother, God rest her soul."

Obeying, Amanda sat stiffly, the high color in her cheeks and the angry silver sparkle in her eyes at odds with her compliance. It was quite likely that she would have swallowed her pride and accepted her aunt's suggestion had Lady Marlowe not been so unwise as to choose that moment to belittle Roger and Katherine Marlowe. This was but one in a series of slighting remarks that Amanda had endured since coming to live at Birchfeld Manor, and she had known it was only a matter of time before she lost her temper. Amanda would have liked to have forestalled its eruption, for she fully appreciated that the consequences of losing one's temper were never pleasant. Even so, at the moment she was still so indignant, she told herself that she would rather die than retract what had been a decidedly hasty refusal.

To her credit, Eve never joined her mother in her disparagements of Amanda's home and family, but neither had she ever tried to discourage her mother's behavior. Amanda found herself wondering, as she had done many times in the past, just how Eve's mind worked, and inwardly marveled at her cousin's ability to dissociate herself from any unpleasantness. Where another person might have felt embarrassed or uncomfortable, Eve appeared totally oblivious to the tense atmosphere in the room. She had retrieved *Ackermann's Repository* from where it had fallen to the floor, and was studying with single-minded absorption a fashion plate depicting a jaconet muslin walking dress over a peach-colored sarcenet slip.

"Look, Mama!" she now interjected, twirling the periodical around and holding it aloft. "Isn't this the most luscious gown? 'Tis exactly what I have been wanting! Don't you think it would suit me?"

Lady Marlowe's cold eyes softened as they rested upon her daughter. "Yes, indeed it would, my angel, and you shall have it! I intend to spare no expense in launching you upon society. And when you are 'my lady' we'll have the satisfaction of knowing that every guinea was well spent."

"Lady Vale," Eve murmured, with the air of one hearing the name for the first time. "I shall quite like being a Marchioness, I think."

"Er, yes, perhaps my Lady Vale." Lady Marlowe sounded a little dubious.

Eve shot her mother an inquiring glance. "Perhaps, Mama? You think he may not come up to scratch?"

Her ladyship winced. "You really mustn't use such vulgar phrases, my love," she pleaded. Directing her frosty gaze at Amanda, she added, most unfairly, "Where *can* you learn them, I wonder?"

Eve's beautiful mouth slid into a pout. "Oh, Mama, don't tease! Just tell me what you are trying to say."

Lady Marlowe hesitated, then sighed. "As you know, it is the match your father desired for you. For my part, I have not been entirely comfortable with the idea these last few years. All the Brinvilliers men have

41

sown their oats, but this one, my love, has taken oat-sowing to the extreme! Only last fall, there was such a to-do! These dreadful duels! And then there is worse!"

She paused, gathering her strength for the next part of the story. "His name was linked with a young woman of quality in a particularly shocking scandal about six years ago. I don't choose to relate the details, indeed, the tale is not fit for unsullied ears! Suffice it to say that even your father was disturbed, and Lord knows *he* was inclined to gloss over most such indiscretions as mere . . . mere peccadilloes to which the male sex is ever entitled." This last statement was delivered in an uncustomarily bitter spirit, and Eve looked rather surprised.

"But, Mama," she argued, gazing thoughtfully at her fingertips, "surely whatever story you heard was greatly exaggerated. You yourself always say that three-quarters of all the tittle-tattle one hears is pure fabrication."

"And so it is," agreed her mother heavily. "But a great deal of it is based on fact, nonetheless, and in this case I am convinced that a large portion of it is true. I voiced my concerns to your father at the time, but Sir Hugo did not agree. These men! Once they get a maggot into their heads there is no swaying them! Your father insisted that marriage was bound to improve Lord Vale. I am not so sure. I have never held with the theory that reformed rakes make the best husbands, for one never knows if they are truly reformed until it is too late!"

Lady Marlowe's somber gaze rested on her daughter's face. "It is one thing for one's husband to have an Interest on the side—that is common enough, I assure you! Oh, I know" — she held up one thick hand — "convention dictates that unmarried young girls should know naught of these things! But why must ignorance and innocence go hand in hand? There is a vast difference between life and what you may read between the covers of a romance. Perhaps if more girls were warned, there would be fewer of these sordid little scandals."

"Dear Mama," said Eve satirically, "I am not as ignorant as you seem to think. It is Lord Vale's position in society that concerns me, not his past. If he is not a dead bore, why so much the better!"

Eve's views invariably baffled Amanda, but this, she thought, surpassed everything! Reentering the conversation despite her aunt's obvious disapproval, Amanda said curiously, "But why are you so set on marriage with Lord Vale? You've told me you haven't laid eyes on the man in years."

With a derisive laugh, her cousin's blue eyes narrowed in amusement. "Gracious, Amanda! You can ask that? The man's worth thirty thousand a year, at least! I should think that reason enough!"

Amanda stared in amazement. "But . . . but you cannot really mean that, Eve! Surely there are other considerations!"

"For once, Amanda is right," agreed Lady Marlowe grudgingly. "There will be other eligible gentlemen after your hand, my darling. Your father is dead, and *I* will certainly not compel you to wed Lord Vale. It is entirely possible that you may meet someone who is not only more suitable but more to your taste. There are other rich and titled gentlemen, though perhaps not many as personable."

43

The possibility of a better match had not, it seemed, occurred to Eve. A new, rather speculative look gleamed in her eye but she said only, as if to herself, "So I am free to choose, then. That is good to know."

"It is not necessary for you to repel his lordship, you understand," Lady Marlowe explained punctiliously. "Indeed, within the boundaries of propriety you may encourage him all you like. To have him dancing attendance on you can only be a feather in your cap, for there is no denying he has been a choice prize on the Marriage Mart for years, despite . . . that other business I mentioned. The important thing to remember is to keep your wits about you and not be taken in by fortune hunters. My sister will be able to tell you who those are." She transferred her attention to her niece almost as an afterthought. "And you, Amanda. Allow Lady Besford to guide you and you should go on perfectly well."

It was not until much later, as she sat at her dressing table before dinner, that Amanda had the leisure to think through the odd conglomeration of information that her aunt had hurled at them that morning. She was kept quite busy performing the many duties which normally occupied her afternoons, and when she finally sat down, it was to complete some needlework for her aunt.

Amanda was unused to living such a tightly constricted existence. Never more fully than now did she appreciate the degree of freedom her parents had permitted her to enjoy. She had come and gone as she pleased, made friends with whomever she wished, and consorted with persons of all walks of life. Neither had anyone ever questioned her right to an opinion, as Aunt Marlowe frequently did, though her father had always insisted that she try to be as informed as possible upon any topic she might choose to discuss. He had taken care that she was educated and encouraged her to read widely, himself undertaking her instruction in the classics. How her mother and father would have chuckled at some of Lady Marlowe's remarks! But even her aunt was entitled to her opinions, Amanda reminded herself sternly as she pulled the pins from her hair and picked up her brush.

As unhappy as she had been these past few months, she was still of two minds about leaving the Manor. She strongly resented Lady Marlowe's criticisms, and misliked the state of affairs which necessitated her remaining under her aunt's roof. But was going to London the solution to her problems? Or was it best to relinquish forever this one opportunity to visit the world which had been her mother's, and of which Katherine Marlowe had spoken so much? Employment as a governess would always loom as an option, whispered her rash, impulsive voice. But this might be her only chance to see London, at least under such incredible circumstances!

As she stared past her reflection into her thoughts, Amanda realized that much of her previous ire had already faded. It was simply not in her nature to remain angry for very long, which in part, she supposed glumly, made up for her frightfully shocking temper.

Deciding that she had better go and apologize to her aunt, Amanda began to consider the best choice of words. It was at this precise moment that the door to her bedchamber flew open, and a slight figure scurried halfway across the room before coming to a surprised halt.

"Oh, forgive me, miss! I didn't think you was still in 'ere!" gasped the little maid, bobbing a timid curtsy.

Amanda turned to give the girl a reassuring smile. "Hello, Kitty. Did you want something?"

"Yes, miss," nodded Kitty, rubbing her reddened hands on her apron. "That is ter say, I was sent, miss. I'm ter start packing yer things."

"Packing my things!" repeated Amanda, astonished. "Whatever for?"

"Oh, so you 'aven't 'eard, then, miss?" The maid looked delighted to be the bearer of important tidings. "It be Miss Eve. She be in a rare taking, all right. One o' the kitchen maids 'as taken sick." She paused dramatically. "Wi' chicken pox, miss!"

Amanda surveyed the girl with frank disbelief. "Are you telling me that my cousin is distressed because one of the servants is ill?"

"Well, yes an' no, miss," answered Kitty, who was rapidly forgetting her initial alarm at being drafted from her duties in the kitchen to attend her ladyship's niece. "She be unhappy all right, but it ain't no concern for poor Trix what's got 'er kickin' up such a dust! Miss Eve ain't never 'ad the chicken pox, that's the 'obble, miss!"

"Oh, I see," said Amanda, wrinkling her brow.

Interpreting this as a signal to continue, Kitty nodded. "Yes, miss," she repeated. "Miss Eve says she ain't about ter miss another one o' them Lunnon Seasons, not because o' no silly disease. One o' the 'ousemaids

46

'eard Miss Eve say she'd die afore she'd sit around wi' spots all over 'er phiz and let some other girl steal all the Markisses—whatever *those* are! That's why 'er ladyship says yer both ter leave on the morrow, and *that's* why I got ter start apacking yer togs, straight-away, miss!"

Amanda watched as Kitty, stronger than she appeared, hauled her small trunk out of the corner and across the room. "Poor Trixie," she said presently. "I hope she has seen a doctor?"

"Aye, she be well taken care of, miss, and Lor' bless you for askin'. Miss Eve, now. She don't care tuppence for such as us!"

Aware that she ought not to encourage such confidences, Amanda responded uneasily, "Now that is untrue, Kitty, and a most improper sentiment. I . . . I am ashamed of you."

Kitty hung her head. "I'm sorry, miss. 'Deed I am. I got no wish ter make you angry. It's just that you be different, miss. More carin', like. I thought you'd understand, being as 'ow you stood up ter 'er ladyship this mornin', and all. We all 'eard about that below-stairs. Old Jenkins, he told us, *'that Miss Amanda's been snubbed once too often, and she's let 'er ladyship 'ave it'!"*

"Oh, no!" cried Amanda, chagrined by Kitty's enthusiasm. "How did he—? No, don't tell me! Pray, don't discuss it anymore, Kitty. I must go and apologize to my aunt."

As she anticipated, she found Lady Marlowe in her cousin's bedchamber, and one glance around the room, which resembled a scene out of Bedlam, was enough to assure her that Kitty's information had indeed been correct. Her cousin's long-suffering abigail was attempting, despite a series of ceaseless and often conflicting commands from her mistress, to create order out of chaos, a task rendered all the more difficult by the fact that Eve appeared to be flinging items of apparel in all directions without discrimination.

"Parsons, do be careful with that! I don't want it mussed. Not that shawl, dolt, the new one! Give that one to my cousin. I daresay she'll—oh, there you are, Amanda! Have you heard—?" Eve tossed a blue velvet pelisse carelessly onto the bed and plopped herself down on its edge. "I could not have believed that such ill luck could befall me!"

"But that is absurd, Eve. It is not you who are unwell," Amanda pointed out, in a reasonable tone.

"Oh, what has that to say to anything? Provoking creature! I shall be next if I remain in this house. I feel it in my bones!"

"Certainly you must go at once," concurred Lady Marlowe from her chair near the fire. "It is regrettable that you must arrive on my sister's doorstep without a word of warning, but I know Emily will understand. She is looking forward to your coming and will not care if you are a week early." She scrutinized Amanda rather coldly. "Under the circumstances, it would have been impossible for me to have provided you with any additions to your wardrobe, Amanda. Perhaps it is as well that you have decided to spend your own money."

Amanda squared her small shoulders. "As to that, Aunt, I . . . I want to apologize. I realize my behavior this morning was very much at fault. It was unforgivable of me to fly off the handle at you the way I did."

48

Her ladyship inclined her head and permitted herself a small, rather sour smile. "Very well, Amanda. We shall say no more about it. Now you must be sure you have a good rest tonight. I have instructed Kitty to assist you in the morning as you will be leaving very early. I suggest you retire immediately after dinner."

"I shan't leave my room tonight!" declared Eve. "I will take a tray in here, Parsons. Pray, see to it immediately. And don't allow that wretched girl to so much as *touch* my food!"

Amanda peered through the half-open window of the coach into the growing darkness of the London streets. Here and there, lamplighters were going methodically about their business, and what meager illumination resulted from their efforts availed her a fascinating glimpse of the hodgepodge of humanity populating the outskirts of the metropolis. Weary apprentices and liveried footmen wended their way toward unknown destinations; raffish bucks strolled arm-in-arm with buxom, painted ladies; a portly shopkeeper waved his hamlike fist threateningly at a cowering, pale-faced urchin; a pair of pickpockets stalked a finely garbed gentleman swinging a malacca cane; a crippled soldier on a three-legged stool held out a battered tin cup to those who passed. These were but a few of the sights that caught Amanda's wide-eyed gaze, though she was too naive to comprehend the implications of much of what she saw.

Despite the hour, carts, coaches, and carriages filled the cobblestoned streets, and the scent of horses and their droppings mixed with the foul smell of the whale oil lamps. The sharp blast of a horn startled her, and she watched as one of London's famed maroon and black mail coaches lumbered past, setting out on its nightly journey piled high with passengers and luggage. The guard standing on the boot at the rear blew his long brass horn once more, causing Eve to utter a soft moan and open her eyes.

"What a frightful sound! My poor, poor head aches so dreadfully, Amanda. If it should be this noisy at my aunt's, I don't think I'll be able to bear it!"

"I'm sure it won't be," soothed Amanda, patting her cousin's hand. "This cannot be the fashionable quarter of the city." Eve only moaned again in response, and lay back against the velvet squabs. Amanda regarded her sympathetically but soon turned back to the window, drawn by the strangely exhilarating stirrings of the restless city.

It was almost completely dark when they drove into the quieter West End area, where the streets lined with grand mansions were brightened by lights of a dazzling brilliance. Set in elegant lamp-posts of wrought iron or burnished copper or bronze, the new gas-lit lamps shone like splendid beacons compared with the feeble flicker of the old oil lamps.

In a way, it was the most beautiful sight Amanda had ever seen. Though the hues and colors of daytime were lost, the pools of light melting into deepening shadows gave the tall, symmetrical, brick buildings of Berkeley Square a mysterious look. To one who had lived her entire life in the country, it was almost exotic. Something in the scene awoke a vague longing within her, not a new sensation but one which was achingly familiar. It was that same longing that touched her when she wished to share a joke — and there was no one to tell. It came to her each time she watched a red-gold sun sink behind dark hills, throwing its last rays up to gild the edges of a summer cloud — and there was no one else watching. And it came to her at night, often, as she lay alone staring past the curtains at a cold, glistening moon when she had nothing but her pillow to press her face against.

No, she had *not* come to London to entrap some gentleman into marriage. But even while her mind rejected such a grasping, emotionless approach to the sacred state of matrimony, Amanda could not deny her heart was lonely. Now more than ever, she was beginning to realize just how much she had never seen, had never experienced. Was he out there somewhere? Could the man her heart craved so fiercely possibly be near? Did he even exist?

Chapter Three

Outside Amanda's window the sun was shining like an omen of good fortune. It looked to be another beautiful day, she thought, as she swept aside the velvet curtains to gaze upon the stately residences of Berkeley Square. In view of the weather's fairness, Amanda was almost sorry she had not accompanied Lady Besford and her cousin to Bond Street. However, she had already learned that shopping in London was, at least for her, to be a pointless pursuit.

It was her third day in London. Practically the whole of the first and second had been spent rushing from shop to shop, and while Amanda had immensely enjoyed the hustle-bustle and excitement of the crowded streets, she had been appalled by the exorbitant city prices. Everything seemed to cost three to four times what it would in the country, she had noted with dismay.

Eve's aunt had taken the two girls to her own modiste, a Madame Simonnet, in Oxford Street. Madame was actually English, but since everything termed *Parisienne* had long been considered "all the crack," Madame had wisely adopted a French pseudonym. Lady Besford was one in a very select clientele, a clientele which included such ladies of rank as the Duchess of Richmond, Lady Jersey, and Countess Lieven, wife of the Russian Ambassador. Madame's prices were correspondingly dear, and although that small detail had not troubled Eve, who equated cost with quality, it had quite dashed Amanda's last hopes of purchasing a new gown or two for herself. The only items of apparel she bought throughout that first long day were two pairs of silk stockings and a length of Brussels point lace with which to refurbish, as much as possible, her yellow muslin.

Amanda had been embarrassingly aware that Lady Besford had expected her to order gowns for herself from Madame Simonnet, and had been puzzled when she did not. However, the Countess had tactfully said nothing, and Amanda, torn between the wish to explain and the hope she need not, was almost relieved when her ladyship granted her the opportunity to do so in private that first evening.

"Quite frankly, I do not have nearly the energy I used to, my dears. When I was your age, I could spend all day shopping and still dance 'til dawn, but those days are long over. Amanda, I have something in particular to say to you. Pray accompany me upstairs, if you please. I shan't keep you long." Lady Besford bid goodnight to Eve, who was also on the point of retiring, and swept from the room, leaving Amanda to trail after her with a sinking heart.

Amanda was soon seated before a crackling

hearthfire in her ladyship's bedchamber, a handsome room decorated in various shades of rose and silver. It was dominated by a large four-poster bed of carved mahogany, whose counterpane and hangings were of rose silk, and hand-embroidered with tiny, exquisite rosebuds. Before she had the chance to observe much more, however, Amanda became conscious of the Countess's searching blue eyes upon her face.

"Well, Amanda? I daresay you know what it is we have to discuss."

"I suppose so, ma'am," Amanda faltered.

Lady Besford patted her hand reassuringly. "You look unhappy, child. This past year has been difficult for you, I'll warrant."

Accustomed as she was to Lady Marlowe's sharp tones, Amanda was unprepared for the Countess's gentle sympathy. "Yes, ma'am . . . a trifle. My life has changed so much, you see."

"Jane has been kind to you?"

"Very kind," she responded colorlessly.

"But not as kind as she could be," finished the Countess, who had noted the tiny hesitation which preceded the girl's reply.

Amanda flushed. "Oh, no, ma'am. You must not think—! It is only that I have . . . so little in common with my cousin. And I'm afraid Aunt Marlowe disapproves of me," she added in a low voice.

"Of course she does," said Lady Besford mildly. "She disapproves of nearly everyone, so I hope you do not take it too much to heart. She is very straitlaced, you see, and it is a rare creature who can live up to her high standards. Why, she even disapproves of me!"

Amanda looked surprised. "You, ma'am? But why on earth should she—? Oh, *pray* forgive me! I have such difficulty minding my tongue! Aunt Marlowe says it is my besetting sin."

The Countess laughed. "Good heavens, as if you could not ask me a simple question! Jane disapproves of me, my dear, because I am sadly shatter-brained, and am forever saying the most foolish things!" She reached out to pat Amanda's hand. "Do not look so serious, Amanda. Indeed, you truly may say what you like to me. You will not wish to stand on points with me, I hope."

Amanda gazed at the Countess's round, motherly features in amazement. It had been more than a year since anyone had spoken to her with real kindness, and for a moment she was as close to tears as she had been in a long while.

"It has been difficult," she admitted, dropping her eyes to her lap. "But I am fine now, ma'am. Truly I am."

"Now why do I have the feeling you are telling me a whisker?" wondered her ladyship. "You have not told me the whole, of that much I am certain. Come, child, talk to me as a mother. I have a daughter of my own, grown and married, and I miss her girlish chatter more than you can imagine."

Amanda smiled, blinking back an unshed tear. "Do you, ma'am? What is her name?"

"Her name is Priscilla," answered Lady Besford, "and I shall tell you all about her on another occasion. But right now, I want to hear about you."

And so, haltingly, Amanda told the Countess the entire tale—the unbearable pain of her parents' deaths, the shock of being left homeless, the dubious welcome she had received in her aunt's house. When she came to the part where she had lost her temper with Lady Marlowe, the Countess grimaced.

"Jane never did have a grain of tact," she remarked. "Whatever possessed her to say such a thing? However, I assure you, Amanda, that Jane did not mean to imply that the deaths of your parents was a piece of good fortune! I daresay she would be astonished to discover how it sounded to you."

By this time, Amanda had lost much of her initial reserve in speaking so freely on what she considered a delicate topic. "But that was the least of it," she tried to explain. "She was forever sneering because Papa didn't have any money. She claimed that Mama had disgraced her family by marrying beneath her, and . . . well, you would not credit some of the things she would say! At times, it was as if she were testing me, to see how much I could take. And then, that last morning . . . I simply could not accept her charity when I was so angry. I know it was wrong of me to feel so, but . . . but I could not help it."

"Why was it wrong?" queried Lady Besford. "One cannot help how one feels, my dear. Jane can be oppressive, at best, and I know the circumstances were particularly trying. Remember,

56

though, it is to her credit, and Eve's, too, that neither one of them apparently begrudged you this Season. Most girls would resent such an intrusion into their moment of glory, my dear. And you are exceedingly pretty!" She waved aside Amanda's incoherent protest.

"Moreover, it is perfectly true that your parents' marriage was a mesalliance in the eyes of the world — you must face that, Amanda. But from what you tell me, it seems obvious that they were happy, and that is what really counts. You have the satisfaction of knowing that to be true, and no one can take that away from you."

Amanda smiled shyly at the Countess. "I know you are right, ma'am. Thank you so much for your kindness! I'm afraid I have been feeling quite wretched over the whole business. I . . . I will try to put it behind me and enjoy myself while I am here."

The Countess beamed. "Good! Now we must discuss something else that is going to make you a trifle uncomfortable, I fear."

"My clothes," guessed Amanda, with a sigh.

Her ladyship nodded apologetically. "The gown you are wearing may do very well for the country, but here, to put it plainly, it will not do. You will only hinder your chances of making a respectable marriage, my dear."

"But, ma'am, I truly am not here to find myself a husband! I came simply to . . . oh, enjoy myself for a while, and to get away from —" Amanda broke off, almost biting her tongue at her own stupidity.

57

"My sister," stated the Countess calmly.

"No!" protested Amanda. Then, "Well, perhaps, in a way, but you must not think me insensible to the fact that I owe my Aunt Marlowe a great deal. She has given me a home for the past year and asked for little in return. I *am* grateful, however it may appear."

"I know you are, my dear. But I think we're drifting from the subject, don't you? In London, young ladies of your station in life *must* dress well. Not to do so is to fade into social obscurity, or worse, risk ridicule. There's no denying that upon occasion Polite Society can be terribly impolite, not to mention, cruel. I do not wish to appear deliberately unkind, Amanda. I am merely trying to explain to you why we must put our heads together, and come up with a solution. Since you feel unable to spend any great sums of money, I propose that you allow me to purchase several gowns for you. Believe me, child, it will cause me no hardship whatever. In fact, it would be rather fun!"

But Lady Besford's words, carefully rehearsed, did not have the effect she hoped. Amanda appeared a little pale, but her voice was without a tremor as she politely refused the Countess's suggestion.

"For you know as well as I do, ma'am," she explained, "that there is no reason you should have to buy me anything. I am not your niece. I have no claim whatsoever upon you. What would people say if they learned you had furnished me with a wardrobe? They would label me a . . . a

58

hanger-on, I think. And I would hate that."

"But Amanda, my dear," responded the older woman gently, "no one need know."

"I would know," said Amanda with resolution. "And I didn't come here expecting to go to balls and . . . and such." With more nobility than truth, she added, "In any case, I have no interest in such things. I shan't mind in the least."

"Now, that is a great piece of nonsense!" exclaimed Lady Besford with conviction. "I would have credited you with a little more sense, Amanda. You are far too young and pretty to sentence yourself to such a dull existence. In fact, I refuse to allow it!"

Perceiving the stubborn set to Amanda's jaw, the Countess looked a little daunted. "Oh dear! Well, we shall try it your way for a while, but I think you will be changing your mind very soon. You are young, Amanda, and at your age standing up for your beliefs seems a fine thing to try to do. I remember very well how it is."

When Amanda said nothing, Lady Besford continued brightly, "At any rate, I am determined to give you every opportunity to meet well-connected, unmarried gentlemen. You may not be on the lookout for a husband, but in my view, there could be far worse things than acquiring one!" She stood, and held out her hand to Amanda. "Well, things have a way of coming about, I always say," she added, linking her arm through Amanda's. "The ball I am planning for a fortnight from now is just as much for you, Amanda, as it is for Eve. Once you have given all this some more thought, I know you will change your mind and let me buy you some gowns. It really is the most sensible solution, my dear. But pray do not think upon it too long, for ball gowns are not made in a day, you know!"

In her kindly, enthusiastic manner, Lady Besford continued her chatter until they reached the door to the guest room which was Amanda's. "So you see, my dear, we are going to have such fun! And very soon you will make some acquaintances, and can begin to settle in and feel at home. And you *will* have suitors, never mind the fact that you are not . . . not wealthy! There are plenty of men who will not allow that to weigh with them in the least. I promise you, Amanda, you are going to enjoy yourself a great deal more than you seem to anticipate."

What Amanda actually did anticipate was unknown, even to herself. There was no question in her mind but that she must go to the Countess's ball, though it would be more practical if she did not. After receiving such kindness from that good-natured lady, she would not for the world risk offending her in such a way. Whether it would be the pleasant experience which Lady Besford prophesied was another matter, for ever since that conversation Amanda had remained adamant in her refusal to allow Eve's aunt to buy her a ball gown. Why, to accept such an offer would place her under a tremendous obligation to Lady Besford, no matter that the Countess claimed she could well afford the price of a few gowns. It was unthinkable even to consider it!

But saying "no" hadn't been easy for Amanda, when every particle of her being had longed to accept. It was merely foolish pride, foolish most of all because she clung to it like a drowning man clutching at a shard of wood. The stubborn need for independence had burned inside her since childhood, fostered by a lifetime of parental example. How many times over the years had Mama refused to go to her relations for help? How many times had they gone without something they wanted or needed because Papa had been unable to pay for it? At times, she acknowledged bitterly, such pride could be more a curse than a blessing. For the first time in months, Amanda allowed herself to think about the accident. Perhaps, just perhaps, if they could have afforded to keep their own carriage . . . Amanda's hands flew to her face as a wave of pure anguish rose in her throat.

It was several minutes before she completely regained her control. Then she turned once more to the sunshine and was filled with an uncontrollable urge to be out in it, alive and free and able to draw fresh, crisp air into her aching lungs. Unused to the rigidity of London propriety, it did not occur to Amanda that she ought not to go out alone. With eager hands, she tied the strings of her bonnet under her chin, snatched up her shawl and reticule, and headed for the door.

Hurrying down the two flights of stairs to the ground floor, Amanda paused and glanced around. None of the servants was to be seen. Good! If no one knew she was gone, then no one would be worrying about her whereabouts. She tiptoed across the main hall, eased open the huge front door, and nearly dropped her reticule in startled surprise. A gentleman stood outside, his hand raised halfway as if caught in the act of reaching for the iron bellpull.

Unmistakably a man of rank and fortune, he was garbed in quiet yet fashionable elegance. Perhaps because they were just above her eye level, Amanda noticed his shoulders first. They were just perfect, she found herself thinking, solid and dependable-looking the way a gentleman's shoulders ought to be. As if mesmerized, her eyes traveled up. High, rather prominent cheekbones and a faintly aquiline nose gave a saturnine cast to what was undeniably a handsome face. His hair was black as jet, his jaw, aggressive. It was not until Amanda actually looked into the gentleman's bored blue eyes, however, that she realized she was guilty of staring. And then it was too late, for one black brow had already risen inquiringly and his gaze was sweeping over her in an equally appraising manner.

Color suffused her cheeks. In an effort to regain her composure, Amanda raised her chin and stammered out the first thing that came into her head. "G-Good day . . . sir. May I . . . be of assistance?"

The remaining brow flew up to join its mate, and the boredom disappeared from his eyes. "I trust not," drawled the gentleman, looking lazily amused. "Er, unless you are the butler?"

Under his piercing blue gaze, Amanda began to feel strangely discomposed. "Well, of course I am not the butler," she replied. "Higgins is about somewhere, I expect."

"Then perhaps you would be so good as to summon him," suggested the gentleman, with gentle dryness.

Something in his tone annoyed her, for it held an autocratic note of assumption that she would immediately go and do as she was bid. It annoyed her so much, in fact, that she was prompted to reply, rather curtly, "That's quite unnecessary, I assure you. I can tell you just as well as Higgins that both Lord and Lady Besford are out. Do you wish to leave your card?"

Almost languidly, the gentleman's hand went to his quizzing glass, and for several seconds Amanda found herself subjected to the most insolent examination she had ever experienced. She was extremely put out, for while her pride would not allow her to retreat, the man's tall, very solid body was effectively blocking her exit. There was nothing for her to do but put up her chin and stare back, ignoring as best she could her own embarrassment.

"My dear girl," he finally drawled, "I am unable to fathom your function in this household, but I am reasonably certain it is not to answer the front door. In fact, it is my opinion that you should not even be using the front door."

"Is that so?" Amanda gasped, her sense of outrage reaching a new height. "Well, I am *completely* certain that you are quite the rudest man it's been my misfortune to meet! And I have not the smallest interest in your opinions! Now if you will you please move out of the way, I would very much like to get by."

Somewhat to her surprise, he did as she requested, an almost gallant gesture of his hand inviting her to pass. She looked at him suspiciously, then dropped her haughtiest curtsy and swept regally past him down the steps. She was so occupied in preserving her wounded dignity, in fact, that she missed the appreciative gleam in the eyes that followed her progress. With pointed indifference, she ignored the elegant high-perch phaeton in the street and the gentleman's tiger, but found she could not refrain from darting an admiring glance at his horses, a perfectly matched pair of bay geldings.

At the outset, she had intended to stay within the confines of the Square, but all such thoughts now fled from her mind. Her back stiffly erect, she chose a street at random, and was soon well away from the vicinity. Still seething with indignation, she mentally reviewed the recent episode. Never in her life had *anyone* ever looked at her like that! What an arrogant man! How dare he treat her so! She well knew he had mistaken her for some sort of menial, which in her present frame of mind made everything seem worse.

Of course, once again it all came back to clothes. She had donned one of her older gowns that morning, her shawl was faded, and her simple straw bonnet was a relic from her days in the country. To him, she must have looked and sounded very much like an impertinent servant! Finding this an utterly lowering reflection, Amanda wandered listlessly along some of London's most fashionable avenues without taking the least notice of her surroundings. Perversely, she relived the same scene again and again in her mind. Odious, odious man! If she had been attired in the first style of elegance, he would not have dared to treat her so!

A short while later, it suddenly occurred to Amanda that she had not the slightest notion where she was or how far she had walked. As yet unalarmed, she began to retrace her steps—or at least that was what she hoped she was doing. Surely *something* would soon start to look familiar!

She continued on for some time, pausing now and then to stare around her in perplexity. Had she passed that house before? Or that one? Indeed, they all looked very much alike, and the names of the streets meant nothing to her at all. Oh, how stupid she had been to allow her ruffled feelings to interfere with her sense of direction! Beginning to grow apprehensive, Amanda tried to decide what to do. Well, she had a little money in her reticule—perhaps she could hire a hackney to take her back. After careful consideration, Amanda decided that this was probably the wisest course, and set about to locate such a conveyance.

Although she had observed a number of hackneys earlier, now that she wanted one, of course, there were none to be found. Her frustration increasing by the minute, Amanda bit her lip. The obvious thing to do was to ask someone, but with the exception of a squat, middle-aged gentleman who had ogled her in a most uncivil manner, the few people she had seen had either been too far in the distance or driving past in carriages.

Narrowing her eyes against the bright sun, Amanda studied the nearest house. Would it be considered improper, she wondered, if she simply knocked at the door and asked for directions? Before she could make up her mind, however, a perch phaeton swooped around the corner of the avenue, not ten feet from where she stood. In itself, this was not unusual, for already several others of its kind had done the same—though not, perhaps, at quite so smart a pace. What startled Amanda was that it rolled to a very abrupt stop almost directly in front of her.

Even before his head turned, she recognized its driver. "Well, well, look who's turned up on my doorstep," he drawled, in the same soft voice he had used before. "Were you coming to visit me, sweetheart?" His bold blue eyes trailed over her from head to toe.

This simply could not be happening, Amanda thought wildly. Her instinct was to flee, but for the space of several seconds it was as though roots had suddenly affixed themselves to her feet. Then, before she realized what he intended, he had passed the reins to his companion and leaped to the ground.

Amanda's paralysis ended abruptly. Without any conscious plan of escape, she spun around, and might actually have gotten away if her slipper had not caught upon the rough cobbles. In two easy strides he was beside her, well in time to keep her from falling. "Still angry with me?" he inquired, his strong fingers clamping around her forearm.

Her dignity destroyed, Amanda wrenched her arm from his grasp. "Please . . . please leave me alone!" she cried, the rise and fall of her breasts displaying the measure of her agitation.

"Why, certainly, if you're quite sure that's what you want," he replied, with an infuriating laugh "But if you were not coming to see me, then I suppose you must be lost. At least you *look* lost. And if that's the case, you must allow me to offer my assistance."

Amanda turned to look up at her tormentor, whose lips had curled into a rather curious half-smile. "You are quite right," she admitted with reluctance. "I am lost, and if you would like to atone for your *reprehensible* behavior, you may direct me to Berkeley Square."

He bowed. "I'll do better than that. I'll take you there myself." He glanced up at the other gentleman within the dashing perch phaeton. "That is, if you don't object to riding bodkin. Charles, this is the charming lady I told you about!"

Amanda's cheeks reddened. "It may please you to mock me," she told him, her low voice sounding a little hurt, "but I cannot think what I can have done to deserve it."

For a long moment he studied her, and something seemed to flicker in his eyes. "Why, nothing," he said at last, dropping his flippancy. "Only tell me your name, and I'll promise to see you safely home."

"I most certainly shall not!" she protested, unconsciously clutching at her reticule as if it were a lifeline.

He sighed. "Then I shall have to christen you myself. What name would suit you? Arabella, perhaps? Belinda? Or how about—Prudence?"

"My name," Amanda informed him desperately, "is Miss Marlowe."

"Miss Marlowe!" He looked rather taken aback, and then murmured, "Ah, I see. A relation."

"As you say," replied Amanda, a little wryly. "Now, please. I . . . I beg you to have the goodness either to assist me or leave me alone, I care not which. This whole conversation is most improper, as you must know."

One dark brow shot up. "And what will you do if I leave you?" he said with a quizzing look.

"Summon a hackney!" said Amanda promptly.

He glanced lazily up and down the empty street. "Yes, well, there's never a hackney around when you need one, is there? I think we ought to convey Miss Marlowe home, eh, Charles?"

Until now, Mr. Perth had been making a polite and very determined pretense at deafness. However, since Jack seemed bent on dragging him into the conversation, he obligingly twisted about in his seat and essayed as civil a bow as he could contrive. "No trouble at all, Miss Marlowe," he said handsomely. "Always pleased to oblige a lady. Allow me to introduce myself. The name's Perth . . . Charles Perth."

Relieved that at least one of them knew how to behave properly, Amanda gathered her skirts and allowed herself to be assisted into the perch phaeton. "Thank you," she said stiffly. The seat seemed absurdly high in the air, and she gazed down at the ground far below in slight trepidation.

Mr. Perth caught her look. "Don't worry," he assured her. "Vale, here, is a capital whip! Drives to the inch, 'pon my honor!"

Vale! The man swinging himself into the seat beside her was the infamous Marquis of Vale! Amanda was so dumbfounded, she could make no answer to the Marquis's next outrageous remark.

"It's a good thing you're so small, Prudence. Phaetons were never meant to carry three. Perhaps we should set you down, Charles."

"Not a chance of it," responded Charles, whose sidelong glance had taken in Amanda's horrified expression. "You promised me a go at these bays of yours, and I don't mean to budge before I've had a turn at the ribbons!"

No one more than Charles Perth realized how much the little lady squeezed in between them needed his chaperonage. She had a remarkably sweet face, and he simply did not have the heart to abandon her to the Marquis's advances. Lord only knew what Jack was about, he mused. To Charles's knowledge, at least, the Marquis had never in his life brought his cattle to such a halt — at least not to address some dowdy little chit on the street!

Amanda, meanwhile, was suffering agonies of embarrassment. She had not realized just how cramped would be the space in which he expected her to sit. She was squeezed tightly against both men, but it was the proximity of the Marquis's muscular thigh which for some obscure reason disturbed her the most. "Now, isn't this cozy?" drawled the thigh's owner, evidently bent on making her mortification as complete as possible.

This dreadful man was ruining her whole day, Amanda fumed silently. If he had not driven her to it, she would never have left Berkeley Square, and therefore would never have gotten herself lost! And now look what a scrape she was in! If she arrived home with her reputation intact, it would be more than she expected.

She was stunned when, seconds later, Mr. Perth said, "I say, Jack. This ain't the way to Berkeley Square!"

"We're not going directly there," stated the Marquis equably. "I promised you a drive in the Park, Charles, and that is where we're going."

"What!" cried Amanda, aghast. "Oh, indeed, you must not! You said you would take me to Berkeley Square!"

"Don't be such a grudgeon, Jack," protested Mr. Perth. "Take the young lady home first. It's too crowded in here by half."

"Calm yourself, Charles. You, too, Prudence! It's quite likely the carriage way will be empty at this hour." The Marquis glanced at Amanda. "Therefore, Charles can tool the phaeton once around the Park—if he can manage not to overturn it—while you and I, Prudence, take a little stroll and become better acquainted."

Amanda's hands clenched into fists. "I should have known this would happen," she exclaimed, glaring up at him. "You are obviously no gentleman so I suppose it is foolish of me to be surprised. But you may as well turn around at once, for I can assure you that I have absolutely no intention of strolling anywhere with such an insufferable, odious . . . *ooh*, you are not listening to me!"

The Marquis smiled slightly. "Yes, I am," he corrected, as the phaeton swung through the Stanhope Gate into Hyde Park. He pulled up a short way along the drive and once more thrust the reins into Charles's hands.

"Here you are, Charles. Take care of my horses or I'll have your head!" Before either of his companions could think of a thing to say, the Marquis was out of the carriage and had reached up to grasp Amanda by the waist. "Out you come!" he commanded carelessly.

Amanda had every intention of remaining precisely where she was, but there was no thwarting the strength in the powerful arms that lifted her down from the carriage as though she weighed no more than a bundle of feathers.

Highly alarmed, she appealed to the Marquis's friend. "Mr. Perth!" she called, over her shoulder. "I cannot believe you mean to abandon me to this . . . this reprobate! You, at least, seem to be a gentleman."

"Drive on, Charles," commanded the Marquis, in bored tones.

"Don't know as I should, Jack," Charles responded miserably. "The lady don't seem to want your company."

The Marquis rolled his eyes. "I'm not going to ravish her here in broad daylight, for God's sake!

71

Do give me credit for a little natural restraint! Now, don't keep my horses standing about, Charles. You are very much *de trop* at the moment, you know."

"Tell you what," wavered Charles, trying to compromise. "I'll drive as far as that group of trees down there, then turn around and come back. Shouldn't take more than ten minutes at the outside. Then I'm going to take Miss Marlowe home!"

Amanda watched him drive off in frustrated dismay. Then she rounded on the Marquis. "Why are you doing this to me?" she demanded, trying her best to hide how very small and defenseless he made her feel.

The Marquis shrugged. "Call it the whim of the moment," he replied, once again wearing his mocking smile. He offered her the crook of his arm. "Shall we?"

There seemed little she could do other than submit gracefully. There was no one nearby, and screaming for help seemed not only extremely undignified but would be, Amanda thought pragmatically, very likely of no use at all. Whatever his motives, the man was unlikely, as he himself had pointed out, to molest her in such a place.

"There, now, isn't this better?" he inquired after they had walked a few steps.

"I have nothing whatsoever to say to you," stated Amanda, instantly contradicting herself by adding, in scathing accents, "If I were a man I would hit you, but alas I am not, so I must suppose you will go unpunished for your . . . your *infamous* conduct!"

"By all means, go ahead and hit me," he challenged, flashing her another of his oddly disturbing smiles. "I won't strike back, I promise."

"Now you are being ridiculous," she said in a dampening tone.

He looked amused. "And you, my sweet, are being delightful, despite this extremely unbecoming bonnet you are wearing." Halting, he reached to loosen the ribands and push the offending article back. "Ah, chestnut hair," he murmured under his breath. "I thought so."

Despite Amanda's very real attempt to prevent him, the Marquis easily pulled her close, trapping her arms against his broad chest. For one heart-stopping moment, their eyes met. "Don't look so frightened," he whispered. "I'm not going to hurt you."

Even before his lips touched hers, Amanda's heart was hammering wildly in her chest. The mere sensation of his warm, hard body pressed against hers was enough to drive all rational thought from her head. Never, never in a thousand years would she have believed something like this could be so exciting. And when his mouth finally came down to claim hers, she was even more shocked to discover that a part of her longed to return his kisses . . . .

"No, no . . . you must stop," she heard herself cry weakly, as if from a great distance. In answer, the Marquis drew her closer still, and kissed her again, one hand trailing down the length of her spine in a thoroughly shocking caress. Beginning to panic, Amanda tried once more to push him away, and in doing so managed to free her right arm.

The stinging slap she dealt him contained every ounce of her strength, and judging from his wince, she knew that she had hurt him. Still trembling, Amanda swallowed hard and forced herself to meet the Marquis's incredulous stare. Watching nervously, she could see the clear mark of her hand staining his lean cheek.

It was obvious he had not expected the slap. "I might have known you would do it!" he remarked, rubbing his cheek in disbelief. "You only required adequate provocation, I gather."

"Well, I hope it will teach you a lesson!" she blurted, instinctively using sharp words to conceal her profound agitation. When it became apparent that, true to his word, he was not going to react in a violent manner, Amanda's courage began to creep back. "But I daresay it won't," she added, her voice gathering strength. "It may interest you to learn that I know exactly who you are, Lord Vale!"

The Marquis's eyes narrowed. "You do, eh? Do I detect some underlying meaning in that?"

"You do, indeed!" Amanda answered warmly. "You are a thoroughly scandalous person, my lord. I am near to swooning with the shock of finding myself in your . . . your *disreputable* company!"

To her complete amazement, he burst out laughing. "If you're near to swooning, Prudence, then I'm the Prince of Wales. You seem a most redoubtable girl!"

Observing the approach of the Marquis's phaeton, Amanda made no reply, for her outraged emotions still churned at the memory of what had just occurred. She supposed that most gently bred girls would either have succumbed to strong hysterics or fainted completely away, so obviously she had not the requisite amount of sensibility. Moreover, after having been treated so shabbily, she ought to have conceived a sound disgust for the Marquis, but oddly that was one emotion she did not feel. Dear lord, could she actually have been so shameless as to enjoy the encounter? No, of course she had not. How perfectly shocking that would be! Taking a covert survey of the man at her side, Amanda frowned. He *was* dangerous, she acknowledged, recalling her Aunt Marlowe's insinuations about his past. Dangerously attractive!

Afterwards, she could never quite remember how it happened. One minute, Mr. Perth was out of the phaeton, assisting her to mount with all the gallant courtesy of a true gentleman. Then the next thing she knew, the Marquis was sitting beside her, waving a mocking farewell to poor Mr. Perth, who was left standing at the side of the carriage road, looking exceptionally put out.

Amanda maintained a rigid silence on the return trip, hoping to convey to her companion the gravity and magnitude of his offense. Whether she achieved that goal was uncertain, for although he glanced her way a number of times, she could not even begin to fathom his thoughts. If he was regretting his impulsive action, it was not immediately obvious.

She did not feel equal to the task of sorting through her confused emotions and so began to mull over the possible repercussions this escapade might bring upon her head. She arrived back at Berkeley Square more than two hours after she had left, but miraculously, no one observed from whose carriage she climbed, or remarked upon her flushed countenance as she entered. The Countess and her cousin had only just returned to discover that the Marquis had left his card during their absence, and beyond gently admonishing Amanda for leaving the house unattended, Lady Besford was far too ecstatic to say very much.

Of course, she might have said a good deal more, had Amanda not lost her courage and omitted to mention her own encounter with the Marquis. It was not exactly lying, Amanda told herself, to say that she had gone out for some air, become lost, and wandered around for a while before finding her way.

Her meeting with the Marquis had evoked emotions too complex to discuss, or even analyze, just yet. Of course, Amanda knew she was thoroughly shocked by the Marquis's presumptuous, inexcusable, *scandalous* behavior! Unwilling to delve any further than that into her feelings, she decided to put him entirely from her mind, a resolution that was to prove extremely difficult to keep in the days ahead.

Chapter Four

"But *why* can't you stay, and *where* are you going? You treat me abominably, Jack!"

The baronet's widow could not resist the questions, though instinct warned her the Marquis of Vale was in no mood to answer them. An elusively private man, he seldom warned her of his visits, preferring instead to keep his comings and goings a matter of personal whim. His unannounced entrance into her boudoir an hour ago had caught her quite by surprise, in fact. She wondered if he had somehow sensed her dismay, for his behavior this evening had bordered on the brusque. Even between the sheets he had seemed unusually remote, and she was assailed by the new and unwelcome suspicion that her aristocratic lover was no longer enthralled by her charms.

She watched him as he dressed, her black-fringed violet eyes moving possessively over the hard planes of his tall, very masculine form. It was almost a pity he was so attractive, she thought. He would have been so much more malleable were his lineaments less appealing to the female sex. Perhaps then he would have been suitably grateful for her favors, instead of treating her as if she were of no more account than a common opera dancer. He might even have been eager to marry her, as the lately departed Sir Neville Claverley had done.

Lady Claverley's fingers curled in an unexpected rush of frustration. Her liaison with the noble Marquis had now lasted almost a twelve-month without the smallest sign of its leading to a more permanent arrangement. She knew he could not possibly have misunderstood her hints, yet she had been unable to elicit a single response from him upon the subject. Another woman might have let the matter rest, but not Alexandra Claverley. The marriage of the Earl of Ogmore, in October, to a Mrs. Throdley—his mistress of seven years (and in Lady Claverley's opinion, a very plain, vulgar sort of woman)—had set a torch to ambitions which until then had only smoldered in secret. It had been her hope that the woman's marriage would plant a similar seed in his lordship's mind, but in this she was doomed to disappointment. Vale's reaction to the happy event had been restricted to a short laugh and the observation that he was sorry to see the Earl make such a cake of himself, a warning which the lovely widow was unwise enough to ignore.

"Do come back to bed, darling," she urged, trying a different tack. "I'll be so lonely without you. Why, I've scarce set eyes on you these past few weeks. Who can be occupying so much of your time, I wonder? Is she very pretty?" She stretched with calculated languor, and rolled gracefully on to her side.

Vale glanced at her dispassionately, wondering if

she knew how petulant she sounded. Her position was deliberately provocative, one smooth white arm draped along the curve of her hip, the silken sheets falling forward to reveal full, voluptuous breasts. Coal-black hair framed an oval face with features so perfect they might have been carved from ice.

"Pitching it a little strong, aren't you, Alex?" he suggested, his voice full of its usual flippancy. The mattress sagged under his weight as he sat to pull on his boots.

Lady Claverley rose up on one elbow. "Damn it, Jack, answer me! I'm entitled to know if you've taken a fancy to someone else!"

"Are you indeed?" He turned and subjected her to a cold scrutiny. "And I, too, would consider myself entitled to know if you've, er, taken a fancy — as you so tactfully phrase it — to anyone else." His blue eyes did not waver from her face. "Have you?" he demanded, his tone so emotionless it caused her to shiver.

Startled, Lady Claverley said uneasily, "How can you even ask such a thing? You must know how steady I am in my devotion to you. My feelings for you, Jack, are as indestructible as . . . as a fortress!"

The Marquis sneered. "A fortress, Alex? How very poetic, to be sure. But you neglect to mention that your fortress is built on a hill of sand."

He reached past her and plucked a hair from one of the pillows. "Too light to be yours, too straight to be mine," he mused. "Whose can it be, Alexandra? Do you want to tell me or shall I hazard a guess?"

Lady Claverley paled. "Why, I've no idea where it came from!" she stammered. "What can it signify?"

Under his ironical gaze, she added shrilly, "Am I to be condemned on such slim evidence? It could as well belong to one of the servants!"

"God forbid!" Vale dropped the offending hair fastidiously onto the floor, and sighed. "Frankly, Alex, I don't feel like sparring with you anymore. You have played me false once too often." He stood and reached for his coat. "The time has come for our association to end."

"No! You can't mean that!" she sobbed, and lunged forward to fling her arms around his waist. "Will you judge me guilty because of a single hair? I swear I've been faithful to you!" she insisted.

"Then you are a liar, madam," Vale replied inexorably. Her clutching fingers suddenly filled him with revulsion and he pushed her away. "Devil take it, woman, let be! There was never any chance that I would marry you! Save your histrionics for Frome. Perhaps you can bamboozle him into doing so, but I doubt it. The proud Baron is many things, but hardly a fool."

"How dare you!"

The widow's despair turned to rage at the insult, and she flew at him, thrusting long, elegant fingernails upwards at his face. "I'm not well born enough for you, am I?" she stormed. "The daughter of a Cit just isn't good enough to wear a Marchioness's coronet!"

He captured her hands quite easily and held her off, though she twisted wildly in his grasp, her beautiful features contorted with rage.

"I wouldn't have stated it quite so bluntly," came his brutal reply, "but yes, I owe my name a better bride than you, Alex. Besides birth, the woman I marry must possess honesty and loyalty, virtues of which you apparently know nothing. Good God, Alexandra, did you think that fool, Ogmore, would set a new fashion? There's not a damn reason that I can think of for a man to marry his mistress. It's a mutton-headed thing to do!"

Further enflamed by the Marquis's cool words, she tried to strike him, and he gave her a rough, exasperated shake. "If you must have it, I've been pledged for years to a girl of my father's choosing, and I mean to honor that commitment! But that's not a subject I mean to discuss with you, Alex. My marriage is not, and will never be, your concern."

Despite her rage, the widow recognized the finality in his voice. Her struggles ceased, but her eyes gleamed oddly and her voice turned venomous. "You'll regret this, Jack. You can't insult me and not answer for it."

"You alarm me," he retorted dryly. "Come, Alex, this is ludicrous. You could not seriously expect me to marry you—such a thought would never have crossed your mind before last October. In any case, you're not a woman who enjoys being tied to one man, which is what I will demand of the woman who becomes my wife, believe me."

He decided that something of his logic must have gotten through to the lady, for she relaxed slightly and forced an abrupt, rather harsh laugh as she jerked out of his grasp.

"Well, Jack, it looks as if you've won this hand, at any rate. I can't deny I like my freedom." She tossed her head defiantly and reached past him for her dressing gown. "However, before you go, I've a trifling problem I hope you'll assist me with one last time."

"Let me guess. You want me to settle more of your gaming debts," he said cynically. "You've never lacked for nerve, have you? Well, let it be my parting gift to you, my sweet."

Looping the white satin tie about her waist, Lady Claverley smiled tightly. "In matters of nerve, I suspect we are quite well matched."

The Marquis bowed slightly as he took the stack of crumpled gambling vowels and shoved them into his pocket. By the time he emerged from Lady Claverley's house, both his step and expression had already lightened. Feeling for the first time in weeks as if a small but irksome weight had been removed from his shoulders, he paused and drew a deep breath of cool night air thankfully into his perfume-drenched lungs. Women could certainly be the very devil, he thought.

To be sure there were other, more disturbing things on his conscience than the knowledge that he had grown to dislike the very expensive woman whom he'd been keeping as his mistress. However, there were few things more distasteful to him than Lady Claverley's temper tantrums, and he had found himself procrastinating, waiting for a ready excuse to provide him an expeditious means of escape. The hair had only been a welcome confirmation of what he'd already known—that his mistress was on over-friendly terms with the man whom he considered his enemy, a man who hated the Marquis of Vale for a very personal reason.

The Marquis found himself thinking of marriage

and Eve Marlowe. She would have to be nearly twenty by now. Twice in the past two years a member of her family had died, forcing her to cancel her plans for a Season in London. Twice now, he had been given a reprieve, and he could hardly hope for another. He heaved a sigh. Well, now she was here and was already creating quite a stir among the gentlemen, if what he heard was correct. If he was going to offer for her, he had best get on with it. He could feel the noose beginning to tighten.

Certainly, he knew his duty. It had been drilled into him time and again since he was old enough to be out of leading strings. As the fifth Marquis of Vale, and the only living male who bore the family name, he had been brought to understand from his earliest years that the words *marriage* and *duty* were synonymous. He needed an heir, and marriage to a healthy girl of good birth was of paramount importance. For personal reasons Vale had never understood, his father had selected the daughter of his childhood friend as his son's future bride.

Brinvilliers always had sons. It had been considered a major flaw in his mother that she had failed to conceive a child for almost the entire first decade of her marriage to Vale's father, but when she did, at the age of seven-and-twenty, finally present the fourth Marquis with a male heir, she was generally accounted to have redeemed herself. Four years later she successfully delivered a second child, but since it was of the female sex, this achievement did not merit as high a degree of praise as the first.

The birth of Vale's sister, Frances, had been a difficult one, and for the sake of her health the

Marchioness was warned by her physicians to make no more attempts at childbearing. This proved to be no great hardship for Lady Vale, for she heartily detested her husband and could think of nothing more desirable than to be relieved of any further obligations requiring an encounter with her lord. She promptly retired to Stirlings, the family estate in Sussex, where she proceeded to live quite happily for a number of years surrounded by her servants and a multitude of dogs of indeterminate ancestry. When her husband was in residence, she simply kept to her apartments and ignored his presence. Vale remembered her as a rather eccentric woman, fond of dogs and horses, and tolerant of her children provided they made no noise. Though he had loved her, she had not played a large role in his life, and when she died at the age of forty he had not particularly missed her.

The Marquis frowned at the memory, for it inevitably led to less welcome recollections. His mother had been but a shadowy figure in his life compared with his father. The fourth Marquis had been of a despotic temperament and had ruled his household with intolerance and an almost total disregard for the wants, needs, and opinions of his family. However, when he discovered that his son was not so easy to bully as his wife and daughter, things began to change. The years passed, and the old Marquis's grudging respect for his first-born blossomed into a pride and admiration that was nearly as suffocating as his previous ill-temper. Any young whelp, he had been fond of saying to anyone who would listen, who had the courage to take a stand and defeat *him* in a verbal dispute (by employing the older man's arguments twisted about in a perfectly reasonable manner) deserved to be granted his wishes upon occasion. Though it might have appeared to anyone not intimately acquainted with the Brinvilliers family that father and son were more frequently at loggerheads than in accord, they had actually reached a tolerable degree of understanding. That state of affairs continued until the day the younger man met Miss Charlotte Elizabeth Wythe.

The Marquis could still recall how he had thought her perfect. From the topmost hairs on her golden head to the tender soles of her tiny feet, her angelic beauty had entranced him, and sent his callow senses reeling. She had about her an air of shy fragility and innocence that awakened his most chivalrous instincts, and he had set about to win her as gently and honorably as he knew how.

He was startled out of his romantic daydreams by an interview with his father. Bushy brows drawn heavily together in disapproval, the old Marquis informed his infatuated son that marriage with Charlotte was out of the question and forbade him to continue in his courtship. It was his heartfelt wish, he told his stunned offspring, that his son marry the daughter of his closest friend, Sir Hugo Marlowe, a schoolroom miss then at the tender age of thirteen summers.

Nothing could have been more clearly calculated to set up the younger man's back. In a voice as carefully controlled as it was grim, he consigned his father, in no uncertain terms, to the devil. The ensuing scene was one that even now continued to haunt him.

Somehow the vein of their argument became something more than just a simple quarrel over a girl. For years he had put up with his father's high-handed attempts to run his life, and the cumulative effects of this frustration erupted in one white-hot explosion of fury.

The Marquis's expression grew bitter, as he remembered the events of that dreadful year. There had been that awful episode with Charlotte, followed by his own confusion and retreat from her life. Her suicide had come next and, days later, his father's fatal heart attack. He had grown almost ill at the thought that the rift between them, as well as the scandal of Charlotte's death, had contributed to the old man's demise. The public mask of indifference he adopted was pure self-defense, for there was something in him that demanded he conceal his grief. In truth, he felt somehow responsible for Charlotte's death as well, and in the beginning it had been all he could do to hide from prying eyes his shock and horror at her self-destructive and unfathomable action.

Would marrying Eve Marlowe in some measure alleviate that guilt or was he a fool to think so? This was his hope, for quite frankly he was tired of the guilt, tired of the disturbing dreams that still held the power to rob him of his sleep. He remembered Charles's reaction to his announcement and smiled grimly. No, he was not made of the stuff from which admirable husbands were cast. Not anymore, at any rate.

Though his love for Charlotte had actually been of short duration, there was little doubt that she had

had a profound effect upon his life. Even now, it was difficult for him to dwell upon the hurt and guilt he'd been made to suffer. After her death, he'd resolved never to allow a woman to matter to him again. It didn't take a great deal of intelligence to realize that if one didn't love, one didn't get hurt. Perhaps he was missing something into the bargain, but he'd managed to convince himself he didn't care. He'd settled for a series of sexual liaisons instead, and decided that he could make do with that.

For no definable reason, a picture of the girl he had met that morning entered the Marquis's mind. She was evidently related to the Marlowe family in some way, though to judge from the style in which she had been dressed, she was clearly in some sort of impecunious, servile position. He almost chuckled aloud at the word, his black mood lifting for an instant. He couldn't imagine a less servile sort of girl than little Prudence. A pity she was a member of a respectable family, he reflected. He would have liked to pursue her acquaintance to its obvious conclusion.

He wondered briefly what she had thought of him, and was conscious of an unpleasant stab of guilt. It was precisely the last emotion he wanted to feel at the moment, but nevertheless he faced it, turning it over in his mind. She really had been quite agitated, he decided. He rather admired the way she had stood up to him, and a reluctant smile crept into his eyes when he remembered how she had slapped him. Well, he had not liked it at the time, but he had to admit it had brought him to his senses. He had no business treating a respectable girl in such a manner, and he knew it. But for some inexplicable reason, kissing her had been the most satisfying sensation he'd experienced in a very long time. He wondered why that should be so.

Charles Perth was still spluttering. It was outside of enough to have abandoned him, he wrathfully informed the Marquis, when that miscreant dared set foot in his lodgings later the same day. That was bad enough, Charles told him, tossing off a glass of brandy with indignant expertise. But to have promised to deliver the young lady safely home, then carried her off to the Park against her will and forced his highly improper attentions on her—! Well! Charles had a great deal to say on that head, and proceeded to do so for a number of minutes.

The Marquis remained impassive during most of his friend's expostulations. When he was finally granted an opportunity to speak, he merely said, "I told you before, Charles, I'm not the paragon of virtue you seem to think. When will you give up and admit it?"

Charles scowled. "Damn you, I should!" he answered bitterly. "You behaved like a curst scoundrel, Jack! Admit it!"

"Yes," agreed the Marquis, his features set in an expressionless mask.

"It's all a dashed game to you, isn't it? You don't care who you step on or hurt in the process. I wonder if you give a fig about anyone but yourself!"

The Marquis frowned. "Of course I do, Charles. Come off your high ropes. What I do is my own affair."

Charles stared at the Marquis, an expression of outrage settling upon his countenance. "I see," he said, with awful sarcasm. "Excuse me, my lord, for daring to presume. Never realized you was too high in the instep to take a nudge from a friend, *if* that's what I am, which I'm beginning to doubt."

"I can see I've really done it this time," remarked the Marquis with a sigh. He leaned back in his chair and stretched out his long legs. "Come, Charles, don't be miffed. I'm sorry if I ruffled your feathers. I only meant—"

"Oh, stubble it, Jack," said Charles, rather rudely.

Vale fell silent. Never before had his friend launched into him like this, and it was beginning to dawn on the Marquis that he had genuinely angered one of the only two people in the world for whom he felt any real affection. Preoccupied with this thought, he poured himself another glass of brandy and went to stare out the window.

At last he spoke. "I'm sorry, Charles. I don't know what came over me. There was something about that girl that made me—oh, I don't know! What can I say? Will you forgive me?"

Charles was not about to let him off that easily. Though his indignation had not been assumed, much of his anger stemmed from his concern over the Marquis's growing apathy. They were as close as brothers, yet the Marquis had erected a protective barrier around himself that even Charles had lately been unable to surmount. It was as if the most human part of his friend had been crippled in some way, and could only stand back and observe life with detachment.

Of course, the Marquis had not given up his interest in women. Charles, himself an incurable romantic, found Vale's cynical dealings with the female sex entirely incomprehensible. Females were to protect and cherish and adore, not merely to kiss and bed—or to abduct off the street. Six years before, he was sure Jack had been of like mind, judging from his exemplary conduct with Miss Wythe. But since her death, the Marquis had sought out her opposite—earthy, sensual women like Lady Claverley. That pretty Miss Marlowe was the exception. However, Charles doubted she could hold the Marquis's interest, despite the fact that she had really been quite a taking little thing. She was obviously impoverished, and very likely the paid companion of the girl whom the Marquis claimed he intended to wed! By all the rules, such a circumstance ought to inhibit any gentleman's actions. But Jack did not play by ordinary rules, and Charles was beginning to realize that if he was to help his friend, his own rules would have to change. Charles, in fact, had come up with a Plan.

"It's not for me to forgive you!" he therefore lashed out, with uncharacteristic tenacity. "Wasn't my reputation at risk! That pretty little gal was Quality, Jack. Any fellow with half an eye in his head could see that, even if she was alone! But did you care? Not old Jack! Jack does precisely what he wants, when he wants, no matter who gets in his way! Not content with ruining your own reputation, you must try to ruin others as well! Another pretty miss to add to your list of conquests, eh? Or should I say victims?"

"Go to the devil!" responded Vale, visibly stung. "I

90

ought to plant you a facer for that, Charles!"

"Mill me down for telling you the truth?" asked Charles with a scornful snort. "Go ahead, if you wish to start a vulgar brawl in the middle of my drawing room. I warn you, I won't go down without a fight, though I don't carry your weight."

The Marquis's expression grew blacker. "Do you have anything else to say?" he demanded furiously. "Pray do not spare me! I am a regular care-for-nobody, a seducer of innocent girls — why not add the word murderer to your list?"

"Because that's one thing you ain't! Dash it, Jack! The only thing I'm trying to say is that you're selfish! When was the last time you did anything for anyone else but yourself?"

"I've no idea," said the Marquis with cold indifference.

"You see!" pounced Charles, triumphant. "That's the trouble with you. You need someone or something to care for besides yourself!"

The Marquis cast him a suddenly suspicious look. "If this is all some sort of elaborate scheme to unload that mongrel hound of yours, Charles — !"

"No, no," replied Charles hastily. "I wouldn't part with my Betsy, not even for you, Jack." He ran his fingers through his unruly hair in frustration. "Do you remember that young horse of Nick Warden's? The chestnut stallion you admired back last August?"

"Certainly, I remember the horse. Why?"

"Didn't get a chance to tell you yet, what with all the to-do. The poor fellow's all to pieces. Been playing too devilish deep at Watier's, from what I hear. Macao!" he added, rolling his eyes expressively.

"Anyway, his estates are already mortgaged to the hilt, and now he's selling off his cattle. His grays went to Tatt's on Wednesday, but I managed to track him down before he sold the chestnut. Made him an offer he couldn't refuse."

Diverted, the Marquis gave a silent whistle. "The devil! What did you pay for him?"

"Close on two hundred, but he's worth it."

"Congratulations!" Vale remarked. "If only your driving skills equaled your taste in horseflesh, Charles, you'd be elected to the four-in-hand. Though what this has to do with my iniquities eludes me, I confess."

Charles cleared his throat. "Actually, I'm hoping to lose him to you in a wager."

Plainly startled, the Marquis shot his companion a keen glance. "My dear Charles, I think you've had too much brandy."

"You'd like to own him, wouldn't you?" plunged Charles, bravely setting his plan into action.

"Of course! I tried to buy him from Warden, last summer, but he wouldn't sell. Only name your price."

"I told you, he's not for sale," Charles reiterated. "If you want him, you'll have to win him."

The Marquis's reply was swift and smooth. "You're not, by any chance, trying to manipulate me, are you, Charles? I warn you, I don't dance to anyone's music but my own."

"Selfish!" remarked Charles to the surrounding air. "Just as I said. Arrogant, too. Won't give a fellow so much as half a chance to explain before he pokers up."

Rather amused, the Marquis relented. "All right,

Charles. Explain, I beg you. Though I'm not yet convinced you aren't a trifle above par."

Charles gulped down the rest of his brandy. "You want Warden's chestnut? Then do something unselfish! That's it, Jack. Just do something to please someone besides yourself for a change. Mind you, it can't be just anything," he cautioned, noting the Marquis's incredulous expression. "I'm not talking about helping some old woman find a sedan chair, or tossing a gold guinea to a beggar on the street. I mean, really putting yourself out for another person. Going to a deuced amount of trouble to make someone else happy."

"You must be out of your mind!" pronounced the Marquis with emphasis. "That's the most confounded wager I ever heard!"

"Naturally, you'd think so," Charles told him, nodding wisely. "Not quite as simple as it sounds, though. Conditions, Jack, that's what we need."

"But, of course," agreed the Marquis, vastly entertained.

Charles knit his brow thoughtfully. "First, we must set a time limit. Say, one month? Then, whatever it is you do must fulfill certain requirements. You must do something that will really matter. That's it! If it don't make a difference to someone, over the long term, then it's no good! Nothing too simple, mind. If you can do it, the horse is yours. If not, you refund me the blunt I put out to acquire the horse."

The Marquis sat down and regarded his friend with amazement. "My dear Charles, this is wholly unnecessary. I'm impressed that you would go to such pains to redeem me from my follies, but really!

93

All you will accomplish is the losing of your horse. It will take more than this wager to reform me, I fear."

"Afraid you won't succeed?" goaded Charles.

"Merely reluctant to take unfair advantage of a friend!" flashed the Marquis angrily.

Charles adopted a belligerent tone. "Are you going to accept this wager or not?"

"You're serious, aren't you?" Resigned, the Marquis shrugged, and finished his brandy. "Very well, Charles. If you wish to be robbed of your horse, I'll be more than happy to oblige you. I accept your ridiculous wager."

Chapter Five

If the truth were to be known, the Marquis was altogether floored by Charles Perth's extraordinary and none-too-subtle ploy. He had not considered himself so far gone down the path of Vice as to be branded, in effect, nothing but a self-centered fribble. To be the target of such unrestrained criticism from his closest friend had shaken him more than Mr. Perth would have imagined. If it had been anyone else but Charles, he would have called the fellow out, but coming from Charles—! The Marquis needed no one to remind him that Charles was a thoroughly loyal friend and, in general, a most amiable, uncritical fellow. If Charles believed him selfish, and was sufficiently perturbed to go to all the trouble and expense as to offer him this preposterous wager—why then, he supposed it must be true!

It had never occurred to the Marquis to think of himself as selfish, and he was finding it a most distasteful notion. Of course he organized his life to please himself, for who did not? His immense wealth enabled him to indulge in any of the variety of pursuits open to men of the nobility. He boxed at Jackson's, practiced his shooting at Manton's, attended the races at Newmarket, and availed himself of the company of beautiful women, whenever he was so inclined. Was that being selfish? He attended house parties and shooting parties and any other sort of party which offered the possibility of relief from the boredom which frequently assailed him. Was that being selfish?

He was a member of several prominent men's clubs, and had even been known to visit the gaming hells of Pall Mall, where the perils of roulette and French Hazard brought devastating losses to many poor unfortunates. He was spared that lot, for although he enjoyed the challenge of calculating odds, games of pure chance held no real allure for him. He refused to pay homage to so fickle a mistress as Lady Luck, and invariably listened when his almost infallible sixth sense told him to walk away from the hazard tables. When he won, he felt no sympathy for the other fellow, when he lost, he felt no sympathy for himself. Was that being selfish?

No, by God, he'd be hanged if he'd admit to such a charge! Charles had a damned lot of nerve suggesting such a thing, and as for the absurd notion that he cared for nobody but himself—*that* was a complete bag of moonshine! He cared a great deal for his sister, Frances, and bore as much affection and loyalty for Charles as Charles did for him. Moreover, he was almost always courteous, and paid his servants extremely well for their services. He conscientiously managed his estates, and had never neglected the needs of the families who lived on his lands and depended on him for their livelihood. Charles's accusation was glaringly abroad, the Marquis decided, acutely annoyed. He would make Charles cry pardon, too. He would win that wager, and then magnanimously refuse to take the damned horse! That would show Charles how unselfish he was!

After reaching this satisfactory conclusion, the Marquis turned his thoughts to Eve Marlowe. It was unfortunate that he had missed her. He had been hoping to assess her before she had a chance to acquire a flock of besotted gallants trailing at her heels. He remembered her as being an extremely pretty schoolgirl, and if nature had fulfilled her early promise, Eve was by now, in all probability, something of a diamond of the first water. On the whole, it would be less trouble if he was to stake his claim early, before the girl's head was so turned by compliments that she might choose to play coy with him. Though he enjoyed flirtation, he found the idea of marriage sufficiently depressing as to deprive him of any enthusiasm for the project. He had seen too many unhappy unions to look forward to the wedded state with any emotion other than resignation.

He was consequently pleased to discover, when ushered into Lady Besford's drawing room the following day, that only one gentleman besides himself had chosen that particular time to pay a call. Since that gentleman was none other than his own cousin, Mr. Godfrey Forrester, the cards appeared to be in his favor. At his best, Godfrey was nondescript, and his mild temperament made it unlikely that he would try to compete with the Marquis for Miss Marlowe's attention.

Across from Mr. Forrester was seated the young lady in question, already rigged out, the Marquis noted, in the highest kick of fashion. Her gown of sapphire blue had been artfully chosen to match the exact shade of her eyes, and its modish design displayed her tall, shapely figure to perfect advantage. She reminded him of a statue, he found himself thinking, for her exterior was as cool and beautiful—and as hopelessly remote. The Marquis was rather startled by his own dismay, for physically, she was just the sort of girl he usually admired.

Yet if the hand he bowed over was extended with the composure of an empress, there was a most unempresslike calculation in the gaze that touched his. He recognized it as surely as if he had read her mind, for it was the same look that women had been sending him all his life. It had a great deal to do with his hereditary title, and even more to do with the size of his bank account. It was a look he had come to despise.

"Lord Vale," she murmured, with what he thought remarkable self-assurance for a girl in her situation. "You do us honor. We did not expect that you would call so soon."

"But naturally I would call as soon as I heard you were in town," he replied, keeping his voice neutral. "It is what my father would have wished, as well as your own, I presume."

Lady Besford was hovering flutteringly nearby. "Yes, indeed! So very kind—! Pray allow me to present my other guest, my lord. Miss Amanda Marlowe is my niece's cousin from her father's side of the family. Amanda will also be making her come-out this Season. And, of course, you know Mr. Forrester."

The Marquis barely concealed his surprise. It appeared that little Prudence was not a lady's companion after all, though her drab gown was as unbecoming as it was inappropriate to her station. Now why the devil would she be dressed like that, he wondered, feeling vaguely annoyed.

All at once, he knew that she was nervous. There could be no mistaking the anxiety in her expression, so she must have had the good sense not to mention their meeting to Lady Besford. Those lovely silver eyes were plainly beseeching him to keep quiet, and as he acknowledged the introduction, he sent her a quick, reassuring smile.

She relaxed almost imperceptibly, her relief apparent to him though it went unnoticed by the others. He felt absurdly pleased that she had understood his wordless message, for among other things, he disliked unintelligent women. To himself, he acknowledged that Miss Amanda Marlowe had every right to bear him a grudge, so it was with a certain amount of amazement that he realized there was no trace of ill-feeling in her gaze. Her cheeks did seem a trifle pink, and there was, perhaps, a hint of shy reserve in her expression, but of coldness or animosity he saw nothing. Was it possible she had forgiven him?

"Welcome to London, Miss Marlowe," he told her quietly. He nodded briefly at his cousin. "How are you, Godfrey?"

Mr. Forrester had risen when the Marquis was announced, and he now stepped forward to somewhat unnecessarily shake Vale's hand. "I am in my customary good health, my lord. And yourself?"

Lord Vale lifted his quizzing glass and critically inspected Mr. Forrester's oddly arranged cravat. Out of the corner of his eye, he could have sworn he saw Amanda's lips twitch.

"Oh—well enough," he answered, and flashed her a swift look. "You've managed to steal a march on me, Godfrey. I'd hoped to be the first to welcome Miss Marlowe—or both Miss Marlowes, I should say—to London."

"You are certainly one of the first," inserted his hostess, waving him into a chair. "We've been from home nearly every morning save this one, haven't we, my dears? Though I swear we must have come across half of society in Bond Street! That is how we happened to meet your cousin, my lord. My niece was jostled by some uncouth fellow on the walkway, and Mr. Forrester was kind enough to catch her as she stumbled."

"My dear Godfrey," drawled the Marquis, once more leveling his quizzing glass. "How very fortuitous! To render the lady such timely assistance—! I am all admiration, I assure you."

"It was nothing," replied Mr. Forrester, looking modest. "I was happy to be of some small service."

Feeling a little sorry for the man, Amanda spoke up. "Mr. Forrester has been telling us of all the interesting things there are to do in London. I can see I will have to purchase a guidebook." She glanced encouragingly at Godfrey, who promptly lapsed into an unresponsive silence.

"And a map," advised the Marquis helpfully. "Familiarity with the area one wishes to visit can be a tremendous advantage, I have always found." Although his remark earned him a look of burning reproach from Amanda, he was positive those pink lips twitched yet again. Little Prudence, it seemed, possessed a sense of humor.

"Amanda is interested in the oddest things," Eve informed him, before the other girl could think of a suitable retort. "Good heavens, the very notion of wanting to prowl through some musty old church! I still say it sounds too dreadfully dull and dirty."

The Marquis shifted his attention to the girl he had come to meet. "Oh? Then what sort of entertainment appeals to you, Miss Marlowe?" he inquired blandly.

"Why, Vauxhall, of course, and the theaters, and the opera. After spending so many years of my life buried in the country, bored out of my mind, I am longing to be where people talk about something other than crops and horses." Eve waved a hand toward the window. "And I enjoy driving out when the weather is pleasant. I understand, my lord, that you keep several carriages in town?"

The Marquis had never been accused of being slow to recognize a hint. "I do indeed, Miss Marlowe. You must do me the honor of allowing me to drive you," he responded, steeling himself to remember his duty. "Today, perhaps? Or tomorrow, if you prefer?" He caught himself taking another look at Amanda, but this time her expression was unreadable, for her eyes were in her lap.

It was duly arranged that he would collect Eve Marlowe later the same day at the hour of five o'clock for the daily parade of fashionables in Hyde Park. The remainder of his visit passed quickly and both he and Godfrey soon took their leave.

As soon as they were gone, Lady Besford's plump face was wreathed in smiles.

"Well! That went off rather well, did it not? To have Lord Vale paying you a morning visit so soon is more than I had bargained for! I wonder who told him you were here? Well, I fancy he is a man who makes it his business to know such things. Such an air! Such shoulders! And already to be taking you for a drive in the Park! You are to be congratulated, my dear girl." She gave her niece an affectionate hug.

Eve smiled, but said, "Oh, Aunt! You speak as if he is the only gentleman in town of any consequence."

"Nonsense!" pronounced her ladyship. "You must be as pleased as I am. It is perfectly clear he intends to honor the agreement between your father and his. What a brilliant match! Just wait until I tell Robert!" she added gleefully.

"Perhaps, Aunt Emily, but let's not talk about it. It is not at all a settled thing."

"Of course not, my dear," Lady Besford assured her, recalling the need for discretion.

"Mr. Forrester is a rather odd gentleman," Amanda put in. "Why did Lord Vale seem to be needling him, do you think?"

"Oh, was there ever anything more awkward?" marveled her ladyship. "He is Vale's heir, did you know? If Vale marries, it quite cuts Mr. Forrester's chances of ever succeeding to the title. Though I must give the man credit, for he wears no outward sign of concern. Still, I cannot quite like him, and no doubt his lordship feels the same. How Godfrey Forrester can be related to a fine-looking man like the Marquis is more than I can comprehend! It's ridiculous, of course, but I once had an aunt who told me she always judged a man by the breadth of his shoulders. A nonsensical, skimble-skamble creature she was, but I cannot help thinking what Aunt Caroline would have said about these two!"

"What did you think of them, Eve?" asked Amanda curiously.

Eve shrugged. "Mr. Forrester seems to lack a personality of any sort, so him I would classify as a dead bore. Lord Vale is certainly not a bore, but I did not care for some of his remarks. I felt as if he mocked us all."

"Yet you accepted his invitation!"

"Of course, Amanda. I am not a fool," replied Eve, her scoffing tone earning her a surprised look from her aunt.

Peeking furtively from the window of her bedchamber, Amanda was able to observe the Marquis's arrival shortly before the hour of five o'clock. She had pleaded a headache to avoid being downstairs when he arrived, but instead of lying upon her bed, she found herself pacing the room like a restless cat. She watched the Marquis's tiger run to the horse's heads, while his lordship swung his long, lithe body out of the curricle.

She wished she could hear what he was saying to her cousin when minutes later, he handed Eve into

103

the two-wheeled carriage with a courteous and very charming smile. He was probably flirting with her, she decided, feeling illogically cross at the idea. Abruptly, Amanda realized that what she was doing was nothing short of spying, and she withdrew from the window and sank into a nearby chair.

Propping her chin on the palm of her hand, she stared blindly at the scarlet and green flowered design of the carpet beneath her feet. Why had she been unable to resist watching for him? It was not at all the type of thing she normally did, Amanda reflected uneasily. Of course, he *was* very handsome, but somehow that did not explain all of it. When the Marquis had walked into the drawing room earlier that afternoon, she had expected to feel embarrassed and uncomfortable in his presence. However, the instant their eyes met, those emotions had faded away, leaving her with a curious aura of contentment and the feeling that everything was just as it should be. She had actually almost laughed aloud at his clever sally about the map.

But things were *not* as they should be, she told herself, jumping to her feet. She clenched her small hands into fists. Good Lord! What kind of thoughts were these? He was *Eve's* suitor, and she had better remember it! It was all nonsense anyway, foolish meanderings from the mind of a girl who longed, not for a suitor for her hand, but for a *friend*. If he were not so handsome and she were not so lonely, such thoughts would never have entered her head.

Briefly, she smiled, recalling Lady Besford's remarks about the Marquis's shoulders. Yes, physically he was everything a girl could wish, and most probably this was only a case of admiration for a handsome face. She would just have to be strong and sensible enough to ignore him. Even as this thought went through Amanda's mind she rejected it. It was not going to be that easy.

She knew she ought to dislike him. In one short hour, he had managed, not only to place her reputation at stake, but to make her feel furious, frightened, shocked, helpless, and confused. And God only knew there was a name for the way she had felt when he had kissed her. She had never before experienced the power of a man's touch, and she had been half appalled and half elated by the discovery of how extremely agreeable it was. Even remembering the way his lips had ruthlessly invaded hers made her tremble, and the memory of her own shameless response brought a blush to her cheeks. Well, now she knew what he could do to her, she would certainly be careful never to let it happen again. Not that it would, she mused. After all, it was Eve in whom Lord Vale was interested. Now that he had set eyes on her beautiful, elegant cousin, it was unlikely he would give Amanda a second thought.

Or a second look, she added silently, as she turned to glance at her reflection in the guest room's attractive, gilt-edged mirror. Her gown did not become her—the color was all wrong for her complexion and it was beginning to show signs of wear. Amanda sighed. She had always believed that somewhere there existed a man who would look beyond the exterior, and love her for who she was on the inside. Somehow, it did not seem very likely at the moment. The Countess seemed to think everything in London depended on appearance. What if she was right? She only hoped Eve appreciated the good fortune that had come her way, but familiarity with her cousin's disposition told her not to depend upon it.

Actually, Eve was enjoying herself very much, but not for the reason that Amanda might have supposed. There was the normal afternoon assemblage of carriages in the park, and she was very much aware of the many glances, both envious and admiring, which were being aimed in her direction. Indeed, everyone was curious about the beautiful young blond woman who rode with the Marquis in his curricle. More than one person remarked on the charming picture they made—the gentleman so dark and the lady so fair, with the Marquis's jaunty little tiger perched on his small padded seat at the rear. There was none who questioned the lady's birth and quality, for unlike some, the Marquis was not in the habit of flaunting his bits of muslin before the eyes of the Polite World.

Eve had lost count of the times they had been greeted by some aristocratic lady or gentleman of the *ton*. Many of those who gave her the nod were among the ladies whom she had met when shopping with her aunt. One who was not was the indomitable Lady Jersey, who greeted the Marquis with an imperious nod and cheerfully demanded to be introduced to his companion. To be so accosted by one of the patronesses of Almack's was for Eve a heady experience. She was sure she would be granted one of the much-sought vouchers of admittance, for Lady Jersey, before ordering her coachman to drive on, made reference to their "little Wednesday night gatherings" and voiced the belief that Miss Marlowe might wish to attend.

"Vouchers for Almack's," remarked the Marquis flippantly, when Lady Jersey was gone. "You are now to be assured of social success, Miss Marlowe. I trust you and your cousin will be able to endure the stale cake and insipid company in exchange."

"My cousin—" Eve repeated blankly. "Oh, I don't think Amanda is very likely to go there."

"No?" he said, and gave her an unexpectedly probing look.

"Well, how can she? You've seen her, my lord. It is the stupidest thing, but she will not purchase any fashionable gowns for herself. Everything she owns is shabby and outmoded."

"My friend, Charles, has a grandmother like that," he said, raising his black brows a little. "Rich as Croesus, and still wears the same atrocious gowns that were in style thirty years ago."

"Oh," said Eve, unamused and a little nonplussed. "Well, Amanda doesn't have a large fortune, so it is not the same at all. She is simply too stubborn to borrow from me. My poor aunt has even offered to frank her but without success. I own I cannot understand the girl at all. Aunt Besford is soon to give a ball, and Amanda will have no ball gown to wear to it. She is placing me in an excessively awkward situation with her foolish behavior," she finished peevishly.

"So very thoughtless of her," he agreed.

Ignoring the irony in his voice, Eve presented him

with a serene smile. "I daresay I should not be telling you such things, my lord. You will be thinking me a shameless gossip which, in the general way, I am not. Let us speak of something else."

Vale turned and gave her an inscrutable look. "What would you like to talk about?" he inquired in an unencouraging tone.

Before she could form an answer, they were distracted by the sound of approaching hoofbeats. A lone horseman came cantering down the Row, leapt gracefully over the rail adjoining the carriage road, and trotted up to the curricle.

While not precisely handsome, the gentleman looked well astride a horse. He was obviously tall, perhaps taller than the Marquis, though of a more lanky, loose-limbed build. Eve judged him to be somewhere in his middle thirties, and could find no fault in his appearance. True, his wavy, light brown locks were in dashing disarray, his complexion was a little swarthy, and his black eyes contained something brittle in their brilliance. But his smile was really quite attractive, she noticed. She thought it softened the rather harsh lines surrounding his mouth.

"Why, if it isn't my old friend, Jack," drawled the gentleman, his voice surprising her for some reason with its deep timbre. "What an — unexpected — pleasure." Still smiling, he added deliberately, "Or perhaps that is not quite the right word."

The Marquis stiffened. "Admittedly an odd way to phrase it. To what do I owe this . . . honor?" His tone was so close to insulting that Eve gave him a sharp look.

The man's lip curled a little. "Why, to our so-great

friendship, of course." He made an airy gesture, reminiscent of a fencing feint. "Why else would one come to the Park at this hour, Jack, if not to greet one's friends?"

"Why indeed?" concurred the Marquis with blighting candor. "And when you number among them, Everard, I will be sure and let you know."

"Tut, tut, my boy," said the other gentleman, his eyes glinting strangely. "Such plain speaking! Why do you not strive for a little more subtlety? The lady beside you is wondering where you have left your manners."

Vale's expression was grim. "I save my manners for those who rate their use. As I do my temper."

"Are you, by any chance, threatening me, Jack?"

"If that is how you choose to interpret it."

The other man's eyes narrowed for a moment, and then he laughed. "Such a prickly fellow you are. Why should I wish to force a quarrel? 'Tis far too lovely a day to bicker. And speaking of lovely—I believe I have not the pleasure of the lady's acquaintance." He made no effort to conceal his blatant admiration, and as accustomed as she was to being so regarded, Eve felt her cheeks growing hot under his bold stare.

The Marquis sighed. "You are bound to meet eventually, I suppose. Miss Marlowe, allow me to bring Lord Frome to your notice. He is no proper person for you to know, and I strongly advise you to give him a wide berth. Now, may we continue? My horses grow impatient."

Lord Frome ignored him. "How do you do, Miss Marlowe? But that is a foolish question, is it not? You look to be doing—very well indeed," he said, quizzing her with his dark eyes. "You must pay no heed to anything Vale tells you. He will warn you that I am a dangerous blade, but he is merely afraid I will steal you away from him. I am known to have a great deal of address."

"But not a great deal of modesty," inserted the Marquis sarcastically.

"A show of false modesty can be so irritating," explained Lord Frome, parrying the Marquis's thrust with expertise.

Eve spoke up. "Why, I think I must agree with you, Lord Frome. So many people are shocked when one says something about oneself that is complimentary. But why should we criticize ourselves? There are always others more than willing to do that."

Lord Frome groped for his quizzing glass. "A beautiful woman with all her wits about her!" he marveled. "What an unusual combination. We simply must meet again, Miss Marlowe. Only tell me where you are staying, and give me leave to call upon you, I beg." His black eyes seemed to devour her with their intensity.

Eve smiled coolly. "I am staying with my aunt, the Countess of Besford, in Berkeley Square. And, of course, you may call on me, my lord."

"I shall live only for that moment," he promised. With a mockingly triumphant glance at the Marquis, he briefly doffed his beaver hat, and rode away.

"Why were you so rude to him, my lord?" she inquired, as Vale sent the curricle rolling forward.

The Marquis hesitated. "That is a personal matter, Miss Marlowe. It would be better, I think, if I did not explain."

"I see," she said, a little piqued. "It is none of my affair. Will you tell me nothing about him, then?"

He shot her a penetrating glance. "Did you like him? I warn you, he is a gazetted fortune hunter, a womanizer, and a hardened gamester. Ask your aunt, if you don't believe me. I'm sure it would please her no more than it would me if you allowed him to start hanging on to your sleeve. He is no fit escort for an innocent girl like yourself."

"Forgive me, my lord, but it occurs to me that the same might be said of yourself," remarked Eve, calmly pushing back a curl.

"It might," he answered frankly, "if my intentions were not strictly honorable. You must know why I have made the effort to seek you out. We must decide if our fathers' wishes coincide with our own."

"This is rather abrupt, is it not?" said Eve, wrinkling her brow.

"Forgive me, Miss Marlowe. This is something that had best be discussed when we know each other better. I had not meant to imply that the matter must be settled immediately."

She startled him by replying, with amazing composure, "That is unnecessary, my lord. I shall consider your offer, and give you my answer when I reach a decision."

The Marquis began to feel as if his neckcloth were tied too tightly. Now what the devil had made her think he was making her an offer? *Had* it sounded like an offer? This was utterly ridiculous, the Marquis told himself furiously. Everard Frome was not the only one who was supposed to have a great deal of address! Here he was making a total mull of a situation in which he ought to have been in complete control!

He glanced at her, eyes narrowed. Cool as a queen, she was, and completely indifferent to the fact that he was eyeing her like this. Should he set her straight? Lord, what a set-down that would be! But then he would lose his only chance to right the wrong he had done his father, and he would never be rid of his guilt.

The truth was that nothing about this whole infernal episode had gone as he had planned. Damn Everard Frome and his interference! The man was like a thorn in his flesh, always popping up at odd times to torment him. In the beginning, Vale had felt great pity for Lord Frome, for he was aware the man had suffered a great deal over the loss of his sister, Charlotte. But after years of taunts and pinpricks from the fellow, he no longer felt any sympathy.

The Marquis returned Miss Marlowe to Berkeley Square, and took his leave of her with inward relief. She was a beautiful girl, there was no denying, but to spend the rest of his life with her—! Damn it, he didn't want to be married to a statue!

Well, he supposed he would feel the same about any woman, since the mere thought of marriage was so repugnant to him. His own parents had demonstrated just what a living hell the wedded state could be. And now he had Frome to worry about, and that damned wager. Why could not life be a little simpler?

Chapter Six

Lord Frome glanced idly at his riding companion. As always, Lady Claverley was magnificently clad, the dashing velvet habit of deep crimson contrasting vividly with her dark hair and alabaster skin. With detached interest, the Baron's eyes slid downward to explore the alluring expanse of smooth, creamy flesh exposed by the habit's very low cut bodice.

There was something fundamentally common about the woman, he decided. Despite all her pretensions of gentility, she seemed incapable of the smallest act of restraint. Her self-consequence had been deeply wounded by her former lover, but where a woman of breeding would have gracefully acknowledged defeat, Lady Claverley had become obsessed with her desire to strike back at the Marquis of Vale. His eyes gleamed, and his lips twisted into a cynical half-smile. Jack had erred in not assuaging the lady's ire with greater finesse. Perhaps his enemy had forgotten how very adept he was at making use of the Marquis's mistakes.

113

Lady Claverley had noticed his smile. "You find me amusing, Everard?" she inquired, the flinty hardness of her voice jarring with the femininity of her appearance.

"Of course not," he soothed, his answer more mechanical than honest. "I find you as enchanting as ever. I was merely pondering the fate of our mutual friend."

"You have a plan?" she asked eagerly.

"Of course. You were right about the girl. She's quite lovely, and unquestionably a lady. He means to marry her, I'll wager." The Baron rubbed his chin thoughtfully.

"Marry!" Lady Claverley spat out the word as if it were foul. Something that was not at all beautiful distorted her features as she said, "A baronet's daughter is good enough for him, but a baronet's widow is not. How I loathe the man!"

He laughed, knowing it would irritate her. "I thought you loved him, Alex. You really must learn to be consistent."

She drove her spur into the horse's side, and for a short while they cantered along the Serpentine. When at last they slowed, she tossed her head defiantly. "I don't love him. There's not a man alive worthy of my love."

"The blow to my ego is profound," Frome responded, his smile sarcastic. "I assume these impassioned sentiments spring from devotion, my sweet? To your dearly departed husband, of course."

"Neville?" She tittered mockingly. "What an amusing idea, Everard. The poor sot was always so

114

foxed he scarcely knew if it was me in bed with him."

"The man never drank until after he was married," he reminded her with gentle malice.

She threw him a resentful look. "So what is your plan?" she queried, rather sullenly. "Do you actually have one, or are you just trying to impress me?"

He laughed harshly. "Oh, most assuredly I have one. Do you think I've waited all these years without having devised a suitable punishment for him? The small cuts he has received thus far are nothing to the way I plan to lacerate him."

"Well, tell me!"

He leaned a little closer. "His future bride will provide the means for my revenge. Although 'tis possible he may not wish to marry the lady when I am through with her."

Her gaze widened. "You will seduce her?"

The Baron sneered. "Why not? Isn't it fitting? I shall spirit her away right from under his arrogant nose. By the time he finds her, she will be nothing but soiled merchandise. Perhaps I can even be sure she is *enceinte*."

"Marvelous!" she breathed. "But what do you need me for? What can I do?"

"That we shall see as the play unfolds," he retorted. "I'm quite sure you can make yourself useful, love. After all, women tell each other things they will not tell a man."

She nodded, pleased with the role. "And whisper the most shocking rumors to one another. Have you heard, my dear Miss Marlowe—!"

"Precisely," he murmured. "I appear to have underrated your intelligence, my dear. Your comprehension seems dramatically improved."

Lady Claverley ignored his gibe. "What if he begins to suspect?" She shivered suddenly. "He has not forgotten Charlotte. He may guess what you mean to do."

His brows snapped together, and a soft, faintly menacing note crept into his tone. "Don't mention her name, Alex. I will not have my sister brought into this conversation." His arm shot out as he spoke, and his long, strong fingers clamped tightly around her wrist, bruising the tender flesh.

"Loose me!" she hissed. "Loose me at once, Everard, or you can look to the devil for assistance!"

He stared at her briefly, then flung her hand away.

"I hate you! You are no better than Jack!"

"No?" he responded coolly. "I wonder if you really believe that. Who was it that helped you, my sweet, after Neville died and there was not a well-bred soul who would receive you? Do you remember how many gave you the cut direct? They all thought you drove the poor devil into his grave—as of course you did. Neville Claverley was a good and decent man until he fell into your web. But it was I, Alex, who made sure you were accepted again. A word here, a whisper there, and, voilà, a miracle was accomplished. Just remember how much you stand in my debt when you speak of the better man."

"I do know it, and I am grateful," she replied

bitterly. "But do not lay hands on me, Everard."

"You did not say that last night," he jeered, wondering if she would have the grace to blush.

She did not, but he saw her jaw tighten. "You are despicable," she told him.

"Perhaps," he answered indifferently, weary of her spite.

They walked their horses for a while in preoccupied silence, each engrossed with reflections that, though completely unalike, were similar in emotional intensity.

Whenever he thought of the Marquis of Vale, Everard Frome invariably began to brood over his sister's death. He had loved Charlotte—or Lottie, as she had been called—more dearly than anyone, and the memory of her suicide still had the power to distress and anger him. Though it had been six years, and the freshness of the pain had naturally abated, he had never lost his desire to avenge her death.

Even as a child Lottie had been unique. Possessed of a sparkling, sprite-like quality, she won the devotion of everyone around her, most of all himself, the doting brother eight years her senior. No one outside the family knew about Lottie's strange moods—moods that were as unpredictable as they were worrying. At those times, her sunny nature would alter suddenly, and another creature would emerge—high-strung, irrational, deeply depressed. To her family's relief, those periods grew more and more infrequent as she matured, until that fateful spring of her eighteenth year—the last in her short life—when Lottie's parents decided she had grown out of her "moodiness" and into a healthy, normal young lady for whom a husband must be found. Neither parent being physically able to travel, Lottie was sent to visit her godmother in London, while Frome himself had dutifully abandoned his life of riotous living to guard over his sister as best he could.

Lottie's first days in London were blissfully uneventful—until she met the man who now held the title of fifth Marquis of Vale. Frome was still unable to deny that initially she had thrived under the young man's flattering attentions, and to this day he could not recall an instance where Vale's behavior had seemed anything but circumspect. But what was now clear was that Lottie had not been as mentally stable as they had all thought.

Her deterioration was gradual. If Lottie had fallen directly into one of her moods, of course, he would have seen to it that she was removed from London before the sun had time to set. Maturity, however, must have increased her ability to conceal her feelings. His first faint clue that something was amiss was her sudden tendency to fidget when the Marquis was near, a restiveness that could have had any number of perfectly reasonable explanations. On one occasion, he remembered hearing his sister respond with unusual sharpness to a compliment which should have pleased her highly. In retrospect, he believed it had been a sign that her moods were returning, and he still cursed himself for not recognizing it as such.

However, he blamed the Marquis entirely for what happened next. After besieging Lottie with

118

flowers, driving her in the Park, and dancing with her at balls, he suddenly ceased singling her out, and was seen with several other ladies. Lottie had always needed so much to be loved, even pampered, by those around her, and the defection of her suitor confused and hurt her deeply. Although both he and Lottie's godmother made every effort to distract her from her sorrow, Lottie sank into gloom, refusing even to leave her room or see any visitors.

Dismayed, they decided to send her to Bath, in the hopes that the waters and the rest would do some good. Alas, they had not been quick enough! He would never forget that terrible morning when his beautiful Lottie was discovered dead in her bed, the bottle of laudanum on the table nearby. His grief was nothing to the wild fury which seized him when it was discovered that his sister was with child. No wonder the poor girl had behaved so strangely with her lover! Having indulged his passions, the Marquis had abandoned his sister, callously leaving Lottie to suffer whatever consequences should arise. The scoundrel! Frome knew not how the man had managed it, but he swore then and there that the Marquis of Vale would be made to pay for his infamy.

Almost the worst part of that whole horrifying episode was the frustration of being unable to call the blackguard out and put a bullet in him. Despite his rage, Frome had the sense to realize that his sister's good name depended on his forbearance, and as it was, rumors flew wildly. Of course, Lottie's family put out the story of an accidental overdose, a version of the tale that no one had ever dared challenge within his hearing.

There had been a time when the Baron had considered wreaking his vengeance upon Vale's own sister. This, perhaps, the Marquis had foreseen, however, for Lady Frances Brinvilliers had been more strictly chaperoned than was usual, and was hustled into marriage with the Earl of Rosebery before she had even completed her first Season. The lady's choice of husband had unwittingly been her salvation, for Lord Rosebery's political influence was on the rise, and Everard Frome did not quite dare to harm the wife of a peer of his lordship's power and influence. Nonetheless, he could not forget that had Lottie lived, she would have been utterly ruined, condemned to a lifetime of social ostracism for the Marquis's sin. The effects on her mental condition were not even to be considered.

No, it would be a far better revenge to deflower his enemy's future bride, a lovely girl whose assets did not include a powerful protector. He would drink from the nectar of the Marquis's rose, and considering the beauty of that particular rose, he would enjoy it mightily. Perhaps then he could begin to forget the past, and carve out some sort of a sane life for himself.

The Marquis was thinking about the wager. It was really the most absurd wager he had ever accepted, mainly because its outcome must be a foregone conclusion. At least, that had been his opinion before he had spent an entire hour cudgeling his brain over the matter.

He had thought it would be the simplest thing in the world to come up with any number of ways he could win. He had actually sat down at his huge mahogany desk with the intention of making a long list of possible strategies which would guarantee him victory, but his paper remained maddeningly blank. He had no wish to put himself out for anyone whom he actively disliked, and he could think of no reasonable act of altruism to perform for any of those he did. In fact, every scheme he considered seemed likely to be vetoed by Charles as being too simple to qualify. The Marquis toyed with the notion of increasing his cousin's allowance, for Godfrey was almost wholly dependent upon him, but gave up the idea almost immediately. It held little appeal to him, for he felt he gave Godfrey quite enough as it was. The fellow appeared to manage nicely on what he had, and in any case, he was sure that was not the sort of thing Charles had in mind. It galled the Marquis to realize just how difficult the winning of this wager was proving to be.

Vale threw down his quill in self-disgust and gazed out the window. It was cloudy, but not so overcast that it looked to threaten rain. He rose from his desk and reached for the nearby bellpull.

"Send a message to the stables," he instructed the footman who appeared. "Tell them to have my curricle brought round in half an hour."

He had made no arrangements to see Eve Marlowe this afternoon, but if she was at home, he

121

might as well offer to take her for another drive. Perhaps a second meeting with the girl would prove more felicitous than the first, a faint hope upon which the Marquis did not dwell with much optimism.

He was about to go and change his clothes and was halfway across the room before he remembered something, and returned to his desk. An indecisive frown marred the sun-browned skin of his brow as he stood still, drumming his fingers on the smooth wooden surface. Then he reached into the top drawer and took out a small book, which he slipped into his pocket.

The forbidding expression which settled upon his countenance as soon as he left his house did not abate until he forced it determinedly away moments before he entered the drawing room of No.12 Berkeley Square. Its lingering remnants vanished in truth when he learned that his invitation was to be declined. Miss Marlowe, it seemed, had made other plans.

"I am sorry, my lord," Eve apologized, her dazzling smile slim testimony to the verity of her regret. "But I promised another gentleman I would ride out with him in a little while, and I must soon go and make myself ready." She cast an inscrutable look at Amanda, who was sitting nearby. "Why do you not take my cousin?" she continued, with rare amiability. "Amanda never misses a chance to take the fresh air, isn't that right, Amanda? I am sure she would enjoy it, Lord Vale, for she was forever tramping the hills and meadows back in Hampshire."

Jolted by the unexpectedness of the suggestion, Amanda could feel the color rising in her cheeks. Oh, how could Eve be so insensitive! Could her cousin possibly be blind to the fact that she was placing both Amanda and the Marquis in an awkward position? Why, this man was here to court her cousin with matrimony as his object, and could hardly be expected to appreciate being foisted off in such a casual manner. Now, out of common civility, she reflected, he must be forced to extend his invitation to herself—which he might well be disinclined to do! Amanda had never felt so out of charity with her cousin as she did at this moment. It was one thing to be invited for one's own company, but she had no desire to play proxy for Eve.

She had to admit, however, that not by so much as a flicker of an eyelid did Lord Vale betray chagrin at being so fobbed off. He bowed in her direction, and said, quite formally, "I should deem it an honor, Miss Marlowe, if you would care to join me."

Despite his pleasant manner, Amanda could not help thinking there was a tiny note of challenge in his voice. She hesitated, glancing at the window to give herself time to think of a reply.

"I . . . well . . . it's not going to rain, is it?" she said weakly, wishing her normal confidence would reassert itself.

"I don't think so," replied the Marquis, smiling a little.

"Why don't you go, Amanda?" put in Lady Besford surprisingly.

Eve's aunt was still reeling from what she could

only call perversity on the part of her niece, and felt that for both girls to refuse his lordship would border on insanity. Not an hour before, she had suffered from the shock of hearing her sister's only child consent to go riding with a dissolute fortune hunter, a shock which was worsened by the discovery that the girl was both unfazed and uninfluenced by her aunt's obvious disapproval. Only the Countess's hartshorn succeeded in reviving her to the point where she felt able to receive another caller, but since it was her ladyship's custom to push anything unpleasant from her mind, she eventually recovered, and managed to greet the Marquis, when he arrived, with a tolerable degree of calm. Her leading concern, she now decided, was to forget the unsavory Lord Frome, and see to it that an outstanding matrimonial prize like the Marquis of Vale did not think himself unwelcome in her house.

"You have been shut in for several days, my dear," she therefore continued. "The air will do you good. I'm sure Lord Vale knows that, as a *gentleman,* he must take the strictest care of you." This last statement was delivered with an undercurrent of meaning, for as partial as she was to the Marquis's suit, her ladyship did not forget that he, too, possessed something of a reputation.

The Marquis bowed ironically. "Miss Marlowe will be quite safe with me, ma'am," he assured her, the small, rather cynical quirk to his mouth indicating that the point was taken.

Though she told herself she did not wish to go, Amanda was irrationally glad she was wearing her

124

yellow muslin, for it was the least dowdy of her gowns. With the addition of the pointlace, it could even pass as a fairly attractive morning dress—well almost, she amended silently.

She hurried to her room to fetch her best bonnet and shawl, the latter, the sole cast-off garment she had allowed herself to accept from her cousin. Darting a quick look at herself in the mirror, she put up a hand to tuck in a stray curl. Did she look her best, she wondered anxiously. And what did it matter if she did not, a voice inside her demanded. The next hour was likely to be an ordeal, not an exciting adventure designed to put a flush on her cheeks and a sparkle into her eyes!

As she had half known it would, the Marquis's formality vanished as soon as they were in his curricle. "Well, Prudence?" he said lightly, a small flick of the reins sending the horses prancing forward. "Dare you give me another chance? Or do you fear that your virtue is about to be assaulted? With the *strictest* care, of course."

Amanda eyed him reproachfully. "Somehow, I do *not* think the Countess would approve of that remark, my lord," she said. "And you did promise to behave the gentleman."

"Ah, but that would be so dull," the Marquis responded, his lazy blue eyes gleaming with good humor.

She shifted uncomfortably. "Nevertheless, I would prefer that you honored that promise. I do not enjoy your efforts to put me to the blush."

He flung up his hand, as if to ward off a blow. "Not another word, I swear. I'm determined to make up for my previous behavior, which you informed me was, ah, reprehensible. Do I have the correct word?" He cast her a quick look. "Yes, I see by your expression that my memory is not at fault. However, today I shall endeavor to keep my behavior exemplary."

"You cannot imagine my relief," she returned, her flippancy matching his own.

"You doubt me?" Though he was tooling his curricle around a corner as he spoke, he shot a frowning glance in her direction.

"Well, it would be a trifle strange if I did not," Amanda told him severely. "After the way you conducted yourself, Lord Vale, I would be a fine fool to trust you now. You've shown me your true colors."

"Nonsense!" Unaccountably nettled, the Marquis cleared his throat. "I admit I acted badly, Miss Marlowe, and I apologize for it, but that does not mean you have anything to fear from me. You were quite right to slap me, by the way." He dug his hand into his pocket, and withdrew the book, thrusting it at her. "Here—I brought something for you."

Caught off-guard, Amanda took it automatically, her eyes widening as she read its title. *"The Picture of London,"* she murmured in astonishment. She touched the small guidebook reverently, admiring its red leather cover and gold embossing. "H-How extremely kind of you, my lord," she stammered. "I cannot believe that you actually—" She drew a breath, and forced herself to add regretfully, "But, I fear I cannot accept it."

His brows rose. "You did not purchase one already?" he asked, conscious of a slight feeling of disappointment.

"No," she admitted slowly. "It's a bit difficult for me to explain."

The Marquis's expression altered subtly, and a sneer crept into his voice. "I suppose I ought to have known better. Believe it or not, Miss Marlowe, this was *not* an attempt to throw you a lure."

"A lure?" Amanda echoed, confused by his abrupt change in manner. "I . . . I don't understand."

He did not look at her, his attention diverted by the business of navigating his curricle and pair neatly around a hay wagon as it emerged from the entrance to Lambeth Mews. "An inducement," he explained coolly. "To behave in an unvirtuous manner."

Unprepared for his words, for the space of a few seconds Amanda simply stared at him. "I certainly thought no such thing, Lord Vale!" she said at last, her low voice filled with indignation. "You are determined to insult me one way or another, I see."

Vale sent her an appraising look. "Well, then, why won't you accept it?"

Visibly distressed, Amanda clenched her hands tightly together. "Because I am not at all certain it would be proper to do so," she said defensively. "Lady Besford spent more than an hour last evening explaining to me what I may and may not do, but I have not quite gotten it all sorted out yet. I—I am not used to living by so many rules, you see. As you know, I already made one mistake."

Though his mouth was still set in a hard line, the Marquis's voice lost its harsh note. "Then I must beg your pardon once more, Prudence. Obviously, I did you an injustice. Have I offended beyond all possibility of forgiveness? Do you wish me to take you back to Berkeley Square?"

Amanda blinked, unsure whether he was serious. "Why, good heavens, of course not. I hope I am not so . . . so *missish!* I expect you did not realize how it would sound."

"You credit me with too much virtue," he retorted in an odd tone. "Nevertheless, it is generous of you to make excuses for me. I have done nothing to deserve it."

"No, you haven't," she agreed, a twinkle entering her eye. "Nothing except give me this lovely book—which you still have not told me whether I may accept! You are a man of experience, my lord, are you not? With such a wicked reputation to guide you, I'm sure you must be acquainted with the rules of propriety—and impropriety."

The Marquis's lips twitched. "A guidebook is a perfectly unobjectionable gift, you little vixen. However, anything of a personal nature, such as a piece of jewelry, would be considered extremely improper. If you require any further elaboration on the subject, I suggest you apply to Lady Besford."

"So I may keep it then. I am so glad," said Amanda ingenuously. "It is something I would dearly love to own, and I thank you. And I don't know what virtues you think you do not possess, but I know of at least one that is quite apparent."

"Oh?" he said, rather startled. "What's that?"

"You are very thoughtful," she replied.

Her words, combined with the singularly sweet smile she bestowed upon him, caused the Marquis to be attacked by a tiny twinge of guilt. The gift had cost him no effort, for he had merely instructed one of his servants to see to its purchase, and he realized suddenly that he had never even taken the trouble to glance inside. Now, for some reason, he found himself wishing he had selected it personally.

Of course, there was another, more well-grounded reason for that twinge. It actually *had* occurred to him that he might steal a kiss or two as a reward, though it had been little more than a passing daydream. But since it was true, it was strangely hypocritical of him to be vexed at the idea she might interpret his gift as some sort of bribe. He puzzled over his anger from a moment before. He had leaped to the wrong conclusion and was startled to discover his feelings had literally been bruised. What was it about this girl that caused him to act so unlike himself, the Marquis wondered uneasily. It was his intention to amuse himself only; feelings had no business entering into the matter.

Hiding these thoughts behind an impassive countenance, Lord Vale studied Amanda's profile as she leafed through the book. Her features pleased him, he decided arbitrarily, especially that pert little nose and those beautiful eyes. To be honest, everything about her pleased him, though she was a mere wisp of a girl, lacking the curvaceousness he normally looked for in a woman. Still, despite the slightness of her build, she did manage to fill out her gown in all the important places, he noted, with the exacting eye of a connoisseur. His daydream, with a few embellishments, floated once more into his mind, and he abandoned his brief effort to understand his own motivations.

From whence was born his next idea, he had no notion, but the words were out before he had time to reconsider.

"So, Miss Marlowe, tell me where you would like to go," he said, an almost imperceptible movement of his hand sending the bays the command to slow their pace.

Surprised, Amanda turned a little in her seat. "Do you mean that you are willing to take me to see some of the sights?"

"Well, we've already been to Hyde Park," he told her in a reasonable tone. "Come, here's Piccadilly. Make your decision, Prudence. What shall it be?"

The outcome of this was that they were soon headed toward the official city of London, it being one of Amanda's principal desires to view for herself the magnificence of St. Paul's Cathedral. She had seen much of Mayfair, and was impressed by the grandeur and solemnity of its residences, but what she most longed to see was something that would help bring the city's fascinating history to life in her mind. The Marquis, who was not in the habit of taking virtuous young females sightseeing, was pardonably amused by Amanda's enthusiasm, and assumed his role as tour guide with an aplomb that would have caused Charles Perth to stare.

He pointed out Devonshire House to her as they

130

slowly made their way up Piccadilly, and Amanda gazed curiously at what little she could see of the huge, rather plain, two-storied mansion hidden behind its brick wall. She found it interesting, for she remembered hearing her mother speak of the glamorous, auburn-haired Georgiana who had lived there as Duchess of Devonshire, and worked so tirelessly for the Whig cause, and the election of Charles James Fox.

Close by, opposite Green Park, the Marquis directed her attention to Pulteney's Hotel. Its key claim to fame, he told her dryly, was its housing of the Emperor of Russia and his sister, the Grand Duchess, when the ruling heads of Europe had convened in England two years earlier after the defeat of the Corsican upstart. Amanda studied its bow-windowed exterior intently, trying to picture the tall, handsome Czar waving from the balcony to the cheering crowds below, while the Prince Regent sulked in his palace, unhappy and unpopular.

The Marquis was quite frankly enjoying himself, a fact which he attributed less to his having escaped the daily parade of the *monde* in Hyde Park than to the innocent charm of his pretty companion. Long before they reached the Strand, he realized that Amanda had lost all wariness of him, and he found that with a little encouragement, she became surprisingly talkative. In general, he did not consider volubility an asset in a female, but Amanda, he discovered, did not talk unless she had something to say. He found her both intelligent and direct; she could discuss a topic without chat-

131

tering like a magpie, and she laughed without making him wince. However, her most sterling quality, he soon decided, was her failure to play the coquette. He had seen much in the way of female guile, and was delighted to find it was possible to converse with her in a perfectly ordinary way, much as he did with Charles.

They passed by St. Clement's and, shortly after, entered the city of London through the gateway at Temple Bar. It was just after this that the Marquis suddenly noticed Amanda's silence. A small frown had taken the place of the cheerful expression she had worn a moment before, and her hands were clenched together, as she did when she was nervous.

"What is it, Prudence?" he asked curiously.

When she answered, there was a certain constraint in her voice. "Do you think that the Countess might object to your bringing me here? Please do not be offended, my lord. I know I should have thought about it before, but I cannot help wondering if she might not say it was not . . . not right."

The same thought having crossed his own mind, the Marquis measured his answer carefully. "Well, since it is too late to worry about it now, I can only advise you to put it out of your mind. It is possible she might disapprove, but frankly, I don't see the harm in it. After all, my tiger is here to lend us countenance. You'll do that for us, won't you, Jerry?" he added, turning his head.

"Lord love yer, guv'nor, you know werry well I do whatever yer lordship tells me!" replied the Marquis's tiger, a diminutive lad with a cocky gleam in his eye. "Course, you ain't never asked me to play chaperon before, but if you and the young lady want to kick up a bit of the breeze, why it's yer business, and I'll keep me gab closed! And if they cut up rough when you get back, miss, you just tell 'em Jerry was with you!"

Directing a pained look over his shoulder, the Marquis said dryly, "Thank you, Jerry, but a simple 'yes' would have sufficed." He then distracted Amanda by saying, "Look, Prudence, there it is! Do you see it?"

In the distance, rising above the roofs and chimney pots of the unending sea of brick houses, Amanda could see the great dome of St. Paul's, the apex graced by its golden ball and cross. Their progress up Fleet Street toward the church was necessarily slow, for the bustling activity in the roadway nearly defied description. Everything from pedestrians and carts, bullocks and brewer's drays blocked their path, but for Amanda it was incredibly exciting. Not a little of her excitement stemmed from the presence of the darkly handsome man who sat beside her, and the part of her that was sensible whispered dire warnings in her ear. However, the not-so-sensible part of her shrugged them aside, and gave herself over to the enjoyment of the hour. Once they had reached their destination, the Marquis's tiger took charge of his master's horses, while Vale escorted her into the interior of Wren's wonderful cathedral. Half an hour later they emerged, Amanda, dazed by what she had seen, and the Marquis, strangely thoughtful.

"Tell me, why did you come to London?" he

asked her as he assisted her back into the carriage.

Amanda was surprised. "Why—I came because I was invited to do so."

"Nothing more?" asked the Marquis, lifting his brows. "No dreams of marriage? No thoughts of providing for a comfortable future?"

She flushed a little. "Marriage is the last thing on my mind at the moment. I must say that is a rather personal question, my lord. My reasons are my own."

"Of course," he agreed, climbing in next to her. "Do you plan to attend the usual round of social events?"

Amanda was silent, wondering why he was asking her this. At length, she shrugged, and said, "Does it look to you as though I have the means to do so?"

He looked down at her proud little profile. "No," he replied, rather gently. "I suppose not. Please forgive my cloddish tactlessness, Prudence."

Knowing she had spoken rudely, Amanda smiled and said impulsively, "It's of no account, my lord. I hope you will not feel sorry for me. I should dislike it above all things."

He smiled. "Then I won't. I wish, though, that a way might be found so that you might enjoy some of what the Season has to offer."

"Well, I will get a taste of it," she replied, feeling oddly breathless. Was it her imagination, or had he moved a fraction of an inch closer? "Lady Besford is quite insistent that I come to her ball, and it would be churlish of me to refuse. I expect she'll be sending out the cards in a day or two."

"Then, you must do me the honor of allowing me to lead you out," he said smoothly. Those blue eyes in that dark, lean face held her transfixed. Instinctively, she knew that every detail of his features would stay frozen in her memory. She would recall this moment exactly, feel again the warm breeze on her face, and hear the horses' hooves striking the flagstoned pavement as they began to move down the street.

"I'm not sure whether I'll be dancing," she finally answered, pulling her gaze away from his with difficulty. "But thank you very much, my lord. It is kind of you to offer."

"You see?" he remarked. "I told you I was going to make up for my reprehensible behavior. And I'll make up for it even further by taking you to visit Westminster Abbey someday soon. You'd like that, wouldn't you?"

Taking her discomposed, rather incoherent reply for an assent, he promptly advised her to study her guidebook, teasing her so skillfully that she was able to recover her equanimity. Once he was sure she was relaxed, he turned to more serious topics, and before she knew it, Amanda found herself giving him a short sketch of her parents' accident and the ensuing events in her life.

The Marquis was elated, for when they had been standing inside St. Paul's, it had come to him in a flash that the little lady next to him might supply the answer to his problem of the wager. Leavening his probing with a fair dash of flirtatious nonsense, he now learned enough to banish any doubts on that score. Little Miss Marlowe, he decided with

135

satisfaction, would serve the purpose quite nicely. Her difficulties posed the necessary challenge; solving them without her knowledge would require both ingenuity and a certain amount of subterfuge. Certainly Charles was unlikely to object to the scheme, for he more than anyone would sympathize with a desire to aid a lady in distress.

Yes, the more the Marquis tossed the idea around in his head, the more he liked it. By God, he liked Amanda as well! Her matter-of-fact recital of her story aroused his sympathies far more than she would ever have suspected. He could commiserate with her about the senselessness of her parents' deaths, and from its pointed omission, he was able to make a shrewd guess at the way she felt about her present situation.

The idea really ought to have occurred to him sooner, he mused. From the moment she'd put her nose in the air and given him that set-down on the steps of the Besford residence, he'd known a distinct urge to see her more becomingly attired. Well, perhaps that was not entirely accurate. His urge had been somewhat more basic than that, for even at their first meeting he'd been able to appreciate Amanda's trim figure and the hint of an interesting wiggle he'd thought he'd detected in her backside.

Well, all that was going to be changed. Miss Marlowe was no raving beauty, but she possessed engaging manners and an intrinsic charm that many girls lacked. He thought her silver-gray eyes were truly beautiful, and her complexion was like the petal of a flower. The Marquis smiled to himself. Little Prudence would cast half the debs in town into the shade before he was through loading the dice. Because of him, she would undoubtedly acquire a swarm of town beaux, marry one of them, and retire from society to dutifully present her spouse with a pack of hopeful brats.

But even while he pondered upon how neatly it was all going to work out, the Marquis experienced a very real pang of regret. For although he did not yet realize it, a part of him was already yearning to claim Amanda as his own.

Chapter Seven

When Amanda reentered the house at Berkeley Square a short while later, she was informed that her ladyship wished to speak with her at once. Higgins went on to add that the Countess could be found in her favorite retreat, the Yellow Saloon, along with her cousin Eve. Amanda hesitated only an instant, wishing she could run upstairs first to deposit the precious little guide book safely among her things. However, if the Countess wished to speak with her, it would be rude to keep her waiting any longer than necessary.

"My goodness, Amanda, what took you so long?" inquired her ladyship as soon as her young guest entered the Saloon. "I would have thought you'd be back much earlier, my dear. In fact, I was beginning to fear some accident had befallen you."

Amanda bestowed a warm smile upon the plump little woman who had treated her so kindly. "Oh no, ma'am. We had no problem at all. And I had a wonderful time."

Opposite the Countess, Eve was sitting with a

copy of *La Belle Assemblée* upon her lap, leisurely chewing on comfits. "I did not see you anywhere in the Park, Amanda," she remarked rather curtly. "And I looked for you most particularly." She reached over to pick up another little sweetmeat and pop it into her mouth.

Making a determined effort to speak lightly, Amanda began to untie the ribands of her bonnet. "Well, that is because we did not go there. We went to see St. Paul's instead!"

Lady Besford's smile faded abruptly. "You went *where?*" she uttered, her mouth falling open in a most undignified fashion.

Beginning to feel like an errant schoolgirl, Amanda repeated, a bit more hesitantly, "St. Paul's Cathedral. His lordship seemed to think you wouldn't mind. At least, it did not seem to . . . to concern him."

"But, Amanda, my dear!" protested her hostess, showing signs of consternation, "He was supposed to be taking you to the Park! Why on earth would he choose to take you into the city instead?"

Her spirits sinking rapidly, Amanda laid her bonnet on a nearby chair cushion. "Well, he did not exactly do the choosing," she said reluctantly. "I do not think he cared where we went. He asked me where I would like to go, and I said St. Paul's. Have I . . . have I made another mistake?" she faltered.

Searching the nearby surfaces in vain for her hartshorn, her ladyship remarked unsteadily, "All the way to the top of Fleet Street in an open carriage . . . with the Marquis of Vale! Oh, my dear Amanda!" She closed her eyes and moaned, with a faint shudder, "Burnt feathers! *That's* what Aunt Caroline used to hold under her nose."

Quickly, Amanda crossed the room to retrieve her ladyship's bottle of hartshorn from where it sat upon the shelf above the fireplace. "Here, ma'am," she urged, pulling the stopper from the small vial. "Perhaps this will help. Do not tease yourself about this, I beg of you. There is no reason, I promise."

Lady Besford inhaled the potent fumes for only an instant, then waved the bottle away. "Thank you, my dear. Now I can be sensible." Straightening her posture, she gave her anxious young guest a beseeching, rather puzzled, look. "Now, tell me the whole story, Amanda, and do not, pray, leave anything out."

"Yes," inserted Eve sharply, "do not leave anything out, Amanda. We are all agog to hear of your adventures." Her penetrating eyes dropped to Amanda's hands. "What's that you're holding?"

Amanda glanced down. "It's a guidebook. Lord Vale gave it to me."

Eve's eyes narrowed. "Oh, he did, did he?"

Diverted, the Countess's brows shot up. "Oh? Well, that was rather odd of him. He scarcely knows you, after all. I suppose it was because of our conversation the other day."

Amanda decided it was time to sit down. "Yes, well, it was very kind of him, also. He said it was perfectly proper for me to accept it . . . I hope he is right? For it is the most fascinating book, ma'am!" Flipping the small volume open to a random page, she went on, "For example, listen to this description of —"

140

"Please, Amanda," interrupted her cousin in a bored tone, "spare us the commentary. You sound like a veritable bluestocking."

Frozen silence filled the few seconds before Amanda, with a slight shrug, closed the book with a snap. "Very well, Cousin," she said, her voice clipped. Turning to her ladyship, she went on, "But it was most advantageous to have along. It explains everything one might wish to know—"

Once more Eve cut in. "What I wish to know," she said with a sneer, "is how you managed to bamboozle him into taking you in the first place. Good lord, the man must have been bored out of his mind!"

"Eve," reproved her aunt with a frown, "that is hardly a charitable remark. Amanda is going to tell us how it came about."

"I do not think he was bored," objected Amanda, very much indignant.

"No?" said Eve softly. "You made very sure of that, did you?"

Stiffening with anger, Amanda stared at her cousin. "If you mean to imply that I . . . I *flirted* with him, you are laboring under a grave misapprehension! I have not the remotest intention of trying to . . . to engage Lord Vale's interest. And do not forget, Eve, that it was you who suggested I go!"

Unexpectedly, Eve went into a peal of laughter. "No, I did not forget it. To own the truth, Amanda, the very notion of you trying to flirt with a man like Lord Vale makes me want to go into whoops! Especially in that gown! Why, what a figure you should cut!" she added, with another chuckle.

"Eve!" Lady Besford's flushed face was a study of

141

incredulity and dismay. "I cannot believe what I am hearing! What would your mother say if she heard you speak in such an uncivil, unkind way to your own cousin?"

Eve's shoulders rose and fell in an indifferent shrug. "I daresay she would agree with me," she retorted, quite coolly. "But you are perfectly right. It was rag-mannered of me, and I am sorry, Amanda. I should know better than to think you capable of duplicity."

Her feelings considerably bruised, Amanda had to force herself to nod slightly. She directed her next words to Lady Besford. "And I am very sorry if I have caused you distress, ma'am. Am I to understand, then, that I should not have permitted him to take me there?"

The Countess made a helpless gesture. "Well, Amanda, it was not exactly the wisest thing to have done. In an open carriage, my dear, where anyone could have seen you! But then, of course, a closed carriage would have been much worse," she added hurriedly. "While I am sure Lord Vale behaved with complete propriety—he did, did he not? Well, thank God for that!" she added, when Amanda nodded affirmatively. "Now, as I was saying . . . You see, if he were a relative, it would be one thing, of course. Oh, dear, I do not seem to be explaining myself very well."

"But I thought it was only in St. James's Street and . . . and Bond Street that a lady could not be seen in the afternoon," ventured Amanda. "Between two and five, was it not?" she recited. "Because of the gentlemen's clubs?"

Clearing her throat, her ladyship shifted uneasily. "Strictly speaking, Amanda, that is correct. And it is not only because of the clubs, my dear. Most of the gentlemen do their shopping in the afternoon, and what with the number of lodgings and 'sporting' hotels in that area, it is not the place for a lady who values her reputation." Her bosom rose and fell in a short sigh. "However, in the situation we are speaking of, it is more a question of *who* you were with, rather than *where* you went."

Having just finished another comfit, Eve made a slight guffaw. "What she means, my innocent little coz, is that Lord Vale's reputation is far from unblemished. And since no one is likely to believe his intentions toward you are honorable, people may be inclined to believe the worst. Isn't that right, Aunt Emily?"

Lady Besford was once more clutching her vial of hartshorn, as if the mere presence of it in her hand could somehow sustain her. "I am sorry to say, Amanda, that what Eve says is perfectly true. Although naturally I am pleased that you were able to see something of interest and have a pleasant outing, perhaps it would be better if next time you told me what it is you want to see. I suppose I could take you there myself," she finished dubiously.

Amanda was conscious of a pang of regret. "But his lordship invited me to go with him to Westminster," she revealed unhappily. "And I was very much hoping to go."

Observing the girl's disappointment, Lady Besford's blue eyes grew troubled. "I cannot allow you to go off with him unchaperoned, but . . . perhaps

Eve would like to go with you? That would make it perfectly unexceptionable, especially if you took one of the maids, as well!"

"I have not the slightest desire to go to Westminster," Eve informed them with a derisive curl to her lip. "Nor do I particularly care whether Amanda goes or not. Good God, do you think me jealous? She is welcome to enjoy the Marquis's company, since she finds it so edifying. Why do you not go with them, Aunt Emily? I daresay you have not done anything of that nature in years!"

Lady Besford gaped at her niece in amazement. "Are you certain you do not object, my love? I mean, to being excluded from such an expedition?"

"Quite," replied Eve, with complete indifference.

Amanda was too well acquainted with her cousin not to regard such generosity with the suspicion it deserved. Eve was up to something, she reflected.

Wondering if for once she could throw her cousin a little out of countenance, she inquired, in a casual tone, "And how was your ride in the Park with Lord Frome?" It would not hurt for Eve to know what it was like to experience discomfiture, she reasoned.

"Very well, thank you," replied Eve, with unimpaired calm. However, she did not deign to meet Amanda's eyes, for her attention was suddenly riveted upon the magazine in her lap.

"And her ladyship's mount?" persisted Amanda. "The mare suited your liking?"

Eve glanced up at the question, but her eyes fell on her aunt. "Sugarplum needs more exercise, Aunt Emily. You have not ridden her enough and she is getting fat."

Lady Besford nodded sadly. "Yes, indeed, it is most provoking. The problem is that *I* have gotten a trifle fat, and do not enjoy riding as much as I used to. I leave her exercising to the stable-boys most of the time, you see."

Eve's voice took on a critical note. "You cannot place your trust in stable-boys, Aunt Emily. They have not the intelligence to be given such responsibility."

"Why, I am persuaded they do their best, my dear. All our servants receive handsome wages, and your uncle's groom has been in his service for the better part of twenty years!"

Eve made a dismissive gesture. "All the same, why do you not let me take care of exercising Sugarplum while I am here? I shall take better care of her, and I need the fresh air and exercise."

Amanda was only human. "Why, Eve," she was unable to resist putting in, "I never realized you enjoyed being out-of-doors as much as that. You always tell me how much you dislike being out in the elements. The sun and wind are injurious to your complexion, remember?"

There was a glint of humor in Eve's eyes as they rested on Amanda's face. "Dear me, what a memory you have, coz. But in this case, I fear I must correct you. I am as fond of riding as you are, let us say, of visiting historical sites."

"I—I see," said Amanda, reluctant to cross swords with her ruthless cousin in front of the Countess.

Eve smiled complacently. "Yes, I rather thought you would."

* * *

Lady Besford shivered resignedly, and squinted up at the lofty interior of the huge gothic Abbey of Westminster. "Such a damp, chilly place," she complained to her personal maid, Ellen, whom she had brought along to make the party of a more respectable size. "Oh, I do hope Amanda does not want to stay very long!" Ellen nodded in glumpish silence, her thin mouth clamped tightly shut in disapproval.

To be sure, it was not of Amanda that Ellen disapproved. Her fears that Amanda would turn out to be an ingratiating, low-bred female bent on taking advantage of her lady's generosity had been put to rest practically the first night Amanda arrived. After observing her for some days now, Ellen had reached the conclusion that, far from putting on airs that did not become her, Miss Amanda was just about as prettily-behaved a young lady as anyone could wish for! And she was pleasant-spoken, too, which was more than Ellen could say of Miss Eve, never mind the fact that the statuesque blonde was her ladyship's blood relative, and little Miss Amanda was not. Why, it was plain as the nose on your face that Miss Amanda was Quality, simply by the nice way in which she conducted herself. In fact, Ellen did not find it nearly as remarkable as her ladyship that the Marquis had offered to bring them to Westminster. What was odd, Ellen felt, was that Miss Eve had not come along, for wasn't his lordship supposed to be her suitor? Too sure of herself, was Miss Eve, and too full of the knowledge of her own consequence. And wouldn't it serve her right if she lost her Marquis to Miss Amanda! *Not* that the poor mite had any such thought in her head, as any sapskull with half a wit could see! And this was largely the source of Ellen's frowns, for Miss Amanda, she worried, was very likely headed for a nasty fall. 'Twould be a shame if she was to get overfond of his lordship, and what with him being such a handsome gentleman and all, how could she help it? Why, it was enough to turn any normal girl's head the way he looked at her with those wicked blue eyes of his! Ellen would not have trusted the Marquis as far as she could jump, for when it came to a pretty face, weren't all men the same? Yes, and it didn't take too much to guess what it was he wanted from Miss Amanda, the worldly maidservant told herself, her brow puckering even more. Her ladyship ought not to allow them to be together, it was that plain and simple!

They were in the nave of the Abbey. Ahead of Ellen, Amanda was standing to the Marquis's left, her head tipped back to better assimilate the magnificent gothic arches of the ceiling. The Marquis, on the other hand, had seen the Abbey before, and was deriving considerably more entertainment from watching Amanda.

"Well, Miss Marlowe?" he inquired, a slight smile twisting the corners of his firm mouth. "Does it meet with your approval?"

She glanced at him. "How could it not? It is . . . extraordinary. It defies description. And to think that the coronations of many of our kings have actually taken place here! How can I ever thank you, my lord?"

"How, indeed?" he murmured, a glint in his eye

that would have shocked Ellen. "Come. Henry the Seventh's chapel is this way." His hand at Amanda's elbow guided her forward toward the east end of the Abbey.

Their approach was reverent, their footsteps making but little noise in the great hush of high-walled silence. Not even Lady Besford spoke as they slowly mounted the black marble steps which led up to the entrance of the chapel of the Order of the Bath, which served as final resting place for so many of England's monarchs.

Indifferent to the intrusion of visitors, Henry himself lay within, close by his wife, Elizabeth of York. Side by side, beneath effigies of brass they slumbered, as they had throughout the long centuries. Other monarchs lay nearby, resting beneath superb monuments to their glory: the tempestuous Elizabeth and her unfortunate cousin, Mary, Queen of Scots; James I and his queen. Further, at the east end, slept Charles II, William III and Mary, his consort, and Queen Anne, all sharing this abode with other rulers from a far dimmer past.

"The tombs of the great," said the Marquis, swinging around to survey the three women. He pointed to a large marble sarcophagus several feet away. "George the Second and his queen," he told them knowledgeably, and even Ellen began to look impressed at their proximity to a king of whom she had heard.

"And Queen Caroline?" asked Lady Besford, her curiosity roused at last. "Where will she lie, poor lady? They say her health is so indifferent, she cannot last much longer."

The Marquis pointed again, directing their attention to where a vault had been prepared beneath the floor for the present royal family.

"It's a bit depressing, isn't it?" said Amanda quietly.

Tilting his dark head, the Marquis considered her question. "Perhaps, in a way. It certainly humbles one, at any rate. Would you like to go?"

"Not yet," answered Amanda, gazing around her. "There is so much more to see. I am most particularly interested in the poets' corner."

"And the shrine of Edward the Confessor," he added teasingly. "And the coronation chair, and anything else you have read about, I daresay!"

She smiled back at him. "I am a regular bluestocking, am I not? You will have to pretend not to know me if we meet in society."

"Gammon," he responded, but his smile faded, as if her joking words had reminded him of something unpleasant.

To Amanda's distress, she saw that what she was beginning to call Lord Vale's cynical look had slipped back into place. She studied him uncertainly, noting how the faint lines on either side of his mouth appeared to deepen with his change of expression. By this time, Amanda had begun to feel so at ease in the Marquis's company that she nearly asked him why he looked so grave, and only just caught herself before doing so. Such a question would be considered unseemly, even brazen, she lectured herself, and would doubtless have shocked both the Countess and Ellen.

Surprised by her own audacity, it crossed Amanda's mind that she had nearly forgotten that this was the same man who had forced his insolent kisses upon her in Hyde Park. Of course, it was only her perception of him that was changing, for every hour she spent in his company, Amanda was increasingly aware of his good qualities. She already knew him to be kind; she was also discovering that he was well-informed and amusing. And when he chose to display interest in something, she noted with approval, it was sincere rather than superficial, a sure sign of intelligence, according to her father. Even in this past hour, her opinion of him was undergoing enough of a change that it was difficult to make the connection between the man who had insulted her with his kisses, and the man who stood and explained the architectural planning that had gone into Westminster Abbey. In fact, he was the first person in a long while whom she would have liked to call her friend, for there existed a sort of camaraderie between them that she had never experienced—except with her parents. Peeping up at him as they left the chapel, she wondered, rather wistfully, whether he would be at all interested in playing that small part in her life.

To her relief, he seemed to perk up when they reached the poets' corner, located in the south cross of the Abbey. "Here lies the aristocracy of the quill, ladies," he said with a wave of his hand. "The creators of some of the finest poetry and literature ever written. Miss Marlowe, I see you are already deep in admiration, so I will cease my prattle and let you explore in peace."

Her eyes alight with excitement, Amanda began

reading some of the names aloud. "Cowley, Dryden, Prior, Rowe . . . oh look, my lord, this memorial is to Chaucer! And this one is Milton's! Oh, and Dr. Johnson is buried here as well!"

Lady Besford clutched her shawl more firmly around her. "Amanda, my dear, do you think you are nearly finished? I vow I've never heard of half these people. Are you sure they are all poets?"

Having very nearly forgotten her ladyship's presence, Amanda's expression changed to one of contrition. "Are you getting tired, ma'am?" she asked, concealing her disappointment. "Would you like to go?"

"I am a little weary, I think, though of course, all this is . . . is excessively diverting! Is there anything else you wished to see?"

The Marquis's voice interrupted Amanda as she began to reply. "May I direct your attention to one more monument before we go?" He sent Lady Besford one of his most charming smiles. "Somehow, I feel sure Miss Marlowe will be sorry if she misses it," he added, by way of explanation.

Following his gaze, Amanda stood quite still for a moment, then walked closer, touching her fingers to the cool stone. The name sculpted into the marble was that of William Shakespeare; beneath his monument was buried the incomparable Garrick, who had made the bard's lines come alive for so many audiences.

Impulsively, Amanda turned to the Marquis, her eyes filled with gratitude. "You were right, my lord," she said softly. "Coming here today was like a dream come true for me. You can have no notion how much I enjoyed it. Thank you so much."

His blue eyes studied her upturned face. "Think nothing of it, Miss Marlowe," he replied, deliberately keeping his voice neutral. "It was a pleasure for me as well."

Amanda was surprised by his sudden lack of enthusiasm, yet she sent him a warm smile before taking one last look around the poets' corner. It was this smile which caused the Marquis, as he shepherded the women back to his carriage, to question for the first time his own ability to remain detached. Since when, he asked himself restively, had a virtuous young lady been able to send his blood racing like this? Since when had a mere pretty smile filled him with such an ache? Such feelings would be a damn sight more appropriate in another time and place, and with a woman whose birth and breeding did not preclude his making her the object of his masculine attentions. It was extremely disconcerting to feel this way with Amanda Marlowe, and was not at all what he liked. One did not, he knew, think of respectable, gently bred females in such terms— certainly not unmarried ones!

Still, to be realistic, how long could that smile of hers possibly continue to affect him this way? Not long, if he knew anything at all about himself, he thought cynically. Once this wager between Charles and himself was concluded and Amanda Marlowe had been converted into a fashionable London belle, things were bound to be different. That refreshing spontaneity, that appealing openness which he found so damnably attractive, would get lost in the process, and she would learn to simper and coquet with the best of them. There was, however, a distinct consolation in this: she would then be safe from him, and he would be safe from his emotions.

"Wait for me here," Eve commanded, pointing her riding crop toward the North Lodge at Hyde Park's Stanhope Gate.

Looking irresolute, Lord Besford's groom doffed his cap and scratched the back of his neck. "Beggin' yer pardon, miss, but I dunno that 'is lordship would like me to do that. I reckon 'e'd say 'twas my responsibility to stay close to yerself, miss. To see that ye come to no 'arm, so to speak."

"I require no protection," replied Eve haughtily. "Your duty is to mind your betters, my good man, not to make impertinent comments. Pray remember it." Jerking the reins, she turned her mount around and, with a sharp kick of her spur, sent Sugarplum loping off with an energy the horse had not displayed in over a twelve-month.

Dismounting from his nag with a sigh, the groom raked a hand through his thinning hair and retrieved his pouch of tobacco from his pocket. "Uppity female!" he mumbled in disgruntlement. "Impertinent comments, my arse!"

Paying no heed to anyone she saw, Eve kept Sugarplum at a steady gait until, about halfway along the south side of the Serpentine, she spied the person she sought, waiting patiently beside a cluster of spreading yews. Under her expert guidance, Sugarplum slowed obediently, approaching the other horse and rider with dainty steps.

"So you came!" said Lord Frome, urging his gray hack into a position adjacent to Sugarplum. "I did not think you would." He gave no intimation that such a breach would have inconvenienced him to no small extent.

Eve's brows arched in surprise. "Of course I came, my lord. Did I not say I would?"

"Ah, but what a lady promises and what she does are seldom one and the same," he explained with a glimmer of laughter. "At the least, I thought I'd be cooling my heels here for some time to come. Does this mean you are predictable, Miss Marlowe?"

"Hardly," she scoffed. "It means, my lord, that I do what I choose. And I chose to meet you — on this occasion."

"And how did you manage that?" he inquired lazily. "Surely you did not tell your aunt the truth?"

Eve studied Lord Frome appraisingly, taking in his easy posture and carelessly knotted cravat. Though she still thought him more dashing than handsome, she had to admit that he possessed an air of rakish distinction, sitting there with his right hand resting lightly upon his buckskinned thigh, his topboots gleaming in the sunlight.

"I tell Aunt Emily only what she needs to know," she informed him tranquilly. "And that, my lord, is very little."

The Baron's shoulders shook with laughter. "How very resourceful," he remarked, his glance appreciative. "Let us walk our horses, then, while you tell me how you contrived to deceive poor Lady Besford. You perceive me brimming with curiosity, Miss Marlowe."

Beginning to recognize the authority of her rider, Sugarplum responded with alacrity to the first nudge of Eve's heel. "Actually, my aunt believes I am at home," she told him pensively. "My uncle is at his club, and Aunt Emily and Amanda have gone sightseeing with Vale."

"Sightseeing!" he repeated, a good deal startled. "With *Vale!*"

"Yes, is it not odd?" she agreed. "I cannot think why Amanda wished to go. She is a strange girl."

"But where did they go?" he asked in some amusement.

She shrugged. "Westminster Abbey, I believe."

Slowly, his mouth spread into a broad smile. "And you, lovely lady, did not wish to see the Abbey? It is a magnificent structure, and well worth a visit."

"I am sure it is very dirty," pronounced Eve, wrinkling her aristocratic nose in distaste.

"But think of all the famous people who have been interred there," he protested, grinning.

"I am thinking of it," said Eve frankly. "And I have not the slightest desire to go and stare at a lot of dead people."

He gave a shout of laughter. "What a neat way you have of expressing yourself! Eve, my love—may I call you Eve?" At her short nod, he continued, with another chuckle, "No doubt you find the living much more worthy of your interest?"

Sensing that his laughter was not aimed at her, she considered the question seriously. "Not excessively. Most of humanity is as dirty as these old churches. And you, Lord Frome? Do you find these masses of humanity roaming the streets . . . of interest?"

155

"Not in the least," he confided. "I am beginning to think that you and I are very well suited to one another. We are both essentially self-centered."

"And I think you presume far too much, my lord," she reproved, without batting an eyelash.

"Everard," he corrected gently.

As if making a decision, Eve frowned, then gradually her brow cleared and her mouth relaxed into its first smile. "You presume too much . . . Everard."

Everard Frome's lips curved in response. "Do I?" He reached out to take the reins from her grasp, thus bringing both horses to a simultaneous stop. Appropriating her hand, he turned it over, and with practiced fingers, undid the small button of her tan riding glove. With a tantalizing lack of haste, he drew it off and carried her hand to his lips.

"Do you know how lovely you are, Eve?" he whispered, his black eyes gleaming in a manner designed as much to devastate as to woo. His lips burned their way along her wrist, trailed the curve of her palm, and slid down each delicate finger to its tip, where he planted tiny, playful kisses.

"You'll meet me again, won't you, princess?" he said caressingly. "When we can arrange it?"

As accomplished as he was at the art of dalliance, Lord Frome was unable to divine Eve's thoughts. Albeit he had employed his most successful blandishments, he had no idea whether he had made any impression upon this aloof beauty whose very reticence had caught his baffled fancy. Had his boldness caused a spark of excitement to flare briefly in those heavenly blue eyes—or had he merely imagined it? While he awaited her answer, Eve pulled on her glove and, to his amusement, wordlessly presented it to him to rebutton. Though he did so willingly, he was confounded to discover how tense he had become. Good God, she practically had him holding his breath in suspense! The little witch! She had cast her spell over him when he had meant it to be the other way around—!

To his genuine delight, she finally nodded. "Yes, Everard, I rather think I shall. You amuse me very much and that pleases me."

Immediately, she dug her spur into Sugarplum's flanks, and without hesitation, Lord Frome followed her lead. It would seem that seducing this delectable siren was going to be as much a challenge as a treat. But 'twas better so, he thought in exultation. *Lest too light winning make the prize light . . .*

Chapter Eight

The Countess of Rosebery was reclining upon her couch when her brother was announced. Hearing his name, she gave a small but delighted shriek and sat up at once, one hand instinctively flying up to pat her dark, saucy curls. "Jack!" she exclaimed, sounding as though he were the last person on earth she expected to see. "Whatever are you doing here? Rosebery is out, but I daresay it is me you have come to see, anyway!"

"Of course it is, goosecap," he said cheerfully, dropping a kiss on her cheek before drawing up a chair. "What could I possibly have to say to that husband of yours? Where is he anyway? Is he never at home?"

Frances made a wry face. "Seldom, unfortunately. I am quite out of patience with him. Not that I expect him to live in my pocket, you understand, but it is very lowering to feel that one is of less importance to one's husband than the corn laws. Duty calls, and all that flummery!"

The Marquis smiled. "The corn laws were passed last year, Fran," he corrected gently.

"Well, I am sure I cannot possibly remember such

dull details," she retorted, pouting a little. "I have other things on my mind these days that are of far greater import."

Vale took out his snuffbox and helped himself to a pinch before replying. "Just as long as you remember that it was you who insisted upon this marriage, and don't hold me to blame if you are bored now."

Frances frowned. "I am not bored in the least, Jack! I do wish you would not speak in that odiously cynical way. My William is a good, sweet man, and I love him dearly. It is only that I have been feeling a trifle out of sorts these past few days. I have something in particular I wish to tell him, and I have not been able to.—" She broke off, her lips curving into a rather secret smile. "Well, it is of no consequence. Tell me why you are here."

The Marquis ran his eye over his sister. She was looking unusually pretty—her complexion positively glowed, and she seemed to have acquired a new softness about her features.

"Is it possible that I'm to be an uncle at last?" he inquired shrewdly.

His sister blushed. "Is it that obvious?" she inquired, sounding a little anxious. "I do so want to surprise William, and it would be too provoking for words if he first got wind of it from someone else. After all our false hopes, I did not like to mention it until I was completely certain. And now, of course, I'm waiting for just the right moment. I want to be sure I have his full attention, you see," she confided.

"Well, tell him, goose, and I'll wager you'll get it

fast enough," he advised. He yawned loudly and leaned back, linking his fingers behind his neck. "It's what you've both wanted, after all. He'll probably be cast into such transports of delight that you won't be able to shake him off for a month."

"You think so?" she said wistfully.

"Yes, I do," he said, studying her with concern. "How are you feeling?"

She smiled, displaying a dimple. "Oh, beyond a touch of melancholy I am very well, I assure you. I am fortunate that my constitution is not delicate, though perhaps t'would make William notice me more if it were! But you didn't come here to discuss such things as this. Tell me about this girl that everyone has seen you with! Is it true you're actually courting her?"

The Marquis's cordial expression faded, and he dropped his arms to fiddle with his snuffbox. "I suppose so," he said in a depressed tone.

"You *suppose* so?" echoed his sister disbelievingly. "My dear brother, either you are or you aren't, and I trust you'll soon make up your mind! Expectations are bound to be raised, especially since you've made it your pleasure to ignore all the marriageable girls for so long."

"Expectations be damned!" he shot back, scowling darkly.

His sister regarded him thoughtfully. "Well, I can see something must have happened to cast you into a miff. You don't normally snap my nose off like this."

The Marquis hesitated. "I'm sorry, Fran. I've a few things on my mind. Frome has been bothering me again, for one thing. I've an urge to throttle the man and be done with it, but of course, I can't. It puts me in the devil of a humor."

"That dreadful man!" Frances shuddered. "I can never see him without feeling I must run to the mirror to make sure I've put on my clothes. The way he looks at me is positively indecent!"

"The swine," he responded swiftly. "If he ever touches you, I'll kill him."

"But if Lord Frome were going to do me a mischief, surely he would have done it years ago. It's you he means to harm, Jack! I'm sure of it!"

"I can take care of myself," he said. "I was an idiot to mention it to you! You must not worry about me, you hear me? I came only to request your help on another matter, not to put you into a fidget on my account."

His sister raised her brows in slight alarm. "My help? Good heavens! What in the world have you done this time?"

He smiled wryly. "A sisterly remark if I ever heard one! Fear not, it's nothing disreputable. I've merely accepted a wager, and I think you can help me to win. It's . . . important to me, Fran."

"What sort of a wager?" she asked, instantly curious.

Her brother grimaced. "An extremely foolish one." Briefly, he told her the story, and sketched out his own plan, which necessitated an account of his acquaintance with Miss Amanda Marlowe. This took longer than he expected, for his sister found the entire story difficult to credit and interrupted him with a great many questions. He found himself

161

telling her of his so-called abduction of the girl, although he had had not the least intention of doing so when he'd begun. It was unlike him to be so frank with his sister about his doings, but he knew she was unlikely to overreact, and for some reason he seemed to have a need to talk about it.

As soon as he was finished, Frances said bluntly, "What is this girl to you, Jack? Is she to be just another one of your flirts?"

After the smallest pause, the Marquis said easily, "Amanda, my flirt? Nonsense! She's a respectable young lady, Fran. I don't trifle with the affections of innocents."

"Amanda, is it? She gives you permission to address her so familiarly?" she queried, decidedly suspicious.

He lifted his shoulders, and the shuttered look he so often assumed slipped back over his features. "Of course not. A mere slip of the tongue, Fran. Come, do not put on that stiff attitude with me! I know you are no stickler for the conventions. Will you help me or not?"

Frances rubbed her forehead. "It's a mad, scandalous plan, my dear," she sighed. "How could I possibly deceive the girl? And you *do* know, of course, the interpretation that will be placed on any call I make upon the Countess of Besford? After all, I scarcely know the woman!" She hesitated, eyeing him curiously. "And can you assure me this girl is indeed an innocent? I won't embroil myself in any scandals, even for you, Jack. Why, what Rosebery would say if he knew, I quite tremble to contemplate!"

The Marquis leaned back in his chair and stretched out his long, muscular legs. "You will have no trouble deceiving her if you are half the actress you were when we were children! She is a green girl, I promise you. As for making a common morning call, it will seem perfectly natural, since I imagine the Countess already has a fair notion that I intend to marry her niece. And as for Amanda's innocence, I leave you to be the judge of that. Two minutes in her company should put those fears to rest. Any other objections?" He was not watching her, and so missed the gamut of emotion that crossed his sister's face.

"So you do mean to marry the girl!" she cried, slapping him lightly on the knee. "How wonderful! But why could you not say so in the first place?"

"I mean to marry Eve Marlowe only out of respect for our father's wishes, and because it is my duty to beget an heir," he said dampeningly. "Otherwise, I would choose not to marry at all. You, more than anyone, ought to be able to understand my reasons."

"Well, I don't!" replied his sister, disappointed. "Papa may have ridden roughshod over us while he was alive, but I see no reason for allowing him to continue to do so now. You ought to marry to please yourself, as I did. You may mock my husband, but I'll have you know I am happier now than I ever was before I married. You can have no notion how pleasant it is to have one's wishes respected and . . . and one's comfort considered."

"I intend to have that no matter who I wed," retorted the Marquis acidly.

"Now that," remarked Frances candidly, "sounds much more like Papa than you! I would take care if I were you, Jack. I think marriage with the wrong woman will make you into a selfish and sour-tempered old man just like Papa! I'm beginning to think this wager may turn out to be a very good thing!"

Even if she had not, in the end, agreed to help her brother, Lady Frances would have found some excuse to call at Berkeley Square. She desired very much to meet the two young women who, in such a short time, had obviously cast her brother's life into complete disorder. That he was willing to go to such lengths for the one, yet expressed his intention to marry the other, she found extremely interesting. The wager she immediately dismissed as irrelevant. He had made wagers before, and none of them had ever affected him as profoundly as this. For he *was* different somehow, though she was at a loss to put her finger on exactly what it was that had altered.

Well, this whole affair had certainly provided her with some food for thought, and if she was not mistaken, would probably need some sorting out before it got out of hand. Of one thing she was certain, and that was if she had any say in the matter, Jack was not going to marry a girl who would change him into another such as their father had been. She loved her brother far too well not to make a push to prevent such an occurrence.

These reflections occupied her for some time after the Marquis's departure, but eventually the young Countess lay drowsily back upon her couch. Her visit to Berkeley Square could wait.

At much the same time of day, another lady was also resting. She was very nearly asleep, in fact, and so was unaware that the door to her boudoir had swung quietly open, and a gentleman stood in the doorway. He moved into the room and gazed silently down upon her, his mouth marred by a sneer. Then he turned and slammed shut the door with such violence that the lady's body jerked and she sat bolt upright, her face rigid with fear.

"You!" she uttered in her low voice. "What do you want?"

He threw his hat and cane on a nearby chair and approached her with a loathsome smile. "Why, I want what I always want from you, Alexandra. What you're so skilled at providing, I should say."

She swung her legs to the floor and would have risen, but was forcibly prevented by the gentleman's strong arms. "Gently, gently, my love," he whispered. "No fights between us this time. Variety is the key, don't you think? I shan't hurt you very much, if you're good. And you can be very, very good, can't you, my love?"

He pressed her down upon the elegant daybed, and drove his tongue into her mouth until she tasted blood. Lady Claverley despised herself as she began to respond, but his power over her was far more than just his knowledge of her past indiscretions. Some primitive urge within her enjoyed his brutality, and he knew it. His strange ways fascinated her, for his cruelty was oddly mixed with an extraordinary, bewildering tenderness, a bizarre combination that defeated her entirely, and made her his puppet.

"Do not bruise me, I beg you," she murmured, when he raised his head to breathe. "I go to the opera tonight. How did you get in? Did anyone see you?"

He laughed bitterly. "No one ever notices me, love. It's my lot in life, don't you see? Jeanne let me in. She dared not do otherwise, so do not blame the wench. She is as afraid of me as her mistress is."

"I'm not afraid of you," she protested, but immediately regretted her words. There could be little doubt that he wanted her to be afraid, for it was part of his enjoyment of the game. He was the sharp-clawed predator, she, the defenseless prey. He was smiling again, his pale lips drawn mirthlessly back to reveal rather large teeth. Perhaps it was his smile that frightened her the most, for it certainly did not signify amusement. And his eyes were the coldest she had ever seen.

To punish her for her defiance, he ripped open the bodice of her new gown. "You're not afraid of me?" he said softly. "Why not, Alexandra? Haven't I given you just cause to fear me? What do you think your lovers would say if they knew what you had done? What would the fierce Lord Frome say, or the arrogant Marquis? More to the point, what would they do?" He rose, and began to remove his coat.

"No," he continued reflectively, "I think you're lying, my beautiful one. I think you're very afraid of me. Or else you're very, very foolish." He came

166

back to her then, stirring her this time with that astonishing, puzzling gentleness.

After a little while, he paused. "Alexandra, love. I've something that I want you to do for me."

She gazed up at him in mute appeal.

"It pleases me that you are spending time with Lord Frome. I know all about his desire for vengeance and I'm interested in his plans, Alexandra. I want to know all about them."

"Please," she whispered. "Later."

He touched her cheek, wiping away the glistening tear that hovered at the corner of one of her lovely violet eyes. "Oh, very well," he said, kissing her forehead. "You can't talk now, that's clear. You're no better than a Covent Garden trollop, my love. Only more expensive, of course, and far, far more beautiful . . ."

"What did you think of Mr. Wilcox?" inquired Lady Besford one morning a few days later, after that gentleman had paid them a morning visit.

Caught up in memories of her visit to Westminster with the Marquis, Amanda found it difficult to concentrate on her ladyship's question. "Why, I . . . I thought him a very pleasant young man. Not very confident in himself, but honest, and . . . and good, I think." She reached to pick up her embroidery.

The Countess studied the girl carefully, but could find no evidence of concealed interest. "He is not married, Amanda, and seemed very taken with you. You could do worse than attach such a man."

Amanda smiled slightly, and began threading a needle. "I suppose that is true, ma'am. Yet I could not see myself wed to him. We should not suit at all, I'm afraid."

"Then, what of Lord Castlebury or Sir Edward Tymalt? They were both very courteous and gallant to you, and they are both single gentlemen rumored to be on the lookout for a wife."

Amanda's eyes gleamed in sudden amusement. "I do not mean to seem contrary, ma'am, but Lord Castlebury is old enough to be my father! And his gallantry did not prevent him from laying his hand upon my, ahem, thigh, three times as we talked. You did not notice, I fancy, as you were busy speaking with Lady Westhaven at the time."

"Good gracious, Amanda! Truly? Three times?" asked her ladyship, quite dismayed.

"Three times," Amanda replied firmly.

"Well, what of Sir Edward?" the Countess persisted. "He, at least, has never been accused of the least impropriety. I'm sure he would not dream of doing such a thing!"

Amanda sighed, but her eyes held a distinct twinkle. "Yes, ma'am, but Sir Edward has a butterfly collection."

"Oh?" said the Countess, bewildered by this seemingly innocuous objection.

Amanda wrinkled her straight, little nose. "We spoke of nothing but butterflies for twenty minutes, ma'am. He did not make the least effort to get to know me, or inquire how I liked London, or . . . or anything else. We spoke only of butterflies. He has a room filled with them. Stuck up on pieces of wood with little pins."

"Heavens!" The Countess looked rather revolted. "You do not care for butterflies, I suppose?" she inquired, after a moment.

"Well, ma'am," answered Amanda frankly, "I think I may safely say I like butterflies as much as the next person. But only conceive of being obliged to discuss them each day for the rest of one's natural life! I suspect that I might develop quite an aversion to them. Did you know there are hundreds of varieties flying about, if one includes moths?"

"Really?" the Countess managed rather weakly.

Amanda jabbed her needle into her pin cushion and once more set her stitchery aside.

"You must not worry so much about my future, dear ma'am," she said, softening her words with a warm look. "I really have no intention of marrying anyone just yet. I am too much like my mother, I suppose, for I refuse to make a marriage to suit someone else's convenience. Perhaps I will never marry at all."

Lady Besford's automatic protest was drowned out by a sudden and most incongruous trample of footsteps, followed by a penetrating, high-pitched wail.

"Mamaaaa—!" howled a youthful voice. "Perry pushed me!"

"Good gracious!" exclaimed her ladyship, a hand to her cheek. "Am I hearing aright—?"

A crash against the wall just outside the door to the drawing room appeared to confirm her suspicions.

"It is!" she cried joyfully. Without hesitation,

Lady Besford sprang to her feet and was nearly to the door when it crashed open and two small figures literally fell into the room.

"Grandmama!" they both shouted, nearly in unison.

At once, the Countess bent to assist the smaller of her two grandsons to his feet. "My goodness, Robin, just look at you!" she marvelled, straightening his little coat. "You've grown into such a little man since last I saw you! And you, too, Perry, my dear. You look so tall and handsome! Where is your mama? And what on earth are you *doing* here?"

"They're both outside. Mama's waiting for Papa, and Papa is giving directions to the coachman. They said to come ahead and see if we could find you!"

"Perry! Robin! Where are you? Did you find your grandmother?" called a female voice from the foot of the first-floor staircase.

Lady Besford hurried out of the drawing room. "Priscilla, darling, what are you doing here? What a wonderful surprise!"

Mounting the stairs, the Countess's daughter protested, with a helpless little laugh, "A surprise? Oh, but Mama, I *did* send a letter! And you didn't receive it? But this is a great deal too bad! I was most careful to post it in time, just so this would not happen!" Exchanging an affectionate embrace with her mother, she went on, "Then if you were not expecting us . . . oh, dear! You do not have guests, do you? I would never have allowed the children to run up here in such a boisterous fashion if I thought—but Higgins would have told me, wouldn't he?"

"No, no," said her ladyship, beaming happily. "Only Eve and Amanda, and Eve has gone visiting for the afternoon. But why are we standing out here? Come into the drawing room, and let me introduce you to Amanda."

They reentered the room to find both Amanda and the boys gazing out the window on to the Square. "There is my papa," Perry was saying proudly. "I told you we could see him from here!"

"You did indeed," replied Amanda. "Are you here for a long visit?"

His mother answered. "Not this time, I'm afraid. We are only passing through on our way to visit friends."

Smiling a little shyly, Lady Priscilla Braxton stepped forward and held out her hand to Amanda. "I am very glad to meet you, Miss Marlowe. Mama told me in her last letter that you were planning to come to London."

As far as Amanda could see, Lady Besford's daughter resembled neither of her parents. She was a slender, dainty-looking young woman, with delicate features and soft, doe-like brown eyes. Though it was not inclined to curl, her finely-textured hair was an attractive shade of brown, rather like coffee which had been laced with a single drop of cream.

"And where is Papa? Is he out?" continued Priscilla, her eyes on her sons.

Lady Besford sighed. "Oh, he has gone off to White's, as usual. And I believe he had to visit his tailor, for I heard him grumbling about it this morning! I'll send a message to him presently to let him know you are here. In the meanwhile, let us be comfortable!"

Lady Priscilla sat down gracefully. "Boys, come away from the window and make your bows to Grandmama and Miss Marlowe. I am sure you neglected to do so when you came plunging in here like a pair of wild beasts."

As her sentence ended, Priscilla's husband appeared in the doorway. "Well, that's taken care of," he said, strolling over to place a dutiful kiss upon his mama-in-law's cheek. "You're looking as lovely as usual, ma'am," he told Lady Besford with a smile.

Sir Julian Braxton, Baronet, was a capable-looking gentleman in his mid-thirties. His curling blond hair and regular features were still very much admired among the females of his acquaintance, but not once since his marriage to Lady Besford's daughter had his deep-set gray eyes lingered upon any woman but his own wife. While his mama-in-law liked to believe that the match had been largely her doing, the truth was that Sir Julian was a man who walked into nothing unless it was of his own volition.

He, too, shook hands with Amanda. "I trust you will enjoy your stay in London, Miss Marlowe. It's an interesting place to visit—at least occasionally." He exchanged glances with his wife. "I assume she has met the little monsters?"

Priscilla smiled fondly. "Yes, but they have yet to make their bows."

Perry was first to come forward. He was tall for

his age and resembled his father, for his hair was just as blond and his smile as engaging.

"I'm six," he told Amanda when she inquired. "And Robin's not quite four. His name is Robert but we call him Robin. He's named after my grandfather."

"I see," said Amanda, smiling at the seriousness with which he offered this store of information.

"And how old are you, miss?" he asked with polite interest.

"Perry, darling, you do not ask a lady that question," reproved Priscilla. "It is not done."

He looked at his mother in puzzlement. "Why not? I want to know."

Amanda leaned forward. "Actually," she told him in a confidential tone, "I am nineteen. But I beg you will not spread it about. I would prefer to keep it a secret."

Satisfied with this, Perry retorted, "A secret? Oh, that's all right, then!"

At this point, Robin, who only moments before had climbed onto his grandmother's lap, began to wriggle. "I want to get down!" he said emphatically. "I want to talk to the lady." Approaching cautiously, Robin stared at Amanda in seeming fascination.

"Make your bow, Robin," commanded his father sternly.

After a brief pause, the little boy shook his head. "No," he stated decisively. "She is not a duchess. Nanny says bowing is for duchesses."

Maintaining a straight face with difficulty, Amanda replied, "And how do you know I'm not a duchess? I might be, you know."

His older brother laughed. "You're not a duchess! She's gammoning us, isn't she, Papa? You can't be a duchess until you're quite old!"

Playing along, Sir Julian said easily, "Well, she could be if she were married to a duke. You can never tell about these things, Perry. It's always best to do the civil, just in case."

To everyone's amusement, little Robin proceeded to execute a wobbly bow in Amanda's direction. "Nanny's sick," he explained. "We left her home so I can't ask her if you're a duchess."

"Nanny says duchesses are almost as good as queens," Perry informed them with a giggle.

"Perhaps," remarked Sir Julian meaningfully, "the boys might go down to the kitchen and visit with your cook for a while. They got on very well with the fellow last time we were here, I believe. He gave them too many sweets, but other than that . . ."

"An excellent idea," agreed Priscilla immediately. "Mama, is it all right?"

Before Lady Besford could answer, the smallest Braxton stepped back into the conversation.

"I'm right gutfoundered, Grandmama," he announced hopefully.

"You're *what?*" repeated Sir Julian in astonishment.

Robin grinned self-consciously. "Gutfoundered," he repeated. "I want something to eat."

"And where," inquired his father in a terrible voice, "did you learn that unpalatable expression?"

Abashed, Robin immediately stuck his thumb in his mouth, leaving it to his brother to respond,

"Oh, that is what Bob Coachman says, Papa!" Eagerly, Perry jumped up, stuck out his stomach, and pummeled it with his fists. "I'm right gutfoundered, I am," he mimicked, lowering the tenor of his voice. "Got to get me some mutton and a pint of ale!"

Apparently, his son's performance must have struck an authentic chord, for Sir Julian's mouth began to quiver. "Dear me, where *did* we get these children, Cilla?" he said to his wife. "Did the gypsies abandon them on our doorstep?"

Priscilla sighed. "I cannot seem to recall, Julian. But what with Nanny being ill, we're going to have to take them in hand for the next few days."

Lady Besford investigated the nearby surfaces for her handbell. "I will ring for one of the footmen to take them down to see Cook—if only I can locate my bell! I could have sworn it was right here next to my hartshorn a moment ago. Now where could it be? I'm sure the poor darlings must be quite ravenous!"

"Oh, to be sure," concurred Sir Julian with irony. "We only went through an entire picnic basket of food on the journey."

Believing that the three family members might like to speak privately, Amanda said, "Why don't you let me take the children down to the kitchen, ma'am? They are such splendid little fellows, I'm sure it will be great fun."

Sir Julian gave her an amused glance. "You are quite free to change your mind about that, you know."

"Are you sure it's no bother, Amanda?" said Lady Besford gratefully. "Don't let them keep you

175

long, my dear. Just leave them with Alfred and come right back."

Taking Robin firmly by the hand, Amanda surveyed Perry reflectively. "Are you too old to hold my hand? I cannot quite remember at what age that occurs."

Perry hesitated, then came toward her with an impish grin. "Not when it's someone pretty like you, miss."

When they had gone, Sir Julian sat back in his chair, looking mildly stunned. "Good lord, the boy's turning into a miniature Lothario! Since when did he learn to turn out a compliment like that, Cilla?"

"Now, Julian," replied his wife, blushing slightly, "you know what they say about children's ears. And when we are at home, I have known you to make just that sort of remark. To me, of course," she added, for her mother's benefit.

"Dear me!" said Sir Julian, much struck. "I see I shall have to watch what I say!"

Her ladyship's head bobbed in agreement. "Yes, indeed, one must be very careful. And now, Priscilla, love, do put me out of suspense! I am still waiting to hear what brings you all here! And how long you are meaning to stay!"

"She did not get my letter," explained Priscilla at her husband's surprised look. "You see, Mama, we are on our way to visit Julian's sister in Oxford. But Julian has some business to conduct here in town, and I need to do some shopping, so we thought we would stay here a day or two. If it is inconvenient, I suppose we could put up at a hotel—?"

"A hotel!" echoed her mother in horror. "My grandsons in a hotel? You cannot be serious, Priscilla! What happened to the boys' nurse, by the way?"

"Oh, Nanny came down with one of her mysterious ailments the day before we left. The poor woman is prone to them, you know. I believe it was something to do with her chest, but it was a trifle unclear. Naturally, Julian summoned the doctor, who declared her to be unfit for travel." She sighed. "He said she must remain in her bed for at least a week."

"How excessively provoking of her!" exclaimed her mother. "And just when you were going to need her the most!"

Priscilla shrugged. "Well, she does not do it on purpose. And the children love her dearly, so we put up with her constitutional idiosyncracies. I daresay I can send them to the Park with my abigail for a few hours in the morning, and in the afternoon, Julian says we can take them to see the performance at Astley's Amphitheatre. Didn't you, dear?" she added, with a guileless smile at her spouse.

"Did I really?" retorted Sir Julian, a laugh in his eye. "Dear me, what a lamentable memory I must have, for I cannot recall saying anything of the sort." The look he shot his wife must have contained some private meaning, for Priscilla's cheeks turned quite pink. *"Julian—!"* she said, her lips quivering in response.

"Ah, well," relented Sir Julian, meeting her gaze with an enigmatic smile. "If we must, we must!"

Since it was Sir Julian's surmise that a single morning would be insufficient to complete his business, the Braxtons decided to remain at Berkeley Square for two days rather than one. This arrangement delighted Priscilla, whose goal it was, she confided to her mother at breakfast the next morning, to squeeze in as much shopping as she could while she was in town.

"And it will give us more time to be together, which you can be sure Julian took into account. As it is, I hate to make such a short visit, but you can depend that Louisa will be in a complete stew if we do not arrive in time for her birthday celebration on Thursday!"

Reaching for her cup of chocolate, she went on, "Of course, the dressmaker and the milliner must come first, but I hope to get a chance to visit that perfumery shop in New Bond Street, you know the one I mean, Mama! And I need to purchase some artificial flowers as well. Where is the best place for that, do you suppose?"

"Botibol's," said the Countess instantly. "They are in Oxford Street, my dear, and I recommend them highly. I buy all my ostrich feathers there. Their merchandise is of the finest quality."

Sir Julian had left for the city an hour before, and Lord Besford, finding himself the only man in a houseful of females, had ventured into the breakfast room only on his wife's assurance that he would still be allowed to read his newspaper. Finding, however, that a lively discussion of feminine fripperies was to be conducted concurrently, he ate rapidly, refolded his paper, and prepared to flee the room.

"Now, don't you go wearing your mother out!" he told Priscilla, tucking his paper under his arm. "And just what were you proposing to do with the boys? You ain't planning to drag them all over London, are you?"

"No, of course not, Papa," said Priscilla, a shade reproachfully. "You don't need to ask me that. I was planning to send them to the Park with Yvette."

The Earl eyed his daughter sternly. "Who the devil is Yvette? I can't keep track of all these people you've got traipsing in and out of my house!"

"Oh, Papa! Yvette is my abigail! And she is perfectly capable of handling the boys for a single morning."

"She sounds foreign. Is she French?" he asked suspiciously.

"Excessively so," his daughter told him with a faint sigh. "And very temperamental."

His lordship glared at his daughter. "Do the boys like her?"

Priscilla hesitated. "Well, it does not matter whether they like her, does it? As long as they mind her?"

"It matters to me! She ain't that long-nosed female that nearly knocked me down the stairs this morning, is she? Demmed Friday-faced creature with squinty little eyes?"

"It . . . it sounds very like her," responded Priscilla, trying not to laugh. "She does have a squint,

179

I'm afraid."

"Perhaps Eve and I could take the children to the Park," offered Amanda, who could see that the Earl's complexion was becoming alarmingly suffused. "You would not mind, would you, Eve? They are very nice little boys."

Eve's coffee cup rattled loudly. "I hardly think that is a good idea, Amanda," she replied, with a betraying shudder. "I have not the faintest notion how to deal with children."

"You could take any one of the housemaids, Amanda," put in Lady Besford quickly. "Or Ellen, for that matter! She came from a large family, and no doubt deals extremely well with children."

Lord Besford's thick brows snapped together in disapproval. "A sorry plight we've come to, Emily, when one of our guests must start playing nursemaid! Why the devil should Amanda be imposed upon when we've a houseful of servants?"

"But, my lord," said Amanda, rather amused by the Earl's attitude, "I really do not mind. I am very fond of children, and I have nothing better to do this morning—truly!"

Recognizing the sincerity in Amanda's voice, Lord Besford barked out a laugh. "Too polite to tell me I'm talking humbug, ain't you? Very well, I'll keep my nose out of it. But I'd sooner trust a Chinaman with my grandsons than some long-nosed Frenchie! You're a good girl, Amanda, and I hope my daughter appreciates it."

After her father had stomped from the room, Priscilla gave Amanda an embarrassed look. "I'm so sorry, Miss Marlowe. My father is right. It is

180

shocking of us to impose on you like this."

"Fiddle!" responded Amanda, with a good-natured laugh. "One would think you had a dozen children, Lady Priscilla, instead of merely two. I have already made their acquaintance, you know, and we got along famously. Perry has told me all about his rock collection, and little Robin has decided that even if I am not a duchess, he will still bow to me!"

Priscilla looked relieved. "Well, that is very good of you, then. I confess I was not any more pleased than Papa about sending them with Yvette, for although she is very capable, she is sometimes much too sharp with them."

Hearing a series of peculiar thumps from somewhere overhead, Amanda pushed back her chair. "It is settled then," she said with a smile. "I'll go find the boys. I expect the sooner they are out where they can run around, the better it will be."

In the end, it was decided that Ellen would accompany them, in case the two little Braxtons' high spirits should prove more than Amanda could manage. The distance to the Park being too considerable for a small child to walk, they were sent off in the Besfords' landaulet, along with a great many admonitions to behave.

When they were out of sight, the Countess heaved a comfortable sigh. "Well, now we may be easy," she said to her daughter, "for Amanda is a dear, reliable girl. So, my love, off we go to Madame Simonnet's! How unfortunate that Eve does not feel well enough to come with us. The poor girl gets so many headaches!"

Chapter Nine

Hours later, after the Braxton family's rather noisy departure for Astley's, the house at Berkeley Square began to settle back into its ordinarily peaceful state. It was one of her ladyship's "at home" afternoons, so with Amanda in tow, Lady Besford led the way to the drawing room to await the arrival of possible callers.

"You could have knocked me over with a feather, Amanda, when Robert said he would go with them!" confided her ladyship, sinking gratefully into her favorite chair. "Pray do not repeat this to the children, but the truth of it is, my husband does not care for Astley's at all! Nor do I, for that matter. Oh, I admit the equestrian ballets are entertaining, but I see nothing wonderful in forcing eight noble horses to perform a country dance. It seems so . . . so *unnatural!* However, it is very popular, and I daresay the children will love it."

"It gives Lord Besford a chance to spend some time with the children," suggested Amanda. "Perry was absolutely delighted he decided to go."

"Well, we *do* spend nearly half of each summer at Sir Julian's estate in Kent, so it is not as if we never see our grandchildren, my dear. But even so, it's my belief that he felt we neglected them this morning and that is why he chose to go. Of course, we could scarcely have sent them to the Park with Robert! The very notion is laughable! My husband has many good qualities, Amanda, but coping with children is not one of them. He has very little patience, I'm afraid."

Amanda smiled. "Yes, they are a handful," she concurred. "But no more so than other children. Which reminds me of something I wish to say to you, ma'am."

"Oh? And what is that, my dear?"

"Since I knew you and your daughter were planning to do more shopping, I promised Perry that I would take them to the Park again tomorrow, if the pleasant weather continues. I hope that will be all right?"

Lady Besford assumed a determinedly casual tone. "Why, of course that is fine, Amanda, but are you quite sure you wish to? Ellen could take them if you have something else you would like to do. I was hoping to persuade you to come shopping with us."

Amanda shook her head. "No, ma'am, I would rather not, if you do not mind. But I would enjoy taking the children again. And what I wanted to suggest to you is that it might be better if . . . if Ellen did not come with us."

The Countess's brows went up. "Oh?"

"While I am sure that Ellen is an excellent abigail," said Amanda, choosing her words with care,

183

"I do not think she would make a very good nanny. For some reason, despite having had a vast number of siblings, she holds the unrealistic belief that Perry and Robin ought to behave like little pattern cards of virtue—merely because they are of the nobility! And you know as well as I, ma'am, that it is natural for all children to be active. Their liveliness simply needs to be guided, not . . . not *squelched!* But Ellen seemed quite shocked to see Perry attempting cartwheels in the grass, and I thought she was going to have a fit of the vapors when I had to take Robin behind some bushes to—well, you know what I mean! But there was no one about to see, so I cannot see what difference it made!" she added with lingering obstinacy. "Anyway, ma'am, I swear I spent as much time in soothing Ellen's offended sensibilities as I did in watching the children!"

Lady Besford looked amused. "Yes, well, Ellen has always had very high standards. I'm sure we all must disappoint her quite frequently."

The sudden appearance of Higgins put an end to this conversation, for Lady Besford's first visitor had arrived.

"The Countess of Rosebery," intoned the butler in majestic accents.

That the lady who entered the drawing room was related to the Marquis of Vale was immediately obvious, for she bore an astonishing resemblance to her brother. Thick black brows arched over eyes just as piercingly blue; her nose had that same slight aquiline curve, and her face, the same bone structure. On the Marquis, those features were strikingly attractive; on Lady Rosebery, they were both elegant

184

and unusual. She looked rather younger than her age, which was four-and-twenty, but her mien, as she greeted her hostess, was one of complete poise and dignity.

"My brother suggested that I call," she explained after a few minutes of general conversation. She glanced at Amanda, her look both friendly and subtly assessing. Judging from the girl's mode of dress, she had guessed at once that this must be Jack's Amanda, and although she greatly desired to meet both cousins, she was not altogether displeased to have the chance to form an opinion about this one first.

"Well, we are delighted you came," Lady Besford told her with a beam. "Unfortunately, my niece is slightly indisposed at the moment. Amanda has been kind enough to bear me company this afternoon."

"My brother mentioned you, Miss Marlowe," remarked Lady Rosebery, noting with interest the tinge of color in the girl's cheeks. Her tone grew dry. "Yes, my brother is the notorious Marquis of Vale. I believe he took you to visit St. Paul's the other day," she added.

"Yes, he did," replied Amanda, a little flustered. Feeling that some other comment was expected of her, she added, "It was a most enjoyable and . . . and informative outing."

"Informative?" The young Countess's black brows lifted. "Dear me, that sounds ominous! Do you mean he has been flirting? If he steps beyond the line, Miss Marlowe, you need only drop a word in my ear, and I will give him a trimming! Believe it or not, he listens to me occasionally, though he is the elder of us two."

Amanda's telltale blush confirmed Frances's suspicions. "Oh, no, ma'am. Lord Vale behaved with perfect propriety, I assure you! I merely meant that he was kind enough to take me somewhere that . . . I mean, it was a place I had very much longed to see. It is a magnificent church," she added, feeling like a fool.

"Yes, isn't it," agreed the Marquis's sister, observing Amanda closely. The girl was *not* a flirt, she decided. It still remained to be seen what she *was*. God willing, one or the other of the two girls would prove to be the right woman for her brother, for she was of the opinion that Jack desperately needed to love and be loved, and that time was running out.

Satisfied for the moment, Frances changed the subject. "I hope your niece is not seriously ill?" she inquired, turning to Lady Besford.

"Oh, no," the older woman responded. "It is merely another of the poor girl's headaches. I do hope she'll be feeling well by tomorrow, for we go to the opera in the evening, and I know she is looking forward to it."

"Ah, yes." Frances smoothed her skirt absently. "The Catalani will sing. One cannot help admiring the purity of her voice, though they say she is a regular virago of temperament behind the scenes."

"Her voice is lovely," agreed Lady Besford doubtfully, "but I cannot quite like the way she smiles so incessantly, even while singing the most tragic lyrics."

The young Countess chuckled. "Yes, I have noticed that also. Will you go to hear Catalani, Miss Marlowe? I heard her sing in *Semiramide* last season, and despite all her smiles, her performance was indeed outstanding."

It was more than a polite inquiry, Amanda knew, for there was genuine kindness in Lady Rosebery's voice and true interest in her gaze. It impelled her to give a forthright answer.

"I had not planned on it, ma'am." She smiled shyly. "I would truly love to go, but for me, it is sadly impractical. I cannot afford to play the part of fashionable lady." Frances's sympathetic expression prompted Amanda to continue, with pretty hesitancy, "I am only here in London because of Lady Besford's kindness, and I will quite likely be seeking a post as governess after my visit. So you see, ma'am, it just would not do."

Absolutely incredible, thought Frances, startled. How many girls Miss Marlowe's age, in her situation, could make such an admission without sounding even a little self-pitying? Either the girl was the best actress in the world, or she was genuinely as unaffected and, yes, as *nice* as she appeared! If she behaved as refreshingly natural with Jack, it was no small wonder she had triggered his interest.

Fascinated, Frances found herself responding, "But, Miss Marlowe, you are so young! Surely marriage would be a better solution?"

"That has been suggested to me," Amanda replied with an apologetic smile at Lady Besford. "But, you see, I have the great misfortune to be extremely romantic. To marry for the sake of expediency seems to me a worse fate than earning my living. I know it is very contrary of me," she added, trying to sound repentant.

There was, however, a distinct twinkle in Amanda's eyes, and observing it, Frances began to grow excited. If this girl could laugh at herself, then she ought to be able to make Jack laugh as well. And a little laughter would do her brother a world of good, thought the Marquis's sister approvingly.

"It certainly is contrary!" said Lady Besford, diving back into the conversation with vigor. "My goodness, Amanda, this is the first I have heard of this! What on earth makes you think you should become a governess? Just because you enjoyed taking Perry and Robin to the Park this morning, does *not* mean you would derive the least enjoyment from becoming such a drudge!" She turned to the Marquis's sister for support. "Surely you agree, Lady Rosebery, that a governess's life leaves much to be desired!"

Frances sat back, regarding Amanda quizzically. "I do, indeed! Yet I sympathize with you, Miss Marlowe, for I know what it is like to possess a romantic disposition. Who are Perry and Robin, if I may ask?"

Lady Besford gave her a brief explanation. "And now she wants to take them to the Park tomorrow morning as well!" she finished in exasperation.

Very much intrigued by Amanda Marlowe, Frances found herself wondering what the other cousin was like. An idea occurred to her, and she leaned forward.

"Take my advice, Miss Marlowe. Forget your circumstances, put on the best gown you have, and

188

come to the opera tomorrow night. Lady Besford, may I invite you all to join us in our box? I plan to be there, and my brother, too, for my husband cannot come and I need an escort. He would be delighted to see you, I promise. And it would give me an opportunity to meet your niece."

Several thoughts went through Lady Besford's mind, but the foremost of these was that Lady Rosebery's gesture stemmed from the knowledge that her brother intended to make Eve a formal offer. Her matchmaking instincts told her to accept, and she reminded herself that her own box was available should Priscilla and Sir Julian decide they wished to go. She had a strong suspicion that they would not, however, as Sir Julian seldom displayed an inclination to be anywhere but at home with his wife in the evenings, a preference which her daughter seemed to share.

"How very kind!" she therefore responded. "We shall be delighted, shan't we, Amanda? Now, you absurd child, don't you dare say you will not come! We shall find you a dress to wear, never fear."

All Amanda's strongest resolutions failed her at this instant. Having always had a desire to attend the opera, it suddenly struck her as incredibly foolish not to do so when she had the chance.

"Oh, very well, ma'am. You are right, I know." She smiled, a warm kernel of delicious anticipation rising within her. "My mother always said that life was too short to waste in useless vacillation!"

By the end of her short visit, the Marquis's sister was completely won over, and had reached the conclusion that Amanda would do very well for a sister-in-law. Spontaneously, she found herself saying, "Would you care to drive out with me a while later, Miss Marlowe? I drive myself, and am considered no mean whip, if that reassures you without sounding braggish."

Surprised, Amanda glanced at Lady Besford, who nodded encouragingly. "Why, thank you, Lady Rosebery, I should like that very much," she replied, her pleasure obvious.

"I shall be outside at about four-thirty, then. Best be ready, as my pair do not like to stand in the street for very long."

Amusement flashed in Amanda's silver eyes. "Do you know you sound a great deal like your brother?" she asked, rather teasingly.

Frances's dimple quivered in response. "Who do you think taught me to drive, Miss Marlowe?"

At four-thirty, Amanda descended the shallow stone steps of the house, eagerly inspecting Lady Rosebery's dashing little wine-colored phaeton with its silver trim. Her new friend waved cheerfully, and she hurried forward, allowing the groom to assist her into the carriage.

Frances flicked the reins. "How do you like my turn-out?" she inquired as the phaeton rolled forward.

"It's marvelous," Amanda answered admiringly. "I've never driven anything other than a gig myself, and that only a few times. I'm not very good at it."

From the corner of her eye, Frances shot the other girl a mischievous look. "Truly? I should ask

Jack to teach you, Miss Marlowe. He is first-rate himself, and was amazingly patient with me, though I was a sore trial to him in the beginning."

"Oh, no!" Discomposed by the suggestion, Amanda said a shade unsteadily, "I hope you are not serious, Lady Rosebery. I'm sure he would think it a great imposition, and anyway, it is not something a governess needs to learn."

The Marquis's sister smiled knowingly and made an unconventional suggestion. "Why don't we use our Christian names? We are practically of an age, after all, and I am tired to death of titles. Although they can be very useful at times," she added with a hint of her brother's cynicism.

All ceremony being summarily dispensed with, Frances chattered away, guiding her horses as expertly as she had claimed. Having no wish to subject Amanda to the stares of the *ton* who paraded in the Park at this hour, she instead chose to drive a circuitous route through the Mayfair streets, her path encompassing such squares and avenues that were most pleasurable to view. It did not take her long to steer the conversation in the direction of dressmakers, for Amanda was willing to talk about anything the Marquis's sister wished.

"You know, Amanda," ventured Frances quite casually, "I sympathize with your situation, but I was thinking that there is really no reason for you not to purchase some new gowns in London. I am surprised that Lady Besford took you to someone like Madame Simonnet. She is shockingly expensive! It is no small wonder you felt overwhelmed by her prices."

Receiving no reply, the young Countess hurried on, feeling absurdly treacherous. "There *are* dressmakers who could serve the purpose. Of course, I cannot promise you that they can create anything as fine or as fashionable as what your cousin may be wearing but, forgive me for saying this, would it not be something to consider?"

Amanda's clenched fingers betrayed her feelings, though she did not realize it. "Yes, I—suppose so. Do you know of anyone?"

Frances knew this was her cue, and suppressed her guilt. She had promised Jack, and she would not go back on that promise.

"Well, I have heard of a woman who might be a possibility. I understand she is just opening a business, and her prices are reputed to be very . . . low."

Amanda's hopes stirred. "Really?"

"Y-Yes," continued her friend, her eyes fixed straight ahead. "Her name is Madame Claret. She is French, of course, and from what I understand, she is supposed to be extremely clever, though quite elderly. I believe she and her daughter have only recently settled in London. Their cloth may not be of the highest quality, but they should be able to fashion you some modish-looking gowns."

Amanda frowned thoughtfully. "You think I could afford them?"

"I think it's quite likely," declared Frances, who had the advantage of knowing exactly why those prices were so low. "I don't believe they have acquired much custom yet. No doubt they will charge more as soon as they become more well known. If

192

TAKE ADVANTAGE OF THIS SPECIAL OFFER, AVAILABLE *ONLY* TO ZEBRA REGENCY ROMANCE READERS.

You are a reader who enjoys the very special kind of love story that can only be found in Zebra Regency Romances. You adore the fashionable English settings, the sparkling wit, the captivating intrigue, and the heart-stirring romance that are the hallmarks of each Zebra Regency Romance novel.

Now, you can have these delightful novels delivered right to your door each month and never have to worry about missing a new book. Zebra has made arrangements through its Home Subscription Service for you to preview the three latest Zebra Regency Romances as soon as they are published.

3 **FREE** REGENCIES TO GET STARTED!

To get your subscription started, we will send your first 3 books ABSOLUTELY FREE, as our introductory gift to you. NO OBLIGATION. We're sure that you will enjoy these books so much that you will want to read more of the very best romantic fiction published today.

SUBSCRIBERS SAVE EACH MONTH

Zebra Regency Home Subscribers will save money each month as they enjoy their latest Regencies. As a subscriber you will receive the 3 newest titles to preview FREE for ten days. Each shipment will be at least a $11.97 value (publisher's price). But home subscribers will be billed only $9.90 for all three books. You'll save over $2.00 each month. Of course, if you're not satisfied with any book, just return it for full credit.

FREE HOME DELIVERY

Zebra Home Subscribers get free home delivery. There are never any postage, shipping or handling charges. No hidden charges. What's more, there is no minimum number to buy and you can cancel your subscription at any time. No obligation and no questions asked.

TO GET YOUR 3 FREE BOOKS
ILL OUT AND MAIL THE COUPON BELOW

3 F R E E B O O K S

Mail to: Zebra Regency Home Subscription Service
120 Brighton Road
P.O. Box 5214
Clifton, New Jersey 07015-5214

YES! Start my Regency Romance Home Subscription and send me my 3 FREE BOOKS as my introductory gift. Then each month, I'll receive the 3 newest Zebra Regency Romances to preview FREE for ten days. I understand that if I'm not satisfied, I may return them and owe nothing. Otherwise, I'll pay the low members' price of just $9.90 for all 3 books and save over $2.00 off the publisher's price (a $11.97 value). There are no shipping, handling or other hidden charges. I may cancel my subscription at any time and there is no minimum number to buy. In any case, the 3 FREE books are mine to keep regardless of what I decide.

RG0693

NAME

ADDRESS _____ APT NO.

CITY _____ STATE _____ ZIP _____
( )

TELEPHONE

SIGNATURE _____ (if under 18 parent or guardian must sign)

Terms and prices subject to change. Orders subject to acceptance by Zebra Home Subscription Service, Inc.

GET
3 FREE
REGENCY
ROMANCE
NOVELS—
A $11.97
VALUE!

ZEBRA HOME SUBSCRIPTION SERVICE, INC.
120 BRIGHTON ROAD
P.O. BOX 5214
CLIFTON, NEW JERSEY 07015-5214

you let them make up a few gowns for you, you'd probably be doing them a great favor. I'm sure they could have something ready in time for Lady Besford's ball."

Amanda touched the older girl's arm imploringly. "I should not ask, I know, but . . . do you think you could take me there? It could not hurt, just to see if this woman might answer the purpose."

"Of course, Amanda. I would be glad to, but, er, not today. I shall have to discover when she'll be ready to—I mean, *able* to see you. And exactly where she is located," added Frances, wondering why her so-called acting skills were deserting her.

"Oh yes, of course. I should have thought of that." For a few seconds, Amanda was silent. "You know, I do not mean to be mercenary, and indeed, I try not to mind, but sometimes I wish so much just to be able to look nice and . . . and not have people stare—"

"People are so rude!" said Frances with sudden ferocity. "That is one thing I hate about London— all the hypocrisy and deceit that exists here. Why, when my brother—"

She broke off, and cast Amanda an apologetic look. "Well, it's early days to be thrusting our family trials at you, my dear. What do you think of Jack, by the way?"

Amanda gazed down at her hands and wondered how to reply. "He's very nice," she said awkwardly. "I've never met anyone like him. He seems a trifle impulsive . . ." Her voice dwindled off, as she realized that none of the words she would have used to describe the Marquis were at all appropriate to repeat to the Marquis's sister.

"He has acquired a notorious reputation," remarked Frances a little sadly, "but the stories are greatly exaggerated." She turned a little, and pressed Amanda's hand. "You will not let it influence your opinion, will you? I swear to you my brother is one of the kindest, most wonderful men alive. I only wish . . ."

"What do you wish?" Amanda could not resist inquiring.

Frances sighed. "I wish he were happier. I wish he could find some peace within himself. Things have happened . . . oh, my father's death, for example. Jack blames himself, I know. And there was another problem. There, what a ninnyhammer I am! Didn't I just say I would not besiege you with our problems?"

"I don't mind," Amanda said truthfully.

"No, I can see you don't. You're a nice girl, Amanda. Jack said I would like you, and he was right. Oh, lord! There is Mrs. Warfield and her daughter. The daughter has had her cap set at Jack for the last two Seasons! She hasn't a prayer of catching him, of course. He can't abide girls who simper and clutch at his arm, which is exactly what poor Maria does! Some girls can be so foolish, can't they?"

Yes, they can, agreed Amanda silently, remembering her own preoccupation with the handsome Marquis.

"You know, Amanda, I am quite looking forward to tomorrow evening. You shall sit in my box, and I will meet your cousin, and I promise I will make

Jack come—though he is not really fond of opera. You *will* be there, won't you?"

"Of course," Amanda told her slowly. "I suppose it was silly to think I could not. I'm looking forward to it more than you can know."

"Good!" Positive that Amanda's enthusiasm was due to the knowledge that she would see Jack, Frances smiled to herself. She could hardly wait to see the two of them together!

"And by then I should be able to tell you when we may visit Madame Claret!" she added.

Initially, the news that Frances had already accomplished so much had buoyed the Marquis's spirits, but the following morning found him pacing the length of his study, his movements stalking and restless. He was dressed for riding, and the casualness of the attire, combined with the distracted, rather mulish expression upon his face, gave him an ungovernable look, as if some less civilized element of his nature had been unleashed. So little Prudence would be in the Park this morning, would she? Slowly, an anticipatory smile lifted the corners of his mouth. During the night, he had reached the conclusion that this was a golden opportunity, for if he happened upon Amanda, it would appear to be nothing more than a coincidence, an adjunct that suited him perfectly. And this time, he reflected with satisfaction, Charles would not be around to rake him over the coals.

Well, and why should he not choose to exercise his mount on this particular morning? he asked himself stubbornly. His intentions might not be perfectly honorable, but damn it, he'd endured all he could of Eve Marlowe the past few days and was now in the mood to reward himself. And good behavior merited a treat, did it not? It was specious reasoning, of course, but it was time for a little self-indulgence.

His nobler instincts repressed, Vale paused to pick up his riding crop, slapping it purposefully against the hard muscles of his thigh. At first, when Frances had related the details of her visit to Berkeley Square, he hadn't given much thought to that business about Amanda going to the Park. But last night, as he had lain sleepless in his bed, it had struck him that herein lay a way to achieve a twofold objective. Despite the nudgings of his conscience, he still had an urge to dally with the girl, and it was this, first of all, that drew him uncontrollably, so that neither argument nor scruple could sway him from his chosen course. His second goal was to rectify this very weakness in himself.

His own peace of mind demanded it. After all, it was deuced unsettling to find himself hankering for a girl of respectable birth and breeding as if she were some kind of trollop he might take to his bed! However, experience had taught him that the heart seldom grew fonder, and that women almost never improved upon acquaintance. Therefore, another hour or two in Amanda's company would undoubtedly cure him of this damnable infatuation, and he would prove to himself that she was as easy to lock out of his thoughts as any other woman.

Approximately three-quarters of an hour later, he

was to spy his quarry standing at the base of a small beech tree near the center of the Park. She wore no bonnet, and even from a distance of thirty yards he could see that her shining hair was tousled, as if the small fingers of her charges had wrought their playful damage upon her normally tidy curls. Something in the tree above had evidently caught her interest, for her head was thrown back, making the delicate line of her throat clearly visible to his hawklike gaze. A determined gleam entered the Marquis's eye, and he directed his mount quietly forward.

"Perry, come down!" For the third time in as many minutes, Amanda peered up into the tree. "You've gone quite far enough!" she called.

"Just a minute!" The elder boy's voice floated down, along with several dislodged leaves.

"I want to sail my boat now," wailed Robin, one chubby hand tugging at Amanda's skirt, the other clutching his wooden toy.

Amanda gave the little boy beside her a patient glance. "We shall do just that, love, in just a few moments. Perry, I mean it!" she added, her gaze shifting back to his brother.

"Look how high I am!" shouted Perry from his precarious perch near the tree's topmost branches.

Slightly exasperated, Amanda strengthened her tone. "I see how high you are, and I do not think your mama would approve! Or your papa, either! Now, come down at once!"

"Don't worry, Miss Amanda, I do this all the

time at home," he assured her blithely. "Only there, I go even higher!"

However, the consequences of misbehavior having been clearly represented to him by his father earlier that morning, Perry began a reluctant descent. His dangling heels were nearly to the level of Amanda's upraised hands when he halted.

"Oh, bang-up!" he cried, jabbing his finger in the direction of the nearby bridle path. "Look at that sweet-goer, miss! Now, *that's* just what I want, at least someday, when I'm older!"

Dropping her arms, Amanda turned to look where he was pointing, and was astonished to see the Marquis of Vale advancing toward them upon a strikingly handsome and very large-boned black gelding. She stared at him in surprise. "Why, hello! What are you doing here?"

"Exercising my mount," replied Vale quite smoothly. "I frequently do so at this hour of the morning. And I might ask the same question of you, Prudence," he added, lithely swinging himself to the ground. "Wherever did you get these two bantlings?"

"Her name is Miss 'Manda!" corrected Robin vociferously. Glaring at the Marquis, he yanked so hard on Amanda's gown that she was forced to bend down to disengage his fingers.

"Robin, dear, do not pull so," she said gently. "You will rip my dress."

Studying Amanda curiously, the Marquis was about to speak when a flash of movement from above caught his eye. Perry had decided to hang upside down by his legs, and was in the process of readjusting himself into the proper position to do so. However, at just this moment one of his hands slipped, and being off balance, he was unable to save himself.

Although the Marquis's reflexes were excellent, he was not quite fast enough to catch the boy. He did, however, succeed in breaking his fall, which was fortunate, for Perry would undoubtedly have crashed squarely on top of Amanda had he not intervened. As it was, it was the Marquis who knocked her over instead, the momentum from his leap forward sending him sprawling on top of her, just missing Robin in the process.

Finding this absolutely hilarious, Robin promptly erupted into a fit of giggles, but Perry jumped up instantly, full of shocked remorse. "Oh, Miss Amanda, I *am* sorry! Are you hurt? Oh, be quiet, Robin! It's not funny!"

Rising up on his elbows, the Marquis stared down into Amanda's startled eyes. "This is not quite my usual method of attack," he murmured, an apology in his voice, "but it has the advantage of being different. I trust I have not hurt you? You don't look like you're in any pain."

"No, no, I am perfectly fine, but do get off me at once!" Amanda gasped, beginning to push frantically at his chest. "Quickly now, before someone sees!"

For an instant he did not move, for the faint scent of her skin made him think of roses in summer, and the feel of her soft, feminine body beneath him delighted his senses. Then, with great effort, he tethered his baser impulses and obeyed, glancing ruefully at the children.

He desired her, all right. In fact, his need for her was still twisting inside him, along with a most unwelcome stab of guilt. Now, why the devil should he start to feel guilty, he wondered in irritation. Considering the way he had hunted her down, it was absurd to feel badly over an incident that was purely unintentional. Ah, of course, that was it. His damned conscience was objecting to his waylaying her like this. This innocent girl, it was whispering, did not deserve to be tracked down like a piece of game. If he wanted to fight his yearning for her, he ought to find some other way to do it.

Of course, after what had just occurred, it would have served him right if she had fallen into a swoon or behaved in some other nonsensical fashion. Come to think of it, if she had been so obliging as to pull such antics, it would have made it simpler for him to banish her from his thoughts. Hardly to his surprise, however, the focal point of Amanda's attention was the anxious six-year-old.

"No, Perry, I am not hurt, but you must thank Lord Vale at once for his assistance! I hope you, too, are unharmed, you foolish boy? Well, thank goodness for that!" she added when Perry nodded penitently. Paying no heed to the Marquis's scrutiny, Amanda accepted his hand to rise, and began brushing the grass from her skirt.

"Yes, Robin, I daresay we *were* very amusing, weren't we?" she continued in a humorous tone. "We were all tangled up like a pile of spillikins, weren't we, my lord?"

Her comparison made his lips twitch. "Indeed,"

he agreed, a little wryly. Then, almost without his consent, his mouth curved into a genuine smile. "I'm sure we looked very odd—to a small child."

At least she was wise enough to make light of it in front of the children, he noted, barely conscious of his own approval. In fact, she was taking the whole thing remarkably in stride, as if she were quite accustomed to being tackled in such a hurly-burly fashion. Offhand, he couldn't think of another woman who would have reacted so sensibly. Most, he thought cynically, would have gone into hysterics despite the presence of the children; the rest would probably have tried to wring a marriage proposal out of him.

"But why must I thank him?" inquired Perry after puzzling over Amanda's instruction. "He didn't even catch me!"

Vale's amusement grew. "Ungrateful brat!" he remarked mildly. "I suppose you have no idea what an upbraiding I shall get from my valet when he sees the grass stains on my knees."

Perry cast a doubtful look at the Marquis's soiled riding breeches. "I'm truly sorry, sir. Will you be in a great deal of trouble?"

"Yes!" responded the Marquis with considerable feeling. "One's servants can be the very dev—" Intercepting Amanda's frown, he quickly rephrased his remark. "—can be difficult," he amended.

Perry nodded wisely. *"Dashed* difficult," he agreed.

The Marquis laughed. "Aren't you going to present me to your small friends, Miss Marlowe?"

Having ascertained that the sole witnesses to the

preceding episode were a pair of squirrels in a nearby tree, Amanda relaxed and introduced the Marquis to the two Braxton offspring. Perry, she was pleased to see, remembered enough of his manners to say everything he ought, but Robin, obsessed as usual with titles, found it necessary to inquire whether a marquis was as important as a duke.

Regarding the youngster thoughtfully, the Marquis dropped down on one knee. "No," he told Robin with the air of someone about to divulge a dark secret. "But I don't mind, you know, because marquises are usually *taller.*"

Robin's eyes grew very big. "Oh . . . ! Nanny never told me that," he whispered back, in obvious awe.

A quiver of laughter crept into Amanda's voice. "One should be very careful what one tells a child, my lord," she said primly. "I warn you, they have very long memories!"

"So do many adults," was his obscure reply, and for an instant it seemed as if his good humor might fade.

Meanwhile, Perry's worshipful eyes were trained on the Marquis's magnificent black gelding, grazing peacefully a few yards away. "When I'm an adult—" he began.

"A *dolt!*" shrieked Robin gleefully. "Perry says he's a dolt, Miss 'Manda!"

"Oh, cheese it, Robin!" cried his brother angrily. "That's not what I said!"

With an apologetic glance at the Marquis, Amanda reached for Robin's hand. "Don't tease

202

your brother, love. Shall we go sail your boat now?"

"Would you mind if I joined you?" asked the Marquis rather quietly.

Caught off-guard by his question, Amanda gave him an uncertain glance. Though she suspected he meant to flirt with her, and though common sense warned her of the impropriety of his presence, there was something in the disarming way he looked at her that caused her to waver. His hat had fallen off, and between his ruffled hair and the stains on his knees, he seemed almost as much a little boy as Perry. She knew a brief longing to keep him as carefree as he was at this instant, and said, with a note of severity, "If you stay, my lord, you must behave yourself and be helpful."

"Yes, ma'am," said the Marquis meekly.

She regarded him suspiciously. "I am *serious*, my lord!"

"I promise I'll be very helpful," he replied, scooping up his hat. "Where is your bonnet? Ah, I see it," he added, and presented it to her with a gallant bow.

By this time, Perry had forgotten his transgressions, and wandered over to stroke the gelding's glossy neck. "What's his name, sir?" he threw over his shoulder.

"Caesar," replied the Marquis, ambling over to join the boy. "Do you like him?"

"Oh, very much! He's a *prime* stepper! When I'm an adult, I'm going to have just such a horse! Could I sit on him, do you think?" asked Perry hopefully.

"Not without your parents' permission," said the

Marquis firmly. "Although he would not hurt you, we can risk no more accidents. I am a little acquainted with your papa, and I suspect he would not care for me to allow it."

Fortunately, Perry seemed to accept this, and trotted quite amiably at the Marquis's side while he led Caesar the short distance to the Serpentine. Vale allowed Perry to tether the horse, then they wandered over to where Amanda and Robin were trying to launch the child's vessel.

"Hold tight to the string," Vale advised, striping off one of Weston's finest coats and laying it on the ground. "Here, Miss Marlowe, sit down," he commanded.

For a while, they all sat upon the riverbank, watching Robin's boat toss and bob in the tiny, lapping waves. Then the Marquis suggested they pretend there was a storm, and both children took turns poking the boat with a stick until it overturned, cheering with bloodthirsty delight when all the imaginary people were drowned. All three males scoffed at Amanda's suggestion that they use life boats to rescue the people, so she fell silent, content merely to listen to their nonsense.

He was good with children, she thought, observing how patiently he was able to divide his attention between the two boys. Then, remembering her cousin's indifference to the little fellows, sadness crept over her, only some of which was alleviated by the reflection that Eve's children would have an excellent father.

At length, Perry began to practice his cartwheels. "Not like that," said the Marquis, watching him

204

critically. "Keep your legs straight, and fling them higher over your head."

"Miss Amanda said she used to do them, too," panted Perry between attempts. "But she would not show me."

Conveniently forgetting his promise to behave, Vale edged closer to Amanda. "Come, come, Prudence," he said mischievously. "How unreasonable of you! I should very much appreciate a demonstration. The view itself would be worth a thousand words."

"Oh, do hush!" she replied, trying not to laugh. "You are worse than the children, you know."

"Am I?" He stared into her silver eyes with something akin to fascination. "Do you know you smell like roses? It makes me want to kiss you again."

Though her pulses leaped, Amanda said briskly, "You merely say these things to see what sort of a reaction you will get. It is just what Perry does, which leads me to wonder how old you really are, my lord!"

A trifle disconcerted, his look turned quizzical. "And how did you come to know me so well, 'Manda dear?"

She flushed slightly. "I do not! Forgive me, my lord. In such a setting, it is easy to forget that I should not speak so . . . so plainly."

"Lord, I don't regard that," he replied easily. "Say what you like to me, but I beg you won't let it become generally known."

She glanced at him. "Let what become known?"

"That I never grew up!" he joked.

"Sir, can you do a cartwheel?" inquired Perry,

dropping down next to the Marquis with a thud.

"Not anymore!" he said firmly. "My dignity don't allow it!"

Amanda gave him a saucy look. "Come, come, my lord," she said softly. "How unreasonable! Surely you could not be so stuffy as to refuse!"

"I can be as stuffy as I choose!" replied the Marquis with a glint in his eye. "Minx!"

Chapter Ten

Draped in one of Lady Priscilla's most elegant gowns, Amanda stood still, awaiting Lady Besford's pronouncement. Unfortunately, Lady Priscilla was taller and her proportions of a less diminutive scale than Amanda's, so the dress hung much too loosely upon her slender frame. Though the gown must have been stunning on the Countess's daughter, Amanda had no doubt that on her it looked perfectly ridiculous.

At last, Lady Besford was forced to agree. "There is no help for it, Amanda," she said finally, her voice filled with regret. "My daughter's gown simply will *not* fit you, and neither will any of Eve's. Oh, dear, I was afraid this was going to happen." Frowning thoughtfully, her fingers drummed the arm of her chair. "Ellen, let me see Amanda's blue gown once more. It *might* serve, if some sort of ornamentation were added. Otherwise, it is far too plain."

"Blond lace," suggested Ellen with a stoic expression. "We could borrow it from your ladyship's gown of nearly the same shade. The one that is too tight," added the abigail with faint disapproval.

The frown faded from Lady Besford's brow. "An

excellent idea, Ellen! How clever of you! Do fetch it at once, if you please." Continuing her critical study of Amanda's only evening gown, she went on, "I could wish it were flounced, Amanda, but at least the cut is good."

"I hate to put you to all this trouble, ma'am," said Amanda in distress. "Are you quite sure the gown will not do as it is? I have my mother's pearls, you know, to dress it up a trifle."

Concealing a sigh, the Countess said kindly, "I do not wish to hurt your feelings, my dear, but the gown really is sadly outmoded. If we can make it look more stylish, then it would be foolish not to do so. Do not look so concerned! Ellen is a positive wonder with the needle when she chooses to be, and one of the maids can assist her if she wishes. Never fear, your dress will look quite different by the time we leave for the opera!"

There remained a hint of doubt in Amanda's face, but having no wish to argue, she forbore to comment, and instead inquired whether Sir Julian and Lady Priscilla planned to come with them.

"No," sighed Lady Besford. "Between her visit to Astley's yesterday, and all the shopping we have done, Priscilla says she is quite worn out. And Sir Julian has urged her to spend a quiet evening with him. Dear Sir Julian! I find it so gratifying to see how devoted he is to her!"

"Here it is, my lady." Ellen bustled back into the room with the Countess's gown, her expression less dour than usual. "From the looks of it, there should be plenty of lace to do the job."

"Oh, more than enough, I should think!" retorted

Lady Besford rather merrily. "My gowns are considerably larger than Amanda's!"

"Oh, but, ma'am, the lace will have to be cut!" objected Amanda suddenly.

"Very true, but if it is not, you will have no lace. And I cannot wear the dress anyway. So let me hear no more protests, my dear." With less than her usual energy, the Countess pushed herself out of the chair. "And now I am going to take a nap. Ellen, I will leave Miss Marlowe's dress in your capable hands. It must be ready by seven o'clock, do not forget."

Ellen curtsied respectfully. "As your ladyship wishes."

Left alone, Amanda decided that she, too, could use a rest, and even more importantly, an opportunity to marshal her disordered thoughts. Curling up on the bed, she released the latch on her mind, and drowsily allowed it to drift at will, like a leaf cavorting in the wind. So much had happened in the short time she had been in London. Back at Birchfeld Manor, life had been tedious and lonely, filled only with chores and fantasies and memories of happier times. In contrast, she now had so much to reflect upon that she felt herself almost unequal to the task of sorting it all out.

With no effort at all, an image of the Marquis's face rose before her eyes. They had spent nearly two full hours together in the Park, and if she had been aware of him before, it was nothing to what she was feeling now. There had been a dreamlike quality to the morning, which, replayed in her mind, imbued her with the odd sensation that she had lived a scene in someone else's life. They had not spoken of this evening's opera, for nothing had seemed to exist outside the isolated spot of grass on which they sat. Yet knowing that in a few short hours she would see him again, a tingle ran down Amanda's spine, reminding her of those seconds she had been pinned under the Marquis's hard, masculine body. At the time, she had not even dared to acknowledge the magnetic pull of his attractiveness, or her own shuddering awareness of his arousal. If she had allowed herself to believe, even for an instant, that his passion held any true meaning, or that it was for her alone, she would not have been able to cope, either with the children, or with her own quivering emotions. Had the children not been there, she would still have tried to brush the whole thing off as nothing, for that was all it had been, she told herself dispiritedly. Having come to this rather dreary conclusion, Amanda decided that the wisest thing to do was to forget that the entire episode had ever taken place. But when had she ever been wise?

The Royal Italian Opera House in the Haymarket was one of the most splendid edifices Amanda had ever seen. Its entrance, lit almost as bright as day when a performance was about to take place, was choked with people, making it difficult to penetrate the inner foyer without being shoved or jostled. Yet by placing Lady Besford on his right arm and Eve on his left, and positioning his sister and Amanda in front of him, the Marquis managed to maneuver them safely through the throng without incident.

As soon as they were comfortably seated in Frances's box, Amanda took the opportunity to study the great horseshoe-shaped auditorium. Its five tiers of boxes seemed to her to be almost overflowing with bejeweled ladies and fashionable gentlemen, although, Lady Besford explained, this was nothing compared to what it was at the height of the Season. Absorbed as she was in her perusal, Amanda was yet very conscious of the Marquis, and could scarcely be blamed for noticing how very well he looked. Indeed, having been fashioned by one of London's finest tailors, his bottle green coat was cut to perfection itself, even while his buff-colored pantaloons clung so tightly to his long legs that only the most prudish female could have failed to take (surreptitious) note.

Almost to her surprise, Lord Vale had greeted her with the correct measure of formality, his words so conventional that they might have been barely acquainted. His slightly narrowed eyes had taken in her dress (which had been vastly improved by the addition of the blond lace) but there had been no hint of approval in their expression. Ellen had put a great deal of effort into her stitchery, and Amanda had felt very fine indeed when she had first tried the gown on. Nevertheless, in comparison to the other women, she began to perceive that she still looked dowdy. She reached up nervously to finger the dainty string of pearls at her neck — the only jewelry she owned — and wished the Marquis would make one of his amusing remarks and put her at her ease.

To her disappointment, all traces of the Marquis's former good humor had vanished. He was leaning back, his arms folded across his chest with what appeared to be an air of bored resignation. Like many others, his eyes roamed the theater, pausing here and there as if to study someone he knew. Then suddenly his gaze veered to Amanda's face, and she knew he must have sensed her watching him. Embarrassed, she offered him a tentative smile, which he returned, his mouth curving just enough to send a message of reassurance.

Not once since their arrival had Eve displayed the smallest inclination to converse with the Marquis, and instead had entered into a desultory conversation with Frances. After a while, Amanda noticed that her cousin's attention kept straying to a box about fifty feet away, where a familiar-looking gentleman lolled next to a woman of absolutely incredible beauty.

Though Amanda would not have credited it, for the first time in her life Eve Marlowe was feeling a small tug of dissatisfaction with her own appearance.

"Who is that woman with Lord Frome?" she whispered to her aunt.

Lady Besford frowned. "Do not look at the dreadful man, my love. You will only encourage him to think that — oh!" Her lips pursed with dismay when her eyes fell upon the woman in question. "Oh dear! *That* is Lady Claverley, my love. *Not* a person whose acquaintance you should seek. She is shockingly fast," she added condemningly. "Why do you ask?"

Eve shrugged, the gesture emphasizing the faultless symmetry of her shoulders. "No reason, Aunt. I merely wondered."

The Countess cast a quick look at the Marquis, who she was certain could not possibly hear them over the cacophony of voices. "Well, do not let Lord Vale see how curious you are," she pleaded.

It's too late for that," Eve reminded her coolly. "I have already gone riding with the man."

The Countess moaned softly. "And I should never, *never* have allowed it. I shudder to think what he will say when he finds out. As for Lady Claverley, she is . . . is . . ." Words failed her. "Now why didn't I think to bring my hartshorn?" she sighed feebly.

Eve's eyes slid back to Frome. "I want to invite him to my come-out ball, Aunt Emily. But not the woman, of course."

Lady Besford gasped. "That odious man at your ball? Oh, no, Eve, it will not do! It will only serve to antagonize Lord Vale."

"I care not," Eve answered. "If I am to wed the man, he must learn that I do what I want."

Her distress clearly visible, Lady Besford made no reply.

Owing to the seating arrangements, which placed her between her cousin and Lady Besford, Amanda had been made privy to this exchange. Curious as to what sort of man would attract her cousin's notice, she leaned forward to take a look at Lord Frome. He was laughing at something the lady beside him was saying, and she caught a glimpse of his profile as he whispered in her ear. Was Eve enamored of this man, she wondered. He was not exactly unhandsome, but she could not imagine preferring him to the Marquis. However, where Lord Frome's expression was relaxed and amused, the Marquis's countenance had taken on an icy aspect, which she supposed did make him look a little formidable. He was probably displeased by her cousin's interest in this Lord Frome, Amanda decided.

With an inaudible sigh, she sat back in her chair, for it was time for the opera to begin. Catalani was to sing the part of Dorabella in Mozart's *Cosi Fan Tutte,* and as the curtain rose, Amanda pushed all else from her mind, determined to enjoy what might well be her only opportunity to hear the famous singer.

For his part, the Marquis was not in a good mood. The prospect of spending the evening cooped up in a box at the opera with Eve Marlowe held no appeal, it having the oddest effect of increasing the trapped feeling she engendered in him. Moreover, his interlude in the Park with Amanda had served only to strengthen her allure — the opposite of what he had intended — and what he was going to do about it he had not even begun to decide. Two very different young women were causing him untold mental stress, and confronted with this, the Marquis had known a brief, rather craven impulse to tell Frances to find herself another escort. Yet he had not done so, for the knowledge that Amanda would be facing the critical eyes of the *ton* for the first time (and most probably in one of those unfashionable gowns of hers) acted on him as a powerful incentive to be present. Though he would have been reluctant to admit it, the worldly young Marquis was plagued by the worry that Amanda was going to be snubbed. He was, after all, fully conversant with the Polite World's tendency to look down its aristocratic nose at those it did not consider its equal, an attitude he had hitherto taken very much for granted. However, if anyone were so mannerless and unkind as to try to cold-shoulder Amanda, he thought belligerently, they would find themselves answering to him.

No, he did not know how he was going to deal with his preoccupation with Amanda Marlowe, but his motives for wanting to defend her were perfectly clear. He had liked her from the beginning; this morning's piece of work had taught him to respect and admire her. She was like a breath of spring in the dead of winter, he mused, and it was crackbrained to try to liken her to other women he had known. For that matter, his notion that her character was going to be altered by the acquisition of beautiful clothes now seemed so preposterous that he wondered if there was something wrong with his own mental processes.

As Amanda suspected, Eve Marlowe's interest in Everard Frome had not escaped the Marquis's notice. Her indifference to his own charms did not trouble him, and although he could not admire her taste, it was not until Amanda also leaned forward to look at the man that he'd found himself actually grinding his teeth. What was it that females saw in the damned fellow? He hoped that she, at least, would have enough sense not to be taken in by that dissolute ne'er-do-well. Surprisingly, this caused him to feel an odd stab of—could it be jealousy?—and he found himself wondering yet again what the deuce he was going to do.

Of course, there was one rather obvious course of action he had not yet pursued. There was an extremely lovely opera dancer who, if he was not mistaken, had been attempting for some weeks to ensnare his interest. It was said that this voluptuous redhead, Angelina, by name, had dismissed her previous protector, Lord Kilbarchan, and was casting about for someone to take his place (an event which had sparked a near-frenzy of betting in the clubs). With a humorless smile, the Marquis sat up a bit straighter and raised his quizzing glass, determined to consider this potential strategy to eradicate from his mind the girl he really wanted.

Despite the noisy and obnoxious dandies in the pit, the voices of the singers held Amanda enthralled throughout the first act. As the curtain slowly descended, she shook her head and glanced around, trying to bring herself back to reality. The Marquis chose that moment to look her full in the face, and she colored a little, wondering if he would speak.

Oblivious to this exchange, Lady Besford began waving gaily to someone across the room. "There is my dear friend, Lady Brockport, beckoning to me," she exclaimed. "I know she wishes to tell me about her daughter's wedding plans, so I had better go alone, my dears, for she would only bore you to tears! I shall tear myself away as soon as I can."

Frances rose as soon as she was gone, having discovered a sudden and overwhelming urge to introduce Eve to one of her own dear friends. Eve's docile acquiescence astonished Amanda until, by the merest chance, she saw that Everard Frome's quizzing glass was leveled in their direction. Was it only a coincidence that he, too, was gone from his box the next time she looked?

Abruptly, she became aware that Lord Vale was looking at her.

"So, Prudence, what do you think of tonight's performance?" he inquired, his eyes resting on her face with a curious expression. "Are you enjoying yourself?"

216

Amanda's eyes dropped to her lap, then she flashed him a smile that, incredible as it seemed, made his heart turn over.

"Very much, my lord. The music is delightful. Of course, the theme of the story is absurd, don't you think? To suggest that women are incapable of being faithful is stupid and insulting . . . but I suppose one must remember it is meant to be entertaining," she added prosaically. "It reminds me of one of Miss Austen's stories."

The Marquis did not answer, and something in the rather intense way he was gazing at her caused Amanda to feel suddenly shy. He seemed to be searching her face, looking for signs of — what? Then his eyes were on her gown.

"Is that the best dress you own?" he shocked her by saying.

She was not to know the number of times the Marquis would curse his unthinking words, that they leaped from his tongue without calculated thought, unpremeditated and heedless and damnable. The stricken expression in her silver eyes lanced him in return.

"I — I beg your pardon?" Her voice was hardly more audible than a whisper.

"Oh, God, I never meant to say that!" he protested, his face aghast. "Forgive me, please, Amanda. I swear I didn't mean it!"

Close to tears, Amanda said faintly, "I did not think I looked so very bad."

Appalled that his clumsy words had caused her pain, he floundered, "You don't! You look . . . beautiful, Amanda. You *are* beautiful! But you lay yourself

217

open to snubs and insults when you go about in such a . . . a countrified gown."

"Yes, I can see that I do," she replied, a little shakily.

"Amanda, for the love of —" he began, his voice low and tight. Without thinking, he reached out and squeezed her hand. "Don't poker up at me, Amanda. You may not believe this, but I spoke only out of concern for you."

"Well, it was an odious thing to say," she told him, still fighting for composure.

The Marquis's expression flattened. "I'm aware of that. Come, then, let me escort you to my sister," he said, standing up. "I don't blame you for being angry."

Amanda rose immediately, but amazed him by laying her hand on his arm. "I'm not angry with you," she told him hesitantly. "We are friends, are we not? What you said did startle me, but I know you did not mean it the way it sounded." She paused and took a breath. "And I know you are right. I did not realize it until . . . until a little while ago. I should not have snapped at you just now. It is just that I am a trifle sensitive about it."

He looked at her incredulously, but saw nothing to indicate that she did not mean exactly what she said. Frances, arriving back at that precise instant, took in the expression on her brother's face with a gleam of satisfaction. Evidently, the time she had left him alone with Amanda had been well spent!

Outside the box, they paused briefly, and it was then that a grimly determined woman in puce satin and a redhaired girl wearing far too many diamonds bore down on them. Amanda recognized them at once as the women Frances had pointed out to her during their

218

drive. It was Mrs. Warfield and her daughter.

"Good evening, *dear* Lady Frances," cooed Mrs. Warfield in high, nasal accents. "How very well you are looking! Oh, and here is your charming brother. We did not even see you, my lord."

Frances drew herself up haughtily, causing Amanda to suspect that she did not care for the woman's manner.

"Indeed?" the Marquis's sister remarked coolly. "It seems he must possess extraordinary talent, then. I had never suspected him capable of invisibility."

Miss Maria Warfield tittered at the remark, and gazed soulfully up at the Marquis, who bowed slightly. "Oh, my lord! What did you think of Catalani? Was she not simply divine? But it is *your* opinion which counts, Lord Vale," she babbled, her small hand trying without success to attach itself to his sleeve.

"Which one was Catalani?" inquired the Marquis.

Miss Warfield stared at him, unable to decide whether he was joking or serious. "Why, what can you possibly mean, my lord?"

Amanda choked, and tried unsuccessfully to turn her giggle into a semblance of a coughing fit. At this, Miss Warfield turned, sweeping her from head to toe with eyes as hard as quartz. "Have we been introduced?" she said icily.

Amanda murmured a negative, and sent the Marquis an imploring look. He shrugged slightly, and glanced at Frances, who was left to make the introductions.

Mrs. Warfield murmured a short greeting, but her daughter was not so wise. "Why, you cannot be the Miss Marlowe who is niece to the Countess of Besford,

219

can you? I have heard how very beautiful and elegant the niece is and—" She crimsoned suddenly, realizing her gaffe.

Anger blazed through the Marquis. "You know, if one stretches one's imagination," he drawled, regarding the girl contemptuously, "one can begin to understand why you were denied a voucher for Almack's, Miss Warfield."

Dead silence greeted the set-down, for Miss Warfield appeared to have been struck dumb, and was gaping up at him with all the composure of a beached fish. Within seconds, the embarrassed girl was being dragged off by her irate mother, whose own complexion had taken on something of the hue of her puce gown.

"Really, Jack!" exclaimed Frances, between amusement and dismay. "How could you?"

"She deserved it," he snapped. He was furious over the incident, for it was just the kind of slight he feared Amanda would be facing repeatedly if his plan did not work.

Ignoring his sister, he turned to Amanda. "I'm sorry about what just happened," he told her quietly. "I hope you won't allow it to ruin your evening. Maria Warfield will not trouble you again, I promise you."

Amanda smiled slightly. "Well, you warned me, did you not?" she said, without acrimony. "In fact, everyone has warned me, so I have only myself to blame."

The Marquis gazed down at her, and though he was unaware of it, there was more than a trace of tenderness in his expression. What he would have said next neither of them would ever know, for Eve appeared out of nowhere to place a proprietary hand on the Marquis's arm.

"I'm back now," she remarked, her tone suspiciously sweet.

The gesture brought the Marquis back to earth with astonishing rapidity. Devil take the girl, this must be a sign that she meant to accept his "offer"! A string of curses went through his mind at the thought. How, he wondered irately, had he ever been so bacon-brained as to get himself into this insupportable position? He hated being manipulated, and it was becoming evident that manipulation was Eve Marlowe's particular forte.

Frances was standing some few feet away, ostensibly chatting with an acquaintance, and took in Eve's arrival with an inward sigh of vexation. Having observed both her brother and Amanda very closely the entire evening, the Marquis's sister decided she had a very fair notion which way the wind was blowing. She only hoped this business of Jack's wager would come off without a hitch, and that "Madame Claret" would cooperate as well as Jack predicted.

As soon as she could politely do so, Frances freed herself and made her way over to Amanda. "I did not have the chance to tell you before, but the matter is settled," she said in an undervoice. "I shall take you to see Madame Claret on Thursday, at eleven o'clock." Paying strict heed to her brother's instructions, she added, "Madame will be most happy to receive you, and believes she is able to satisfy your needs. She is extremely anxious to acquire custom and says her prices are very reasonable."

For Amanda, the remainder of the evening passed in a haze of new optimism. After all, the Marquis had told her she looked beautiful, and she was soon to have something fashionable to wear! The two events mingled in her mind, as though they were somehow related. Though her eyes were fixed dutifully on the stage, Amanda actually took in little of the second act, and it was not until later when she crawled wearily between the sheets that the implications of her euphoria began to sink in.

Amanda had not given much serious thought to the possibility that her cousin really intended to marry Lord Vale. Since Eve had demonstrated no partiality toward him at all, it had seemed far more likely that she would simply make some other selection. But now Amanda was beginning to wonder. Eve was capable of almost anything—even marrying a man she disliked because he was rich and titled. And if Lord Vale married her cousin, Amanda was not going to like it one bit.

She blushed in the darkness, remembering how great a significance she had dared to place upon his compliment. Simply because he had told her she was beautiful, did that mean he would turn to her, ignoring the wishes of his father? And even if he cared for her, was it likely he would wed a girl who was nearly penniless? No, shouted her sensible voice, and this time, her less sensible self was silent. Engulfed by a wave of pure misery, Amanda buried her face in her pillow.

The Braxtons departed the following morning, and Amanda pushed aside her problems so that she could concentrate on bidding farewell to Perry and Robin with appropriate enthusiasm. Priscilla graciously invited Eve and Amanda to visit them in the summer, to which both boys added chants of agreement. Then Sir Julian ushered his family into their coach, and with much waving and commotion, they rolled off down the street.

The remainder of that day, as well as the following three, were filled with preparations for the ball. Amanda had spent two entire afternoons helping Lady Besford write out the invitations, and acceptances were already beginning to stream in. She learned a great deal about what was involved in planning such an elaborate affair, from ordering food from Gunther's to the hiring of extra kitchen help for the grand occasion. Both Eve and Amanda began taking daily instruction with a dancing master, and they rehearsed their steps each day. The Countess professed herself ready to drag Amanda by the hair to Madame Simonnet's until Amanda told her of Madame Claret, and even then her ladyship seemed dubious. However, Lady Rosebery's endorsement of the woman put an end to any objections she might have voiced. As long as Amanda was to have a suitable gown in time for the ball, then Lady Besford was satisfied.

Thursday morning arrived at last, and Amanda awoke to discover it was raining. Yawning, she stretched her arms above her head, then memory surged through her—today she was to visit Madame Claret! If only she could afford the woman, she would purchase something so extraordinarily becoming that *he* would immediately approve.

Sitting up in bed, Amanda wrapped her arms around her knees and stared blindly at the coverlet. This, then, was the real reason she wanted some new gowns, for in the beginning, it hadn't really mattered.

Her motive for coming to London had not been to live the frivolous, fashionable life of a debutante, whatever everyone else chose to believe. She had actually thought to content herself with living quietly, visiting some historic sights, and making a few friends. But the maddeningly attractive Marquis had managed to change all that. Now she wanted only to talk to him, to be near him, and to look beautiful for him.

Abruptly, she remembered a dream she had had in the early hours of the morning. They had been in a field somewhere in the country; he had called her sweet names and kissed her, pressing her into the grass with all the gentleness of which he was capable. Amanda's hands flew to her cheeks as she recalled the remainder of the dream. In it, she had called him John, rather than Jack. Jack seemed too rakish a name, and he was not a rake at all, just a dear, caring man—of that, she was certain, no matter how many scandals he had caused. Darting a self-conscious glance at the door, she whispered his name aloud. "John . . ." She repeated it a little more loudly, and jumped when the door swung open, in seeming response to her voice.

It was only the maid, of course. If the girl noticed her high color, she said nothing, but merely wished Amanda good morning, and set the basin of warm water next to the soap and towels on the washstand. As it was Amanda's custom to wash and dress herself, the girl left immediately, much to Amanda's relief. She needed a little time to compose herself, and prepare for the day ahead.

By eleven o'clock, Amanda had herself well in hand. The rain had been intermittent, and had begun to let up to the point where she was unlikely to get a soaking.

"Where are we going?" she asked Frances as she settled into Frances's chariot.

"Madame Claret resides in Elizabeth Street, in Hans Town. It's just south of Hyde Park, a perfectly respectable location, I assure you, though quite middle-class. It won't take us long to get there."

"How did you hear of Madame Claret?" asked Amanda, thinking how curious it was that her friend would know of this woman.

"Ahem . . . do you know I can't quite recall. Perhaps my Aunt Cordelia mentioned it. She lives with me, did I tell you? She is quite impoverished, so I daresay she keeps her ear open for such things." Somehow Frances managed to steer the conversation into safer channels until they reached Elizabeth Street.

Madame Claret was not at all what Amanda had expected. She was a tall, gaunt woman, with a great beak of a nose and an intimidating manner. Dressed in black bombazine, she looked more like an elderly bird of prey than a lady struggling to start a dressmaking business. Moreover, Amanda did not think she appeared nearly as gratified to see her new customer as Frances had led her to believe.

The first thing she said, in a stern, almost reproachful tone, was, "But you are short, mademoiselle!" Her French accent was very thick, and unlike Madame Simmonet's, entirely unassumed.

"I'm afraid so," Amanda replied in some amusement. "I stand but five feet and two inches in my stocking feet, madame."

"Eh bien," continued Madame, eyeing her critically. "At least you are not fat. For an English girl, your

figure is of a fineness and proportion I cannot fault."
She nodded emphatically. "We shall manage."

Amanda cast a speaking glance over her shoulder at
Frances, but the Marquis's sister was staring in seeming fascination at Madame Claret and did not appear
to notice.

Unconcerned with the impression she was making,
Madame began making odd, clucking noises with her
tongue. "Ninon! Ninon! Where are you, *imbécile?*"

In answer, a woman emerged from one of the interior rooms of the house. Like Madame Claret, she was
tall, but there all resemblance ended. Ninon possessed
a smooth, rather placid face, with lashes and eyebrows
so pale they gave her a look of perpetual surprise.

"I am here, *Maman.* Is this the young lady?"

"But, of course," Madame snapped impatiently to
her daughter. She rattled off a series of instructions in
French, then turned back to Amanda.

"This drab gown you wear, *c'est incroyable!* You will
want to burn it when we are finished." She took in
Amanda's appearance thoughtfully. "Hair, dark
brown. Eyes, gray. Complexion, typically English.
You are lucky, Mademoiselle Marlowe. Many colors
will suit you. Pale blue, primrose, lavender . . . oh,
you have many choices! But do not wear black or
brown or gray or purple — they do not suit. Ninon! *Ou
ès-tu?*" she shouted.

"Here, *Maman!*" Ninon puffed back into the room
carrying a small silver tea tray, which contained, besides tea and cakes, a measuring tape and a pin cushion. The tea and cakes were for Frances.

Amanda stood motionless in the center of the room
while Madame poked and prodded and measured to

her satisfaction. Then, Madame retreated to a small desk in one corner of the room, where, with an inscrutable expression, she proceeded to scrawl with feverish intensity upon a sheet of paper for several minutes.

Finally, she said, "I have finished, mademoiselle. You will be very pleased with my recommendations. I have decided that you will need a minimum of twenty-five to thirty *ensembles*. For the morning dresses, at least six, the walking dresses, again, six. *Alors,* for the evening and dinner and ball gowns, a minimum of twelve will do, fifteen, *si vous préfèrez*. Ah . . . the carriage dresses, perhaps four or so. And, of course, the riding dress. In addition, you will need a number of pelisses, spencers, shoes, gloves, stockings, hats and bonnets, and of course, undergarments. I will provide everything but the shoes, stockings, hats, and gloves, and of these you must purchase exactly what I have written, or the effect will be completely ruined."

Amanda's jaw dropped during this recital. "Madame!" she gasped. "I cannot possibly afford so many—"

"Bah!" barked Madame, in a tone that left no room for argument. "It is necessary, mademoiselle. Besides," she added, looking sly, "is there not some gentleman you wish to impress? The young ladies, they must have their compliments, *oui?*"

"You do not understand, Madame!" Amanda protested. "Frances, tell her I cannot possibly purchase so much!"

Unexpectedly, Frances did not come to her support. "Don't be so hasty, Amanda. Why don't you give Madame Claret a chance? Perhaps it will not be as costly as you imagine."

"Ah . . . cost. What is cost?" remarked Madame, waving her hand in a dismissing, rather Gallic gesture. "Cost is nothing. Fashion is all."

Amanda began to feel desperate. "Nevertheless, it is important to me. I cannot promise to purchase a thing until I have some idea of how much—"

"I will tell you the cost presently, mademoiselle. You must have patience," Madame interrupted testily. Then, she rubbed her hands together in anticipation. "Ninon! Fetch the fabrics!" she commanded with almost childish glee.

There was a large oak table in the next room, and this was soon covered with a rainbow of gay colors. India and jaconet muslins, French cambrics, tulles, crapes, and gauzes—it was impossible to say which was the most beautiful. From ice blue to sea green, lilac and lavender to peach and jonquil, apple green to celestial blue, they all dazzled Amanda. Never in her life had she owned a single gown made of such fine cloth. How could she possibly leave without buying— at least something?

"To commence," said Madame, consulting her list, "I have written . . . one ball gown of white spyder gauze, worn over a slip of rose satin. We shall put trimming at the bottom, as is *le dernier cri*—perhaps artificial corn-flowers? That I must decide. The outer robe we will leave open at the left side and edged in a double row of pearls. The bust will also be decorated in pearls. The sleeves will be short, of lace over satin, and slashed in the Spanish style. Elbow-length white kid gloves, and corded silk shoes will finish. Ninon! Drape the fabric around Mademoiselle Marlowe. There! What think you of that, mademoiselle?" she

228

smirked triumphantly. "I am an *artiste,* am I not?"

"Oh!" breathed Amanda, forgetting everything but the thought of the Marquis seeing her in such a gown.

"You look *très belle,* mademoiselle!" Ninon assured her, unknowingly setting the seal upon Amanda's decision to buy this particular gown, even if it was the only purchase she made.

As Madame outlined each *ensemble* on her list, Amanda grew more and more dazed. The woman was undoubtedly skillful in her choices, but some of her remarks were distinctly baffling. The dressmaker possessed a streak of mischief, too, for she obstinately refused until the very last to quote Amanda a price.

Finally, she said, with a strange glint in her eye, "And for all this, mademoiselle, a very small fee. Oh, very small. You are fortunate to be one of my *first* customers. I am so *new* to this business, you see." Her chin wagged up and down in secret amusement.

"What is the fee?" Amanda asked calmly.

Madame's small black eyes gleamed. "Such *sangfroid!* You have all my admiration, *ma petite.*" She caught Amanda's steady look, and sighed. "Thirty pounds, mademoiselle," she announced with a philosophical shrug.

Amanda stared at the dressmaker in blank astonishment. "Madame Claret," she said flatly, "you are hoaxing me. You cannot possibly sell me all this for such a small amount. The fabric alone must be worth many times that sum."

Madame Claret nodded. "Ah, *oui, oui.* You are no fool, mademoiselle. But I, I am no fool either. I have my reasons, *ma petite,* which are no concern of yours. My next customer will pay most dearly, I promise you." Eyes narrowed, she tilted her head consideringly. "You are pretty, mademoiselle. In my creations, you will be beautiful. You will be my walking—how do you say?—costume plate. You will bring me much business, *n'est-ce pas?* So poor Madame Claret does not starve?"

"But, madame—" Amanda began.

"Amanda," said Frances hastily, "we are taking up much of Madame's precious time. She will have much to do. Madame Claret, Miss Marlowe's come-out ball is in six days. Can you have a ball gown ready by then?"

"Certainement, madame. Ninon, she plies the needle with a quickness *extraordinaire!* She will work hard, and I will direct." Noting Amanda's frown, she added roguishly, "There is no cause for worry, *ma petite.* Your lover will soon see you in all your finery."

As they entered the front hall, and were about to leave the house, Madame called Frances back. Slightly surprised, Amanda turned to watch as Madame addressed Frances in a low voice. She did not hear the soft words, only the thin cackle that accompanied them.

"Extend my compliments to your so-generous brother, madame. I think he will be *very* pleased."

Chapter Eleven

"What did she say to you?" inquired Amanda as soon as they were in the carriage.

Frances avoided her gaze. "Oh, nothing to signify. She just asked me how soon you would need your other gowns. What a pity it's starting to rain again! I was hoping to take you to the botanical gardens while we were right here!"

"Frances, didn't you think there was something odd about Madame Claret? She said some very strange things."

"Odd?" repeated Frances faintly. "Well, I suppose one could say she's a trifle eccentric. After all she is French, and quite old," she offered in an excusing tone. "I daresay she must be over seventy."

"Yes, but don't you think that was the oddest part? Why would she be just starting a business at her time of life? I'm sure she is not what she pretends. And I can't quite believe I won't be saddled with a staggering bill. That would put me in a dreadful fix." Amanda shuddered at the thought.

"Yes, well, you can always return everything and

refuse to pay. But, Amanda, why don't we forget about her? Let's just wait and see if she actually delivers the gowns. There's no need to make more out of this than there is."

"I suppose you're right," said Amanda doubtfully.

"I know I am," responded the older girl, hoping her powers of persuasion were better than her ability to act.

Actually, Amanda would have liked very much to believe that Madame Claret was exactly what she claimed, but the more she thought about it, the more suspicious she became. She said nothing of this to Lady Besford, for whom she provided a slightly edited version of her adventure, but her doubts would not be quelled. The Countess did express some misgivings over the business — such an excessively odd location! — but was, all in all, relieved to hear of her young guest's purchases, and was far too practical to look a gift horse in the mouth.

However, the advent of the ball soon drove everything else from Amanda's mind. As Madame Claret had promised, three bandboxes arrived well before they were needed, giving Amanda adequate time to shop for accessories. The first bandbox contained the gauze and rose satin ball gown, the second, a high-waisted morning dress of pale yellow jaconet muslin, whose elegant adornments included a demure lace and muslin collar, and six rows of ivory-colored satin ribbon at the hem. The third box contained another evening dress, a selection of petticoats, and detailed instructions on what she should purchase to complete each *ensemble*.

Could the Marquis have witnessed Amanda's expression as she opened these boxes, he would undoubtedly have been pleased. He would not have been so pleased, however, had he also been privileged to read her mind. Why was fortune so suddenly smiling on her, Amanda was wondering. There was a mystery here, and she knew she could not rest until she got to the bottom of it. Abruptly, Amanda knew she would pay Madame Claret another visit as soon as she was able.

But meanwhile there was the ball to be considered, and Amanda would have been more than human if she did not eagerly anticipate wearing her beautiful new clothes. When at last it was time to put on the ball gown, Amanda shivered with excitement, imbued with the oddest fancy that a new phase of her life was beginning. A young housemaid by the name of Hettie had been assigned to assist her, and Amanda stood quietly in her thin chemise while the girl pulled first the slip and then the overdress carefully past her chestnut curls. Hettie, whose aspirations included a desire to become an abigail, meticulously smoothed and rearranged the silken folds until she was satisfied that the gown hung perfectly.

"Coo, miss!" uttered Hettie admiringly. "You look just like a princess from a fairy story! I reckon you'll be stealin' a few hearts tonight!"

When Amanda moved to the mirror, she found it hard to believe that the girl looking back was herself. In the soft glow of candlelight, the velvet-black pupils of her eyes were huge, and her hair was a smoldering halo, like the dying embers of a fire. Undoubtedly the most becoming gown she had ever owned, the rose and white evening dress fulfilled Madame Claret's predictions, transforming her into a singularly ravishing young woman. For the first time in her life Amanda was fully conscious of her attractiveness, and it was with a sharpened sense of her own femininity that she studied her reflection. A new confidence budded within her, and she began to believe once more in the power of positive thinking—until Eve swept into the room.

"Well, well," stated her cousin, staring critically. "What a change! Your bourgeois dressmaker obviously knew what she was about. Who would have thought it possible? My own dear cousin ready to cut her dash in society! Does this mean you've changed your mind?"

Amanda took time to thank and dismiss Hettie before inquiring, somewhat reluctantly, "Changed my mind about what?"

"About marriage, ninny! I've never seen you looking so well, Amanda. Your cheeks are quite pink, you know. You haven't been dipping into the rouge pot, have you?"

"Don't be absurd." Rather nettled, Amanda searched for a fresh topic of conversation. "That corsage is very pretty. It complements your gown nicely. It's from Vale?" Somehow she managed to say his name normally.

Eve looked down at the flowers with a complacent expression. "No, the one he sent was the wrong color. This was from Lord Frome."

Amanda's eyes narrowed. "How could it be the wrong color? Lord Vale asked you most specifically what color you planned to wear. I know, Eve, for I heard him."

Her cousin's expression turned almost smug. "Yes, well, I found the slightest stain on the other gown. Quite vexing, of course, but what can one do?"

"One could make some effort to choose another gown of similar color," said Amanda dryly. After a short hesitation, she added as casually as possible, "I thought you wanted to marry Lord Vale. Won't he disapprove of you wearing the Baron's flowers?"

"I don't care if he does." Eve sounded indifferent. "Do you think he will be jealous?"

Her cousin's response told Amanda nothing, so she tried again. "I've no idea, but if you really plan to marry him, ought you to be encouraging Lord Frome so openly?"

Surprisingly, her cousin laughed. "Perhaps not. What would dearest Mama say, do you think? My Lord Frome's reputation is decidedly wicked." Briefly, she moved to examine herself in the mirror, then swung around. "At any rate, my dear cousin, I find that I enjoy the company of gentlemen. Therefore, whoever I wed will have to be understanding in that respect."

"Well, I wouldn't count on Lord Vale understanding," said Amanda in annoyance. She avoided Eve's mocking blue eyes and began to draw on her gloves.

"Oh, really?" drawled Eve, rather maliciously. "And what do you know of him, pray? Can it be that my little cousin has set her cap for my own intended? Those two little sightseeing jaunts seem to have gone to your head, Amanda. Perhaps I should have gone with you after all, if only to keep an eye on my own interests."

"Don't be ridiculous," Amanda retorted, her back stiffening. "It's just that I find it difficult to understand how you can mean to marry one man while encouraging another under the very nose of the first. Lord Vale seems much more the ideal suitor, according to your own standards."

"Oh, Vale is the wealthier and better-looking, I'll grant you that. And I fully intend to marry a rich man. But I find Lord Frome . . . interesting . . . for some reason." Eve stared off into space for a moment, then let out a sigh. "Unfortunately, I have it on the best authority that he is shockingly poor. And I, as you know, am shockingly expensive. So I have no intention of relinquishing Lord Vale to anyone else." Casting Amanda a taunting look, she walked to the door. "And on that note, dear Coz, I shall leave you. Do ponder it, won't you?"

When Eve was gone, Amanda stood frozen, a heaviness in her chest that made movement out of the question. Was she that transparent? If her normally undiscerning cousin could guess her secret preoccupation with Lord Vale, how could she possibly hide it from anyone else? The magic had evaporated, the floating-on-air sense of anticipation melting away before she had time to grow used to its presence. For the space of a few minutes, she had been sure that Eve would not wed the Marquis. And for a shorter period than that, she had believed *she* was the woman for him, and that in time, he was bound to discover it. How foolish! How hopelessly unrealistic!

"What's the matter with me?" she whispered, closing her eyes. Then with a sharp movement, she pivoted around. "You are a fool," she told her reflection sternly. "You must stop feeling sorry for yourself. You will go down there and enjoy yourself. If you see Lord

Vale, you will behave normally. If he asks you to dance, you will decline."

And with that rather depressing resolution, Amanda picked up her fan and left the room.

In recent years, the Marquis of Vale had not been known to frequent the come-out balls of innocent young girls, so his arrival early in the evening became cake in the mouths of every gossip present. When his name was announced, more than one unmarried young lady vowed to seize that rare opportunity to form an acquaintance with one of the most sought-after bachelors in England. For despite the scandal attached to his name and the warnings of disapproving mamas, there were few girls present who had not, at some time, cherished a *tendre* for the Marquis and his fortune.

He was garbed entirely in black and white, in the severe style popularized by Beau Brummell only a few years before. In both physique and pure masculine presence, Amanda could not doubt that the Marquis was the most distinguished man in the room. Standing in the receiving line, she watched him approach with Frances on his arm. Was it her imagination, or did his eyes fly to meet hers, even before he paused to bow over Lady Besford's hand?

As it transpired, there was no way to decline the Marquis's invitation to dance, for he simply removed the dance card from her unprotesting fingers and, with an easy smile and a practiced remark, reserved his place as her partner for one of the quadrilles. Positioned next to Lady Besford and Eve with the eyes of many of the *ton* upon her, Amanda found she lacked the courage to refuse him a dance. She gave him a swift, rather unhappy smile and turned her attention to Frances, not noticing the way the Marquis's blue eyes raked her face in concern. Then there were others taking his place, and the Marquis was swallowed by the mass of fashionably clad bodies.

Lady Besford's ball, one of the Season's first, was a grand affair, and already promised to be a veritable squeeze. It opened with a country dance, and Amanda's first partner was a sallow-faced young man with a large nose. Mr. Forbes proved to be perfectly amiable, and as much as the movements of the dance allowed, he kept her entertained until the end of the set. It was at the moment when she was looking around for her next partner that she spied Lord Frome.

He was leaning against a wall with a wineglass in his hand, watching the dancers with the appearance of sardonic amusement. He must have arrived late, she thought, for he had certainly not come through the receiving line. As usual, it appeared that her cousin had gotten what she wanted. Amanda wondered what the Baron's purpose was in coming and whether he would be able to contrive a meeting with Eve. Sometime later her curiosity was to be satisfied in an unexpected way.

Amanda's fifth partner that evening was Lord Castlebury (or Lord Wandering Hands, as she had privately christened him). To her dismay, when his lordship arrived to claim his dance, he immediately begged to be excused from indulging in it, on the grounds that dancing was a form of exercise not conducive with his size and years. He chuckled, patted

Amanda's hand, and said, rather wheezingly, "Alas, Miss Marlowe, I cannot dance the quadrille to save my poor soul. Imagine a man of my girth making such a cake of himself! Heh, heh! Why those *entrechats* look silly enough when the young gals do them! Look at that poor girl over there trying to clap her feet together before she comes back to earth. Preposterous! Can't think why Sally Jersey thought she was doing us all a favor bringing that abominable dance back from Paris. She should have left it with the Frenchies! Takes a Frog to leap about like that!" Tucking Amanda's hand around his arm, he escorted her to an empty couch.

"I cannot agree, my lord," replied Amanda, fanning herself desperately as she sat down. "When properly done, I think it a most graceful dance."

"Graceful! Pah! You know nothing about it, my dear." Lord Castlebury inched his large frame a trifle closer and patted her knee. "You are young, Miss Marlowe, and have therefore had no time to form opinions," he said leniently. "The waltz, now, *that* is a graceful dance. A pity you can't waltz yet. That would be one dance I would not sit out." His speculative gaze rested on Amanda's bosom.

"Good heavens!" Amanda said involuntarily, trying to envision his lordship whirling around the floor in such an exuberant fashion. "Do you indeed waltz?"

Her portly companion looked mildly offended. "I know the steps, Miss Marlowe. Though some consider it an immoral dance, I hold it the more acceptable of the two. At least it can be performed with dignity."

Amanda wriggled an inch farther away from his lordship. "It is a warm evening, is it not? I should be so grateful, my lord, if you could procure for me a glass of ratafia."

"Right now?" Lord Castlebury looked dismayed.

"If you would be so good," Amanda replied firmly. "My throat is quite parched."

With obvious reluctance, Lord Castlebury hoisted himself to his feet. "When I return we shall continue our tête-à-tête, Miss Marlowe. I have something in particular I wish to say to you." He bowed to Amanda and left to thread his way through the knot of people crowding the perimeter of the ballroom.

"For which you will wait with bated breath, I am sure," remarked the Marquis of Vale, stepping around the potted plant at Amanda's elbow.

Amanda jumped. "Where did you come from?" she demanded, with an indrawn gasp. "Were you *hiding* behind that plant, eavesdropping on our conversation?"

With a courteous bow, the Marquis took Lord Castlebury's place on the couch and leveled his quizzing glass at the dancers, unaware of the effect he was having on Amanda.

"My dear Miss Marlowe, I was not hiding behind anything. I was simply standing on the other side of the deuced thing, leaning against the wall, like any number of other people at this wearying event. Can you perform the quadrille? I own I thought I could, but now my confidence is ebbing. Perhaps I should seek out a partner and you could watch and give me your opinion?"

Amanda went through a series of emotions during this speech, but her sense of humor prevailed. "As usual, my lord, you are being ridiculous," she told

240

him, her lips twitching. "I am sure you can dance the quadrille most creditably. You have not Lord Castlebury's . . . dimensions."

"I should hope not!" The Marquis let fall his glass and gave Amanda an approving look. "I have not had the opportunity to tell you how lovely you look. That gown suits you admirably."

The warmth in his voice and the unmistakable look of male assessment threw Amanda back into a fluster. "Thank you, my lord," she managed with an effort. "Your sister has been so kind to me. She is very like you, I think."

"I'm glad you like each other," he said quietly. "It's what I was hoping."

"You, too, have been very kind," she continued, her voice shy but determined. "I hope we can continue to . . . to remain friends, my lord."

"My friendship won't do you any good," he informed her, his mouth hardening with bitterness. "Don't go around telling anyone that I am your friend, for the love of heaven! You yourself accused me of being a rake, m'dear. Or to be exact, the word was reprobate, was it not? That means I am morally unprincipled, Amanda, and no fit friend for an innocent girl like yourself."

Amanda looked at him sadly. "I may have said it, but I no longer believe it. You have allowed yourself to be sadly maligned, my lord. You are no more a rake than . . . than your friend Mr. Perth."

Stunned, the Marquis's blue eyes fixed on her face. "Oh, I'm not? And what makes you think that?" For some reason, the question seemed to hold importance to him, and Amanda hesitated, searching for the right

241

words.

"Here is your ratafia, Miss Marlowe. My lord!" Lord Castlebury stood over them, displeasure plainly writ upon his florid face. "Miss Marlowe, has Lord Vale been bothering you?"

"On the contrary," Amanda affirmed, ignoring the Marquis's warning glance. She accepted the ratafia with murmured thanks, and added, "He has been extremely affable."

Lord Castlebury cleared his throat meaningfully, and the Marquis got to his feet. "I believe our quadrille is quite soon, Miss Marlowe. We must finish this conversation later." He gave Lord Castlebury a sardonic look, bowed to Amanda, and sauntered away.

"You should not be seen talking to such a man," Lord Castlebury admonished her. "His reputation is tarnished and his morals are sadly lacking. It is unpermissible of you to risk your own reputation, merely for the sake of feminine vanity."

Amanda regarded him in astonishment. "I'm afraid I do not understand you, my lord. How can speaking to Lord Vale in full view of everyone in the room hurt my reputation?"

Lord Castlebury frowned. "You are naive, Miss Marlowe. Do not question me in this matter, if you please. As my future wife, you must—"

"As your *what—!*" Her gasp held a horrified note that caused him to fidget.

"Forgive me for speaking of marriage in so unromantic a spirit, Miss Marlowe. I had meant to bring up the subject before you mentioned your need for refreshment." He leaned toward her, his thick hand fluttering in the air as if ready to pounce on her knee. "No, let me speak, I beg you. I am a wealthy man, Miss Marlowe, but to my great sorrow, I have not been blessed with an heir. My wife died two years ago, and since then, I have debated the wisdom of taking another. When I saw you, however, I made up my mind. You will not find me a demanding husband, Miss Marlowe. Only provide me with an heir and you shall have—"

"No!" Amanda leaped up, nearly spilling her drink. "Forgive me, my lord, but such a marriage is not possible. I am sorry to cause you pain, but you must excuse me!" She shoved the glass into Lord Castlebury's pudgy hand and fled.

The combined heat of hundreds of candles and human bodies seemed to close in on Amanda, and instinctively, she headed for cool air. Someone had left the balcony doors partway open, and it was through these she slipped, pressing her hands to her cheeks in confusion. How could Lord Castlebury have asked for her hand on so short an acquaintance? And how could she feel as if she had known Lord Vale for years when it had hardly been more than a fortnight? Nothing in Amanda's experience had prepared her for this, and she didn't know how to deal with either situation.

Spinning away from the iron railing, she descended the stone steps to the garden below, upon which a crescent moon was shedding its thin illumination. She sat carefully down on the first bench she could find and sighed deeply, taking in the sweet, earthy scent of flowering plants. Folding her arms around herself in the self-protective gesture she had used as a child, Amanda closed her eyes and tried not to think about anything at all. How many minutes passed was uncertain, but she was suddenly aware of low voices not far away.

"How did you know?" It was Eve.

"Come now, my dear. You are not talking to a novice. You know very well there is no Mr. Slingsby at this ball. In fact, the only Slingsby I know is in Paris at the moment. Confess, now. You wrote this fictional gent's name on your card because you wished to reserve a place for me should I come to claim you—as I have."

"Everard, you are quite, quite vain." Despite the reproving words, her cousin sounded amused.

"Guilty as charged." Lord Frome laughed softly. "And as vain and clever and witty as I am, I have no interest in any woman not equally so. And you, my love, are that woman. You are also as beautiful as life itself." His voice dropped almost to a whisper. "So here we stand in the garden of Eden . . . with you . . . tempting me . . ."

There was a long silence, broken only by sounds which bespoke an impassioned embrace. Dismayed, Amanda sat frozen, afraid to move and embarrass everyone by betraying her presence. Finally, the couple drifted away, and Amanda was able to make out the two figures remounting the steps—separately—and reenter the house.

Though the night air was cool, Amanda was not yet ready to leave the garden. Chafing her upper arms absently, she wondered how Lord Vale would react if he discovered her cousin was secretly meeting Lord Frome. Would he be jealous? Angry? It seemed unlikely, for her own observations told her that he and Eve were no more than civil to one another. Yet it was bound to distress him, for no man would care to see his future wife meeting another man clandestinely. It seemed so addlepated to Amanda for two people who did not love — or even like — each other to contemplate marriage. Yet such matches were not at all uncommon among members of the upper class.

Sighing wistfully, Amanda commanded her thoughts into less disturbing channels. Immediately, the puzzling scene with Madame Claret began to nag at her, unfolding from start to finish in her mind. There *was* a mystery, she was sure of it! Could Lady Frances possibly know something more than what she claimed? While Amanda pondered the question, a tall figure stepped quietly out of the shadows.

"Miss Marlowe?" said a cautious male voice.

Amanda started violently. "Lord Vale, you must stop leaping out at me like this!" she declared. "I don't believe my nerves will be able to take much more of it."

"Good. I thought it must be you. I've been searching all over for you, Prudence. We're missing our quadrille."

"Oh!" Amanda's hand flew guiltily to her mouth. "I'm so sorry. I'm afraid I lost all track of the time."

The Marquis sat down next to her on the bench. "No matter. I've lost all confidence in my ability to execute the *entrechats* without making a spectacle of myself. Of course, we could practice out here, but it's rather dark and we would probably end up leaping into the fishpond."

His banter dispelled her somber mood, and she chuckled softly. "What nonsense you talk! Anyway, there is no fishpond."

The Marquis smiled in the darkness. "I like to hear you laugh, Amanda. It's a pleasant sound — not high and screechy, like some." After a pause, he said bluntly, "When I first saw you tonight, I thought you looked unhappy. Was anything wrong?"

Amanda swallowed. "Wrong?" she faltered. "What could be wrong?"

"You tell me," he suggested gently.

Suddenly, Amanda was acutely aware of the Marquis's physical nearness. He was only inches away, and though it was quite dark, she could picture every detail of his appearance, even down to the expression upon his face. More than ever before, she was aware of his attractiveness, of his strength and virility, and of his charm . . . and it was overwhelming.

Her heart slamming against her ribs, Amanda groped for something—anything—to say. "You really ought not to call me by my Christian name, my lord . . . just as we ought not to be out here alone. It is extremely improper and frightfully indiscreet."

"Yes, it is, isn't it." He sounded exasperatingly indifferent.

Clenching her hands, Amanda went on, "Lady Besford has taken pains to teach me all the rules and codes of manners we are supposed to follow to avoid social disgrace. Why do you continually flout them?"

"Lord, Amanda, I fell into the pit of disgrace years ago!" he answered satirically. "But you're quite right. I must take care not to drag you in with me, mustn't I? Therefore, I promise I will call you Miss Marlowe whenever anyone else is near—which is what I am doing anyway, if you notice."

"A great concession, indeed," she retorted, her half-laugh dying away before it was complete. "Look at it this way, would you not be quite shocked if I suddenly began calling you . . . Jack?" she asked daringly.

"Shocked?" The Marquis considered this. "No, I don't think so. Surprised, perhaps—pleasantly so, I should add. I give you leave to do so, if you like."

"As if I should! This conversation is ridiculous."

"Maybe so, but at least we're not boring each other." He reached out and draped his arm around her shoulders. "You're cold! You're not properly dressed to be sitting out here like this."

Amanda fought the desire to relax against him and allow his arm to warm her. "Please, my lord. I . . . I must be getting back to the house. And I'm quite tired of hearing you criticize my mode of dress."

His grip on her shoulder tightened, forcing her to remain seated. "Don't be so jumpy, Prudence. That's not really the right name for you, is it? If you were truly prudent, you'd run like hell every time you saw me."

"Oh? Is there some reason I should fear you?"

The Marquis's voice took on a dangerous, husky quality. "There is every reason, my sweet. Have you not been warned about my wicked ways? Oh, yes, I forgot. You think I am not really like that."

And then it happened, as some part of her had known, even hoped, it would. With gentle determination, his iron arms were pulling her toward him, drawing her close so that the gap between them grew virtually nonexistent. Then his mouth came down to cover hers, ravishing her lips in a scalding kiss that was by far more intimate and disturbing than that other one, so many days before. Caught up in passion, his tongue nudged insistently at her lips until they parted, then began a staggeringly sweet exploration of her mouth. Dizzy with pleasure, Amanda could only cling to him and match his kisses with her own.

The next moment he was tearing himself away, thrusting her from him as if he found her distasteful.

"Now do you understand?" he said harshly. "Do you still think me fit to be your friend, Amanda? Am I as fine a fellow as Charles Perth? Why don't you answer me, Amanda?" His voice told her his mocking look was back in place.

Amanda felt herself start to shake, a reaction to the combination of chill and heat. "You must think me a fool, my lord. I was not unaware that there is . . . an attraction between us. You need not have demonstrated it!" She struggled to control the unsteadiness in her voice. "I am determined to believe the best of you, my lord, so perhaps I *am* a fool!"

She jumped to her feet, and this time he made no effort to stop her. "If, for some absurd reason, you are trying to shake my good opinion of you, well, you did not succeed! You are spoiled, my lord, and I know you have been working very hard to be a rake. But I sense nothing in you but kindness. I don't believe you could really do anything dishonorable, despite . . . despite what people say. Whatever happened to that poor girl, all those years ago, I know it was not your fault. In fact, I am astounded that anyone could think so."

The Marquis sat very still, straining to discern her features in the darkness. *"Are* you?" he whispered in a wondering tone.

"Yes." Amanda wrapped her arms around herself in an effort to still the shivering. "I imagine it's nearly time for the supper dance, my lord," she pointed out as calmly as possible. "You must not keep my cousin waiting." Retrieving her fan from where she had laid it on the bench, she turned and walked away.

After she had gone, the Marquis sat hunched, his elbows upon his knees. The last thing he wanted to do was to spend the next hour or more with Eve Marlowe; at the present, all he cared to do was to sit here dreaming of Amanda. He ought to be marrying *her,* he mused, his head snapping up as the idea germinated within him. Then, slowly, his shoulders sagged. He wasn't free to make her an offer, and anyway, he wasn't good enough for a girl like that. Amanda deserved someone who would love and cherish her, someone like Charles, who would strew rose petals as she walked and cater to her every wish. She didn't deserve a dissolute fellow like himself.

But, by God, he was attracted to her. She amused him more than any woman he could remember, and there was about her an enchanting, tantalizing mixture of innocence and passion that he found incredibly desirable. Her belief in his goodness amazed and touched him — she and Charles would really make quite a pair, he reflected wryly. Only he was not hypocrite enough to try to stand upon the pedestal of virtue they had erected for him.

Sitting there in the hush of night, with strains of music seeping from the mansion only a few yards away, he experienced a rush of bitter remembrance. He had arranged to meet Charlotte for a few moments in that other garden, at a house party now long forgotten by everyone but himself. For a few moments, he allowed himself to recall. . . .

She had worn white, and had looked as unreal as a wood nymph as she drifted across the moonlit lawn to meet him behind the hedgerow. That night the moon had been full; he remembered with haunting clarity how her delicate features had been illumined by its glow.

His heart full, he opened his arms to her. "Lottie! At last we are alone!"

To his puzzlement, she did not permit his embrace. "Please, my lord," she quavered, her voice nervous and shrill. "Do not . . . do not touch me." She glanced fearfully over her shoulder. "I should not have agreed to come. If my brother should discover—"

"He's deep in his card game," he reassured her gently. "Why should he notice? Or care? After all, we've done nothing wrong, my love. I just wanted to have a few minutes with you, alone, without someone peering over our shoulders." He reached out to clasp her hand. "Say you love me, Lottie," he urged. "Tell me you love me as much as I love you."

Something akin to horror touched her expression. "How can I believe you love me? How do I know I am not simply a diversion—easily sought and as easily discarded?"

Her question astounded him. "Because you have my word, Lottie. I am a man of honor. Surely that is enough?"

She astonished him even more by starting to cry. "I don't understand you. How can you say that to me?"

"How can I say what?" he repeated, bewildered by her words. "What makes you think I would lie about something this important?"

Lottie stared up at him, her eyes filled with some

250

strange, inner torment. "I wonder if you know what love is. Have you not told me, my lord, that I am your first and only love?"

Her words sounded accusing, and he began to grow angry. "Lottie, why at you talking like this? To what do you refer?"

"You see!" she cried, tears beginning to stream down her pale cheeks. "You don't answer! Do you dare deny that you have taken a harlot into your bed?"

He was aghast. "Lottie, who told you this? Was it your brother?"

"Everard would never dream of telling me such things," she cried hysterically. "He seeks only to protect me from life's unpleasantness. But some things must be told. I will not have a husband who has lain with prostitutes!"

His jaw was rigid; a tiny pulse beat at his temple. "I see. So you are saying you don't love me?"

"No!" Her voice trembled with emotion. "Oh, my lord, just tell me it's a lie. Tell me you've never been with another woman. If you tell me it's the truth, I will believe you."

He captured her arms and held her against him, making soothing noises in his throat. Finally, when the racking sobs had stilled he said, "Whether or not I've ever been with another woman has nothing to do with my love for you. I do love you. I fell in love with you the moment I saw you, and have been faithful to you since."

It was not enough. Softly, she said, "So it's true."

His blood still ran cold when he remembered how her voice had changed, and he had realized with a sense of horror that his beloved Lottie possessed an unstable mind. In a strange, lost, little-girl voice, she'd begun to croon, "Lottie needs love. Nobody else, nobody but me. Just me, me, me."

How long he had stood there, holding her, he never knew. His mind completely numb, he had somehow managed to return her to the house, where, miraculously, the music and lights had seemed to restore her senses. Unfortunately, they could not banish the memory.

Inside, the music had stopped, and the Marquis lifted his head from where it had dropped into his cupped hands. Looking back, he saw that he should have lied, that Lottie's immature mind had been incapable of handling her own fears and jealousy. But the truth was that, at two-and-twenty, he had already had a mistress of his own for over six months. True, this was mainly due to the manipulations of his father, who had felt it necessary to arrange every aspect of his son's life, including his first amorous relationship. The interfering old man had chosen the pretty, young, and far-from-virtuous widow of his former valet, and arranged that she be eager and available at a time when his son was in his cups. Every man ought to have a mistress, his father had told him leeringly the next morning. The young woman really had been very attractive, so he had shrugged his shoulders and taken his father's advice.

When he had fallen in love with Charlotte, however, he had severed the liaison. He had been young enough to believe in idealistic love, a love which included honesty and loyalty between partners. It had been an unfortunate mistake — one he would have to be insane to repeat.

With a conscious effort, he smoothed the pain and regret from his face, and got up. Yes, Eve Marlowe would be expecting him. But at least she would not be expecting more than he could give.

Chapter Twelve

Ensconced in her favorite chair, a handsome Norwich shawl draped over her knees, Lady Besford heaved an ecstatic sigh and beamed at her two young guests.

"Well, my dears, the ball was a splendid success, and you are formally presented at last. Now we may begin accepting some of these invitations which have been streaming in all morning! Ah, here is a card from the Grenvilles for a party tomorrow evening! How gratifying! If neither of you have any objection, I believe I will accept for us all. There will be dancing and card playing, and if I know Sarah, we may expect a profusion of excellent refreshments! It is just the sort of thing I most enjoy! And I am sure there will be any number of eligible young men present, although I cannot guarantee the presence of any particular gentleman." She eyed her niece expectantly. "You have told me very little about Lord Vale lately, Eve, and you must know I have been dying of curiosity! Between ourselves, has he said anything about *you know* what? I could not help noticing that he took you into supper last night, which was a very positive sign, I thought."

Eve's lip curled. "About dear Papa's wish that he and I be married? As a matter of fact, I brought the subject up myself. During the supper."

"You!" Lady Besford blinked and looked mildly shocked. "Oh my dear! What on earth did you say?"

"Well, he had already mentioned the matter to me, Aunt Emily. I merely told him I had given it some thought and was not adverse to the idea. He accepted my decision."

Lady Besford's china blue eyes nearly started out of her head. "But my dear!" she gasped. "That means you're betrothed to the man!"

Visibly unexcited, Eve replied, "I don't think it's quite that settled. We agreed not to send in the announcement just yet. I still want to do some looking around this Season, in case there is someone more to my liking. But this way, he can't very well propose to anyone else, now can he?" Her eyes held a triumphant glint as they shifted to Amanda.

For Amanda, it was like being kicked in the stomach, yet she managed — somehow — to return her cousin's look. "A masterly move, indeed, Eve," she said evenly. "You have my congratulations."

Quite scandalized, Lady Besford expostulated, "But you cannot *mean* that, Eve! You could not seriously consider *jilting* the Marquis of Vale!"

Arching her brows at her aunt, Eve replied, "But certainly I could. Good heavens! Mama herself warned me not to feel constrained to accept his suit. I assume he is not the only eligible bachelor in Lon-

255

don?"

The Countess looked ready to burst into tears. "I am *shocked* at your attitude, Eve! I cannot comprehend how Jane could . . . could . . . why, she knows as well as I do what a matrimonial prize he is! You *must* have misunderstood your mother's meaning, my dear! Jane would never think of telling you to play the jilt!"

"Actually, Aunt Marlowe did tell my cousin something of the sort," put in Amanda, rather ironically. "Though I think what she meant was to inspect the other eligible gentlemen *before* becoming betrothed, rather than *after.*"

Eve made an impatient gesture. "You are splitting hairs, both of you. No betrothal is official until an announcement is made."

"Yes, but meanwhile he is bound to regard himself as good as betrothed to you! As a man of honor, he *must* feel himself tied to you by such an arrangement!"

"Precisely," said Eve, cynically amused. "Oh, do try not to react so violently, Aunt! You think me horrid, I know. But consider, the gentlemen have an advantage over us women in all other respects. Why not take advantage of them occasionally? It seems logical to me."

"Logical, yes," agreed Amanda, gazing steadily at her cousin. "And heartless also, as well as unscrupulous!"

"Amanda, my dear, do hand me my hartshorn," moaned Lady Besford weakly. "I think I'm going to be needing it."

* * *

The days began to fly by in a whirlwind of parties, balls, and all manner of frivolous activities. Knowing she was supposed to be having a wonderful time, Amanda hid her wretchedness behind a mask of smiles—which must have been effective, for even Lady Besford seemed unaware of her unhappiness. Occasionally, Amanda herself forgot it for a while, for she and Eve were invited everywhere and had even been granted vouchers for Almack's, the ultimate achievement. But the fact that the many social functions they attended enabled her to see Lord Vale frequently made it difficult to forget him for very long. When they did meet, he always made it a point to converse with her—though rarely about anything serious—concealing the more sensitive facets of his character. His dry, rather flippant remarks did make it easier to treat him as the man who would soon be married to her cousin, yet she longed to catch a glimpse of the man behind the shield of sarcastic wit. To make matters worse, Eve obstinately continued in her refusal to formally announce their engagement, until eventually Amanda began, once more, to grow skeptical that the event would ever come to pass. And since this notion raised her spirits so considerably, she allowed it to take root in her mind. It became her habit to remind herself, at least once a day, that there was nothing in the Marquis's behavior to lend credence to her cousin's claim that she was to be his future wife. For all she knew, Eve's engagement might be the product of her own invention! It would be just like Eve to do such a thing, reflected Amanda.

The remainder of Amanda's gowns had been delivered, each as exquisitely made as the first, and there was more than one occasion when some envious lady inquired the name of Amanda's dressmaker. Amanda tried very hard to give Madame Claret due credit for her creations, conscientiously providing anyone interested with the Frenchwoman's direction. Very soon, however, she began to realize that something was wrong. A Miss Whitney reported that no Madame Claret resided at that address, and told Amanda a shade frostily that if Miss Marlowe wished to keep secrets she ought simply to say so!

From that moment, Amanda doubled her resolve to learn more of Madame Claret. She had seen Frances upon several occasions, but had never succeeded in introducing the subject into their talks. She had learned that her friend was expecting a child, exciting news which seemed to dominate their every conversation. Frances's husband, the Earl of Rosebery, escorted them both to Green Park one afternoon, and Amanda observed firsthand the love which existed between the young Countess and her husband. The news that his wife was increasing had so affected the Earl that he now rarely strayed from her side, and while Amanda rejoiced for her friend's happiness, she felt a little wistful as well. Perhaps love matches were not so uncommon as Aunt Marlowe had claimed, for the Earl's devotion to Frances was as marked as Sir Julian's had been for Priscilla. The Earl hovered around his wife so much, in fact, that Frances now rarely accepted an invitation, and spent most evenings at home. Therefore, the subject of Madame Claret had never managed to be raised.

So one morning, when both Eve and Lady Besford

were still abed, Amanda asked Hettie, who now assisted her daily with her toilette, to accompany her on an errand of a personal nature. Hettie readily agreed, for the day was warm and sunny, and Amanda set out with high hopes of solving the mystery of Madame Claret. Hettie knew just how to go about hiring a hackney, though she freely expressed her doubts about the propriety of Amanda riding in one.

"T'ain't fittin'," pronounced Hettie, yielding to Amanda's entreaties, "but if you insist on goin', miss, then you'll be needin' me for certain!"

Number 4, Elizabeth Street, looked deserted when they arrived. As they mounted the steps to the house, Hettie looked around. "Don't look as if anybody's at home, miss. All the curtains are drawn, I'd best tell the jarvey to wait."

Amanda glanced back over her shoulder. "Yes, do so, if you please, Hettie." She yanked the bell pull repeatedly until the sound of shuffling feet from within told her someone was coming.

The door opened a few inches. "What do you want?" A long-nosed female of indeterminate age peered suspiciously at Amanda through the crack.

Amanda offered the woman a smile. "Good day, ma'am. My name is Miss Marlowe. I'm looking for Madame Claret. It is most important that I speak with her."

"Nobody here by that name." The woman started to close the door, but was prevented from doing so by Amanda's foot.

"But I visited her here in this house only a few weeks ago, ma'am. Surely — "

"You've got the wrong house," interrupted the

woman.

"Please, may I come in for a moment?" requested Amanda. "You've nothing to fear from me. I just want to assure myself this is the same house. Perhaps I am wrong, of course."

The woman hesitated, but the sight of Amanda's maid appeared to convince her that Amanda harbored no evil intent. With no more than a show of reluctance, she allowed the door to swing open. "Can't be. Nobody here but me and the husband. Our mistress ain't been here for three months," she grumbled. "Gone off to Gay Par-ree with some dandified Frenchman! And *his* name ain't Claret either, though I'll wager he drinks his share of it and more! This is a respectable neighborhood," she added, as if that fact was in question.

"What does your mistress look like?" asked Amanda intently.

The woman must have found the inquiry amusing, for her lips pulled back to display her uneven teeth. "Youngish, but not as young as she thinks she is! Plump as a partridge, too, though she likes to call it her womanly bounty. Ha! Looks a mite better in candlelight than in the full light of day. She must be on the down side of thirty by now."

"Thirty?" repeated Amanda in dismay. She walked farther into the hall and looked around. "But this *is* the same house, I'm sure of it." She glanced at the woman's blank face and her voice dwindled. Obviously, there were no answers to be found here.

Very much disappointed, Amanda left the house and walked slowly back to the hackney.

"Never you mind, miss," said Hettie comfortingly.

"You'll find out whatever it is you want to know, sooner or later. Things have a way of working out."

Owing to Hettie's insistence, they paid off the jarvey some distance from Berkeley Square, it not being fitting, said the maid, for any of the neighbors to see Miss Amanda climbing out of a common hackney. They had progressed about halfway up Berkeley Street when a curricle rolled to a stop next to them.

"Why, it's Miss Marlowe, isn't it?" remarked a soft, masculine voice. "Out enjoying the sun, are you?"

Amanda looked up. "Good day, Mr. Forrester. Yes, it's a lovely day, is it not?"

Godfrey Forrester gazed down at her thoughtfully, and belatedly doffed his beaver. "Would you care to go for a drive, Miss Marlowe? It would give me great pleasure to further our acquaintance."

Amanda hesitated, then smiled her acceptance. "Why not? Hettie, please tell Lady Besford that Mr. Forrester took me up in his curricle. I'll be back in a bit."

"I haven't my cousin's skill as a whip," he told her when they were under way, "but I manage to get myself around. These horses used to be Vale's. Sold 'em to me at a dashed high price, too," he added, somewhat moodily.

"They're lovely animals," Amanda assured him kindly. "Very well matched."

"Good enough," he agreed, "but not the high-steppers they used to be. Past their prime, don't you know? Vale never sells any of his cattle unless he can replace it with something better. Treats his women the same."

"I beg your pardon?" said Amanda, quite startled.

261

Godfrey grimaced. "Beg your pardon, Miss Marlowe. I shouldn't have said that. Please forgive me."

"Very well," Amanda told him stiffly, regretting her decision to drive with him.

His next statement was even less to her liking. "You're fond of my cousin, aren't you?"

"I hardly know him, Mr. Forrester," she disclaimed a little guardedly.

Her companion gave her a sidelong glance. "Oh, come now, Miss Marlowe. I think you know him quite well."

"Mr. Forrester," interrupted Amanda. "If you don't mind, I've just remembered a letter I have to write. It simply must be posted today. Would you mind terribly much if—"

Godfrey nodded, and gave her another, rather peculiar look. "All right. I'll take you back now if you like."

They drove back to Berkeley Square in silence, and Godfrey's groom helped Amanda to descend. She looked back up at Mr. Forrester from the walkway. "I'm really very sorry," she apologized, feeling awkward. "Perhaps another time—"

"Another time," echoed Mr. Forrester emotionlessly. He raised his hat once more. "Good day, Miss Marlowe."

After leaving Amanda in Berkeley Square, the Marquis's cousin drove his curricle directly to No. 29 Chandler Street. His groom sprang down and took charge of the horses, while Godfrey stomped up the steps of the house.

A young girl answered his summons immediately.

"Good morning, Jeanne, my dear. How very pretty you look today. Are you going to let me come in?"

The girl gulped and made a trembling curtsy as she opened the door for him to enter.

Godfrey stepped into the house. "Come, wench. Don't look so frightened. I don't bite, you know. Is your mistress alone?"

Eyes wide, the girl nodded and backed away from him, her hands clutching her apron.

He went up the stairs two at a time and threw open the door to Lady Claverley's bedchamber. "What, my dear Alexandra, sleeping again?" he said as he parted the curtains around her bed. "Time to arise, my love. We have business to discuss."

"What do *you* want?" Lady Claverley blinked and rubbed her eyes. "What time is it?"

Angered, he grabbed a handful of her luxuriant black hair and gave it a cruel twist. "Don't use that tone with me, Alex! I want respect from you and, by God, I intend to have it!"

"Ah, Godfrey, you're hurting me!" Lady Claverley sat up, rubbing her scalp. "You've never come here this early in the day. Is something wrong?"

His lips curved in a snarl. "Why, yes, now that you mention it. Things are not going according to plan."

"What do you mean?"

Godfrey glared down at her. "Damn it, woman! Have you no eyes in your head? Whom do you think Vale wishes to wed?"

Lady Claverley looked puzzled. "Why . . . the Marlowe girl, of course."

Godfrey let out an exasperated snort. "Yes, but *which one?*"

"Which one?" she repeated. "Well, Eve Marlowe, naturally. She's precisely his sort. The other one is pretty, but—"

"But nothing!" he snapped, his lip curling contemptuously. "You and Frome are a fine pair of fools! While he's been exercising his so-called seductive talents on *Eve,* my fine cousin has had eyes for no one but the fair *Amanda!* Haven't you seen the way he looks at her? They're like a pair of lovesick calves!" He dragged his fingers over his face. "I can't believe you haven't noticed! It's as plain as a pikestaff to anyone with eyes!"

"But that means nothing!" Lady Claverley retorted in consternation. Thinking rapidly, she shook back her tousled tresses. "Amanda Marlowe has no fortune at all, and the scandal of her mother's runaway marriage set the *ton* on its heels for months—remember that! With his own scandalous past, Jack would be foolhardy to ally himself to her. And you've told me how it is with him. He feels he must marry Eve Marlowe out of a sense of duty. In fact, he himself spoke of it as a commitment."

"Well, he can't marry her if she's married to someone else, can he?" Godfrey exploded, and started to pace back and forth.

Lady Claverley shot him an incredulous look. "You don't think she'd marry Everard, do you? Why he hasn't a feather to fly with! Everyone knows he's been living on credit for years!"

"Eve Marlowe is an heiress! If he seduces her and then offers to lead her to the altar, don't you think she'd accept? You don't think Jack would take someone else's leavings, do you—especially Frome's?"

"Oh, Lord!" Lady Claverley stared at him. "I see what you mean. Instead of being heart broken, Jack will probably rejoice. It will free him from his obligation to his father."

"Wonderful," jeered Godfrey sarcastically. *"Now* the light begins to dawn! Instead of hurting the bastard, we'll have been helping him! Oh, the damned irony of it!"

"Well," said Lady Claverley in a reasonable tone, "the plan must be changed. Everard must turn his talents to Amanda Marlowe instead."

Godfrey halted, and his expression lost some of its bitterness. "Yes . . . yes, that could work. Eve would probably turn to Vale, out of sheer pique, even if she prefers Frome. But will Frome agree? And is he charming enough to supplant my cousin in Amanda Marlowe's affections?"

"Everard could charm the horns off the devil himself," said Lady Claverley with conviction. "A nineteen-year-old girl is hardly a worthy opponent for a practiced philanderer like Everard. And he's certain to agree to the scheme. His desire for revenge gnaws at him like a rat at a flour sack."

Godfrey left off his pacing. Pressing his fists into the mattress, he thrust his face so close to Lady Claverley she could smell his stale breath. "As does my desire to be the sixth Marquis of Vale. For your sake, Alex, I hope you're right. So far, I am not well pleased with you. You have done little to help me, in spite of all your assurances."

Lady Claverley drew back, a shiver running down her spine. "I have tried," she protested, fear causing her voice to tremble. "I've spoken to Eve Marlowe more than once. I tried to tell her about Jack's chères-amies — hoping to give her a disgust of him, you understand — but the girl was absolutely unmoved! I thought it most unnatural behavior in a gently bred young girl! On another occasion, I tried to bring up the matter of Charlotte's suicide. I tell you, she barely attended to me, Godfrey, so involved was she with the readjustment of the flowers in her hair!"

"Well, you'd best do better with Amanda," he threatened. "It is imperative that *she* be given a disgust of my cousin instead, and as quickly as possible. And don't forget, Lord Frome must know nothing of my involvement in this. Remember my promise to you, if all goes as we wish."

Lady Claverley's eyes dropped to her lap, concealing their exultant gleam. Oh, to be a marchioness! She would do anything to achieve such a position in society, even to putting up with Godfrey as a husband.

Lady Claverley took stock of Amanda from the far side of the ballroom. The girl certainly never lacked for partners, she noted jealously, which was surprising when one considered the chit's total lack of fortune. Of course, the fact that she was sponsored by the Countess of Besford helped a great deal, since Lady Besford held a highly distinguished place in society. As far as Lady Claverley was able to discover, it was primarily Eve Marlowe's fortune and beauty which attracted the swarms of admirers to the Besford drawing room. There, it seemed, a portion of those not actively seeking a wealthy wife switched camps, for more than a few gentlemen found the easy going brunette far more pleasant than her proud and distant cousin. The girl practically radiated purity, she thought, watching her with contempt.

The seething widow reached out to touch her companion's sleeve. "Now watch her when she talks to Jack," she whispered. "Look, there he is, with Eve Marlowe, but he's looking at Amanda. Watch his expression, Everard. Do you see what I mean?"

Lord Frome gazed blandly through his quizzing glass. "Good lord," he remarked. "I do believe you're right, Alexandra. I'm utterly amazed, my dear. I would never have guessed you could be so observant."

Lady Claverley frowned. "This is no time for sarcasm. Don't you see that all your plans are going awry?"

"Indeed, I do. But your unprecedented concern for my happiness overwhelms me, my love. Or perhaps you mean it is your own plans which are on the verge of failure," he continued ironically.

Her voice was tight with fury. "A plague upon you, Everard! You know very well this concerns us both! Have we not agreed to help one another?" When he made no answer, she snapped, "If you still desire revenge, then you must do as I say. Forget Eve Marlowe, and begin fixing your interest with her cousin as fast as you can manage."

Lord Frome pulled out his snuffbox. "Just walk right over there and sweep her off her feet, is that it?" he said sardonically.

Lady Claverley watched him take snuff with an air of impatience. "It's your only choice. Do you foresee a problem?"

The Baron's expression was impossible to read. "No," he said shortly. "For once, Alexandra, your reasoning is flawless. I shall begin to lay seige to the fair Amanda this very night. But I wonder if I will be successful."

"You've got to be. All our plans depend on it!"

"Do they?" he murmured after she had left his side.

Unaware of being observed, Amanda was conscious only of the deliciously heady sensation which enveloped her when the Marquis of Vale sought her hand for the waltz. Although she had been granted the necessary permission to waltz some days past, Amanda had not done so more than a handful of times. And when she had, she had chosen for her partners only those gentlemen with whom she had formed a comfortable acquaintance (such as Mr. Wilcox, whose ardor since that occasion had unfortunately increased). She had never waltzed with the Marquis, however, for not once had he asked her to do so.

She had been doing her best to maintain a cheerful outlook, but for a young girl without the support of a parent it was not an easy state to sustain. Lady Besford was kind, yet seemed so eager for the match between Eve and Lord Vale that it did not occur to Amanda to take the Countess into her confidence. There were times when Amanda skated the edge of a despair so bleak that the only way to cope with it was to blank the future completely from her mind. Certain avenues of thought were dangerous to pursue, and the foremost of these was her feelings for the

Marquis. She had not yet admitted that she loved him, and even now, as she circled the floor in his arms, she felt too vulnerable to do anything but close her eyes to what was so obvious to Godfrey. The only thing she acknowledged to herself was that she cared for him, much in the manner that one cared for a very dear friend, and that she would hate to see him married to her cousin. At least until Eve made up her mind to announce — or break — her "engagement," this seemed the wisest and safest thing to do.

She had nearly declined the Marquis's invitation to waltz, for it was the most intimate of dances, requiring a closeness to one's partner that could only threaten her composure. Her hesitation, however, had caused such an odd flicker to pass over the Marquis's countenance that out of pure, breathless curiosity she decided to accept. Her nerves tingling, she wondered whether he would say anything about his so-called betrothal to Eve.

It was the first time he had touched her since the evening of Lady Besford's ball, and she was very conscious of the warmth of his clasp. He did not immediately speak, and his blue eyes were filled with such seriousness that a twinge of unease pinched at her heart.

"What is it, my lord?" she inquired, forcing herself to smile up at him as though everything was normal.

His gaze had been on her lips, but it shifted as she spoke. "I was just thinking of the first day I met you. Did you ever tell Lady Besford the true story?"

"No, I did not," she answered demurely. "I do have a small sense of self-preservation, you know. She would most probably have been horrified, and I should have been sent home in disgrace."

He smiled briefly. "Are you enjoying yourself, then?"

Her eyes dropped. "Yes . . . at least, some of the time I am," she answered slowly. "At first, things were difficult because . . . because I was so self-conscious about my appearance." She felt his grip tighten as she added, "Of course, some of the people who are so kind to me now were not so . . . so kind before I became fashionable. That still hurts a little. To be sought after because of what one wears rather than what one is inside seems so . . . so . . . oh, I cannot think of the word!"

"Asinine," he supplied, with bluntness. "I hope you don't think *I* seek you for such a reason. In fact, I am very glad you did not change along with your gowns."

The pleasure in her silver eyes made him groan inwardly. "What a nice thing to say! But all the gentlemen are not so gallant, I'm afraid."

The Marquis scowled. "Have you had any offers of marriage?"

"What a thing to ask!" she replied, her insides going cold at the question. "But yes, Lord Castlebury has offered for me—more than once, actually. It seems he has need of an heir, and provided I abandon all pretensions to being able to think for myself, he is willing to give me the protection of his name."

"Pompous ass!" the Marquis growled. "You cannot possibly marry him, Amanda."

Somewhat reassured by these words, Amanda lowered her eyes to study his shirt buttons. "I do not intend to. But I shouldn't be discussing this with you, should I?" She swallowed, and added bravely, "Although when you are married to my cousin, I suppose it will then be quite proper for you to concern yourself with my problems."

His lips tightened. "You remind me, quite properly, that I should mind my own affairs. I spoke out of turn."

It was not the response she wanted. Where were the soothing words she so longed to hear?

"You spoke as a friend," she continued desperately, "so why should you apologize? It is good to know that you . . . that you care, my lord."

Vale looked at her strangely. "Of course I care, I —"

He broke off abruptly, and for a full minute the tension between them grew. Half-hysterically, Amanda studied the soft black curls at his forehead, wishing she could just reach up and —

"When Eve and I are married," he said tautly, "you can be sure I will provide you with a handsome dowry. You will have no need to worry about your future ever again, Amanda."

His words slammed into her like a blow from a mallet.

"I —" She had to clear her throat to speak. "I see. How . . . how kind of you, my lord," she managed, nausea welling in her throat. It was fortunate that the music ended at that moment, for her limbs could no longer support her weight. "Would you escort me to my cousin, my lord?" she heard herself say rather faintly. "I see her sitting on that couch over there."

After he was gone, Amanda sat down next to Eve and, with a long, deep breath, struggled for composure. Fool, fool, fool, she cried silently. Somehow, in her eternally optimistic stupidity, she had actually

271

managed to convince herself that the betrothal was nothing but flummery. Well, so much for that theory, she thought numbly. Now, she would have to face reality.

What she desperately needed was time to be alone, but it would be some hours before that luxury would be hers. In the meanwhile, she was going to have to go on behaving normally and try to survive the remainder of the evening.

Noticing suddenly that her cousin had still made no remark, Amanda went on the offensive. "Alone, Eve? How unusual."

Eve did not glance at her, for her eyes were trained on the shifting islands of people who crowded the ballroom. "Only by choice, Amanda. Most of the gentlemen are nothing more than ridiculous boys, paying one the most absurd compliments. They were giving me the headache so I sent them all away. Lord Andrew is fetching me a glass of the champagne punch."

"Most of them are very nice," Amanda said tartly. "And you must admit Lord Andrew is no mere boy. He may even mean to make you an offer!"

"Quite probably," agreed Eve with indifference.

"Does he mean nothing to you at all?" responded Amanda in perplexity. "Since when does the heir to a dukedom not meet with your approval? I thought you set great store on such things as titles."

"Yes, and when his brother marries and has children, what then?" replied Eve, as pragmatic as ever. "I would rather marry a peer than a courtesy lord. Of course, he *is* wealthy—wealthier than Vale, I believe. How clever of you to notice, Amanda," she added in a complimentary tone.

Suddenly, Eve inhaled sharply. Following her cousin's gaze, Amanda was not altogether surprised to see Lord Frome weaving his way toward them through the throng.

He stood before them and bowed. "But this is incredible!" he exclaimed. "The two most beautiful women in the room, together and alone! Alas, what a dilemma! I cannot ask you both to dance." He cocked his head to one side and appeared to debate.

To Amanda's utter amazement, his eyes settled on her. "Miss Marlowe, would you care to dance with one who has admired you from afar for many, many days?"

Amanda stole a look at Eve. Her cousin's face, though as cool and composed as ever, had paled slightly. "I . . . I don't really think that —" she began.

"Dance with him, Amanda," commanded Eve imperiously. "I see Lord Andrew approaching with my champagne, and he will wish to sit in your place."

"Very well." Amanda rose, and accepted Lord Frome's proffered arm. For once, she understood her cousin's motivations completely.

Waltzing with Lord Frome, Amanda decided, was wholly different from waltzing with the Marquis of Vale. They were both excellent dancers, but something in the way Lord Frome held her made Amanda wonder for the first time whether there was some justification in the notion that the waltz was a little immoral. The Baron's hand at her waist felt uncomfortably invasive, and she did not care for the expression in the bold black eyes that examined her with disconcerting thoroughness.

"It *is* customary, my lord, to converse with one's partner," she finally reproved, hoping to divert him from his perusal of her person.

A slow, very attractive smile transformed his lordship's craggy features. "When one's partner is as lovely as you, Miss Marlowe, I think certain customs can be overlooked," was his suave response. "Your beauty deprives me of all sensible speech."

"*Something* certainly does, but I doubt I can claim credit for it," Amanda countered dryly.

His eyes gleamed. "Isn't it sensible to compliment a beautiful lady?"

"If one is sincere," she allowed, openly skeptical.

"Ah, I see," he drawled. "You don't believe I mean what I say. Miss Marlowe, my admiration for you has just increased tenfold. Genuine modesty is—so rare." Lord Frome's eyes locked on her face, a faint, lopsided smile twisting his lips. It had always been one of his most beguiling expressions, but it failed him now. Amanda was in no mood for such games.

"Lord Frome, your reputation as an unprincipled libertine has not been the best-kept secret. You may believe I speak the truth when I tell you I am not interested in flirting with you, nor do I believe for one instant that you have suddenly developed an interest in me." She hesitated an instant. "Forgive me for asking this, but are you perhaps a little foxed?"

The Baron threw back his head and laughed. "Forgive *me*, Miss Marlowe," he said, shaking his head ruefully. "I do not laugh at you, but at myself. To answer your question, no, I am not foxed, but I think I am in love, which is nearly the same."

Surprised, she said, "Well, if you desire my opinion, my lord, that is not so very bad a thing to be—providing you have the gumption to do something about it."

His expression grew enigmatic. "That's an original viewpoint. So you favor the notion that love conquers all, is that it?" he said quizzically.

"I—" Amanda paused, and the corners of her mouth drooped. The Marquis's words echoed in her ear. *When Eve and I are married* . . . "I'm not sure, my lord. But surely, sometimes—?" She did not hear the ragged despondency in her own voice.

"Seldom," he corrected, his tone oddly gentle. "Very, very seldom in real life, Miss Marlowe."

Her quick recovery earned his respect. "Well, if that's so, Lord Frome, it is because very few people make the least push to overcome the hurdles."

"Are you accusing me of being lazy?" he asked, amusement creeping back into his voice.

She smiled wanly. "You will not bait me into listing your faults, my lord. I'm sure you know them, just as I know mine."

At last the waltz ended, and the Baron bowed. "Miss Marlowe, talking with you has been most elucidating. I would deem it an honor if you would drive out with me tomorrow, so that I may hear some more of your very enchanting views."

Amanda shook her head wearily. "I'm sorry, my lord. I will not drive out with you tomorrow, or any other day."

She missed the brief flash of annoyance which crossed his face. "That's most unfortunate, Miss Marlowe," he replied. "I had counted on your acceptance."

"I'm sorry," she repeated, polite but firm.

As if it had never left, his expression of suave amusement was back in place. "Then I must find some way to make you change your mind."

Chapter Thirteen

Unable to sleep, Amanda tossed and turned in her bed, recalling for the hundredth time the events of the evening's ball. She knew now that she had fallen deeply and hopelessly in love with Lord Vale, had known it, in fact, the moment she heard him declare his intentions to marry her cousin, the words dashing over her foolish, half-formed hopes like a shock of cold water. Aunt Marlowe had been right after all, she reflected bitterly. Her romantic daydreams had been nothing but fanciful rubbish, and her belief that the marriage would come to nothing, quite unrealistic. With a small sob, Amanda buried her face in her pillow. The mere thought of the Marquis's strong arms holding someone else was enough to send hot tears of anguish coursing down her cheeks.

His soul was the echo of her own. All her life she had waited for this man, waited to share her thoughts, her dreams, and her life with him. Jack—no, *John*—was the person with whom she could watch a sunset or share a joke. John was the man—

the only man—to whom she could give the whole of herself—without reservation or restraint. He had tried to convince her otherwise, but Amanda knew that he was neither morally unprincipled nor wicked. What utter nonsense! On the contrary, it had become manifestly obvious that he was, above all, a man of honor, a man she could respect and trust—and therefore love. But, to lie here and catalogue his virtues was useless! Think, Amanda, think! Who was it that said people should have the gumption to fight for what they wanted? But even clinging to this idea, Amanda was unable to fend off the heavy weight of depression that had settled somewhere in the region of her heart.

Reaching for a handkerchief from the nearby stand, Amanda sat up and blew her little nose. The evening had really been a complete failure, she reflected, for even Eve had suffered an unhappy blow. She wondered why the Baron had suddenly chosen to ignore her cousin, for he always seemed to make such a point of seeking her out. Almost immediately, an answer occurred to her, for Lady Besford had warned them both how it was with the man, calling him a *hardened case*. He must have tired of the sport of toying with Eve and begun searching out new game.

But wait, in that case, why had he spoken of love? He surely did not mean Amanda to believe he was in love with *her!* Though his previous remarks had been unmistakably flirtatious, his statement about being in love had sounded different, almost confiding. Eve's aunt had also said that the man never looked seriously at a female unless she came with a gold purse. And Eve certainly came with a gold purse — she was to inherit nearly twenty thousand pounds upon the event of her marriage!

So his behavior made no sense. If he was seriously trying to fix his interest with Eve, he would not have treated her as he had this evening. Anyone even remotely acquainted with her cousin would know that Eve did not possess a forgiving nature. As long as she was in control of her bevy of admirers, her cousin would be content. But let any of them dare to wander—!

And then there was Lady Claverley. Amanda shuddered as she recalled her conversation with the bewitchingly beautiful widow. Until this evening, Amanda had never had either the occasion or the desire to speak with the woman. But tonight, Lady Claverley had deliberately seemed to seek her out.

Amanda had been standing in one of the rooms set aside for the ladies to see to their *toilette*. The room was otherwise empty, and Amanda was pinching at her pale cheeks, trying to restore some of their usually healthy glow. The widow entered quietly and came up behind her.

"You should try rouge, my dear," she murmured, meeting Amanda's eyes in the long mirror. "It's so much less painful, and lasts a good deal longer."

Amanda turned around and managed a small smile. "I suppose so, madam."

"You're Miss Marlowe, aren't you? Miss *Amanda* Marlowe, I mean. The cousin of the much-courted Miss Eve Marlowe."

"Yes, I am," Amanda replied, noting how frankly the woman was assessing her. She also could not help noticing the extremely low cut of the widow's bodice, and the fact that it clung to her curves so snugly that it must have been dampened.

Lady Claverley appeared to hesitate a little. "Forgive me, Miss Marlowe. Perhaps I should not say this, but you are so young, I feel almost like an aunt to you. I saw you dancing with the Marquis of Vale earlier this evening."

Amanda regarded her coolly. "What of it?"

The lady's perfectly formed red lips curved in gentle sympathy. "He is an attractive man, isn't he? I myself have been—intimately involved, let us say, with him for some time." She laughed lightly, and allowed her meaning to sink in. "Of course, I am much older than you, and have been married. So I assure you, I speak as a woman of experience."

"Oh?" Amanda made no effort to check the frosty edge in her voice.

"You are ready to take offense, I see," remarked the widow, watching her closely. "Pray, do not, for my intentions are kindly meant. It is only that I hate to see such men prey upon innocent girls like yourself. He has no thoughts of marriage, Miss Marlowe. He's nothing but a wolf, my dear, looking for pretty little sheep to seduce with fair words and court promises. The only love he will offer you is of the cream pot variety. When you are married, of course, you can do whatever you wish. But for now—"

"Madam!" Amanda interrupted desperately. "There is really no need for you to say this."

"Oh, but there is," the widow assured her silkily. "For you display such a marked preference for Jack, and he, my poor little lamb, is quite obviously hunting you. Has no one told you about poor Charlotte Wythe. She was much like you, Miss Marlowe — young and idealistic, dreaming of marriage to a handsome young man. But he killed her as surely as if he ground her into the dirt with one of his so-elegant Hessian boots. He seduced that girl, Miss Marlowe, then he—"

"Stop!" Instinctively, Amanda threw up a hand as if to ward off the woman's poisonous words. "I refuse to listen to any more of this. I can only say I am appalled that you would repeat such horrid stories. I don't know what your motives are in telling me this, but I know most of it is lies."

Lady Claverley's lovely amethyst eyes bored into her. "You are very frank, Miss Marlowe, and also, I think, rather unwise. Perhaps you deserve the fate that awaits you. Do what you wish, then. I shan't lift a finger to help you."

"Good," Amanda told her curtly. "Help from someone like you is the last thing I need."

The woman's eyes glittered angrily. "Why, you little slut!" she hissed.

Amanda's eyes flashed their own silver-edged fury. "To be strictly accurate, Madam," she said distinctly, "it is you who are the slut."

She thought then that the woman was going to strike her, but to her surprise, Lady Claverley only whirled around and rushed from the room, her satin skirts rustling softly in her wake. Amanda discovered then that her hands were shaking, either with rage or shock, she knew not which. It had been an encounter unlike anything in her experience, and, she thought wryly, a fitting culmination to what had truly been a nightmare of an evening.

Even now, hours later, Amanda could not fathom the reason for the woman's malicious behavior. Was she just naturally vindictive, or could she have had some other motive? It seemed curious, to say the least, that two people who had never before paid her an iota of attention had chosen the same evening to single her out. Beginning to feel drowsy at last, Amanda rubbed her eyes and yawned. There was so much to worry about—too much for one person. She was going to have to talk to Frances.

As luck would have it, Lady Besford informed her the following morning that the Earl and Countess of Rosebery had invited them all to visit Vauxhall that evening. Frances, it seemed, had begun to chafe at her enforced inactivity and had hit upon the splendid notion of making up a small, informal party to visit the famous pleasure gardens. The party was to include Lord and Lady Besford, Amanda and Eve, the Marquis and Charles Perth, and Frances and her husband.

Lord Besford grumbled when he first learned of the scheme, but relented as soon he discovered that Amanda wished him to go. Amanda was very fond of the earl, and had from practically the first evening enjoyed a special relationship with him. And so she told him that when he growled like that he reminded her of an old bear, which delighted the crusty old peer so much he offered to show her his winter cave. Despite her depression, Amanda found she could still laugh, and a small portion of her optimism came creeping back.

The prospect of a visit to Vauxhall did even more to revive her spirits, for not only would it provide an opportunity to talk to Frances, it was in itself a lure. For some time she had been wanting to see for herself the numerous and diversified amusements of this twelve-acre paradise. She had heard of its spaciousness, of the thousands of magical lights glimmering in the trees, of the long walks paved with gravel, and of the hedges and groves, grottos and temples, supper boxes and pavilions. She had been told that the nightingales sang in its deepest bowers, their sweet songs vying with the bands playing upon the lawns or in the Rotunda. And she longed to see the fireworks, which had been a regular part of the evening's entertainment for nearly eighteen years.

Eve had already been to Vauxhall several times, for she had a different set of friends and had frequently accepted invitations which were not extended to Amanda. From her cousin's unusual degree of animation before and after each of these occasions, Amanda had begun to suspect that Eve used these visits to meet Everard Frome. From what she had heard, Vauxhall's famed "Dark Walks" would provide her cousin with the perfect location for any such clandestine encounters. She was even more certain of the truth of her suspicions when Eve greeted the news of their intended visit to her favorite place with complete indifference, a vast change from her previous enthusiasms. However, if Eve was suffering, she hid it well, and Amanda's single attempt to commiserate with her was met with a cold rebuff.

Frankly, at the moment Amanda had not the energy to be greatly sympathetic. There were faint, dark circles under her eyes, caused as much by stress and emotion as from her poor night's sleep. She made sure she took great pains with her *toilette* for the evening, and hoped no one would notice her pallor. After some deliberation, she chose a slip of pale mauve crepe, and an overdress of white French lace, with two rows of lace flouncing at the hem. It was one of her favorite frocks, and one she had been saving for a special occasion. She sighed, and wondered how many more special occasions there could possibly be.

The Marquis of Vale leaned back in his chair and stared at the ceiling in growing exasperation. While Charles Perth did not aspire to the dandy set, he had firm beliefs as to what constituted the correct arrangement of a gentleman's neckcloth. Such was the strength of these beliefs that it was nearly impossible to pry Charles loose from his lodgings before he was completely satisfied with the results of his efforts, efforts which at present struck the Marquis as a trifle overparticular. At Mr. Perth's elbow stood Perrot, his valet, with three of Charles's failures slung over his arm in crumpled disarray. To Vale's relief, Charles's fourth attempt at the Mathematical proved an unqualified success, and the Marquis nearly jumped from his chair, so anxious was he to be off.

"That'll do," said Charles, eyeing himself critically in the mirror. He allowed Perrot to assist him with his coat, then turned to the Marquis. "What do you think?"

"Slap up to the echo," the Marquis assured him sardonically. "Do you think you can face the world now?"

Charles grinned. "I'll try." His grin faded as he took in the Marquis's tense stance, and he dismissed the valet.

"Something's amiss," he said bluntly. "What is it, Jack?"

Vale hesitated, and for a moment Charles thought he was going to deny it. Then the Marquis shrugged. "Damned near everything that I can think of," he responded. "Are you ready to go?"

Worried, Charles rubbed the tip of his nose. "Dash it, Jack! Why don't you tell me? If there's something I can do—"

"There's nothing," the Marquis replied. "I've made a complete botch of this marriage business, that's all, and there's nothing you or anyone else can do about it."

"Hang it, Jack, what have you done?"

Again, Vale hesitated. "In my infinite stupidity, I managed to become more or less betrothed to Eve Marlowe, and to own the truth, Charles, I find I can't stomach the girl."

Charles stared fixedly at him. "What do you mean, 'more or less'?"

The Marquis grimaced. "I brought up the matter the first day I drove her in my curricle. I had no intention of offering for the girl until I knew her better, but damned if she didn't misinterpret what I said and think it a blasted marriage proposal. And like a damned knock-in-the-cradle, I said nothing to set her straight."

285

"But why the devil not?"

"I thought it simpler not to, for it didn't seem to matter," Vale replied shortly. "At any rate, we are not *exactly* betrothed because, I fancy, the lady is wondering if she cannot do a little better for herself. She has, in effect, brought me to Point Non Plus."

"I see," said Charles, shaking his head in bemusement. "But what is it you object to in the fair Miss Marlowe, Jack? Does she lack one of the, ahem, qualifications?"

"Qualifications?" The Marquis looked blank.

"You know—beauty, docility, and, er, fertility."

Vale frowned. "Did I say that? I must have been in my cups."

"Don't think you were," replied his friend cautiously. "Though I can't be sure. You're a devilish hard-headed fellow, Jack."

The Marquis's lips twisted. "I think my list of qualifications has undergone a change in the past few weeks," he said soberly.

Charles nodded. "Thought that might be the case," he said wisely. "Is it the cousin?"

"Yes."

Charles watched the Marquis walk to the window and look out. "You're right, Jack," Charles sighed. "It's a deuce of a coil. Any chance the lady will cry off?"

Vale didn't move. "A small one. She seems to see Everard Frome as some sort of romantic figure. And God knows, he would love to get his hands on her inheritance. So the noose is around my neck, Charles, but the stool is still beneath my feet."

"Well, there's some hope then," Charles said comfortingly. "I'm devilish sorry, Jack. Under the circumstances, I think we should call off our little wager. You've enough to plague you right now, without that."

"Oh, the wager." Vale swiveled around. "I forgot to tell you, I already won it."

Charles was startled. "You did? How? And why didn't you say so?"

For the first time, the Marquis's face took on a satisfied expression. "I transformed Amanda from a rustic to a town belle. Haven't you ever wondered where all her fashionable new gowns came from?"

Charles stared at the Marquis incredulously. "You *bought* the girl's clothes?"

"Come, Charles," replied Vale irritably. "You make it sound as if I made her my mistress. Believe me, she knows nothing of my part in it. She believes she found a dressmaker with bargain prices, and she'll continue to believe it. Actually, I went through more begging and wheedling than I like to remember trying to persuade Albertine Le Rougement to come out of retirement."

"Albertine Le Rougement!" repeated Charles, completely stunned. "The French dressmaker?"

"None other." The Marquis looked rueful. "My God, does that sharp-witted old harridan know how to drive a bargain! That's probably why she managed to escape France with her head attached."

"But she must be in her seventies by now! How could she possibly make all those gowns?"

"Oh, she had enough help, believe me. I chose her for her genius with colors and design, not for her skill with the needle."

"But how can you expect to keep something like that a secret?" Charles expostulated. "Have you considered what people will say if it comes out? Your Amanda's reputation will be hanging in shreds, Jack!"

The Marquis was silent. "I don't see why it should, Charles," he said presently. "Madame Le Rougement gave me her word, and Frances will not —"

"Frances! Your *sister* played a part in this?"

"You surely did not think I escorted the girl to Madame Le Rougement myself, did you?" Vale returned, rather coldly.

"But Jack," exclaimed Charles helplessly. "Your sister and Amanda Marlowe have become *friends*. You, with all your vast experience with women, ought to know that when women become friends they blab *everything* to each other! Dash it, man, I've got four sisters, I ought to know!

"Amanda would understand," said the Marquis confidently. "She's a regular out-and-outer, Charles, not one of these tiresome females who always seem to be swooning and sighing and clutching at your arm. And Frances would never tell anyone else, of that I am sure."

"I hope you're right," retorted Charles dubiously.

The Marquis glanced across the room at the clock on the mantelshelf. "We'd better go, Charles. The delights of Vauxhall await us."

Vauxhall Gardens proved even more impressive than Amanda had expected. As they strolled along the Grand Walk, she saw that the trees on either side of this promenade were indeed hung with lamps so that it looked like a setting from a fairy story. Turning north, they proceeded up the Grand Cross Walk, until Lord Rosebery announced that his wife was beginning to tire and they ought to think about sitting down. The Earl soon located a vacant supper box, and Amanda could not help smiling at the way Frances rolled her eyes while her husband fussed over her with excessive solicitude.

"I am feeling perfectly well," Frances whispered to Amanda once the Earl had moved out of earshot. "The thing is, I've found it necessary to take long naps every afternoon, so William is convinced that I've suddenly turned into some sort of frail, helpless creature."

"I'm very glad everything is going so well for you," Amanda said sincerely. "I only wish I could say the same of myself. Frances, I simply must talk to you. Is there any way we can speak privately?"

Frances glanced around. "Well, if I can convince William that it is for my own good, we might walk a short distance. They are ordering the food already, so let's wait until after we sup. I will tell him I can digest better with some exercise. He will probably follow us, but that's just as well. There are a good many rogues about in a place like this."

The gentlemen had ordered a cold collation of ham and chicken, along with several bottles of port wine and a bowl of rack punch. When the waiter brought the plates of ham, however, the Earl of Besford took instant exception to the meagerness of the fare.

"Is this *it?*" he inquired sarcastically. He twirled

the plate around twice, and then further embarrassed Lady Besford by examining the underside of the dish. "My good man, did we not order four shillings' worth?"

"You did, my lord. And I have brought it to you," the waiter replied in wooden accents.

With two fingers, his lordship dangled one of the ham slices in front of the man's nose. "Did you carve this yourself?"

"Yes, my lord."

"Confound it, man, I can see through it!" burst the Earl, glaring at him.

"I am sorry, my lord," the waiter apologized.

Until now, Amanda had made little eye contact with the Marquis, but the situation was so humorous that their eyes automatically linked in unspoken amusement. "The ham slices here are proverbially thin," he explained, *sotto voce*. "The waiters pride themselves on their dexterity with the carving knife."

The waiter departed to fetch more ham, and Lord Besford warmed to his theme. "Drat the man, we've eight people here! Why, a thin little slip of a girl like Amanda could eat what he just brought us and still be hungry! And these chickens are the size of sparrows!"

"Oh, Robert, do hush!" implored his wife.

"I think, sir, that you will find the rack punch goes a long way toward making up for the ham. I have always found it quite tolerable," offered the Marquis politely.

"How very obliging of it!" cracked the earl, though he appeared somewhat mollified by this intelligence.

290

Though it was more than an hour before Amanda was able to separate Frances from the others, the lingering twilight still held the darkness at bay. They walked slowly, heading in the direction of the orchestra pavilion, with Lord Rosebery trailing behind them like an anxious watchdog.

"It's so good to talk with you at last," said Amanda gratefully. "So much has happened that—well, I will tell about that presently, but first you will never guess what I have discovered! Madame Claret has disappeared!"

"Disappeared?" repeated Frances in dismay. "How did you—I mean, how do you know?"

"Well, as you know, I was suspicious of her from the first. That tale about my bringing her more custom might have been true, but then why has no one been able to find her? I finally went back there myself, and the woman who lives in that house is abroad, and her servant claims never to have heard of either her or her daughter!"

Frances racked her brain for a plausible explanation. "Well, perhaps she decided to go back to France. Or perhaps she died, or—oh Amanda, do forget about Madame Claret! She doesn't matter, truly she doesn't!"

Amanda halted, and gripped her friend's arm. "You know something about her, don't you?"

Frances gave an uneasy little laugh. "Don't be ridiculous, Amanda. What can you mean?"

"Frances, you must tell me," Amanda said earnestly. "I have a right to know what this is all about."

"Oh, Amanda, I wish I could, but I promised

Jack—" Frances clapped a hand guiltily over her mouth.

"What did you say?"

Frances glanced over her shoulder at her husband, wishing she had not told him to stay so far behind. "Oh dear," she sighed unhappily. "Now I am in a fix. Jack will be so cross with me."

"What did your brother do?" Amanda demanded, unconsciously tightening her hold on Frances's arm.

"Do let go, Amanda," Frances begged. "It was only a silly wager! Indeed, he meant no harm, and you must not be angry with him. Don't look like that, Amanda."

Amanda could feel the color draining from her face. A wager! He had used her to win a wager. He had allowed her to make a fool of herself. He had . . . *paid for her clothes!* A sickening wave of pain and anger and humiliation crashed over her. How could he have done such a thing? And how was she to bear it?

"Let's go back," she heard herself say faintly.

"Amanda, are you all right?" Frances peered into her face anxiously.

"No, I don't think so," she replied, smiling tightly. "But I'm not about to swoon away, if that's what you mean."

Distressed, Frances stumbled out the story until Amanda interrupted her. "I have to talk to him."

"Talk to Jack? Do you think that's a good idea?" Frances asked doubtfully.

Amanda didn't answer. A part of her had gone completely numb, while yet another part was churning with the magnitude of her emotions. For some reason, she was suddenly conscious of the sounds of people all around them. Nearby, a raucous gentleman shouted with laughter, while ripples of voices drifted across the lawns from other supper boxes, carried to her ears by the warm evening breeze. Far beyond, in the darkest thickets and groves, the nightingales sang, their haunting trills reaching Amanda's ears at the exact moment a soft eddy of air lifted her curls and gently caressed her cheek. All too soon she found they were back, and as if Amanda's gaze somehow reached out and touched him, the Marquis turned his dark head and looked up at her inquiringly.

"Lord Vale, I should like a word with you," Amanda stated, her voice sounding unnaturally strained even to her own ears.

The Marquis exchanged a swift glance with Charles Perth, and rose to his feet. "Yes, Miss Marlowe?"

"A *private* word," Amanda insisted, ignoring the little warning voice inside her head that was shrieking at the impropriety of her conduct.

All six faces gaped at the two of them, but Lady Besford was the first to recover. She took one amazed look at Amanda, a closer, even more amazed look at the Marquis, and astonished everyone present by saying unhesitantly, "Yes, go ahead, my lord. Why don't you take Amanda to see the Cascade? You will be in raptures over it, Amanda. It's quite charming—so very like a real waterfall!"

Frowning darkly, Lord Besford stood up and glared first at the Marquis, then at his wife. "Dash it, Emily, you can't allow that young rakehell to take

Amanda into the shrubbery! It ain't at all proper and I won't have it!"

"Oh, do be still, Robert!" snapped her ladyship, much annoyed. "I am sure Lord Vale is capable of comporting himself like a gentleman!"

"Your wife is correct, sir," said the Marquis solemnly. "Miss Marlowe will come to no harm while she is with me." He waited for the earl's curt nod, then added, with a small bow, "Miss Marlowe, I am at your disposal."

"Thank you," Amanda replied stiffly. For the benefit of the others, she added, "I should like very much to see the Cascade."

As soon as they were out of sight, the Marquis scanned her face apprehensively. "What's wrong, Amanda? What has happened?"

"I think you know the answer to that, my lord," she retorted, her voice quivering. "I understand that I have you to thank for all my fine new gowns. Indeed, it seems you own practically everything I am wearing!"

The Marquis swore under his breath. "So Frances told you, eh? Charles was right, then. I wonder if there is a woman alive who can keep a secret!" he said in disgust.

"Is that all you can say?" she flared.

"Amanda, please believe me when I tell you that I wanted nothing more than to help you—"

"Help me!" she cried accusingly. "And what of yourself? I believe there was some sort of wager involved, was there not?"

Vale hesitated. "Well, yes," he admitted unwillingly. "You see, Charles felt that I was . . . that is, I had been acting selfishly, of late. He wagered me his new chestnut against my being able to do some selfless act within a certain time period. It occurred to me that you were the person I would most like to profit from it."

"And you thought that making a fool out of me was unselfish, did you? My self-respect could easily be sacrificed for the sake of a *horse?*"

"Don't be ridiculous," he said impatiently. "I didn't care a jot about the damned horse, at least not after a bit. And you did not make a fool of yourself. No one could expect a naive young girl from the country to realize—"

"I don't think you know the meaning of the word *unselfish!*" Amanda interrupted furiously. "To place me in such an infamous position was the very height of arrogant, boorish selfishness! How can I even put on my gown in the morning knowing that you have paid for it? Do you have even the faintest conception of what it means to have your pride stolen from you like this?"

"So you think I am selfish, do you?" he rasped.

"I think what you *did* was selfish, yes!"

They were nowhere near anything that resembled a waterfall, for Vale had deliberately led them, with the unerring surety of one who knows his way about, to one of the more winding, isolated paths. Dragging her by the arm into one of the private arbors, the Marquis jerked Amanda around to face him.

"And the fact that the past few weeks have been made much more pleasant for you does not weigh with you in the least, is that it?" he continued, his tone growing more caustic by the minute.

295

"It has nothing to do with it! You *used* me—"

Reaching out, his hands locked on her upper arms, hauling her forcefully against his broad chest. "Don't delude yourself, Amanda," he warned her softly. "I have not even begun to use you."

Then his lips came plunging down to crush hers with an intensity that was almost violent. There was nothing loverlike in this kiss, for it was fueled by six years of bitter hurt and disillusionment, and it did not end until he felt Amanda's struggles to breathe. He allowed her only a few seconds to recover before his mouth came down once more, but gently this time, as if to apologize for his first assault.

"God, Amanda, you've no idea how much I want you," he groaned at last, his hungry eyes roving over her face.

Though her senses were reeling, Amanda's pride forced her to gasp out, "You forget yourself, my lord. Recollect that it is my cousin you should be trying to kiss."

He smiled unpleasantly. "I'd as soon kiss an iceberg as that cousin of yours. At least you've got some fire in you, sweetheart—and don't think you can hide it from me. I've enough experience with women to recognize when one has some passion in her."

"Thank you very much," she lashed back. "So I am supposed to be flattered, perhaps, that you would rather take your pleasure on me than on the lady you will wed? And what of my feelings? Do they count for nothing?" She brushed an angry tear from her cheek, and added waspishly, "Go back to your . . . your strumpets, my lord, for they know the rules of this little game you play. I am sure you must have at least a dozen of them anyway! Oh, how foolish I am! Lady Claverley tried to warn me about you, and I would not listen!"

Vale's face whitened, and a muscle at the corner of his mouth began to twitch. "What did she tell you?" he demanded tensely.

"Enough to know what kind of person you are," Amanda flung with a sob. "She said she was your . . . " The word stuck in her throat, for it conjured up vague, intolerable images of him with that horrible woman.

"My mistress," he finished, in a hateful drawl. "Yes, Amanda, that she-dog lived under my protection for nearly ten months. I suppose that makes me some sort of a depraved animal in your eyes." His piercing gaze searched her face, wordlessly beseeching her to refute his statement. "Well, does it? Answer me, damn you!" he exploded, shaking her roughly.

His words were left to hang in the air between them like an invisible wall, for at the moment Amanda was incapable of speech. His expression hardening even more, the Marquis released her abruptly, and to keep her balance, Amanda took a step back.

"So history repeats itself, and I have once more put myself beyond the pale," he remarked with savage sarcasm. "If you will allow me to escort you back to the Countess, I will then remove myself from your presence. I do trust that you will refrain from doing anything too dramatic. One suicide on my conscience is quite enough."

Unable to believe he could speak to her in so odious a fashion, Amanda avoided his gaze. "Don't c-concern yourself, my lord. I would not dream of ending my life for so trifling a matter," she managed to whisper, her throat aching with the need to weep.

The Marquis bowed sardonically. "My sentiments exactly, Miss Marlowe."

Chapter Fourteen

Confident of her charms, the girl turned and smiled at him seductively. For the past few weeks, she'd been casting out lures to him from the stage, and now that he was here he planned to reap some of the promises those sly looks had tried to sow. Her thick red hair hung almost to her waist, and experience gleamed in the almond-shaped eyes that had long ago lost whatever innocence they had ever possessed.

Damn it, if only his head would stop spinning! The Marquis had no idea how much gin he'd consumed, but he did not doubt that he was, as Charles would say, full of frisk. His mind was so blurred that he could barely recall why he had drunk so much in the first place. When he tried, a sharp memory quickened within him, but it was like touching a knife wound and he'd given it up.

He studied the girl's voluptuous figure with vague dissatisfaction. As lovely as she was, there was something displeasing about her, something that kept nagging at him. But what the devil fault could he find with such perfection?

"How may I serve you, milord?" Even when she spoke, it was with accents that were soft and pliably seductive. The corners of her full pink lips lifted invitingly, as if to assure him that with her he was free to experience whatever delights he fancied. Moving closer, she slowly entwined her arms around his neck. "Tell me your desires," she whispered in his ear.

"I wan—" He stopped, unable to complete the sentence. What the devil did he want, he thought in confusion. Then, as if by magic, the answer came to him. " 'Manda," he said, relieved that he had remembered, though he had only the haziest recollection of who Amanda was.

Those enticing lips, only inches from his own, slid into a small, reprimanding pout. "My name is Angelina, milord." She rubbed gently against him, a practiced, very effective movement that she had undoubtedly perfected at an early age.

He closed his eyes, unconsciously trying to block her out. "No, 'Manda," he insisted thickly. With his eyes shut, he was barely aware she was there, although he knew she was pressing more than her lips against him in an effort to arouse his interest. There was something odd here, he decided with detachment. Blue Ruin did not ordinarily affect him like this. He reopened his eyes, and pulled his head back to examine the girl more closely. What the deuce was it that was troubling him?

Her hair was the wrong color, that was it. He had no objection to red hair, but lately he rather thought his preference had settled upon gleaming brown tresses with rich chestnut highlights. Her eyes were a lovely coffee brown, a striking combination with that red hair, but that didn't seem quite right either. They ought to have been gray, he mulled, with flecks of molten silver dancing in their depths. And damn it, she was far too tall, her voice wasn't at all right, and her breasts were too full. With a groan of pure despair, the Marquis remembered why he had been drinking.

"Milord?" Angelina drew back, eyeing him in puzzlement. Just what did this gentleman expect of her, she wondered. Of course, he was obviously as full as can hold, but she'd not judged him to be one who would start changing personalities because of his excesses. Well, that was the aristocracy for you!

"Oh, God," he slurred, trying to think. "I'm 'fraid, ah—Angela, ish it?—that my, er, plans for the evenin' have changed . . . ah, quite shuddenly."

"Do I displease you so much, milord?" she asked him quietly. "Or is it merely that my name is not—Amanda."

"That'sh it," he slurred, then nodded gratefully. "It shounds devilish eccentric, I know. But what'sh to be done? I only take women named 'Manda to bed with me." He laughed at his own joke, unaware that Angelina's expression had softened.

"Go home to bed, milord," she advised him. "Then tomorrow, if you remember me at all, remember that I told you to go to her. If you love her that much, you must tell her so."

"I'm 'fraid to," he muttered under his breath, for-

301

getting she was there.

She sighed regretfully, wishing that this tall, handsome man could have been hers. This Amanda was either very lucky or very stupid, she reflected.

Amanda was not feeling very lucky at the moment. She was, in fact, just beginning to appreciate that her actions this evening had been disastrously impetuous. Cursing her own folly, she buried her face in her hands. Oh, why could she not have controlled her wretched tongue? Though her temper had always been quick, for the most part her good sense and ability to recognize the humor in a situation helped her to keep it under control. The times it actually got the better of her were rare, but, Lord, when it did—!

Her foolish pride had been so wounded by the discovery of the Marquis's deception that she had lashed out at him, refusing to consider the possibility that he had genuinely wanted to help her. Now that some time had passed and she was calmer, Amanda realized that it had not been his intention to insult or humiliate her, even if his actions had been somewhat ill judged. She also saw how Frances had come to play a part in the scheme, for the young Countess's fierce loyalty to her brother had been obvious from the first. No wonder Frances always seemed so ill at ease whenever Amanda brought up the subject of Madame Claret. Her friend had not enjoyed the role her brother had asked her to play, and had done it only to please him.

But beyond all of this, Amanda was sickened by the knowledge that she had turned the man she loved against her, that she had destroyed whatever affection he might have felt for her. She had cherished the notion that even if he married Eve they might still continue to be friends, but now this hope was shattered. Even an occasional glimpse of him would have been better than losing him forever, but now — ! Now, she would not dare to show him her face. He obviously believed that he had done her a great service and that she was an ungrateful little idiot, which in a way she supposed she was. My God, she could just imagine the trouble he had gone to on her account!

Immersed in thought, Amanda missed the light tap on her door, and when Lady Besford peeped anxiously into the room, Amanda simply stared at her, a blank look in her eye.

"Ah, Amanda, there you are. Good gracious, child, I thought you would be in bed by now. May I come in?"

"Of course, ma' am, but I'm afraid I won't be very good company," Amanda told her bleakly.

Garbed in her dressing gown, the Countess swept across the room and held out her arms. "Amanda, my poor lamb, why didn't you tell me?"

Amanda hesitated only an instant, and then her face was buried in Lady Besford's bosom, tears streaming down her cheeks. "How could I tell you?" she sobbed. "I thought you would be shocked. I thought you would say I was horrid to think of him at all. And it is frightfully shocking, you cannot deny it! Oh, ma' am, what am I to do? I am so

303

miserable!"

"First you must have a good cry," the Countess said, stroking her hair gently. "Then we will talk."

After a bit, Amanda drew back and attempted a watery smile. "What I did tonight was quite awful, wasn't it?"

Lady Besford withdrew a fresh handkerchief from her pocket and offered it to Amanda. "Well, it was a trifle indiscreet, my dear. Fortunately, there was no one in our party who is likely to spread it about. Lady Rosebery, I daresay, will have some explaining to do to that husband of hers. With his political aspirations, it cannot do him any good to have a brother-in-law who is forever becoming involved with scandals! *He* will see to it that no one finds out. Charles Perth is very close to Lord Vale, and I have never heard that he was a gossip. So I think we may rest easy on that score. But, my dear Amanda, the look on Lord Vale's face when he left us —! I have never seen a man look so — so *black!* I think you had better tell me what happened."

"Oh, it was dreadful!" Amanda said incoherently. "Lady Rosebery told me — not meaning to, you understand, for she is quite loyal to him, which you must admit is perfectly natural! And she would not have told me, but I *did* press her for an explanation —"

"Amanda," soothed her ladyship, "try to calm down. Start at the beginning."

Sighing shakily, Amanda dabbed at her eyes and tried again. "Lord Vale accepted some sort of a . . . a wager that he could do some . . . selfless deed, and

304

he . . . well, the long and short of it is, ma'am, that he decided *I* was the one who needed his help. Somehow, he convinced his sister to assist him, and together they deceived me about that dressmaker, Madame Claret. It seems she was actually someone called Albertine Le Rougement and—"

"Albertine Le Rougement!" echoed Lady Besford, looking thunderstruck. "Good heavens! Do you mean to tell me *she* is responsible for—Oh, lord, Amanda! Do you know who she is?"

When Amanda shook her head, Lady Besford said, "She is, or was, rather, one of the leading French *coutouriers* before that shockingly horrid revolution. At one time, the name 'Madame Le Rougement' was virtually synonymous with the word 'fashion.' My God, Amanda, it is said she even made gowns for Marie Antoinette!"

Amanda's eyes widened. "Then that explains why Frances stared at her so! And why Madame's remarks seemed so odd! I could not understand it at the time."

"Odd is not the word for it! Though her mother was a lowly grisette, it is said her father was a French aristocrat. He must have assisted her financially, for she became astonishingly successful, and did not leave France until that madman Robespierre began signing death warrants left and right. By that time, she was far too rich for it to be safe for her to stay, or to need to work ever again!" She shook her head in frank amazement. "I haven't heard a thing about that woman in more than twenty years. In fact, I would have thought she would be dead by now. Well, then *that* explains why your gowns are so exquisite! But Amanda, do you mean to tell me that Lord Vale actually arranged for Madame Le Rougement to — Good God! The man paid for everything, didn't he?"

Amanda flushed with mortification. "I know what a fool I must look. But truly, ma'am, if it had not been for Frances assuring me that it was perfectly acceptable, I don't believe I would have done it."

"It was very wrong of Lady Frances," pronounced the Countess frankly. "I quite shudder to think of the scandal should the tale leak out. Amanda, a lady does not accept *any* article of clothing from a gentleman, unless she is his mistress, or of course, his wife."

"I know that," replied Amanda in muffled accents.

"The important thing is to discover *who* was involved in the wager beside Lord Vale. Do you know, Amanda?" Lady Besford asked anxiously.

"Frances said it was Charles Perth."

Lady Besford's expression relaxed. "Well, it is probably all right then. If it was a private wager, that is. And it must have been," she reasoned aloud, "for if it was not, you would already have been ruined. I think we may breath easy on that score."

Amanda bit her lip. "But, ma' am, do you think I should make some effort to repay him? It will be a great deal of money, I suppose — "

"Absolutely not!" affirmed her ladyship. "A great deal, indeed! It must have been a staggering sum. I cannot think why he would have done it unless — " She broke off, frowning. "What was he to gain, did she say?"

Amanda looked down at her lap. "A horse, I am given to understand."

"*A horse!* But a horse would not have cost nearly as much as he must have spent on your gowns! I think there must have been another reason, my dear. One that you can guess, perhaps."

"If there was such a reason, it no longer exists," Amanda said despondently. "Oh, ma'am, I said the most dreadful things to him! It was like the time I lost my temper with Aunt Marlowe, only far, far worse! If he comes to the house to see Eve, I simply cannot face him. I think I should go back to Hampshire."

"Run away, you mean?" asked the Countess, raising her brows. "Amanda, there is no need for that. We will go on as before, and pretend nothing has happened. You will continue to wear your lovely gowns, and if the worst happens and the story gets out, I will say that *I* bought the gowns, as indeed I had every intention of doing before you told me of this 'Madame Claret' business! Anyway, do not worry about Lord Vale. I judge him to be a man who will not give up easily. Once his temper has cooled, he will be back, I think. As for his betrothal to Eve, I don't know what to say except that it's amazing how things often work out in the least expected ways."

"This time I find that very hard to believe," Amanda answered, her voice barely above a whisper.

* * *

Mr. Perth slowly made his way up Albemarle Street, an absent frown furrowing his brow. How ironic it was, he thought, that of all the women that Jack had attracted over the years, the only two that he had ever really wanted had succeeded in causing him pain. Dash it, this wager business had not worked out at all the way he had hoped. He had sought to break through the Marquis's defensive shell, that self-imposed wall of indifference that had long ago ceased to serve its original purpose. Instead of protecting Jack only long enough for him to heal his inner wounds, the shell had thickened, hardening his friend in some way it was difficult to pinpoint.

Well, he supposed that in a way he had accomplished his goal. After all, never since that time with Charlotte had Jack shown the least sign that he cared for any of his women. But hang it, he hadn't wanted Jack to be hurt all over again!

It was dashed unfortunate that Jack had allowed himself to be bound to Eve Marlowe in such a way. That young lady, he reflected, seemed to possess an alarmingly Machiavellian lack of scruples that quite frankly made him shudder. Charles sighed, not envying his friend one bit. Well, he'd best go and see how Jack was faring this morning.

The Marquis was shaving when he arrived, and from the dark scowl on his friend's face and the circumstance that the curtains were almost completely drawn, Charles deduced that his friend was suffering from more than a broken heart.

"Feeling a trifle out of sorts, are you?" Charles inquired delicately.

The Marquis cast him a sour look and swore fluently under his breath. "As long as you're here, hand me that towel, will you? And don't talk so loudly," he muttered.

Charles tossed him the towel and sat down. "I always have my man shave me. Can't think why you want to do it yourself."

"I do it myself," the Marquis ground out, "because I can't stand the sight or sound of the fellow when I'm feeling so damned—ouch! Damn it, I cut myself."

"That's why I have Perrot do it," remarked Charles. "Hasn't nicked me once in the five years that—oh, all right. I can see you don't want to hear about it right now."

"Acute of you," remarked Vale, eyeing him grimly. "I warn you, I'm in a damnable mood this morning, Charles. So try not to be too sensitive, will you?"

Charles crossed his legs and sighed. "Where did you go last night?"

Vale dabbed once more at his chin and threw down the towel. "As far as I can remember," he said, shrugging, "I sat down in the bookroom and drank myself into a stupor. Then, I went to find a woman."

Charles frowned. "And did that solve your problems?"

"Damn it, no!" The Marquis winced and lowered his voice. "I searched out that opera dancer, the one with the red hair. But it was no good, Charles. I found I didn't want her after all. So I left."

"Maybe you're not the rakish fellow you think you are, Jack," Charles suggested.

"If you're planning to read me a homily, you can leave," Vale told him acidly.

Charles ignored him and asked the question foremost in his mind. "What happened between you and Amanda last night?"

The Marquis laughed unpleasantly. "Why, you and she would make the ideal pair, Charles. I received a semihysterical lecture on what a selfish bastard I am and how I had used her to forward my own interests. I am quite sunk in her estimation, particularly now that she knows all about my strumpets."

"Your what?" Charles echoed sharply.

"My strumpets," Vale replied bitterly. "My little Prudence is sure I have at least a dozen of 'em. Unfortunately, dear Alexandra seems to have been dripping poison into her pretty little ears. It must please you to know that you were perfectly correct about my beloved sister's inability to keep her mouth shut. My efforts to make Amanda's life more tolerable have only succeeded in damaging her pride and causing her humiliation."

Suddenly the Marquis's restraint cracked. "Oh, God, Charles!" he groaned in despair. *"How* did I manage to make such a mull of everything? After all these years, I finally found a girl I absolutely adore and I've gone and killed whatever affection she felt for me! I love her, Charles! I saw the disgust in her eyes. It was like Charlotte all over again," he added, his blue eyes haunted by the memory.

"Now that's gammon, Jack. You know she's nothing like Charlotte," Charles told him desperately.

The Marquis threw his long body into the nearest

chair. "No, I suppose she's not," he grunted after a long pause in which he grappled for composure. "Look, do me a favor, will you?" he continued brusquely. "Next time you want to make a wager, do it with someone else. Your inspired method of teaching me the fine art of altruism has made my life a worse hell than it already was."

"Dash it, Jack, I'm sorry," said Charles, looking utterly miserable.

Vale saw his expression and cursed himself inwardly. "My God, I am a selfish bastard, aren't I? Look, I shouldn't have said that. It's just that I've a devil of a head right now, along with everything else. Don't blame yourself, do you hear me? It's my own stupid fault."

"I hear you," Charles answered, surprised and gratified. "Y'know, I was wondering, any chance Lord Andrew will come up to scratch?"

"Carisbrooke?" Vale snorted. "I can't in all sanity believe he'd be interested in taking Eve off my hands. Thanks for the idea, but I think not, Charles."

Charles's face fell. "Well, the fellow has been paying her a deuced amount of attention lately."

"Yes, perhaps I ought to drop a word in his ear," agreed the Marquis mockingly. "I say, Lord Andrew, would you mind doing me a bit of a favor? Nothing much, just offer for Eve Marlowe, will you?"

"Well, it was just a thought," Charles pointed out patiently. "Then the only thing left to try is plain reason, though it don't usually work well with females. Tell Eve Marlowe the circumstances and ask her to cry off. Tell Amanda you love her, and ask her

311

to forgive you."

"I'll think about it," the Marquis answered curtly. "But for now I'm posting out to Stirlings. I've got responsibilities there I can't continue to ignore. Look for me to be back in a week or so."

Charles cleared his throat in embarrassment. "Er, any chance you'll be back in time for m'grandmother's ball, Jack?" he mumbled. "It's deuced dull, I know, but she told me to bring you." He shuddered at the memory. "Promised her I would," he added pleadingly.

With resignation and an odd sense of foreboding, the Marquis agreed. "Why not?" he said flippantly. "At least *she* likes me the way I am."

Everard Frome's lazy eyes examined Lady Claverley's face, missing nothing of her displeasure. Objectively, he considered her one of the most beautiful women he had ever seen, but he did not think she would age well. It would be, he mused, her own narrowmindedness that would be her undoing, for Alexandra was the type of woman who believed that a female without beauty was also without worth.

"Well, Alex?" he said, quizzing her as usual. "You're looking a little sullen this evening. Too many late nights, perhaps?"

For a fleeting moment he had pitied her, but the emotion vanished as soon as she spoke.

"To what do I owe the honor of this meeting?" she asked sarcastically.

"Are you aware that Vale has left town?" he said

312

abruptly.

"I am," she responded with equal shortness. "What of it?"

He looked at her curiously. "Well, Alex, would this not be a good time for us to strike?"

"You want to strike when he is gone? Like a coward? I thought you wanted to *snatch the girl right from under his nose!* You have changed, Everard."

He eyed her resentfully. "Nonsense."

"Yes, you have," she taunted him. "I think you're going soft. For God's sake, have you made *any* progress with the girl?"

He shrugged indolently. "She wants nothing to do with me."

She stared at him. "And you'll let that stop you?" she sneered. "Oh, a fine revenge indeed! I had no idea you were so spineless, Everard."

"You think it deters me?" he told her cuttingly. "You have such a simple mind, Alex. If things are not spelled out for you, you think they do not happen. My plans for revenge are the reason I arranged this meeting with you, for I may need some slight aid from you."

She brightened "Why did you not say so?"

He shrugged again. "Why should I?"

"Have you been able to discover what day he means to return?" she asked, following Godfrey's instructions.

"Friday," he answered, "for the Torrington ball." He chewed the tip of his finger. "I thought to be finished with the girl by then."

Her mocking laughter rang sharply in his ears.

313

"You're afraid of him, aren't you? You're seven years older than he, and you're beginning to feel it!"

He flashed her a look of annoyance. "Don't be ridiculous."

She leaned forward. "Then *why* do you want him to be gone? Why don't you wait until he is back, and *do* what you said before. *Snatch* the girl right from under his nose, Everard! I thought that was what you wanted. Now you act as though you fear he will chase after you! If you plan it right, you can seduce the girl before he finds you, and then, Everard, then, with luck, the confrontation you have been so long denied will be yours!"

For a long moment he looked at her. "It *is* a temptation, I admit. I wonder why I hesitate."

"Like I said, you're going soft," she jeered. "Does your sister mean nothing to you anymore? Have you forgotten how he made her suffer?"

Frome's fingers bit into her shoulders. "Damn it, Alex, do not play with me like this! You don't know what I am capable of doing to you."

This time she said nothing, but merely waited for him to release her. Carefully, she said, "Amanda Marlowe will be at the ball also. Perth likes her, and saw to it that she was invited."

"My, you have been busy, haven't you? How do you pay your network of spies, I wonder?" Frome swung around and ogled her briefly. "Never mind, I know the answer to that. Do you have anything else to tell me?"

"I have a suggestion," she offered casually.

"Yes?"

"Use the Countess of Rosebery as bait."

Frome rubbed his chin, his eyes narrowed in thought. "The charming Lady Rosebery is quite friendly with our little pigeon, isn't she? I see what you are driving at. If kind-hearted little Amanda thought her friend Frances needed her . . . why she would rush to her side, wouldn't she? What a diabolical mind, you have, Alex. I am all admiration, for in truth I did not suspect it of you."

"You underestimate me, Everard," the widow muttered softly.

"You've given me much to think upon," the Baron remarked. "I know you'll forgive me if I do not linger. If I do decide to wait until Friday, I will need you to help me. Do you have a card for the Torrington ball?"

"I do," she told him triumphantly. "The Dowager likes to stir up trouble. Why, that's where I finally met success with Jack, only last year. Who knows? Perhaps, I shall be as lucky again."

She waved her hand at him as he let himself out the door, and waited until his footsteps faded away and she heard the front door close. Then without moving from her chair, she called out, "Well, how did I do?"

The door opposite the one Frome had used swung slowly open, and Godfrey Forrester stepped into the room. He smiled broadly, and as always, she noticed how his eyes never seemed to contain much emotion. "You did well, my poppet. You surprised me, in fact." He laughed scornfully. "Frome is not stupid, but he needs his hatred to be hot for it to serve him

315

well. Now, I prefer my hatred cold. It's a far better arrangement, Alex, for then it does not rule you." He held out his hand and she rose and went to him at once.

"Yes, the fierce Lord Frome is falling into my trap very nicely. It does gall me a little to let you take credit for all my ideas, but it matters not so very much. He and my cousin will discover soon enough who controls their strings."

Chapter Fifteen

Despite the fact that Amanda did not relent in her resolve to have nothing to do with Lord Frome, the Baron persisted in calling on her each day. It was both frustrating and depressing to receive so much attention from a man she did not care for, when she had neither seen nor heard from the one she loved with all her heart.

It was ridiculous, Amanda reflected, for what reason could he possibly have for pursuing her? Moodily, she inspected the recently delivered cluster of white roses he had sent, her fingers reaching out to touch one of the soft, beautifully shaped petals. For a brief moment, she allowed herself to pretend that it was the Marquis who had sent the roses, but the fantasy only brought an increase to the throbbing ache that was making her life almost unbearable. She gave herself a mental shake. Why did she continue to torment herself with such nonsense?

But there was no way to check such thoughts. He filled her mind practically every waking moment of the day, the image of his dark, lean face floating in front of her as clearly as if he were really there. She was only a little comforted by the knowledge that Eve had heard nothing from him either, for she knew it was her own sharp words that had driven him away.

Though it must have wounded her cousin to see the Baron dangling after Amanda, Eve made no remark, masking whatever she was feeling as effectively as ever. Lord Andrew Carisbrooke had invited her cousin to a picnic the following week, but even that milestone had failed to rouse the other girl to enthusiasm. Privately, Amanda considered this just another bit of proof that Eve was suffering from the pangs of unrequited love. It was totally unlike her cousin to fail to boast and preen after receiving the attentions of so notable a gentleman as Lord Andrew.

For herself, Amanda continued in her efforts to discourage her more ardent suitors. Mr. Wilcox had made her an offer, which she had politely and firmly refused, while Lord Castlebury had written her a flowery apology and renewed his suit on bended knee. It had taken all her tact and patience to convince him that his hopes were in vain. But to her relief he had finally gone away and not come back. She was spared such a scene with Sir Edward of the butterfly collection, for he appeared to have transferred his affections to, of all people, Miss Maria Warfield. So it was only Lord Frome who continued to be a problem.

Amanda did not think that Lady Besford had even

an inkling that her niece was languishing over the wicked Baron, or if she did, it was not at all evident. Indeed, the Countess had evinced shock at his repeated visits, and had heartily approved Amanda's decision to shun his advances.

"Of course, Amanda, you will know that I mean no offense," her ladyship remarked on the morning of the Torrington ball, "when I tell you that I cannot think why the man is suddenly dangling after you. I don't scruple to tell you that he's a purse-pinched philanderer, my dear, and I'm glad you have the sense to see it. But I would have thought that even *he* would not stoop to such a level. After all, he can hardly wish to offer you marriage, and to be quite frank that leaves us with only one alternative. And *that* does not seem right either, for I see no reason why he should believe you would accept a carte blanche! If only we knew where—oh well, ahem, never mind that. I wonder if we shall be seeing Lord Andrew today. Now *there* is a fine-looking man! If only Eve would try to be a little more conciliating with him. Whatever is the matter with her, do you think?"

"I'm . . . not entirely sure, ma'am," Amanda replied, strangely reluctant to mention her suspicions. It seemed wrong to betray her cousin when Eve so obviously wished to conceal her feelings from those around her. If there was one thing Amanda could understand, it was the desire to maintain one's dignity.

The Countess looked a little dejected. "All this matchmaking business seemed so much easier with

319

Priscilla. Of course, she was very shy, and had difficulty talking to people, but at least I always knew which way the wind was blowing. Now, everything seems to be at sixes and sevens, and no one is behaving in the least predictably."

Amanda flushed a little. "I'm sorry if I've caused you trouble, ma'am. I had no intention of—"

"Oh no, I did not mean you, Amanda," Lady Besford corrected immediately. "I mean these men! And my niece! You know, I can fully appreciate your feelings, my dear, but sometimes I suspect my niece does not even possess any! And the gentlemen are all acting so oddly. Well, at least I was right about Mr. Wilcox. It is too bad you could not like him, but of course I see that he could not even begin to compare with—" She broke off, then continued guiltily, "Oh dear! And I promised myself I would not say anything to distress you."

"Don't worry about me," Amanda said stoutly. "I'll manage. Tell me what you think I should wear to Lady Torrington's this evening."

This question diverted her ladyship long enough to lead her away from a subject Amanda did not feel able to discuss, even with the Countess. Eventually, she managed to slip away to her room, where she made a fair effort at reading a novel she had borrowed from Hookham's lending library before falling into a restless doze for most of the afternoon.

Much later, as she dressed for yet another of the seemingly endless round of balls, Amanda began to wonder whether the Marquis would be present. If he was, would he ignore her? And what would she say to him if he did not? Nervously, she checked her appearance in the looking glass, hoping her fears did not show. She took little notice of the fetching picture she made, her silvery eyes wide and anxious, her short, dark hair curling riotously about her head in a style which became her to perfection. To Amanda, her eyes merely mirrored her pain, and her face looked pale and drawn. This was hardly surprising, she thought morosely, considering how many nights she had lain awake, her heart aching with loneliness and despair. "Oh, John," she whispered, a catch in her voice. "Will you be there tonight? Oh, where are you, my dearest love . . ."

The Marquis had just returned from Sussex, and was at that moment running his fingers through his black hair in an equal state of depression. He was aware that he would in all probability see Amanda this night, and for the first time in a very long while, was feeling unsure and apprehensive about an impending encounter with a member of the opposite sex. He thought he would rather do almost anything than face her as if nothing had happened in front of hundreds of other people. If only he could speak to her privately, but then what good would it do? His sense of honor tied him to Eve, and it was frustrating to know that he had no one but himself to blame. Still, the notion that Amanda held him in disgust caused him no small amount of anguish. His shell—that cynical facade with which he had for so long held his emotions at bay—had at last failed to protect him.

He went and poured out a drink, and had just sat down in his favorite wing chair when a footman appeared, tapping discreetly at the bookroom door.

"A message was just delivered for you, my lord."

"Bring it in," he replied curtly. Accepting the note, the Marquis scanned it quickly before tossing it onto the table beside him with a small snort. "Charles, you puddingheart," he muttered. Closing his eyes, he leaned back, thinking it odd that Charles would wish to arrive at his grandmother's ball so late.

He would have been astonished to learn that Charles was at almost the same instant receiving a similar message, written in a very clever forgery of the Marquis's own hand.

Amanda shivered and pulled the hood of her cloak further over her face as she stepped from the carriage, assisted by an impressively liveried and thoroughly soaked footman in the employ of the Dowager Viscountess of Torrington. He quickly escorted her up the steps to the house, while two more, equally wet footmen lent their supporting arms to her cousin and Lady Besford. The weather was as gloomy as Amanda's spirits, and her fatigue had only been partially alleviated by her nap.

Charles's grandmother resided in one of the finest mansions in London, its enviable location on the Green Park side of Arlington Street. Amanda had met the Dowager Lady Torrington twice before, and she had to admit that the old woman *was* rather terrifying, if one was unwise enough to take her seriously. Mr. Perth had regaled her with stories of his childhood in which his grandmother had figured as some sort of frightful hobgoblin. No wonder he had dreaded having to visit her, she thought sympathetically. A child would not have realized that most of the woman's ferocity was mere bluster.

A purple turban boasting several large peacock feathers adorned the head that turned and fixed its eagle eye first on Amanda, then Eve.

"Where's that grandson of mine?" demanded the Dowager, looking back and forth between the two cousins. "Why the devil ain't he here yet?"

Both girls disclaimed any knowledge of Mr. Perth's whereabouts, and Amanda was grateful to be able to escape from the Dowager's razor-edged gaze. She could easily envisage a reason for Charles Perth's tardiness, but it was scarcely one she could repeat to his grandmother.

The ballroom was rapidly filling with the usual crowd of fashionables, and Amanda paused a few steps into the room, automatically searching the shifting, glittering mass of people for some sign of the Marquis. The din of chattering voices set her teeth on edge, and she was on the verge of retreating on the pretext that her hair needed attention, when someone tapped her on the shoulder.

"Evening, Miss Marlowe."

With difficulty, Amanda swallowed her distaste. "Good evening, Mr. Forrester," she replied with reserve.

Godfrey raised his brows slightly. "Surprised to see

323

you here, tonight. Thought you would have been, well, too concerned about Jack."

The mere mention of his name made her heart begin to thump. "Concerned, Mr. Forrester? I do not take your meaning."

Godfrey shook his head. "His condition looks bad, I hear."

Though she tried to hide the jolt of shock caused by his words, Amanda could not prevent herself from inhaling sharply. "G-Gracious! What has happened to him?"

The ease with which he could manipulate her caused a wave of pure excitement to wash over Godfrey. "Why, he's extremely ill," he said casually. "I'm amazed you haven't heard. I thought everyone knew."

He sucked in his cheeks to hide his smile as she turned away, too distraught to notice her own lack of manners. He had planted the seed, and in a few minutes Frome was going to give it a little water.

Amanda wandered out of the huge ballroom, wrinkling her brow in weary perplexity. Why would such information be kept from her, she puzzled, unless—of course! Lady Besford knew how low she had been feeling and might very well have taken steps to ensure she was not told news which her ladyship would believe she could not handle. Such intentions were kind, but unnecessary, Amanda mused with a frown. She was not such a widgeon that she needed to be cosseted in such a fashion.

Lost in thought, she was surprised when a footman stepped in front of her and bowed. "Miss

Marlowe?" the man inquired politely.

She glanced up. "Yes?"

"A message was just delivered for you, miss."

"Thank you." With foreboding, Amanda took the envelope and examined it, waiting for the man to leave before she ripped it open.

Amanda,
   Forgive me for Disturbing you at such a time but I must speak to you on a matter of Great Urgency. I went first to Berkeley Square, but learn'd you were at the ball in Arlington Street. I await you even now in my chariot, close by in Bennet Street. Do not tell Anyone, for the matter involves Someone whom I am convinced we both Care For, and the utmost Discretion is Essential! Come at once, Amanda, and do not Fail me!

                              Yours most affectionately,
                                        Frances

Beginning to tremble, Amanda crushed the note to her breast. Dear Lord, what had happened? Was he ill, as Mr. Forrester suggested, or had something even worse occurred? Without the slightest hesitation, she hurried to retrieve her cloak, ignoring the curious looks she received from the people she passed. An uninterested footman opened the huge front door for her, and Amanda stepped outside and pulled her hood forward to protect her face from the driving rain.

She found the chariot easily, and though she was a

little surprised that no face peered out the window to greet her, Amanda raised her hand and tapped upon the wet glass. Suddenly, the door was flung open and a pair of strong arms shot out to pull her unceremoniously inside.

"I fear I must apologize, Miss Marlowe," said Everard Frome, depositing her on the seat opposite himself, "for not welcoming you with more formality. Allow me to assist you in removing that wet cloak."

Amanda stared at the Baron in shock. "Where is Frances?" she whispered, her mouth going abruptly dry.

He shrugged, eyeing her. "Home in her bed, I suppose."

The complete indifference in his voice caused a spurt of anger to run through her, banishing the almost paralyzing terror that had threatened her briefly. "How *dare* you sit there and speak like that?" she cried, clenching her hands into fists. "I demand you explain what this is all about!"

Lord Frome chuckled and reached across to pull off her hood. "You are a little spitfire, aren't you? Come, take off your cloak and let me look at you."

She struck at his hand, and he laughed again. "Amanda, this lively display is commendable, but unnecessary. You have lost the game, and must now concede to the victor—myself, in this instance."

She examined him for signs of intoxication. "I don't know what you're talking about, and frankly, I wonder if you do either."

"Oh, no," he told her, shaking his head in amuse-

326

ment. "I am not foxed. There is a good reason for this, which I will tell you as soon as you do as I request."

Reluctantly, Amanda removed her wet cloak and laid it on the seat beside her. "I cannot think of a reason that could justify your actions. If you are not foxed, my lord, then you must be mad. Now, please tell me what you have done with Lady Rosebery."

His black eyes hardened as she spoke. "I am not *mad,* Amanda, and I already told you where she is. The note you received was a ruse, nothing more. It served its purpose, which was to lure you into my chariot." He shifted slightly, glancing at the darkness outside. "Actually, it's the first bit of forgery I've ever done, and a poor effort at that. But it was good enough. It brought you to me and so, at last, I can begin to settle an old score."

"What old score?" she asked, starting to grow nervous again.

This time his smile held no amusement. "Six years ago, the man you fancy yourself in love with seduced and then abandoned my sister. She committed suicide rather than face the shame. For that, he is going to be punished."

"And you really believe he did this?" Amanda inquired, sounding a little scornful.

He leaned forward and took one of her hands, absently rubbing the palm with his thumb. "The story is true. I sympathize with your desire to vindicate him, but you cannot."

She snatched her hand away. "I think it is farradiddle! And what have I done to you, my lord, that

327

you must include me in this? What imagined grudge do you bear me?"

He looked her straight in the face. "None at all, but you happen to be the woman he loves. If I seduce and ruin you, he will suffer immeasurable pain, I think."

Amanda's eyes widened. "You *are* mad!" she protested vehemently. "And you are also quite, quite wrong! Lord Vale does not love me, and even if he did, this is hardly an honorable way to deal with your . . . your anger and sorrow over what happened to your sister."

It was his turn to look scornful. "That's doing it a little too brown, my dear. It's been obvious for some time that he's in love with you. And it may not be honorable, but it will definitely be effective." His mouth twisted bitterly. "As for honor, I don't want to hear the word. Tell me, where was his sense of honor when he used my sister like a common harlot?"

Amanda did not answer, for although she thought him mistaken, it was clear that he sincerely believed everything he said. Instead, she glanced around the interior of the carriage in search of a possible weapon, but her eyes fell on nothing that might serve the purpose. Shivering, she wished he had allowed her to retain her cloak. Ball gowns were not designed for warmth, she thought wryly, but rather to display one's physical charms. She shot him another look, and despite the gloom, she realized that he had fallen to studying her, a new, frankly assessing glint lighting his dark eyes.

To distract him, she said, "Where are you taking me?"

"To an inn," he answered emotionlessly. "A place where people look the other way if they hear a woman scream."

"You are a monster," she told him in a low voice. "If you think I'll make this easy for you, you're insane."

He straightened his position, crossing his arms over his chest. "Come, my dear, I know I'm not the one you want, but sometimes we must make the best of what life grants us. *I'm* not about to cavil, I'll have you know." He tilted his head to the side. "I've always found you very attractive, did you know?"

Amanda's lip curled. "Yes, you've lately made that quite clear, though the genesis of that attraction seems to me of fairly recent origin. I may be naive, Lord Frome, but I am not a complete fool. This game has been going on for some time, has it not?"

He inclined his head, watching her lazily.

"So it began with my cousin. You toyed with her, then when you began to imagine that Lord Vale preferred me, you transferred—"

"It began," he interrupted harshly, "six years ago. Don't imagine that I've just been sitting around doing nothing all these years. This is merely the climax, Amanda. I have been hounding your precious Jack for a very long time. I see to it that every sin he commits gets exaggerated, every fault he possesses becomes magnified. What he wants, I take from him. It's as plain as that."

"What's plain is that you have allowed your judg-

329

ment to become warped!" Amanda snapped. "And what of the other innocent people you hurt? What of me? What of Eve?"

His eyes flickered. "What of Eve? I have not harmed her."

"No?" countered Amanda indignantly. "There is more than one way to harm a person. Do you deny that you've been meeting her clandestinely?"

"No, I will not deny it," he responded, his words a little clipped.

"And did it not occur to you that her emotions might become involved?" she continued sarcastically. "Even I am conscious of your charm, my lord, and my affections are . . . otherwise engaged. My cousin may seem sophisticated, but she has no more experience with men than I."

He frowned slightly. "Did she tell you this?"

"She did not have to," Amanda replied tersely. "It has been obvious to me that she is pining for you. You do not deserve it, of course, but love is not a sensible creature."

"Love," he repeated, sneering a little. "I know well enough that your cousin has the infinite good sense to prefer me to Jack. But love is quite another matter, my dear."

For an instant, it seemed to Amanda that there existed a regretful note in his voice, and she decided to press any advantage she might have gained. "But you admire my cousin, do you not?"

"Eve Marlowe is one of the most beautiful women I have ever seen," he answered. "And yes, of course I admire her. She and I are two of a kind, I suppose."

"And you will not make the least push to win her?"

"You mean ask her to be my wife?" he said incredulously. "What makes you think she would accept? I can offer her nothing, nothing at all. I am a gamester, Amanda. Gamesters do not make admirable husbands."

"You could offer her yourself," she suggested. "If you do not at least try, you will never know what her answer might be."

"I know what her answer would be," he told her irascibly. "She would laugh at me. Your cousin is a practical woman, my dear. She wants wealth, and the title and position to go with it."

"Well, you have the title," said Amanda, attempting to reason with him. "And she has the fortune. You are both unconventional people. Perhaps it would work."

For a long moment, he did not speak. "Amanda, are you seriously telling me that your cousin is in love with me?"

His voice had changed, and Amanda felt a flicker of hope. "Yes, Lord Frome, that is exactly what I am saying."

"But she would never marry me," he argued, half to himself. "She knows I am a fortune hunter, a gamester, a . . . a man with no principles at all . . ."

Amanda smiled for the first time since entering the carriage. "That is no secret," she agreed, "and yet she loves you still. My cousin is an unusual girl, my lord. One thing I know, and that is that Eve will always do precisely as she wishes for she has no one to

331

stop her. Her father is dead, and her mother dotes upon her to the point of folly. However, I do not like to encourage you too much. I sincerely doubt she would marry a man who has seduced and ruined her own cousin."

His glance was both comprehending and a little rueful. *"Ay, there's the rub,* is that it? I believe you have a diplomatic streak in you, Amanda."

"So will you take me back?" she asked hopefully.

He gazed at her ponderingly. The idea of revenge had for so long been a firmly established part of his life that it caused him quite a shock to realize that much of his lust for it had quietly faded away. Other things had lately taken precedence, leaving this insane plan to injure an innocent woman to sour in his stomach.

"No," he sighed at last. "I won't do that. But you have convinced me that this scheme is mad, and I will not force myself on you. You see, I have made certain arrangements with Lady Claverley. Jack will shortly be following at our heels, and I mean for him to find us. I do not intend to pass up an opportunity to, shall we say, make him suffer a little more."

Amanda's newfound hopes evaporated. "What? You do not mean to kill him!" she cried despairingly.

"Kill him?" he echoed mockingly. "Now, Amanda, would Eve approve of that? I doubt she would care if I bloodied him a little, but murder—! I think not."

Privately, Amanda was not sure of even this, but she held her tongue. Just then the carriage lurched a little, reminding her that they would soon reach their destination. It also jarred her memory upon another point. "But what part does Godfrey Forrester play in this?" she inquired suddenly.

Frome had closed his eyes, but at this he opened them and gave her a puzzled look. "Forrester! Why, none at all. What gave you that notion?"

"But it was he that told me Lord Vale was ill. He told me everyone knew. That part is not true, is it?"

Frome's brows snapped together. "He told you Vale was *ill?* But how could he know—? That was my original plan, but I rewrote the note, and omitted that part of it. How the devil would he have known? Why would Alex tell him, unless—" He grew silent, obviously thinking hard.

The carriage began to slow, warning Amanda that they had reached their destination. Without consulting Lord Frome, she redonned her cloak, and attempted to see through the rain-streaked glass. She had just made out that they had entered the interior courtyard of an inn, when the Baron spoke. "Pull that hood over your face," he ordered curtly, "and don't let anyone see you. We shall attempt to preserve your reputation for a little longer."

Amanda did as she was told, and when the coachman pulled open the door and let down the steps, he was, to his regret, unable to take another goggle at the face of the little ladybird his lord and master had so easily captured.

Treading carefully on the wet, uneven cobbles, she peeked out at her surroundings. Dark green ivy crawled up the walls of the old, half-timbered inn, and even Amanda's inexperienced eyes recognized the signs of neglect. She suspected that they had left the main posting road, for the majority of the hostelries and coaching houses along such routes were made prosperous by their considerable trade, as this so obviously was not. That it lacked in upkeep was even more evident when they entered the dingy tap room, where they were greeted by a ferret-eyed innkeeper whose slovenly appearance and ingratiating manner made her shudder.

The man bowed deeply. "Welcome to the Bell and Bottle, my lord. We've been expecting you. Your lordship's rooms have been made ready."

"Excellent," replied Lord Frome smoothly. "We will require some refreshments. Some hot tea for the lady and some brandy for me."

The man bowed again, nearly scraping his nose on the floor. "Certainly, my lord. Allow me to show you the way, my lord."

They followed him out of the tap room and down a long, dark passageway to another room, in which a small fire was struggling against the draught to stay alive. On either side of the fireplace stood a solid oak settle, but the remainder of this room's furnishings, though shabby, were more comfortably modern. It was clearly the inn's best private parlor, but Lord Frome was not satisfied.

"The room is too chilly. I want the fire built up immediately. Where does that door lead?"

The innkeeper glanced at the door on the far side of the room. "Only to another room such as this one, my lord. Smaller and less comfortable — and of course, empty."

The Baron nodded shortly. "Very well. See to the

fire and the tea. Also, I shall not be requiring an upstairs chamber after all. And later, I believe we shall have some company. Do not attempt to stop whoever comes to find me."

The innkeeper gave Amanda a crude, rather speculative glance, and she was glad she still wore the concealing hood. "No upstairs room, my lord?" he whined. "But I took great trouble to prepare my very best chamber for your lordship's, ah, needs."

"You will still be paid, if that's what concerns you," Lord Frome cut in. "Now go and do as I bid, and be sure you knock when you return."

The man shuffled off in disgruntled silence, and Amanda threw off her mantle. "This is a dreadful place, my lord. Whatever made you choose it?"

The Baron smiled wryly, and moved a chair closer to the fire. "My finances, for one, and the questionable character of our so-charming host. His name, by the way, is Oily Tom—a fitting appellation, I am told. For my previous purpose, this place would have served nicely. Here, sit down and keep your cloak ready. I do not want him to see you."

Amanda perched a little uneasily in the chair, and held out her hands to the fire. As she did so, the Baron strode over to glance inside the adjacent room with a heavy frown.

"What is wrong?" Amanda asked him curiously.

He came back to join her. "I'm not sure. What you told me about that Forrester fellow has me worried. When Jack comes, something tells me he will not come alone. I want you to hide, Amanda, no matter how much you want Jack to see you. It's for your protection."

Confused and extremely tired, Amanda rubbed her eyes. "You want me to hide? I don't understand. Where, my lord, and why?"

"In the next room," he replied impatiently. "Give me your word, Amanda. I have a reason, but it's too unclear to try to explain. I don't want to place you in any unnecessary danger."

Wisely, Amanda bit back the response which almost left her lips. These were odd words indeed coming from a man who only an hour before had kidnapped her and coolly declared his intention to ravish and ruin her in the eyes of the world. Yet he seemed to have altered since then, and he sounded sincere now. Dare she trust him? Reason told her no, but instinct prevailed.

"Very well, Lord Frome, I will do as you ask."

He smiled slightly. "Good girl."

When a knock sounded, Amanda jumped nervously, but it was only the innkeeper. A short while later, the fire blazed high, and Amanda sipped at her tea, finally beginning to grow warm. She looked across to the other chair, taking in the tall, brown-haired man who sat sprawled at his ease, gazing into the fire. What was he planning, she wondered fearfully. Was there some way she could prevent the man she loved from getting hurt?

As if sensing her gaze, Frome turned and looked at her. For a moment, his eyes moved over her, assessing the curves of her figure more accurately than she could ever have guessed. Briefly, he allowed himself to wonder how he would have enjoyed the enticing little beauty who fixed him with so innocent a stare. Then he heaved a deep, faintly regretful sigh. The pain he had suffered was nothing to do with her, and he would not harm her. Beside, if there was the smallest chance that Eve would have him, he dared do nothing to spoil his chances. The decision was made.

The chimney smoked a little, and Amanda rubbed her eyes once more. "Lord Frome," she said, giving voice to her fears, "you must tell me what you intend to do to Lord Vale. And what if he does not come? You cannot mean to keep me here all night!"

"He will come," said the Baron, sounding bored.

"But how can you be sure? And what are we to do in the meantime?" she asked, her shoulders sagging wearily.

He did not intend to answer all her questions. "We do nothing, Amanda. We simply wait."

Chapter Sixteen

Charles Perth opened his eyes, blinked twice, and closed his eyes again. Sickening waves or voices punctuated by occasional squeals and shouts of laughter seemed to emanate from the inside of his head, but as he forced himself to think, he realized that the sound was actually coming from the floor below. After another minute in which he struggled to maintain consciousness, he decided that, in all probability, he was on the first floor of an ale house or gin shop. How this had come to be, however, he had not the faintest recollection. He tried to move, and discovered his hands were tied.

A single candle flickered in its holder a few feet away, and when he turned his head to better investigate his surroundings, he saw that he was not alone. A girl sat curled in a chair not five feet away, studying him with dark, pretty eyes.

"So, yer awake now, love," she said, her voice low and rather husky. " 'Ow do ye feel?"

Charles tried to speak, and found he had to clear

his throat first. "Terrible," he groaned. "My head aches like the very devil. Where am I?"

She smiled kindly. "Yer at the Laughin' Pig, love, and 'ere ye'll stay 'til mornin'. Ye'll feel better in a spell. They gave ye a bit of a clout on the nob, that's all."

"So they did, curse them! And who might you be?"

She rose and came to sit next to him. "Ye can call me Nell, if ye like."

Charles looked her over, amused in spite of the relentless pounding inside his skull. "I can, can I? Well, you can call me Charles, if you like. Call me anything you want, only untie my hands, dash it!"

Nell regarded him sorrowfully. "I can't, love. I'm not supposed to."

"Well, what are you supposed to do, tell me that!"

She shrugged. "Watch ye. Make sure yer kept safe. My Hans ain't interested in killin' nobody. 'Specially not a bang-up swell like yerself."

"Can't tell you how relieved I am to hear that," Charles told her feelingly. "But, ah, Nell, these ropes are too devilish tight, and I'm like to lose the use of my hands if something ain't done about it."

Nell frowned, and went to get the candle. "They *do* look tight," she admitted. She touched his brow with a cool hand. "Ye look a mite pale, Charles, love. A bumper of ale is what ye need. I'll fetch Hans to check them ropes."

Charles watched her leave with baffled frustration. What the devil kind of a rig was this? Obviously, that note he received had not been from Jack. He'd thought it a dashed smoky place to meet, but though the envelope had born no seal, he'd not been suspicious. Lord, it had been in Jack's handwriting, after all!

Well, it had been a hoax then, meant to keep him from meeting Jack. But who would play them such a havey-cavey trick as this? He had no enemies that he knew of, but Jack—! It hit him then, plain as the nose on his face. That rascally Frome fellow had finally chosen his moment to strike!

The door opened, and in stalked a giant of a man, with Nell in tow. "Well now, my fine lad. What seems to be the problem?"

Charles gaped at him. "H-Horrible!" he managed, in strangled accents.

Nell appeared concerned. "Feelin' worse, love?"

The giant only laughed. "The cove recognizes me, Nell. Seen me in the prize ring, 'ave ye, young fellow?" He took a penknife from his pocket, and bent down to sever the ropes.

Nell helped Charles to sit up and rubbed his wrists until he was able to hold the mug of home-brewed she had brought. He drank deeply, then stared up at Horrible Hans. "Aye, that I have! Won a pony on you in that last mill of yours." He shook his head in admiration. "But what the devil are you doing mixed up in an ugly business like this?"

Hans folded his great arms over his barrellike chest. "What's ugly about it? A swell promises to pay me an 'undred yellow boys to get ye out of 'is way for one night. You ain't 'urt, are ye, 'sides a small click on the crown office?"

"Small—!" echoed Charles, rubbing the lump on his head. "I like that! Your idea of small ain't exactly the same as mine!"

"Ye 'urt 'im, Hans," said Nell reproachfully. "Hans don't really like to 'urt people," she explained to Charles.

"Tell me something," demanded Charles. "Did the, ah, swell, who hired you bear the name of Frome? Tall, brown-pated fellow with a sneer?"

Hans shook his head. "Never 'eard of no Frome. 'E was sort of a plain-lookin' fellow, not tall, not short. Nothin' outstandin' about 'im 'cept maybe 'is teeth. They was kinda large."

Charles furrowed his brow. The description sounded vaguely familiar, but he couldn't quite put his finger on it. For some reason, large teeth seemed linked in his mind with poorly arranged cravats, but who in the world—?

Then, quite suddenly, he knew. "Forrester!" he breathed aloud. "Tell me, was his name Forrester?"

Hans shrugged, and went to sit in the chair. "Might 'ave been. Said 'is name was Binns. I didn't believe 'im."

"It was Forrester, I know it! *That* explains a great deal—at least I think it does. Jack always felt sorry for him because his father despised the fellow so, but I'll wager the old codger had his reasons. Now is he working with Frome, or—dash it, whether he is or not, we've got to *do* something!"

" 'E paid me to keep ye 'ere, that's all I know," said Hans, wearing a stubborn expression.

"Ha!" said Charles. *"Promises to pay* were the words you used a minute ago. I'll wager a monkey you don't see a single guinea of it."

" 'E gave me ten already," argued Hans, apparently unmoved.

"Oh." Charles was crestfallen. "Well, I still say you can't trust the fellow. Lord, the man can't even tie a decent neckcloth! And I'd stake my honor he's never been to a prize fight in his life! Afraid to get his pretty hands dirty," he added contemptuously. "Dash it, Hans, I'm convinced he and another rogue mean to murder a friend of mine. He wants me out of the way, so my friend will be alone. Does that mean nothing to you?"

Nell gasped, and Hans narrowed his eyes. "Can ye give me a good reason why I should believe ye?" he asked bluntly.

Charles's face fell. "No, dash it!"

Nell spoke. *"I* believe 'im, Hans."

Hans scratched his chin, and sighed. "I do, too, and I'll tell ye why." He gave Charles an inscrutable look. "Because ye didn't try to bribe me just now."

Charles began to struggle to his feet. "Well, if that don't beat the Dutch!" he exclaimed, grinning at the big, blond giant in front of him. "I'll be hanged if this ain't turning into a first-rate adventure!"

The Marquis awoke with a start, and glanced quickly at the clock across the room. Good God, it was after ten o'clock! He'd have to hurry if he was

342

to meet Charles at eleven. Lady Torrington would no doubt be up in the boughs over their absence, and would probably tear them apart the second they walked in the door. The dowager's ill-humor didn't bother him overmuch, but Charles was a lover of harmony and found her tantrums distasteful.

However, when he arrived at Mr. Perth's lodgings, he was surprised to learn that Charles was not there.

"What do you mean, he's left? When did he leave?" he demanded of Charles's manservant.

"Hours ago, my lord. He was to attend the Dowager Lady Torrington's ball in Arlington Street."

"I know that, damn it," said the Marquis in slight exasperation. "But I received a note from him asking him to meet me here at eleven o'clock."

"I know nothing of a note, my lord."

The Marquis frowned. "Go and ask his valet, what's-his-name."

"Perrot, my lord. If your lordship will condescend to wait, I will inquire."

Vale tapped his fingers on a nearby pier table, wondering what was going on.

The servant returned. "Perrot knows nothing of any note, my lord. Mr. Perth departed a little before the time the ball was to commence." The man paused uncertainly. "I have just recalled, my lord, that a moment after my master left the house, I glanced out the window and saw that he had stopped to speak to someone. Not another gentleman, my lord, but a servant. I believe he handed

343

something to my master, but I did not see what it was."

"Could it have been a note, perhaps?" asked the Marquis intently.

"I really could not say, my lord."

Deciding that there was nothing more to be learned from the man, the Marquis headed for Arlington Street. He strode purposefully through the vaulted entrance foyer into the large inner hall, where he relinquished his hat and cloak to an impassive footman. With a quick glance toward the grand staircase, he said curtly, "Has Lady Torrington's grandson arrived yet?"

"You mean Mr. Charles Perth, my lord? I'm not entirely certain. Do you wish me to—"

But the Marquis brushed past him, determined to search for himself.

Godfrey Forrester had positioned himself near the top of the stairs where he could watch for his cousin, and the instant he saw the Marquis, an ugly smile began to form on his face. Everything was going exactly as he planned. Indeed, how could he fail? His intellect was superior to that of his fellows, and it was now time for him to take his place as one of the leading actors in this little farce.

Once more assuming the part of the self-effacing, unobtrusive relative, Godfrey stepped forward to greet his cousin just as the Marquis reached the top. "Evening, Jack. You're just the person I was hoping to see."

The Marquis favored him with a brief, impatient look. "Hello, Godfrey," he replied, attempting to see past him into the crowded ballroom across the hall. The musicians were grinding away upon their instruments, their melody almost drowned by the babble of human voices. He raised his voice a little. "I'm sorry, I can't talk to you just now, I must—"

But Godfrey had him by the arm. "I know. Pay your respects to the Dowager. Before you do, though, perhaps you'll grant me just a moment of your time?" he asked diffidently. "Something on my mind I've been meaning to ask you."

Unwillingly, the Marquis allowed himself to be detained. "First answer me this, Godfrey. Have you seen Charles Perth here anywhere?"

Godfrey appeared to ponder the question. "Charles Perth," he said ruminatively. "Now let me think. Have I seen him tonight? I have a feeling I did. I think—it was down this very hall he went. The Dowager has card tables set up in some of these rooms. Yes, I'm almost certain I saw him go this way."

He hid his amusement at the way Vale's brows snapped together. "You *did* see him? Well, well! Excuse me, Godfrey, I'll be back to talk to you in a minute."

The Marquis hurried off down the long corridor, pausing to glance into each of the various salons whose open doors and attendant footmen indicated that they had been set aside for the use of the guests. In several of these, there were people playing at whist, but of Charles there was no sign.

The last of these rooms appeared at first to be unoccupied, but a slight movement near the window corrected that impression. "Hello, Jack," came a low, sultry voice. It was Lady Claverley.

It struck him as odd that she should be all alone, and for no reason at all it crossed his mind that she had been expecting him. He hesitated, regarding her as warily as if she had been an adder. "Well, Alex?"

As if on cue, the widow left the window and went to seat herself gracefully in a high-backed chair. She smiled, but made him no reply. Unable to stand still, the Marquis swung around, only to find that Godfrey was blocking the doorway.

"Why, hullo, here's Lady Claverley," remarked Godfrey, feigning surprise. "I trust we do not intrude, ma'am. You, ah, already know the lady, don't you, Jack?" he asked, suppressing an urge to snicker at the ludicrous scene.

"We've been introduced," said Vale sardonically. "Look, Godfrey, is this some sort of a game you're playing, tagging around after me? If you've knowledge of Charles's whereabouts, then tell me—otherwise, stop following me around like a tantony pig."

Godfrey sighed regretfully. "Just wanted to tell you I was mistaken. I remember now it was another night I saw your friend Perth. Look, Jack, I only want to ask you for a loan. Dipped a little too deep the other night, and lost a hundred at faro. I thought maybe you'd be willing to give me—an advance."

The Marquis found this a logical explanation for his cousin's strange behavior, for Godfrey did, occasionally, fall a little under the hatches. Chafing at the unnecessary delay, he said, "Of course, Godfrey,

346

but there was no need to accost me like this. Next time, call on me at home."

As if responding to a signal, Lady Claverley rose, smoothing her skirts with her hands. "Who did you say you were looking for, my lord?" she inquired sweetly.

Vale turned. "Charles Perth," he answered shortly. "Have you seen him?"

She shook her head. "Alas, I have not. I thought perhaps you were searching for a certain lady. Someone who I rather imagine has taken your fancy of late."

"Oh?" he responded, his face grim. "Well, I'm certainly in the wrong room, then, aren't I?"

"You are, indeed!" she snapped, and dropped her honeyed tones. "Amanda Marlowe is long gone, Jack. She left this house with Everard Frome hours ago."

The Marquis froze. *"What?* Why the devil would she do that? What kind of gammon are you trying to pitch now, Alexandra?"

She shrugged carelessly, her eyes flitting once to Godfrey for approval. "Is it so difficult to believe? The girl obviously prefers him to you, though I'll wager she's regretting it by now." She laughed nastily. "I warned you I would have my revenge."

In two long steps the Marquis was in front of her, his fingers biting into her shoulders. "Don't play games with me, woman," he ground out. "I swear I'll throttle you if you don't give me an answer. Your poison tongue has already done enough damage."

347

"But I don't understand," Godfrey complained, enjoying himself hugely. "What is the lady talking about? What has happened to Miss Marlowe?"

Vale threw his cousin a brief look over his shoulder. "Never mind. It's nothing that need concern you."

"Let go, Jack! You're hurting me!" Again, the widow darted a glance at Godfrey, resenting the amusement she knew he was feeling at the charade. "I will not tell you anything! I have promised Everard I would not!" she added dramatically, and hoped her act was convincing.

Despite his nap, the Marquis was tired. He was also growing very worried about both Charles and Amanda, and what little remained of his patience was hanging by a thread. If any harm should come to either of them because of this feud between him and Frome, he would—God, he could not even imagine what he would do! His hands slid to Lady Claverley's throat.

"Where is Amanda?" he repeated angrily, his fingers tightening.

Lady Claverley clawed at him with her nails, but did not dare to answer until she saw Godfrey's satisfied nod. "All right," she croaked. "Let go, I beg of you!"

The Marquis released his hold, and she fell to her knees. "Bastard!" she choked out, massaging her bruised neck with shaking fingers.

Vale watched her unsympathetically. "I'm waiting, Alex."

Careful to omit any reference to Godfrey, she

gasped out the story, her voice quivering with hatred and spite. When he learned of the Baron's ignoble intentions toward Amanda, the Marquis swore furiously, his hands itching to strike the woman who still crouched at his feet.

"But this is shocking!" said Godfrey. "What are we going to do, Jack?"

"*I* am going to bring Miss Marlowe back. *You* will be pleased to remember that a lady's reputation is at stake, and keep your mouth shut about all this."

Godfrey's eyes gleamed maliciously at his cousin's back. "Couldn't possibly let you go alone, Jack," he protested. "What if you need help? Someone ought to be there to protect the lady."

Turning, the Marquis surveyed his cousin consideringly. All his life, Godfrey had hovered in the background, something of a nonentity. On his occasional visits to Stirlings with his aunt and uncle, Godfrey had always kept himself aloof, seemingly uninterested in participating in his cousin Jack's pursuits. Vale had never minded him much, for he was no toady, but neither had Godfrey ever done anything to earn his respect. Was he dependable in a crisis? Was he capable of discretion? These were things he did not know, for in truth the Marquis did not know his cousin at all.

If only Charles were here, he thought heavily. Well, perhaps it would be the wisest course to take Godfrey along. He did not dare to underestimate Everard Frome as an opponent.

"She will need a chaperon," he said suddenly.

349

"Where is Lady Besford? Why has she not noticed the girl is missing?"

Godfrey shrugged, and glanced meaningfully at Lady Claverley. "She went home," the widow answered in a sulky tone, "and took the other Miss Marlowe with her. The Countess was quite overset by your Amanda's disappearance. She's probably having the vapours right now."

The Marquis shut his eyes for a second, overwhelmed with frustration. "Damnation, what a mess. Come on, then, Godfrey. Perhaps you can be of some use."

Taking for granted that the other man would follow, Vale strode from the room, determined to waste no more time. Fear for Amanda twisted inside him, but he forced himself to stay calm, and greeted the people he passed in the hall with a cool exterior.

Godfrey turned to Lady Claverley and smiled. "You did well, my love. It was a splendid performance."

How beautiful she was like that, he mused, still cringing on the floor, with liquid anger spilling so deliciously from those lovely violet eyes. Smiling again, he stepped on her hand, crushing her delicate fingers with his foot. So beautiful.

Her cloak tucked around her for warmth, Amanda drowsed in her chair while Everard Frome lounged nearby, not entirely as relaxed as he would have liked. Several times, he rose from his chair and went to the window, but all was silent, and he soon sat down again. Oily Tom did not disturb them, and the Baron quietly attended to the fire on his own, allowing Amanda to sleep as best she could.

It was well past midnight when he heard the Marquis's chaise drive into the courtyard. "Amanda." Lord Frome touched her shoulder. "Amanda, wake up. I want you to go in the next room now.

Amanda straightened, and blinked her eyes, wincing at the stiffness in her neck and back. "Is he here?" she asked, her pulses quickening.

The Baron was at the window. "Yes, and just as I suspected, he has company." He turned and advanced toward her, his features set with determination. "I don't know what this Forrester fellow's game is, but I don't trust anyone who has dealings with Lady Claverley." His lip curled a little. "Excepting myself, of course. For tonight, at least, you can safely place your trust in me."

"But what are you going to do?" she appealed, reaching out to clutch at his sleeve.

Lord Frome's eyes hardened. "Jack and I have something to settle between us. Perhaps I was wrong to let it go on for so long, but tonight, I think, will finish it. You will not attempt to interfere, do you hear me?"

"I will not stand idly by and let you murder him, if that is what you intend!" she flashed.

He took her by the arm and propelled her into the smaller room. "Have no fear on that score, my dear. Having to flee the country does not fit in with my plans for the future."

Ignoring Amanda's next protest, he shut the door in her face. Then he returned to his chair, shifting it a little so that it faced the door by which they had entered. He had waited a long time for this night.

In the tap room, the Marquis was regarding Oily Tom with haughty disdain. "My good fellow, I have absolutely no intention of paying you for the information. I know that Lord Frome and — a young lady — are here in your inn, and I demand that you take me to them at once."

Oily Tom dropped his eyes, his expression becoming resigned. "Your lordship mistakes my meaning," he mumbled. "If you will follow me, my lord."

Halfway down the passageway, the Marquis pushed him aside. "I can find my way from here. Tell the other gentleman where I am when he returns from the stables," he ordered. His long legs carried him swiftly, and he flung open the door with all the driving force of his long pent-up emotions.

Lord Frome put up his quizzing glass. "Why, Jack, what a delightful surprise," he drawled. "What brings you out in such unpleasant weather?"

The Marquis scowled. "Damn it, Frome, where is she?" he demanded fiercely.

The Baron crossed his legs. "Er, where is who, Jack? I confess the abruptness of your conversation has always tended to bewilder me."

"I've not come here to bandy words with you! You brought Amanda Marlowe here, and by God,

352

you shall be made to pay for whatever you have done to her!"

Slowly, Everard Frome rose to his feet, his benign expression fading. "I will, will I?" he said, very softly. "And what of payments yet outstanding, my arrogant friend? You have yet to pay — in full — for your own sins of the past."

The Marquis clenched his fists, his temper barely controlled. "Whatever sins I have committed have nothing to do with Amanda," he growled. "How dare you bring her into this? What right have you to hurt an innocent girl, for God's sake?"

The Baron smiled affably. "Perhaps you and I are more alike than we realize, Jack. We neither of us are overconcerned with *noblesse oblige*."

Vale drew a deep breath. "I never treated your sister any way but honorably."

"You will, of course, forgive me if I say I do not believe you. I have reason to know otherwise," said the Baron curtly, walking to the table to pour himself another drink.

The Marquis frowned. "I don't know what you're talking about."

"I think you do," retorted Frome with a sneer. "Now do we stand here talking all night, or do we settle this thing between us? What happened to your companion, by the way? Did the good Godfrey lose his way?"

Vale glanced around, puzzled. "Why — I don't know. Damn it, the man's useless!" He dismissed Godfrey with a shrug. "So you saw me arrive, and were, in fact, expecting me. Interesting." He gave the other man a grim look, and began to strip off his coat. "I assume you do not mean pistols at dawn? If so, I fear I cannot oblige you. I have no intention of waiting more than another half-minute to plant my fist into the middle of your face."

Provoked by this statement, the Baron sat to remove his boots, all thoughts of Godfrey flying from his head. "Believe me, I have every intention of doing the same to you, my friend," he snapped angrily.

In the next room, Amanda stood rigid with dismay, her whitened knuckles pressed against her mouth. Every word the two men spoke came clearly through the thin wall, and it was only with a supreme effort of will that she was able to refrain from revealing her presence. Dear God, they were going to kill each other after all, she thought, hearing the sounds of furniture being pushed out of the way.

But Amanda was beginning to understand that, as men, they were going to have to fight. She had heard the raw animosity in their voices, and knew instinctively that both men welcomed this chance to vent their hostility for one another. The dispute between them went too deep, and had been building for too long to be settled in any other way. Lord Frome, at least, had allowed his rancor to rule his life, and it was within the realm of possibility that the challenge of a physical contest with the Marquis was what he needed to purge his soul of its bitterness. Unfortunately, it was going to be agony for her to have to listen to it.

Divested of their shoes and coats, the two men had begun to circle each other cautiously. Lord Frome was smiling a little, but the Marquis's features were taut with strain. He knew the Baron to be excellent with his fists, for he had watched him spar at Jackson's, yet he also knew that his own abilities were not without merit. He still had no idea where Amanda was, or what had been done to her, but he could not afford to let his fury or anxiety distract him from the business at hand.

Bending low, the Baron was first to charge, the impact of his lunge sending the two men crashing into the wall. Vale's quick reflexes enabled him to pivot enough to soften the blow, and he twisted loose, forcing the Baron down to the floor. As they struggled, locked in a hold made desperate by six years of ill feeling between them, it soon became apparent that they were closely matched. If Lord Frome had a slight advantage in height, the Marquis's heavier build made up for it.

Vale's fingers dug into the Baron's neck, but his adversary's hand was shoving against his face, blocking his ability to breathe. Then suddenly the hand fell away, its sudden absence serving to throw off the Marquis's balance. They rolled to the side, and he managed to get a quick jab squarely on the Baron's jaw, snapping the other man's head back against the floor. Breathing heavily, Vale started to rise, but Frome recovered quickly, his foot ramming into the Marquis's stomach with enough force to send him sprawling.

Amanda was doing her best to see through the

keyhole, but it offered her nothing more rewarding than a view of the opposite door. Frustrated, she listened as long as she could, wincing at the loud grunts of pain that reached her ears. Then at last, she could bear it no longer. Very quietly, she eased the door open just enough so that she could peer through the crack. What she saw was enough to make her blanche. By this time, the Marquis had Lord Frome in a headlock, but the Baron had not given up the struggle. Blood poured from his nose, yet he thrashed about, attempting to break from the Marquis's viselike grip.

"Where is she?" demanded the Marquis through gritted teeth.

It was so difficult to stand there and not answer, yet Amanda did not dare to distract him, for fear he would lose the upper hand. She bit her lip, silently beseeching Lord Frome to tell him the truth.

The Baron was panting with effort, yet he managed to grind out an answer. "She is . . . safe enough . . . my friend."

Relentlessly, Vale tightened his cruel hold. "And did you—touch—her?" he snarled, his expression so savage that Amanda barely recognized him.

"Did you touch my sister?" Frome shot back, his voice rasping with fatigue.

"Why the hell do you keep harping on that?" the Marquis exploded, relaxing his arm enough to give the other man some air. "I never did more than kiss your sister, damn it!"

The Baron suddenly ceased his movements, and lay still, exhausted and pale. "Lottie was . . . with child . . . when she died," he gasped. "Who else but . . . you . . . could have been . . . responsible?"

Stunned, the Marquis sat slowly back, and wiped the sweat from his eyes with the arm of his sleeve. He stared at the man in front of him, appalled at the realization that for all these years, Lottie's brother had believed such a thing of him. His back was to the door, and he did not notice that Godfrey had entered, and stood listening to their exchange with malevolent interest.

Both men started violently when Godfrey spoke. "Why, I think I must claim that honor," he remarked, smiling pleasantly. "As I recall, Lord Frome, your sister was quite a charming little piece."

Amanda gasped in horror, for Godfrey's hand came up as he spoke. Mr. Forrester was pointing an evil-looking, three-barreled pistol straight at the Marquis's head.

Chapter Seventeen

"I've been at great pains for a very long time to make you hate each other," Godfrey continued meditatively. He sucked at his lower lip and looked at Frome, a flicker of contempt crossing his face. "You failed me, you know. I was counting on you to kill him for me."

Their eyes riveted on the pistol, the two men on the floor still had not moved. Godfrey took a step forward and regarded them broodingly. "It is loaded, of course. My compliments to you, my foolish Lord Frome, for providing me with your own weapon to kill dear Jack. So unwise of you to leave it in your chariot. Unfortunately, Alex couldn't tell me exactly where you kept it, which is why I was so late for the party. But I see you have kept yourselves entertained in my absence."

The shock of Godfrey's announcement had begun to sink in, and the Baron eased himself into a sitting position, his features twisting with rage. "Why, you worthless piece of scum, are you saying it was *you* who seduced my sister?"

A conceited smile hovered on Godfrey's lips. "You never suspected, did you? You blamed poor Jack here, and never even noticed me at all."

"I swear I'll kill you for it, Forrester," the Baron seethed.

Godfrey smirked. "Oh, I doubt that. Haven't you noticed which one of us is holding the pistol, you fool? And rest assured I know how to use it." His eyes shifted to his cousin. "Well, Jack? Haven't you anything to say for yourself? No last requests?"

The Marquis shrugged. "Naturally, I'd like an explanation." He shot a warning glance at the Baron, who appeared ready to hurl himself at Godfrey, pistol or no pistol.

"Naturally," agreed Godfrey, prepared to be indulgent. "It is what I expected." He glanced around suddenly. "Where's the Marlowe chit, by the way?"

It was Frome's turn to send the Marquis a cautioning look. "She's upstairs, asleep," he said curtly.

"Enjoyed her already, have you?" Godfrey said lewdly. "Oho, now, steady, steady . . . I don't want to have to shoot either of you just yet." Keeping a vigilant eye on his two prisoners, he retrieved the chair Frome had used, and pulled it around. "I might as well make myself comfortable. You two can stay on the floor."

Abruptly, his sneer faded and his expression grew tolerant. "Let's see if we can piece together what's going to happen. Obviously, you two have fought — that we cannot change since you are both so . . . untidy. Now, here is where we must fictionalize a little. Frome will have had the amazing foresight to

359

bring his pistol with him. You see where I'm heading, don't you? Our friend Lord Frome will take the pistol and shoot you, my dear cousin, through the heart—or perhaps the head—I haven't quite made up my mind on that detail. Next, you, Frome, are going to have an attack of remorse. How, you will ask yourself, can you bear to live with what you have done? You will—"

The Marquis cut him short. "Extremely unlikely, Godfrey. You've been reading too many romances. And that wasn't the explanation I meant. I want to know why you hate me, as you so evidently do."

"Why I hate you? Are you serious?" Godfrey's laugh rang out bitterly. "Because you are who you are, my dear coz. You have wealth, power, respect, independence—in short, everything I want, including the family title."

Then he snickered. "By the way, old boy, I've never had the chance to tell you how much I applaud your taste in women. I mustn't forget to tell you about Frome's lovely sister. You'll enjoy the story, I'm certain. And did you know Alexandra has been my mistress for nearly half a year? But you don't like to share, do you? You are both fools."

"No doubt we are," admitted Vale calmly. "I won't pretend I've ever understood you, Godfrey, but I never thought you anything but harmless."

It was the wrong thing to say. Godfrey's face flushed, and his voice grew vibrant with loathing. *"Harmless?* Do you think to flatter me? I ought to kill you right now for saying that!"

"I think it's become quite clear to both of us that

ou are a very dangerous man," the Baron quickly nterposed, his tone placating.

Godfrey relaxed. "Good. I don't really blame you 'or being duped. I played the doltish cousin extremely well, I know. Now, where was I?"

"You were going to tell us about Charlotte," prodded the Marquis, with an apologetic look at he man beside him.

"Ah, yes, Charlotte," mused Godfrey. "She didn't eally interest me at first. Not enough passion in her, I suppose. But Jack was acting the doting idiot over the girl, so I began to watch her. I found her wandering in a garden one evening, at the Angleseys' rout. She didn't seem to be herself, which made the whole thing a little more—don't move, Frome. If you want to hear the story, my fiery friend, then you have to sit still."

The Baron's jaw had gone rigid, but the pistol was leveled at him and there was nothing he could do. "Go on, then," he said tautly. "But leave the descriptions out of it."

"Why, Everard, aren't you even curious?" mocked Godfrey. "No, I see not. Would it interest either of 'ou to know that my dear Alexandra had a hand in he business? You see, Jack, even though her husband was still alive, Alex already had her lovely, and very jealous, violet eyes on you. She took it upon herself to whisper a few untruths about you in he girl's ear—shocking, isn't it? Did you never wonder why Charlotte changed toward you? I see comprehension in your eyes. Wonderful. My faith in 'our intelligence is restored."

Frome buried his face in his hands. "My God Jack. Do you hear what this cad is saying? I can' believe it. All this time I thought that it was you—

The Marquis clapped a hand on the Baron' shoulder. "It doesn't matter."

Godfrey bared his teeth in amusement. "Oh, s now we don't hate each other anymore. How touch ing! You two make me sick."

The Baron raised his head. "And you nauseat me, Forrester. You are unfit to walk the earth."

"Nevertheless, it is I, not you, who will continu to walk it. Now stop your whining and listen to th rest of my story. It will be the only time I tell it. Godfrey crossed his legs, his expression pensive. " still wonder if your father knew something of my ways, Jack. The old bastard sent me one of his au tocratic summonses, knowing I would have to com crawling to him like a lackey. Did no one ever tel you of our interview? It was the day after you an he had . . . fallen out, so to speak. Without an explanation, he dared to tell me he was cutting of my allowance. Now I ask you, could I let him d that? Was that *fair?* First, my own fool of a fathe lost everything we had at the gaming tables, an then that!"

Godfrey's voice had risen to a shout, and h wiped at his mouth, visibly trying to control him self. "I came back a day later, and found him in hi library. Now *that* is one memory I cherish. He wa writing a letter to you, Jack. Would you like t know what it said?"

The Marquis had begun flexing his fingers, bu

362

his face was neutral "Somehow, I feel sure you are going to tell me."

"Since you are going to die, I really think I shall. You amuse me, you know. All these ridiculous scruples of yours. You hid your guilty conscience from the others, but not from me, Jack." He leaned forward, his grin malicious. "Your father was writing you a letter of *apology*. A fine joke, is it not? In effect, he told you to marry whomever you wanted, and that he would not withhold his blessing. How ironic is life, that I should happen upon him at such a moment. I need not trouble you with the details, I think. I intended to kill him, just as I am going to kill you, but Fate, in the guise of a heart attack, intervened. Your father ever had a temper, didn't he, coz? He saved me considerable trouble by simply expiring at my feet. So I took the letter and left through the side door. I kept that letter all these years, just to remind myself that Fate was on my side. It has helped me to be patient."

During these last words, the Marquis had surged to his feet, his face darkened with fury.

"Steady, old boy," said Godfrey affably, raising the pistol a bit. "You still have a chance, you know, if you can keep me talking long enough. Perhaps little Miss Marlowe will come running in and save you." He laughed jeeringly. "I tried once before to be rid of you. You never knew that duel you fought with Henry Scorpe was at my contrivance, did you? I managed to convince the fool that you were topping the dice, and the idiot was so cup-shot he actually believed me and called you out!

363

Unfortunately, he made a botch of the business. A pity. It is clearly written in the cards that I mus deal with you myself."

Ignoring all this, the Marquis said harshly, "And what have you done with Charles Perth? Did you kill him?"

"Ah, yes, how did you like my little notes? Forgery is just another of my many skills. Nay, he is safe, never fear. I have nothing against your friend Charles. I don't quite like the way he looks at my cravats, but that's hardly a reason to kill a man, is it? I shall let him live."

"That's big-hearted of you, Godfrey," remarked the Marquis sarcastically.

"Yes, well, I am not quite as bloodthirsty as I seem. I simply want what is my due. Now, any other questions, or are you ready to meet your Maker?"

Through the crack, Amanda was witnessing thi nightmare scene with a growing sense of despair. Lord Frome had been right in his guess that Mr Forrester was up to no good, but unfortunately the Baron had allowed his desire for vengeance to distract him from the real danger. If only he had told the Marquis his suspicions, perhaps they could have been ready for Godfrey!

Both men continued to ply Godfrey with questions, encouraging him to boast, among other things, of his strange relationship with Lady Claverley. The purpose of it all, Amanda realized, was merely to play for time, but how much longer could they stall? Lord Frome, at least, knew of Amanda's

364

presence, and must surely be depending on her to bring rescue. But from what quarter? She was certain that Oily Tom would be of no help, so there was no point in considering him. There was really no one at all, she thought. No one except her.

Biting her lip in nervousness, Amanda put her eye once more to the crack, and felt her first stab of hope. Godfrey had finally risen from the chair and had moved around to stand with his back to her, only a few feet away!

Amanda shut her eyes in an effort to concentrate, desperately trying to recall whether the door in front of her squeaked. If she could just get up behind Godfrey, she could—what? She could not overpower him, that was certain, but she could—why, she could fling her cloak over his head! It would take him only seconds to get it off, but the Marquis was on his feet, and could spring forward and—but, dear lord, what if Godfrey fired the pistol at that moment? Her action could very well cause the Marquis's death.

Faced with this possibility, Amanda still knew she had no choice. As far as she could remember, the door had made no noticeable sound. Gathering her cloak, she pushed the door open a fraction of an inch, and then, slowly, another and then another. Since they were facing her, both the Marquis and Lord Frome saw her at once, yet neither needed the warning finger she put to her lips to tell them to keep silent. With a silent prayer, Amanda stepped into the room and with all her strength, sent the cloak soaring over Godfrey's head.

365

"Who knows, I might even marry her," he was saying. "It's what I told her I would do if she — *Ahhh!*"

The instant his vision was obstructed, Godfrey reacted with the reflexes of a cornered animal. His hand came up to claw at the cloak, even while the other, still holding the pistol, came arcing sideways at Amanda, dealing her a painful blow on the shoulder. She reeled back with a cry, then was thrust even farther out of the fray by the Marquis as he hurled himself at his cousin. At the same time, Lord Frome was diving for Godfrey's arm, and did so just as the pistol exploded, its resounding crash sending Amanda's hands flying to her face in horror.

A string of vicious curses assailed her ears, but these were speedily silenced by what she presumed (for she had not yet dared to look) was a crunching and very effective blow to the face. After that, there was but a short scuffle, then a pair of iron arms was dragging her forward, and her face was shoved, rather roughly, against an unmistakably male chest. Amanda might normally have taken exception to such ungentle treatment, except for the circumstance that her name was being uttered over and over, repeated with such low, fierce intensity that any objection she might have raised was entirely forgotten.

"My God, Amanda, my God," muttered the Marquis, almost crooningly. His dark head bent so that his breath fanned her cheek. "Amanda, are you all right? Are you hurt? Look at me, Amanda. Talk to

366

me, my love."

Lifting her head, Amanda gazed up at him in wonder, the first tendrils of a joy she had never known seeping into her heart. "Only a little," she said shakily. "I'll have a bruise on my shoulder, I expect. And . . . and you?"

"Never better, my darling," he responded with odd fervency. Gathering her closer, he kissed the top of her head, a reassuring gesture that brought a lump to Amanda's throat.

A moan from behind reminded her they were not alone, and she twisted around to see how the Baron had fared. Somewhat to her amazement, Lord Frome appeared to be perched on top of Godfrey, whose arms had somehow become pinned under his own weight. The Baron had firm possession of the pistol, and indeed, was jabbing it rather alarmingly into Godfrey's neck.

"If you will take her out of here," said Lord Frome, his voice soft and very distinct, "I can finish dealing with this—insect." He glanced up at them briefly. "By the way, Jack, I never laid so much as a finger on Amanda."

The Marquis nodded curtly. "You'd better give me the pistol. Murder is not the answer, you know."

Godfrey spat out an expletive, and the Marquis frowned. "Come, my love," he said, taking Amanda by the arm. "This is no place for you."

Pocketing the weapon, he led her down the dark corridor, and back into the empty tap room. Turning her around, he reached for her hands. "And now, Amanda—"

A sudden commotion in the courtyard stopped his words, and they exchanged a questioning look. The next moment, the door to the tap room flew open, and to Amanda's utter astonishment, Lady Besford swept into the room, closely followed by Eve and Lord Besford.

"Amanda!" shrieked the Countess, rushing forward to enfold Amanda in a plump embrace. "My poor lamb, we've been searching for you *everywhere!* I have been quite, quite sick with apprehension, for I could not imagine where you could have—" She broke off to stare about the room. "But what on earth are you doing in such an excessively odd place?" Taking in the Marquis's presence, she added, in bewilderment, "Lord Vale did not bring you here, surely?"

The Marquis bowed. "No, ma'am, I certainly did not. I came to fetch Miss Marlowe back."

Lord Besford forgot his blustery image. "Amanda, my pet, come give me a hug! We've been cast into the fidgets over your safety, and there's no point in denying it. Emily's been nothing short of a watering pot for the better part of the evening!"

"Yes, indeed!" the Countess assured them, dabbing her eyes with a handkerchief. "And I could not find my hartshorn, Amanda! Where on earth did you put it?"

The Marquis's eyes had shifted to Eve. "Well, Miss Marlowe?"

Eve gave him a cool smile. "Well, my lord? Considering that, for all intents and purposes, you are affianced to me, I think explanations are in order."

Is Everard here?"

"He's at the end of the corridor," the Marquis answered, tipping his head toward the door. "I advise you not to go, however, if you don't care for the sight of blood."

"Blood!" she echoed. "What have you done to him?" To everyone's amazement, she turned and hurried off in the direction he had indicated.

"Now, where the devil does she think she's going?" said Lord Besford, scratching the back of his head.

"Oh, dear!" Lady Besford wrung her hands. "She really ought not to show such interest in that dreadful man! You must go and bring her back, Robert."

"Me? Why not you? She's your niece, dash it, not mine! As far as I'm concerned, if the Toast wants to consort with that elbow shaker, then let her. *I've* come to rescue Amanda!"

The Marquis turned to look at the Earl inquiringly. "But, sir, how did you know we were here?"

Lord Besford favored him with a head-to-toe, rather critical inspection, taking in his torn shirt, tousled hair, shoeless feet, and the suspicion of swelling around the area of his left eye. "Your friend Charles Perth learned where you'd gone from your groom. Came and told us that either Frome or that Forrester fellow had made off with Amanda, or possibly both, but he wasn't certain. Thought it a dashed banbury story at first, until he brought in his friends. Demmed odd company he's keeping these days," he added disapprovingly. "I expect he'll be along any minute."

369

The remainder of the Marquis's tension fell away from him. "So Charles *is* safe. Thank God for that."

"Yes, well, ahem. And now, my young buck, I'd like to know what you think gives you the right to chase around after our Amanda?"

A small hand tugged at the Earl's sleeve. "Sir, please," whispered an embarrassed Amanda, who had had time to recall the words she and the Marquis had exchanged at their last meeting. "Lord Vale and I have to talk. Please, don't say anything more."

Eve reentered the room. "It's all right," she announced. "Everard is hitting that Mr. Forrester, but I told him to stop, and he'll be joining us in a moment."

"You told him to stop, and he listened to you?" inquired the Marquis, glancing at her with interest.

"Certainly," said Eve with unruffled calm. "Most of the blood is Mr. Forrester's," she added.

Ignoring the presence of the Earl and Countess, the Marquis once more grasped Amanda's hands. "We do have to talk," he said quietly. "What I said to you at Vauxhall was . . . unforgivable, I know. I—"

The door to the corridor opened, and Lord Frome strolled leisurely into the room. "Why, if it isn't Lord and Lady Besford," he remarked, favoring them with a lazy smile. "What brings you out on such a night?"

Scowling heavily, the Earl waved his fist. "Dammit, Frome, I want to know what the devil you

370

mean by making off with Amanda! I ought to bring you up on charges for this, you black-hearted scoundrel!"

"Oh, Uncle!" interrupted Eve sedately. "For heaven's sake! Amanda is perfectly safe, and we do not want a scandal."

The Baron found his quizzing glass and peered through it. "Eve, my love, do you still mean to wed this fellow, Jack Brinvilliers? I must warn you, he's already holding hands with other females, which don't augur at all well for the future."

Eve looked at him consideringly. "He *is* rich," she said.

"And I most certainly am not," he agreed, letting his quizzing glass fall.

Lord Besford snorted. "He hasn't a sixpence to scratch with," he told her disparagingly.

The Baron's mocking expression faded. "On the other hand, I love you, Princess, and I fear he does not."

"Oh, joy!" said the Earl, rolling his eyes.

Eve ignored her uncle. "You must give up gaming, Everard. I will not live the life of a pauper."

The Baron began to smile. "Of a certainty, my love."

"But, my dear," Lady Besford objected, clutching her handkerchief unhappily. "What shall I tell your mother? She *forbade* me to introduce you to fortune hunters! She will never forgive me! I simply cannot allow it."

Eve smiled sweetly. "But, Aunt Emily, if you won't allow me to have Everard, then I will have to

371

take Vale instead."

Lady Besford cast a helpless glance at Amanda and Vale. "Oh, very well, my dear," she relented, observing their dismay. "But I leave it entirely to you to tell Jane."

Lord Frome's gleaming black eyes were alight with laughter. "Blackmail, my love?" he said to Eve. "I always knew you were a woman after my own heart."

"Well!" inserted the Marquis heartily. "Allow me to offer you my sincere felicitations! I shan't stand in the way of your happiness, my friend. I wish you all the joy in the world." The enthusiasm with which he wrung the other man's hand seemed to amuse the Baron.

Then Frome's expression turned serious. "Jack, I want to tell you—"

Stepping back, the Marquis nodded tiredly. "I know. We'll talk about it. But not, perhaps, to-night?"

"As you wish," responded the other man, with a comprehending glance in Amanda's direction. "You know, Jack, you've got yourself a smooth-tongued little lady."

The Marquis gave Amanda a quizzical look. "Indeed? And now, Amanda—"

The door to the courtyard was once more flung open with a crash, and Charles Perth took two steps into the room before coming to an abrupt halt.

"Good lord!" he exclaimed, viewing the lot of them. His gaze passed speculatively over the Baron's bloody and bedraggled appearance before taking in the Marquis's blackening eye and cut lip. "Missed the mill, have we?" he said, sounding disappointed. He turned, and shouted over his shoulder, "Too late, Hans! We missed it!"

All at once, a blond giant was framed in the doorway, his massive arm clutched possessively by a pretty, dark-haired girl. "Too bad," said the giant regretfully. "Come on in, Nellie, yer gettin' wet."

"The more the merrier," approved Charles, shrugging off his coat. "I don't mind telling you, Jack, it's a devilish nasty night to go racketing about the countryside."

Lord Frome glanced at the Marquis. "Friends of yours, Jack?" he said conversationally.

The Marquis wore an arrested expression. "Charles, *how* and *where* did you manage to find Horrible Hans?"

Charles grinned. "Can't say I really found him, Jack. The truth is, he found me! Some fellow hired him to get me out of the way. I've a notion that cagey cousin of yours is responsible. Is he here?"

"Yes, but he's feeling a trifle indisposed," inserted the Baron.

"Drawn 'is cork, 'ave ye?" asked Hans with interest.

By now, the Marquis had slid a supporting arm around Amanda's waist, for he could see she was starting to droop with exhaustion. "If you will all excuse us, Miss Marlowe and I are going to leave you for a short while."

"Oh, aye!" said Charles, casting a dubious eye

over the room. "We 'll make ourselves right at home in your absence! But dash it, Jack, we came to rescue you, and never a thank-you have we heard! Where's the body?"

The Marquis thanked him solemnly, and left it to the Baron to display Godfrey. In a short time, he had located a small room which had evidently been recently vacated, for it was snug and warm. He guided her inside and shut the door purposefully behind him.

"It appears that our host has abandoned the premises," he remarked, scooping her into his arms. Despite the muffled squeak which came from her throat, he carried her to the couch and sat down, settling her upon his lap.

It seemed the most natural thing in the world to slide her arm around his neck. "My goodness, what are we doing, my lord?" Amanda inquired, with half a laugh. "Do you mean to be naughty again?"

His clasp tightened. "Not before we have a talk," he affirmed, a mingling of good and ill humor in his eyes. "Amanda, my foolish, beautiful, brave little henwit, do you know you probably saved my life tonight?"

Amanda's eyes grew moist at this tender form of address. "I was terrified I would fail you. At first, I could not think what to do . . . but I was so afraid, you see, and then it just flashed into my mind that . . . well, at the time it seemed quite sensible, although I see now that . . . well, when I think what might have happened—" Her voice quivered and broke into a small sob.

The Marquis's thumb brushed a tear from her cheek. "You did well, Amanda," he said seriously, "but if you ever, *ever* take even *half* such an addle-brained risk again, that charming backside of yours is going to be very sore. I mean it, Amanda! Godfrey could have killed you, you know, and if he had, I . . . I don't know what I should have done. Da—I mean, dash it, I almost forgot. The cur hit your shoulder, didn't he? How does it feel?" he demanded, yanking the small puffed sleeve of her ball gown several inches down her arm. "Perhaps we should summon a physician," he frowned, inspecting the nearly invisible mark on her flesh.

Though his action bared an immodest portion of her breast, Amanda made no demur. "I do not think that is necessary, my lord," she protested. "It scarcely hurts at all. Truly!" Then her hand went up to cup the side of his face. "I can scarcely believe you came," she added emotionally. "I was so very afraid that you despised me."

"Never!" he responded, his blue eyes radiating sincerity. "Not for a single moment. And I thought that *you* despised *me!* But you didn't, did you, Amanda?"

She recognized the appeal in his voice, the lonely cry of a man who desperately needed her love. "No, my dear, dear friend," she answered, placing a soft kiss on his cheek. "Not for a single moment."

"I'll be honest with you," he said with difficulty. "There have been . . . other women in my past. But except for Charlotte, none of them has ever touched my heart. I swear it, Amanda!" He frowned. "And

375

what I felt for Charlotte was not love — at least it was nothing like . . . like what I feel for you, for the longer I knew her, the weaker it became." He paused, feeling awkward. "Ever since I first saw you, I haven't been able to get you out of my mind. I love you, Amanda! And I apologize that it's taken me so long to tell you. But how could I, with the way things stood between myself and your cousin? It's been so dashed frustrating!" He ran his hand through his hair in agitation. "You understand, don't you, darling?"

"Yes," she whispered. "It has been difficult for me as well. I have loved you, too, you see."

He stared into her eyes. "I will be faithful to you, Amanda," he promised. "There will be no other women — ever. You have my word."

"I know," she nodded.

"You heard everything my cousin said tonight?" he asked. When she nodded again, he explained, "When Charlotte died, I found that, overnight almost, I had acquired a sinister reputation. I was hurt and disillusioned, and I decided to live up to it. I did a dashed-near perfect job of it, too."

Amanda pressed her finger to his lips. "Shhh, my love. You have been unhappy, and that explains a great deal of your wildness. It does not signify in the least."

"I am not worthy of you," he said humbly. "I courted your cousin for the most selfish of reasons, thinking to use her to bury my guilt. And I acted selfishly with you on more than one occasion." He hesitated, looking deep into her silver eyes. "To

376

night, I learned that my father would have given me his blessing to marry whom I chose. But even were that not so, I have come to realize that I cannot live without you. I want you to be my wife, Amanda. I—if you will have me."

"You cannot know how much I have longed to hear you say those words," she sighed, smoothing the black curl at his forehead as once before she had longed to do.

"Think carefully, now," he cautioned. "I'm no saint, Amanda, despite what it pleases you to believe."

"I would not be happy with a saint," she assured him.

"And I've a devil of a temper," he reminded her.

"I have not forgotten it," Amanda said tremblingly. "I have a temper of my own, my lord."

"And you are going to have to stop calling me 'my lord.' I have a name."

A small laugh escaped her lips. "Yes, my love. Should you object if I called you John, rather than Jack?" she inquired lovingly. "I think it suits you better."

"You can call me anything you like, as long as you keep looking at me like that," he said hoarsely.

He meant it to be a gentle kiss, but even as his mouth came down, her lips were parting expectantly, offering an invitation he had no will to refuse. How could he resist such intoxicating sweetness? By mutual agreement, the kiss strengthened at once into one of wild, engulfing passion, exciting beyond compare. Without any hesitation, Amanda

377

allowed him to possess her mouth, abandoning her
self to the pleasure of his bold caresses. When his
fingers tugged impatiently at the bodice of her
gown, she shifted slightly, so that the fabric might
be more easily pulled away.

"God, Amanda," whispered the Marquis, taking
in the perfection of her small, uptilted breasts.
"You're so damned beautiful, I can scarcely think
straight."

Amanda was a little shocked when his head be
gan to lower, but after that, she was conscious of
nothing but the most exquisite sensations she had
ever known. She did not hear her own soft moans,
did not know how she arched her back so that his
tongue might dance against her hardened nipples.
Then, like once before, he was pushing her away,
but this time, to her startled relief, there was only
love shining in the blue depths of his eyes.

"Well!" said the Marquis, a bit raggedly. "I see it
is up to me to put a stop to this, since you,
'Manda-my-love, are obviously not going to 'do the
proper' and slap my face." At her fiery blush, a
lazy grin spread over his handsome features. "If we
are going to wait for our wedding night, my love,
we really must stop. Or I cannot answer for the
consequences," he explained, helpfully pushing her
bodice back into place.

Suddenly embarrassed, Amanda began an inco
herent speech which ended only when the Marquis
told her, most lovingly, not to talk such birdwitted
gammon. "On the contrary, I am delighted to find
your enthusiasm so closely matches my own. For

378

warn you, my lusty little wife-to-be, I plan to be a very demanding husband." He raised her chin with his finger, so that she must meet his gaze. "Naturally," he teased, a wicked look in his eye, "you must realize that if I'm to give up my dozen or so trumpets, there is going to be a price to pay."

Once more, Amanda blushed rosily. "Naturally," she agreed. To his secret delight, she began teasing him back. "Gracious, John, does not a dozen seem a trifle excessive?" she asked, looking innocent. "It seems a vast number to me."

Laughter welled in his throat. "Why, yes, it does, now that you mention it," he admitted, his voice quivering. "Perhaps I ought to confess that I am not as ambitious as you believe, Amanda. One silver-eyed green girl is enough for me." He stroked her hair tenderly. "You really do love me, don't you? Despite my past, no less. I couldn't ask for more than that."

Amanda straightened her position and looked at him earnestly. "Yes, I do love you. You foolish man, do you think I must be blind to your faults to love you? No, you are not perfect, and neither am I. But it was you who took me to St. Paul's and Westminster, and gave me a guidebook, and many, many times made me laugh so much I forgot to be sad. And though it made me angry at first, it was you who provided me with the most beautiful gowns in the world. Not for the sake of a horse, I know that now, but because you cared for me, and truly wanted to help me. And you came to my rescue tonight, and nearly lost your life because of

me. So you may tell your friend, Charles, that yo
have won that nonsensical wager a hundred time
over! Or so I shall tell him myself!"

Overcome with emotion, he drew up her han
and pressed his lips to her palm, a moving gestur
that was, in its way, a promise of devotion as bind
ing as a marriage vow.

"I suppose we ought to join the others," he re
marked with extreme reluctance. "Lady Besford ma
have something to say about the length of tim
we've been in here. Moreover, we seem to be mc
nopolizing the warmest room in the place."

"Must we?" sighed Amanda blissfully.

The Marquis laughed softly. "Not really. Just thi
once, I think they will forgive us if we are just
little selfish."

In another room nearby, the Countess of Besfor
was heaving a great, sleepy sigh. "Well, Robert,
must own that when I invited those two girls t
London, it never once crossed my mind that :
would all end in a dreadful, draughty old place lik
this. Goodness, why was I looking forward to it s
much, do you think?"

The Earl shook his head. "The Lord only knows
Emily. Launching these young females off is
demmed lot of work, it seems to me."

His wife rested her head on his shoulder. "I'
getting too old for all this. I know I should go an
find them both, but somehow I simply do not hav
the energy. Jane would have my head on a platter i

380

he knew."

His lordship squeezed her shoulder comfortingly. "Forget that mealy-mouthed sister of yours. They're both with the men they intend to marry, at least. I'll go and round them up shortly, for you're already worn to a thread. Amanda will come to no harm with that young fellow of hers, and as for the elbow shaker, well, your niece is perfectly capable of keeping him in line! I swear I never saw the like of it, Emily! It's 'Everard, do this' and 'Everard do that,' and he does it, by jove! That Frome fellow is going to be spending the rest of his life living under the cat's foot!"

Lady Besford smiled. "She'll be the making of him, I think. And you'll have to stop calling him an elbow shaker, Robert. He says he is going to give up gaming."

"Once a gamester, always a gamester," said the Earl cynically.

"I think you are quite out about him," his wife told him. "People can change, you know. After all, you said Lord Vale wasn't the marrying kind, and he most obviously is. Did you see the way he looked at Amanda? The man's completely head over heels!"

"Yes, well, ahem. It seems to me I also told you he wasn't the man for your niece. And I was right about that, wasn't I!" he added, sounding rather pleased with himself.

Her ladyship sat up suddenly. "Robert, I just had thought."

The Earl closed his eyes.

"Your sister's daughter will be eighteen in July. Do you think she will expect me to bring her out next year?"

"No!" said the Earl emphatically.

"No, she will not expect it, or no, you will not allow it?"

"Both," said the Earl. "I'm tired of you running around to all these plaguey balls, Emily. I want to spend some time with my wife, for a change. Whether you know it or not, it just so happens that *I* am completely head over heels for *you!*"

The Countess turned pink with pleasure. "Oh, Robert!"

"And although I am not a dashing young rakehell with a quizzing glass, I am still young enough to want to kiss you! And I am going to do so right now!"

"Scandalous!" murmured his wife happily. "Simply scandalous!"

Author's Note

Julie Caille welcomes letters from readers and invites you to write to her c/o Zebra Books, 475 Park Ave. South, New York, NY 10016.